Praise for Julia London's delightful novels

Extreme Bachelor

"Fun . . . sensual." —*Publishers Weekly*

"London's wonderfully entertaining Thrillseekers Anonymous series is deliciously sexy, clever, and fun." —*Booklist*

"[A] romantic romp . . . a fun, contemporary, second-chance romance." —*Midwest Book Review*

Wedding Survivor

"Wonderfully sexy chemistry [with] plenty of humorous moments . . . Perfect for readers who like sexy contemporary romances liberally laced with laughter." —*Booklist*

"London gives us the pleasure of a celebrity tabloid without the guilt . . . In movie-speak, the novel is *XXX* meets *Legally Blonde*: witty and sweet with plenty of sparks." —*Publishers Weekly*

"A fun romp through the mountains with a side of adventure . . . an irresistible romance with some comic relief." —*Huntress Reviews*

Miss Fortune

"Read this fun and fast-paced adventure of the heart. It will make you laugh, cry, and believe in the power of love." —*The Best Reviews*

"With saucy wit, London brings her delightful trilogy to a triumphant conclusion . . . [with] sharp, snappy writing . . . deliciously entertaining." —*Booklist*

continued . . .

Beauty Queen

"A wonderfully endearing heroine, a delightfully roguish hero, some sizzling chemistry, and writing that sparkles with sexy, sassy charm . . . fabulously entertaining." —*Booklist*

"Another 'knocks your socks off' read . . . funny, sexy, and touching . . . one of the best books of the year." —*Affaire de Coeur*

"Winningly fresh and funny throughout." —*Publishers Weekly*

Material Girl

"Great characters, sassy dialogue, and a feel-good ending."
—*The Oakland Press*

"Simply irresistible. Precious. A polished gem." —*Reader to Reader*

"The romance is great, the sex is fantastic . . . A number one pick for your summer reading." —*A Romance Review*

More praise for Julia London

"Her characters come alive on every page and will steal your heart."
—*The Atlanta Journal-Constitution*

"Witty, absorbing . . . London's fast-paced narrative is peopled with colorful characters . . . and not without its fair share of thrills."
—*Publishers Weekly*

"Will make you laugh out loud!" —Christina Skye

"Delightfully imaginative." —*Booklist*

"Romance and adventure, thrills and chills, sensuality and compassion, and characters you will fall in love with." —*Romance Reviews Today*

"Completely engaging and fun, as well as sensual and exciting."
—*All About Romance*

American Diva

Julia London

JULIA LONDON

BERKLEY SENSATION, NEW YORK

THE BERKLEY PUBLISHING GROUP
Published by the Penguin Group
Penguin Group (USA) Inc.
375 Hudson Street, New York, New York 10014, USA
Penguin Group (Canada), 90 Eglinton Avenue East, Suite 700, Toronto, Ontario M4P 2Y3, Canada
(a division of Pearson Penguin Canada Inc.)
Penguin Books Ltd., 80 Strand, London WC2R 0RL, England
Penguin Group Ireland, 25 St. Stephen's Green, Dublin 2, Ireland (a division of Penguin Books Ltd.)
Penguin Group (Australia), 250 Camberwell Road, Camberwell, Victoria 3124, Australia
(a division of Pearson Australia Group Pty. Ltd.)
Penguin Books India Pvt. Ltd., 11 Community Centre, Panchsheel Park, New Delhi—110 017, India
Penguin Group (NZ), 67 Apollo Drive, Rosedale, North Shore 0745, Auckland, New Zealand
(a division of Pearson New Zealand Ltd.)
Penguin Books (South Africa) (Pty.) Ltd., 24 Sturdee Avenue, Rosebank, Johannesburg 2196, South Africa

Penguin Books Ltd., Registered Offices: 80 Strand, London WC2R 0RL, England

This book is an original publication of The Berkley Publishing Group.

This is a work of fiction. Names, characters, places, and incidents either are the product of the author's imagination or are used fictitiously, and any resemblance to actual persons, living or dead, business establishments, events, or locales is entirely coincidental. The publisher does not have any control over and does not assume any responsibility for author or third-party websites or their content.

Cover art by Bill Diodato/Photex/Zefa/Corbis
Cover design by Rita Frangie
Text design by Kristin del Rosario

First edition: August 2007

Library of Congress Cataloging-in-Publication Data

London, Julia.
American diva / Julia London. 260— 1st ed.
p. cm.
ISBN 978-0-425-21564-7
I. Title.

PS3562.O78745A84 2007
813'.6—dc22

2007007167

PRINTED IN THE UNITED STATES OF AMERICA

10 9 8 7 6 5 4 3 2 1

AUDREY'S BABY BUMP?

(*Celebrity Insider Magazine*) Pop-diva Audrey LaRue and boy-toy, singer Lucas Bonner, capped off a week of R&R in New York at the trendy new Vincente nightclub.

Insiders say the couple were seen cuddling like two lovebirds behind a flimsy curtained-off area. An insider close to the couple says that Audrey's recent weight gain is a baby bump, expected around Christmas. (LaRue's rep dismisses the rumor of a baby bump as "ludicrous.")

Trouble in Paradise?

Audrey LaRue to Lucas Bonner: *I want some space!*

(*Famous Lifestyles Magazine*) Rumors have circulated for weeks that the long-term relationship between Audrey LaRue and her main squeeze, guitarist Lucas Bonner, is on the rocks. "Audrey has gone home to her mother," a source close to both says. "She is trying to finish an album while dealing with Lucas's ridiculous demands, and she has reached her breaking point. Mom is giving Audrey some much-needed TLC before she begins her summer tour in a few months." Reps for LaRue and Bonner could not be reached by deadline.

One

Marty Weiss believed he was the luckiest man in all of Chicago. He'd fantasized about meeting the pop star Audrey LaRue since his ten-year-old granddaughter, whom he'd been stuck baby-sitting one night, had introduced him to her by way of MTV. From the moment Audrey had appeared on Marty's wide-screen plasma TV with that curly blond hair and the bare belly and stiletto heels, he'd been bewitched.

He'd sat on the edge of his seat, his eyes and ears taking in every inch and every sound of Audrey.

The next day, he bought the two CDs she had released and played them over and over in his car. In a month's time, he knew the words to all twenty-eight tracks. He'd read the liner notes until he'd memorized them and had a concert date list for her upcoming summer tour.

He'd also joined an on-line Audrey LaRue fan club where her most rabid fans posted daily. Marty became a regular poster there, offering his opinion about her love life (she'd been with Lucas Bonner, a second-rate musician, too long to Marty's way of thinking); her oft-rumored pregnancy (she looked too thin to be pregnant, and as a father of four, Marty *knew* pregnant); and the meteoric rise of her last CD up the charts (spurred along, in part, by Marty's bulk purchase).

It was only natural that when Marty's wife, Carol, began to plan his sixtieth birthday party, Marty would call an old business acquaintance in Hollywood and cash in a favor the guy owed him. He told his on-line pals that he was certain he could get Audrey to attend his party.

The other cyberfans scoffed at him. They said there was *no way* Marty could get Audrey to a birthday party. One guy said he'd give Marty one hundred bucks if he could get even a reply from her record label.

Marty knew that those cyberyahoos had no concept of the sort of dough he had to work with to make sure it happened. Thanks to his ownership of a series of computer chip manufacturing plants, plus some dubious connections with some "businessmen" in Chicago, Marty had some serious scratch in his pocket.

His birthday party was Carol's brainchild. She'd heard from her cousin in L.A. about an extremely private outfit that would arrange an extremely private outing for the adventurous at heart. "They did Olivia Dagwood's wedding," Marsha said as she and Carol spent a day at the spa. "I mean, *almost*—they had it all ready to go until disaster struck."

"Really?" Carol asked breathlessly. "I read about that in *People*!"

"Mm-hmm," Marsha said. "They've done a *lot* of dangerous stuff like that." She said it as if all weddings were dangerous, and proceeded to tell Carol about this outfit—Thrillseekers Anonymous—that arranged extreme outings for a fee. Their specialty was extreme adventure with guaranteed privacy. But what appealed to Carol most was that TA *worked with movie stars on a routine basis.*

When she told Marty about it, he was all for it. He didn't care so much about the guaranteed privacy aspect, but some of his friends did, as they had some rather strained relationships with the federal, state, and local authorities.

With the help of a couple of women from TA, Carol planned the whole birthday bash. It would be held on a private island off the coast of Costa Rica. They would do some ocean kayaking, some zip-lining through the jungle, and some waterfall hiking up to a volcano. Caterers would be brought in from the finest eating establishments in the U.S.A.

When Carol asked Marty if there was anything special he wanted in addition to all that plus the two hundred names on his guest list, Marty said yes. He wanted Audrey LaRue.

Carol thought he was nuts. "That *girl* you are so enamored with is younger than your daughter, pervert," she reminded him. "And a whole lot younger than the whores you usually hook up with."

There were certain things a woman never forgave, and an extramarital affair or three topped the list.

But Marty was steadfast, and seeing as how he controlled the purse strings for this party, Carol had no room to argue. Besides, as it turned out, Marty's friend in Hollywood knew a friend who knew Audrey LaRue's business manager.

And now, on the day before his sixtieth birthday, Marty was standing on a private beach on a private island off Costa Rica and was already lit, even though it was just two in the afternoon. He was wearing his new Tommy Bahama board shorts whose waist kept folding over below his belly. His fifteen-year-old leather flip-flops were keeping the sand from burning his feet, and he was holding a scotch neat with a little paper umbrella in one hand as he watched the boat ferry Audrey and her crew to the island.

Marty Weiss could not have been happier. And he could not wait to tell the cyber–fan club all about it.

After two days of fun in the sun with the gang from Chicago, the Thrillseekers Anonymous crowd was exhausted. The four partners—Michael, Eli, Cooper, and Jack—agreed that this was one of the hardest gigs they'd ever done. Not sports hard, because what they were doing here could hardly be called *sports*, but hard like a big kiddie birthday party with unruly kids. Of all the trips they'd taken, this one had to rank right up there with Satan's Wedding at the top of the Rocky Mountains, otherwise known as the meltdown of Olivia Dagwood, an A-list movie star.

They couldn't quite put their finger on what, precisely, it was about this group that was making this so hard. The windsurfing had gone off without a hitch, mainly because only three of the two hundred had tried it. The ocean kayaking had turned out to be nothing more than a bunch of fat guys paddling around the shallow end of the pool playing bumper boats. The hike up the waterfall to the volcano had included six trophy wives and one personal trainer—and not one guy from Chicago.

They weren't certain what made this trip so miserable, but as two young Costa Ricans strapped the birthday boy's fat ass into the harness to ride the zip line down to the beach, Jack Price thought he had a pretty good idea—it just wasn't any fun to baby-sit.

As Cooper gave Marty Weiss a healthy push off the rock outcropping, Jack cringed—either at Marty's girlish shrieking or the way the zip line bounced, bungee-like, to the tops of the trees and back up again, high in the air.

"I said we should have done a load test, but no one listened," Cooper sighed as they watched Marty land on the beach and plant his face in the sand.

When TA had signed up to stage this birthday party, they had thought the zip line would be a safe, easy form of entertainment for a bunch of Chicago business moguls who wanted extreme adventures. But what these guys really wanted was extreme adventure without the extreme. Every one of them who'd ridden the zip line from the hilltop to the lagoon had screamed with terror on their way down.

These guys didn't want to do anything but sit on their asses, drink maitais, and eat. And that wasn't what Thrillseekers Anonymous was all about.

"Whatever happened to a little kite surfing?" Michael had complained last night as the fat cats danced a drunken rumba around them. "Since when did we become event planners?"

"Since you saw the green," Eli's girlfriend, Marnie, cheerfully reminded them.

No one could argue with her. It was true that they were being paid a king's ransom by some of the richest men in the United States for this party, and wads of cash did have their own special attraction.

Still, if someone was going to pay *that* kind of money, the least they ought to do is *try* a few of the excursions TA had set up for them. But oh no—more than one man had asked if there was a golf course on the island, and then had complained when told no, as if that was the only sport that interested them.

As Jack and Cooper watched Marty's pals pick him up and toss him into the surf to wash off the sand, a woman said, "Excuse me, Mr. Hunk, but Ms. LaRue would like to ride."

Jack and Cooper turned to see a pretty redhead wearing a pair of board shorts and a very tiny swim bra. She smiled at Jack's crotch.

"Who?" he asked, momentarily distracted by her bold smile.

The redhead glanced up. "Ms. *LaRue*? The *singer*?" she said in a tone that suggested he was a moron.

"So where is Ms. LaRue?" Cooper asked.

The redhead jerked a thumb over her shoulder at almost the same moment Audrey LaRue, arguably the hottest pop star in the country, and dressed in very short shorts and a skimpy tee, picked her way down the path, pushing through underbrush and looking very irritated. "Good God, where *is* this place?"

The redhead sighed wearily as Audrey cleared the brush and inched her way to the edge of the outcropping. She ignored Jack and Cooper as she stepped in between them to have a look over the edge. She craned a very lovely neck to see down, and instantly grabbed their arms. "*Shit!*" she whispered.

"It's a *zip* line," The redhead said. "It has to be high up."

"I *know* that," Audrey snapped.

"What . . . are you afraid?"

Audrey gave the redhead a cool look over her shoulder. "*No* . . . Just a little."

"If you aren't comfortable, you probably shouldn't do it," Cooper suggested.

"I have to," Audrey grumbled.

"Why?"

"Because they promised a sizable donation to my foundation," she said, gesturing to the fat cats on the beach.

Standing behind her, the redhead smiled at Jack again, and let her gaze slide down his body to his crotch again. What was wrong with this girl? He glanced at Audrey. "If you want to ride, strap up, sweet cheeks. We need to wrap this up."

Audrey glanced at him. "Where do I . . . strap up?"

He pointed to the two young Costa Ricans standing a few feet away. One of them held out the harness to her.

"Oh my *God*," she sighed, and started picking her way toward them.

The redhead followed her. Jack and Cooper watched as the Costa Rican boys strapped her into the harness.

"What foundation, do you think?" Cooper asked idly.

"Got me," Jack said with a shrug. And frankly, he didn't care. He'd had about as much fun in the sun as he could stand this weekend. He couldn't wait to get off this island.

Given how lame the entire event was turning out to be, the mystery of Audrey LaRue's presence at this shindig was growing. The TA guys had wondered more than once how the real estate guys, who were currently splashing around like whales in a lagoon, could have enticed her to come to a private island in Costa Rica.

"Money," Eli had hypothesized over beers one night. "What else? That's why we're all here."

"Yeah, but you guys will do anything for money," Leah, Michael's wife, said, oblivious to their startled looks. "They must have offered her a *lot* of money, like platinum record money, because I cannot imagine what would possess *any* woman in her right mind to go to Costa Rica and spend an entire weekend with a bunch of drunks."

Jack was half tempted to ask Ms. LaRue as she struggled to untangle the lines of the harness she had managed to tangle in the space of two minutes. "Can you fix it?" she asked one of the boys. He responded in Spanish as Audrey pushed a thick curl of blond hair from her eyes. She turned to Jack and Cooper. "Can *someone* help me?" she demanded.

The redhead turned her back and snickered.

Jack hoped Cooper would do it. But when he glanced at Coop, he noticed he wasn't exactly looking at her harness. Jack couldn't blame him—with those long tanned legs and green eyes that could light up a stage, this girl was *hot*.

Jack didn't realize just how hot until he stepped up to help her with the harness.

"How did you get the straps so twisted?" he asked.

"I don't know!"

He grabbed the end of two straps and gave them a good tug, cinching the harness up, and almost yanking Audrey into his chest in the process. She looked up at him with remarkable green eyes and raised one dark gold brow high above the other. "I think it's tight."

Jack smiled a little. "You sure?"

"*Yes.* I'm sure."

He let go and stepped back, and gestured for her to precede him to the edge. She carefully inched her way forward to have another look over the end of the rock.

"You sure you want to do this?" Jack asked her most excellent ass.

"Like I have a choice," she said irritably.

"She means she has to if she wants their fifty thousand dollars," The redhead said gleefully.

"*Auuuuud-drey!*" Some numb nuts who stood in the shallow end of the lagoon was shouting up at her, flailing his massively white and flabby arms. "Come on down, baby! I'll catch you!" A roar of drunken laughter went up from his compatriots.

Jack glanced at the sots below, then at Audrey. "Like I was saying . . . are you sure you want to do this?"

She groaned. "Dude, I've been here twenty-four hours now. I think I am battle tested, and besides, a few middle-aged men and a few beers don't scare me." She paused and looked at the beach below. "I mean, they *scare* me, but not like that. I can handle them. I just want to get this over with. So can you just back up and give me some space?"

Jack lifted his hands and did precisely that.

"Let's go over a few things," Cooper said. "Hands on the line," he said as he hooked her harness to the line. "Legs together and in front of you. Eli and Michael will help you at the end of the death slide."

She frowned at Cooper. "That's a funny name for it. So okay, here I go." And before Cooper could tell her not to jump, to step off the ridge, she jumped and bounced.

"*Damn,*" Cooper said, shaking his head. The redhead muscled her way in between them, and the three of them listened to Audrey squeal all the way down, landing on the beach in one huge sprawl. She was immediately swarmed by two or three fat guys, as well as Eli and Michael, who put themselves between her and the others so they could unhook her.

The redhead suddenly started laughing. But Cooper let out a low whistle. "Damn," he said. "*Damn.*"

Jack's sentiments exactly.

Two

The LaRue party was housed in a three-bedroom beach cottage with doors that opened onto a private patio overlooking the ocean. Audrey could be the Queen of England, and still, she would never get used to this sort of wealth. It was gorgeous here, absolutely gorgeous.

Gorgeous notwithstanding, she was still contemplating killing her longtime boyfriend and manager, Lucas, and her publicist, Mitzi—they'd talked her into this deal. She didn't want to do it, but they had promised her it would be fun. They had used words like *vacation* and *relax*, and she'd really begun to feel the vibe.

But then she'd met Marty Weiss and his pals, and discovered that, once again, her instincts were dead on. She had survived twenty-four hours with men who ogled her like a good salami sandwich, then drank and ogled her like a hooker. Her concert—for which Marty Weiss had paid an unbelievable fortune to stage (would she *ever* have the kind of money he had? Did she *want* that kind of money?)—had gone well, she supposed, in spite of the two guys who kept trying to climb up on stage with her. Marty stood below, three sheets to the wind, tears streaming down his face.

The man was older than her dad, for Chrissakes, and furthermore, it wasn't like she was singing opera or something that should really move him—she was singing a song about kicking a guy to the curb, and dancing around on stage as she sang.

It was Lucas who convinced her that the money—a half a million to bring her and the band here—was worth it. It would help bankroll her first national tour, timed to coincide with the release of her third album, the first with a major label. The label wanted her to tour, and they were even kicking in some seed money—but the majority of the tour's costs would be borne by Audrey. After set design, staff costs, transportation, and lodging, that was not a cheap proposition. She'd be lucky if she broke even.

Lucas had convinced her, and it would have been okay, except that Marty would *not* leave her be. She had asked him, threatened him, pleaded with him to stop. And to his credit, Marty had vowed to try, but he had not succeeded. He followed her all day, knocked on the door of her beachfront cabin at odd hours, and seemed to be waiting for her when she stepped out of the communal kitchen. He'd obviously forgotten he had a wife—who, by the look of it, was getting cozy with one of Marty's closest two hundred friends.

Audrey complained to Lucas, but Lucas rolled his eyes and sighed. "It is *one* weekend, Audrey. *One*. Surely you can handle an intense fan in the middle of a tropical paradise for one weekend. Can't you understand what this does for us?"

She hated the way he said it, like she was being a diva or something. "You didn't say I had to *handle* it when that creep broke into my house," Audrey reminded him.

"That's right, because then you *should* have been alarmed. But Marty Weiss doesn't want to hurt you. He wants to put you on an alabaster throne and suck your toes. There is a difference in the two types of stalkers."

"Maybe to you," Audrey snapped.

Lucas grinned, put his arm around her, and kissed her cheek. "Just grin and bear it. It's almost over."

Audrey did not grin. But that night, after her concert was over and Marty was practically prone on the sand, weeping with joy—or more likely, too much rum—she slipped out the back way, grabbed one of the ATVs provided for the pleasure of the LaRue party, and headed for the other side of the island. The *peaceful* side of the island. The side that drunken Marty and his drunker pals could not reach without serious assistance.

After a day of hooking up sides of beef to the zip line, Jack Price was pretty sick of the island, Chicago natives, and party gigs in general. To make matters worse, Marnie and Leah were determined to hook him up with one of the caterers.

He avoided those two like bird flu. It seemed that since Eli and Marnie had hooked up a couple of years ago, the rest of the guys had likewise gone down like tin ducks in a shooting gallery. Michael and Leah had actually *married* a couple of months ago, and even Cooper was seeing Jill regularly now. Now, everyone was "concerned" about Jack.

Okay, so Jack was experiencing a bit of a dry spell in the feminine companionship category. He realized he was getting to the age—thirty-five—where it was time to put up or shut up if he ever wanted to have kids. But it wasn't exactly happening, and it damn sure wasn't going to happen with the caterer. Leah and Marnie acted as if they could hardly stand his single status. It was suddenly their ambition in life to see him happily involved with a woman. It didn't matter that Jack was okay with being single. He figured he was just a cowboy who was best on his own. And besides, now that the guys were settling down, Jack had a new goal.

For years he'd thought TA was the best gig a guy could ever hope for, particularly after coming off a career in the Air Force where he'd learned to fly practically anything. He loved to fly, but at TA, he'd found his second calling—he loved the feature film stunt work they did, loved the movie business in general, and loved the extreme sports outings they arranged. Granted, a couple of their extreme gigs haven't been his cup of tea (a wedding, coaching twenty women to do some pretty wild stunts, and now this one), but he was usually up for anything.

What he wanted was to start his own flight school. But flight schools were expensive—in addition to needing a good, reliable plane, he'd need a hangar, an airstrip, and enough money to get a business off the ground.

He had the plane—an old Cessna Grand Caravan, which he thought was brilliantly designed. But his had an engine problem. He was rebuilding the engine himself, in an old hangar he'd rented in Orange County. If he could get the plane up and running and pass all the FAA inspections, the next step was to infuse enough cash into a down payment to purchase the hangar and start up the school.

That was a hell of a lot easier said than done. He did well with TA, but not well enough to have *that* sort of cash on hand. So Jack was biding his time, rebuilding his plane, and saving every dime he could make.

Frankly, he didn't need a woman around who would prompt him to spend his cash on stuff like flowers and weekend getaways and, God forbid, a *ring*. Which was why, when the rest of the TA guys and their significant others trekked to the other side of the island to catch the Audrey concert, he opted for some alone time on a moonlit beach with nothing but a bucket of beer and his iPod. It was the only way to avoid the matchmaking attempts of Leah and Marnie.

He walked on a path lit with tiki torches, maneuvered one of the big double chaise lounges out from beneath the cabana, and dragged it down to the beach. When he had situated it just so—directly under the full moon, a few feet away from the receding tide but close enough he could still smell the salt—he dropped his bucket of beer next to the lounge, stretched his arms high above his head, and looked out over a Pacific Ocean whose surface was illuminated by the moon.

Sweet.

He'd been waiting for this for three full days and was going to enjoy the hell out of it. Tomorrow, they would pack up and move on, but tonight, he was going to lie under the stars and the moon on a private beach without a soul around and just chill.

He started to sit down, but realized he'd forgotten his iPod. He left the chaise and the bucket of beer and walked back to his cabin to find it. Only he'd misplaced it, and it was another half hour before he made his way back to the beach, thirstier and even more ready to relax. But as he walked down the path, he noticed a movement on his chaise—some . . . some *person* was lying in *his* chaise.

Oh no. *Oh nonononono.*

Jack picked up the pace, striding across the sand until he was standing beside the chaise, staring down in disbelief at the woman who'd hijacked it.

She was wearing a gauzy white top and dark Bermuda shorts. Her feet were bare, and her hair, blond and curly, spilled around her shoulders. As if taking his chaise wasn't injury enough, she was holding one of his beers. No, wait—she was *drinking* one of his beers. And then she had the nerve to look at him as if *he* was bothering *her*.

Audrey LaRue might be a huge pop star, but in this corner of the world, that was *his* chaise and *his* beer on *his* private beach.

"May I help you?" she asked with a definite tone.

Jack shifted his weight onto one hip. "Yeah, you can help me. You can get off my chaise and go somewhere else. Like maybe, the other side of the island."

"*Your* chaise?" She sat up, twisted around, and looked at the chaise. "I didn't see your name on it. There are loads of these things on the island, so how do you figure this one is *yours*?"

"Because I am the one who dragged it down here and set it up with *my* beer," he said, gesturing toward the bottle she was holding, and the bucket, situated at a perfect arm's length.

Audrey looked at the bottle, took a deliberately long swig of it, then lowered it. "Finders, keepers. So if you don't mind, I am in serious need of peace and quiet." And with that, she settled back, shifting her gaze to the ocean.

"Yeah, well, so am I," he said, and nudged the chaise with his knee. "Get up."

"Uh-uh," she said, shaking her head and the blond curls. "I'm not moving. You would not believe my weekend. I *really* need to just chill or I may explode."

"Get up," he said again.

She did not move a muscle, held as perfectly still as a marble statue.

His pulse was beginning to pound at his temple. Jack nudged the chaise again, a little more forcefully. "Get up or I will *pick* you up and deposit you somewhere you won't like," he warned her.

She glanced up at him, incredulous. "Is that a *threat*?"

"Damn sure is."

She gasped—but quickly recovered with another drink of beer as she looked at him curiously. "Who are you, anyway?"

"Jack Price. And just who the hell are *you*?"

He'd meant it only in the rhetorical sense, but Audrey LaRue, Superstar, blinked with great surprise. Then she snorted. "You know who I am," she said with a flick of her wrist.

He knew very well who she was—but he did not like her attitude one bit. "No, I *don't* know who you are," he insisted. "Other than a woman who has hijacked my chaise and my space and my *beer*." Which, to his way of thinking, was about as low as any woman could go.

But Audrey was obviously mesmerized by the idea that someone did not know her. She eyed him—all of him—skeptically. "You know who I am—you put me in that line thingy today."

"I put a lot of people on the zip line today. Are you getting up, or am I going to have to move you?"

"*Seriously?*" she said, swinging her long legs over the side of the chaise. "You seriously don't know that I am . . . Audrey LaRue?"

"I don't know you are Audrey LaRue or anyone else. Why should I?"

Her mouth dropped open. She was clearly unable to fathom that there might be a person on the planet who didn't know who she was. She slowly stood up, the top of her head reaching his chin on his six-foot-three frame. "Because I'm a *singer*," she said, squinting up at him as if he were an alien subspecies. "I *sing*."

Jack shrugged.

"Perhaps you have seen my picture on the cover of *Cosmo*? *Seventeen*? *People*?"

Good lord, her ego was enormous. "No, but speaking of singing, I would like to enjoy some of my tunes," he said, waving his iPod at her. "So you need to go somewhere else," he suggested, and before she could speak, he moved around her, passing so close that his shirt brushed against hers, and flopped down on the chaise. "But thanks for warming it up." He reached down for a beer. "Good night."

Audrey gaped at him. Then she glared at him. "*Fine*," she snapped, slammed her empty beer bottle down on the wide wooden arm of the chaise, and stalked off, her arms swinging, her stride long and sure.

Jack watched her go—or rather, watched her derrière bounce along—then smiled triumphantly, plugged in his earbuds, and cranked up his iPod.

Diva. He'd worked too long in Hollywood not to know all the signs of a woman entirely too full of herself, and *that* chick was entirely too full of herself.

It made him glad he only had four Audrey LaRue songs on his iPod.

He settled back, drinking his beer, watching the ocean move like one living thing, thinking about his plane and the wiring specs for it. He was just opening his second beer when he was startled by a rap on the top of his head—a hard knuckle rap. "*Ouch*," he said, and sat up, his hand on his head, and jerked around.

She stood arms akimbo, her legs braced apart, her smooth, flat belly bared, and the small diamond in her belly button winking at him only inches from his nose. He had an overwhelming and insane desire to press his face against that creamy flesh, but wisely looked up into her green eyes instead. "*Yes?*" he drawled.

"Okay, *Jack*. I'm sorry I took your beer," she said, as if that solved everything.

"Apology accepted. Good-bye." He turned away.

"Okay, all right . . . and your chair," she added. When that didn't get a response, she dropped down on her knees next to him. "But the thing is, this chair is the only one I can find on this side of the island that's on the beach, and this beach is really the only *private* part of the island, and I am *desperate* for some peace and quiet. So listen, I've got an idea. I'll *pay* you for it."

"The beer?" he drawled. "Or the chaise?"

"Both. I'll pay you a thousand dollars for both," she said, gesturing to the chaise and the bucket of beer next to it.

This chick was whacked. She probably was used to snapping her fingers for whatever she wanted and having it magically appear. Jack shook his head. "Not on your life. Buh-bye now," he said, wiggling his fingers at her.

"Come *on*!" she cried, slapping her palms on the arm of the chaise. "One thousand bucks is a lot of money for a chaise that doesn't even belong to you!"

"No way am I giving it up," he said easily, and wiggled his fingers at her again. "You're wasting your time, LaRue."

"Okay. Fine." She popped up and marched around to the end of the chaise to stand in front of him and his view of the ocean. "I'll give you *two* thousand."

Jack gasped. Sat up. "*Two* thousand?" he squealed with false excitement. "*Really?*"

She recognized that he was making fun of her and fell to her knees on the edge of the chaise. "Why not?" she demanded. "Is this really that big of a deal to you? Can't you just get another chaise?"

"I could. But I don't want to. I am tired. I want to relax. I don't think you have any idea how much work goes into a weekend like this. I have been looking forward to a little downtime to myself for three days. I laid this out, and I am not going to just give it up for a pretty smile or a mere two thousand dollars."

For some reason, that made Audrey smile sweetly, and Jack could feel it trickle down his spine. She leaned forward; the gauzy top gaped open and he could see the voluptuous mounds of her breasts encased in a lacy red bra. "Then how about three thousand?" she asked silkily.

He could not help but laugh at her tenacity. He casually took another swig of his beer, taking her in. She was really beautiful—long lashes, lips that would, under normal circumstances, make his mouth water. A toned, tan, and superbly fit body, which he idly wondered how she managed to maintain, given her lack of prowess on the zip line. But Jack knew if he showed the slightest amount of interest, she would take his setup on the beach and not even remember his name the next morning. He grinned and shook his head. "No dice."

"Oh my *God*," she groaned, and swiveled around until she was seated at the end of his chaise, her back to him, blocking his view. She sat that way for several moments, staring out at the ocean. "Could I at least have another beer?" she finally asked over her shoulder.

Jack considered the slender taper of her back into her hips. "If I give you a beer, will you go away?"

She nodded.

God, he was a pathetic sucker for a beautiful woman. He reached down, pulled out another longneck, and opened it for her. "Here," he said brusquely.

When Audrey turned around, he expected her to take it and walk on—but she surprised him by vaulting herself at the beer and at him at the same moment in a half-crawl, half-lunge. She grabbed the beer and landed, wedging herself in the narrow space between him and the arm of the chaise. He could feel the smooth skin of her leg against his hairy one, could smell the lotion on her skin, the scent of magnolias in bloom.

"Thanks!" she chirped, and took a long drink.

"What are you doing?" he demanded.

"Having a beer!" She grinned at him, her eyes shining victoriously. "Share the chaise with me for one beer, and then I will leave you to your private little party. I just want a moment of peace, okay? I can't get it on the other side of the island because those guys are just . . . too much," she said with a funny wave of her hand. She smiled again and took another swig of beer.

Jack thought to protest. She really needed to be put in her place. But then she moved her leg, and he felt a warmth spread through him as the smell of magnolias filled his nostrils. The end of her hair brushed his shoulder, and he thought, what the hell . . .

Three

Audrey intended to drink only one beer, unwind a little, then get on her ATV and drive back to her side of the island. But the night was so mild and the beer so good, and Jack Price, well . . . Seriously, now—Jack Price was a hottie, there was no getting around it. Come on, who could blame her for wanting to hang out with a hunk after all she'd endured in the last couple of days?

It all seemed unreal to her still, because Audrey was new to the big-time celebrity scene. After years of playing clubs and opening for B-list bands, she'd hit it big with her second album. Two of the singles skyrocketed up the charts, and she suddenly became the "it" girl, one of the most sought-after celebrities in the United States. On top of that, she was exhausted from a grueling schedule of recording her third album, film-ing music videos, attending media events, and traveling back and forth between New York and L.A. every other day. She never had the luxury of time to just kick back and drink a beer without the fear of being stalked by some old guys from Chicago or paparazzi or rabid fans.

That she could have a fan as rabid as Marty astounded her. So it was nice to chill with someone who didn't know who she was. Jack was the first person—definitely the first man—she'd met in a very long time who didn't seem even remotely in awe or intimidated by her.

He was *definitely* the first person in months and months who didn't want her around. Usually, people couldn't get close enough to her, couldn't laugh loud enough at her lame jokes, couldn't offer quick enough to do something for her. But Jack Price couldn't get rid of her fast enough. He'd allowed her to stay on his chaise only because she had forced him and he didn't seem the sort of guy to bodily pick her up and toss her off, in spite of his threats to the contrary.

And now that she was sitting beside him, her leg next to his, her arm warm and damp from where it pressed against his, she had another tiny thrill in how damn sexy this guy was. *Incredibly* sexy—he was tall and muscular, had thick black hair and pool blue eyes, and a *very* nice mouth.

As he seemed to have gotten over his aversion to her, she stayed. She stared out at the moon-drenched ocean, squinting at the blinking lights on the horizon and trying to guess what sort of ships bobbed out there. They said nothing at first, until Audrey, in an attempt to sort through the weekend events, asked, "By the way . . . who *is* Marty Weiss?"

Jack chuckled low in his chest. "Got me." He looked at her, his eyes as blue as a cloudless summer sky. "Not a personal friend of yours, I take it."

Audrey snorted. "Never met or heard of him. He knows my business manager somehow, and my business manager spoke to my personal manager and convinced him this was a good thing. And he, in turn, convinced me I should perform at a private gig for a bunch of men important to my recording label."

She'd agreed—but then again, she usually agreed with almost everything Lucas said because she had discovered he was the only person in this world she could trust. She'd been through a lot of changes in the last two years, had discovered people would pretend to be her friend when they were really only using her. She'd already been through two accountants and was seeking damages from a former talent manager.

But she didn't want to think of all that right now, and glanced at Jack from the corner of her eye. "How did *you* end up on this island?"

His grin was snowy white and made the corners of his eyes crinkle. "I've been asking myself that same thing every hour." He gave her a sketchy account of his involvement in Thrillseekers Anonymous, and extreme sports in general. Audrey could imagine him doing extreme sports—he certainly had the body for it. When Jack cracked a second round of beers for them—without protest of her presence, she couldn't help noticing—he asked her about her music.

Audrey skipped over the part about how she had been around the music scene for a while, a Texas native who gained critical acclaim for some alternative rock and folk songs she wrote that other people performed. She started with the stupid pop album Lucas had urged her to write and record. "It's the only way to the top of the charts, kid," he'd said. His instincts had proven accurate—a friend at a radio station started playing the tracks, and the next thing she knew, she was getting calls from around the country.

She told Jack how a dumb little pop song, "Breakdown," had skyrocketed up the charts a little more than two years ago, dragging her up into a different stratosphere along with it. She didn't tell him that, seemingly overnight, she was being followed by the paparazzi and her face was on every magazine cover on every newsstand. Every day was suddenly spent in the midst of hair and makeup specialists, different handlers, and record label people who wanted to protect their investment. She was left without a spare moment to even think about her fame because she was suddenly playing to sold-out venues, appearing on television, and singing at the Grammys in front of some of the greatest recording stars of the decade. She flew so fast and so high that now she had to struggle just to keep a part of herself in the music everyone wanted her to produce and in the kind of star they wanted her to be.

"So you burst onto the scene, huh?" Jack asked.

Audrey smiled a little and shrugged. "I guess. Honestly, everything happened so fast, I never really got to decide if this is what I wanted," she said, surprising herself with the admission.

She obviously surprised Jack, too; his beer bottle paused midway to his mouth. "What are you saying—you don't want to be a star?"

Was she saying that? Her heart skipped a little—she could just see that splashed across the tabloids: AUDREY LARUE DOESN'T WANT TO BE A STAR! She felt safe with Jack at the moment, but for all she knew, he could be just as ruthless and hungry for notoriety as some of her old friends. She shifted uneasily in her seat. "I didn't mean that," she said. "I love my life. Who wouldn't love it?" She flashed a smile at Jack and clinked the top of her beer bottle against his. "I was just talking. Don't listen to me. It's just that I never get to do this."

"Do what?" he asked curiously.

"This," she said, gesturing to him and the beach. "Talk to people."

He still looked confused.

Audrey sighed. "I don't have many opportunities to meet people and just hang out."

Jack snorted and shifted his gaze to the ocean again. "Must be rough—big star, no friends."

"I didn't say I had no *friends*," Audrey said. "I said it's hard to *meet* people. It's not like I can walk into a coffee shop like you and strike up a conversation with the girl sitting next to me. And if I did, forget it—the tabloids would go nuts."

"Well," he said with a chuckle, "the last conversation I had in a coffee shop was with the girl behind the counter, who asked if I had exact change." He glanced at Audrey from the corner of his eye. "I don't think you're missing much."

But he was missing the point. He didn't understand—but no one ever did. Not her family or her old friends. They wondered what she had to complain about. And she *wasn't* complaining, God no. She knew what a gift she'd been handed. It was just that she hadn't been prepared for fame. "I can't do what normal people do," she tried to explain.

"Yes you can," he said.

"No, I can't," she insisted, twisting in the chaise to face him. She was so close that in the moonlight, she could see the shadow of a beard that covered a square jaw. "You can walk down a street in L.A. and not worry about being accosted by photographers or fans. I can't do that."

"Okay," he said, nodding a little. "You can't walk down a street. What else? Are you saying you can't dine out? Go to movies? Drive your car?"

"*No*," she said, exasperated with her inability to get her point across. "But . . . but I can't go into a burger joint without being constantly interrupted." Her gaze inadvertently fell to his lips. "I can't meet a guy and just dance if I want—"

Oh Jesus, had she really just said that? She reluctantly lifted her gaze.

She'd said it, all right—she could tell by the expression on his face. His gaze slipped to her mouth. "No boyfriend?" he asked, his voice warmer.

"*Sort of* boyfriend," she said, feeling a vague and not entirely new regret.

One corner of his mouth tipped up in a lopsided smile. He shifted closer, his gaze still on her lips. "What's a *sort of* boyfriend?"

Audrey had no idea what she was saying. She was only feeling, and at that moment, with the sound of the ocean luring her, the spicy scent of man filling her nostrils, and the aid of a buzz brought on by three beers, she felt like touching Jack Price. She wanted to put her hand on the dark skin in the *vee* of his shirt, to run her fingers over his nipples, to slip her arm around his waist. "You wanna dance, Jack?"

He laughed. "There's no music."

She picked up his iPod from his lap and showed it to him, then turned it on.

"Hey, wait—"

She smiled, yanked it out of his reach, scrolled to SHUFFLE SONGS, and selected that as she dislodged herself from the chaise. She put out her hand to Jack. "Come on, stranger. Dance with me."

His gaze traveled her body—she could almost feel it leave a mark—and he finally hoisted himself from the chaise . . . all six foot three, maybe four inches of him . . . and took her hand. When Audrey tried to lead him to the beach, he pulled back, forcing her to look at him. "I'll take it from here," he said, and put his hand out, palm up, for the iPod.

Audrey deposited the iPod in his hand. He untangled the earbuds and winked at her as he stuffed one bud into her ear, the other into his. He hit the play button, tucked the iPod in the pocket of his shorts, and slipped his hand around Audrey's bare back.

Oh *hell* that was nice. His hand was big and warm on her back, and the other, closed tightly around her hand, felt like a soft baseball mitt.

She felt small and breakable in his arms, but strangely safe. It was odd, she thought, how perceptions cropped up like lilies after a rain. Perhaps it was nothing more than the fact that she felt completely mellow—the heavy and warm moist air, the salty scent in the air . . . was there a sexier setting or a more perfect end to a harrowing weekend?

Audrey closed her eyes as Michael Bublé sang "You Don't Know Me" in her ear, and she leaned into Jack so that her lips were only a moment from his shoulder. He moved smooth and slow, turning her around in a tight little circle, the sand cool and wet beneath her feet.

As they turned lazily on that beach, he brought her hand that he held into his shoulder, tucking it in beneath his chin as he pulled her closer to his body, holding her tighter.

Audrey did not open her eyes, just allowed herself to submerge in the sensations of his body surrounding hers, the heat of his skin over hers. But when his hand began to move on the bare skin of her back, up her spine, to the base of her neck, she began to feel something entirely different. Heat spread through her, spreading through each arm and leg, spreading through each finger and toe, spreading out to the sand around them.

He touched the hair at her temple and pushed it back; she turned her face into the crook of his neck. When he dropped her hand and cupped her chin, lifting her face, Audrey opened her eyes, saw clear blue eyes lined with dark lashes glimmering in the moonlight as Sting took over and sang "Field of Gold." Jack's lips, wet and shining, gave her a shudder of desire. She slid her hand up his shoulder, to his neck. Somewhere, a vague thought in the back of her head told her to stop, to go back to her lodging, but she just lifted her face so that her lips were only a breath from his. She was aware of his body, long and hard against her. She could feel his powerful thighs, could imagine his hips moving rhythmically, his body moving in and out of her.

They had stopped moving; they were barely swaying. Jack was gazing into her eyes, his gone dark with desire. His hand pressed against the small of her back; the fingers of his other hand splayed across her cheek and her jaw, holding her there as he lowered his head to kiss her.

She sighed with pleasure into his mouth as his lips touched hers. His hand skimmed her cheek and neck as he dipped his tongue into her mouth. It was a tentative kiss, soft and tender, but startled Audrey's entire body into a vicious sort of longing.

She moaned deep in her throat, and his hands were suddenly cupping her face, his kiss gone from tentative to ravenous. He nipped at her lips and tongue, swirled his tongue in her mouth. A damp heat began to build between Audrey's legs. His kiss knocked her back, sent her tumbling with an astonishing desire to feel him hard inside her. The strength of her desire matched his, pressed against her belly and in the way he held her.

He released one hand from her face, caressed her body, his hand sliding down the curve of her hip and up again, to the side of her breast. He took her breast in his hand, squeezing it, feeling it, and Audrey could feel it swell in his palm. Her imagination was running wild now, and she pressed against his hard cock, moving suggestively.

But then the song changed, and Audrey's own voice was penetrating her consciousness.

He had her on his iPod. It was "Frantic," the title song from her new album, the single just released. He'd lied—he knew very well who she was, and with an instinctive, protective gasp—she really couldn't trust *anyone*—Audrey rocked backward, away from his mouth and his hand.

She looked up, into Jack's eyes, and saw the hunger shimmering in them. She felt that hunger just as palpably, but took another step backward, stumbling a little when the iPod earbud yanked free of her ear, and then another step—until she was out of his reach. "I thought you'd never heard of me."

Jack sighed. "I lied."

"*Why?*"

"Good question," he said, running a hand through his hair. "I don't really know, to tell you the truth."

"You don't *know*?" she repeated angrily. "I thought I was safe with you!"

That seemed to surprise him. "You *are* safe with me. I would never do anything you didn't want—"

"I don't want this!" she snapped, and started walking almost blindly as a rush of shame and indignation and desire filled her.

"Audrey, wait—*hey!* Let me drive you back!"

"No thanks!" she shouted. Her mind swam with confusion; her body *still* pulsed from his touch. She'd made a terrible mistake, a stupid, horrible mistake.

"Are you okay?" he called after her.

She didn't answer, just walked as fast as she could to her ATV.

She cranked it up and turned it onto the larger path leading to the other side of the island. There was a space of about twenty feet where the trees and palms opened and she could see the beach clearly. He was standing right where she'd left him, his hands on his hips, a dark swath of hair across his brow, watching her. She sped up, hitting a bump in the road so hard that she bit her lip.

"Dammit!" she spat, and drove on into the night.

When she returned to her room in the cottage—skirting around the pool area, where the party was, apparently, still going strong—she'd hardly fit her key in the door before it was pulled open.

Lucas was standing on the other side in his boxers. "Where have you been?" he asked, his brown eyes widening at the cut on her lip. "What happened to you?"

The flush of shame bled into her cheeks and she looked down, sweeping past him. "Nothing," she said. She'd never been unfaithful. Even though there was a lack of intimacy and other problems between her and Lucas, she had *never* been unfaithful, and it galled her that she'd come so close.

But Lucas stopped her with his hand on her arm—a hand that was surprisingly much smaller than Jack's—and made her look up.

He frowned and brushed his thumb across her bottom lip, wiping the blood away. "What happened to you?" he asked again.

"*Nothing*," she said, wrapping her fingers around his wrist and pulling his hand from her face. "I just bit my lip. That's all."

He nodded, glanced at her lip again, then turned away and pushed a hand through his mouse brown hair. "Are you tired?"

Audrey dragged the back of her hand across her mouth where he'd touched her as she walked into the bathroom. "Yes," she said. "It's been a long weekend."

"Okay. We can talk tomorrow when you're rested."

Talk. Audrey sighed and braced herself with both arms against the sink. "Talk about what?" she called from the bathroom.

"About the play list for the next album," he said. "I don't know how you feel about this, but I'd like to include the ballad I wrote."

In the safety of the bathroom walls, Audrey closed her eyes and let her head drop between her arms in frustration. "It's not really a ballad-y sort of album, do you think, Lucas?"

"No, not really . . . but I was thinking we can change my piece up a little. You know, give it a little juice. It would be a nice tie-in to my album."

But you don't have an album! she raged in her head. Yet she said, "Sure," and picked up a washcloth, wetting it. God, she was so tired. She wanted nothing more than to crawl into bed and sleep. But when she did crawl into bed a few minutes later—leaving Lucas to pore over his sheet music—all she could seem to think of was Jack Price, the way his body had felt against hers, the way he'd kissed her with such demanding passion.

Another shiver coursed through her spine, and Audrey rolled over, squeezed her eyes shut. *Just get me off this island*, she thought.

The boats came for the guests at ten sharp the next morning. Some of them were still dressed in the loud floral print shirts and baggy shorts they'd worn the night before and stumbled barefoot onto the beach, clutching a bottle of booze in one hand.

More than one party animal had to be escorted by staff to the waiting boats and deposited gingerly on the white cushioned seats below.

Marty Weiss, the birthday boy, was one of the last to come out of the compound, and only after several sharp warnings from his wife. He winced at the sight of Carol standing and waiting by the golf cart that would whisk them down to the beach and the boats. Her mascara was smudged beneath her eyes, and her unnaturally blond hair was standing practically on end. From where he stood, it looked like she'd buttoned her Hawaiian shirt wrong, and he wondered only mildly where *she'd* been all night.

He hated to leave the island—he'd had the time of his life here. He glanced nostalgically around, and spied Audrey LaRue coming out the back door of the cottage where she had stayed. She was wearing linen trousers and a halter top and her hair was pulled back in a ponytail. The woman was beautiful, he thought with a sigh. Just gorgeous.

He glanced back at Carol, who had shifted her full weight onto one hip, one hand on her waist, glaring at him. He gave her a tentative wave, then instantly started in Audrey's direction.

Marty scarcely gave Audrey time to register his presence before grabbing her up in a big bear hug and lifting her off her feet. "Thank you," he said earnestly. "*Thank* you, thank you, thank you!"

"You're welcome," she said, pushing against him. "Will you please put me down?"

He put her down, held her at arm's length, and beamed at her. "You're really marvelous, Audrey. Do you think that—"

"*Marty!*"

Carol had snuck up directly behind him, judging by the blast of her voice that rang in his ears and made him jump through his skin. "The *boat* is *leaving*," she said, practically foaming at the mouth. "So unless Miss *LaRue* is going to fly you in a private plane to Chicago—"

"N-no!" Audrey LaRue quickly interjected. "I, ah . . . I *can't*. It's not my plane."

"It's not?" Carol asked, momentarily distracted.

"It belongs to the record label. Not me. I have no control over the plane or who flies in it," she said, both hands up and waving.

"*Damn*," Marty muttered, disappointed.

Carol whirled back to him, her bloodshot eyes narrowed on him. "Good *grief*, Marty! Your little birthday fantasy is *over*!"

"And it was the best birthday of my life, Carol," he said earnestly before turning back to Audrey. He grabbed Audrey's hand and ignored her squeal of protest as he brought it to his lips. "*Thank you*, Audrey. You have made this the most memorable birthday—"

"No, Martin, *I* made this the most memorable birthday!" Carol shouted, slapping at his hand. "Stop pawing her!"

Audrey yanked her hand from his grip and smiled a little. "You take care now, Mr. Weiss," she said, glancing uneasily at Carol.

"Take care? My whole life has been transformed—"

"Oh for God's *sake*, Marty! She could be your granddaughter!" Carol snapped as she began marching toward the golf cart.

"Not my *granddaughter*!" he shouted back, offended. "My daughter!"

But as it was apparent that Audrey LaRue was not going to save him from traveling with a postmenopausal woman who had not slept or eaten in several hours, Marty consoled himself with the thought that he would always have the video of his birthday bash concert, as well as the pictures of him and Audrey LaRue, to remind him of his one glimpse at heaven.

And that evening, when he arrived home in Chicago, the first thing he did was head for the computer to download those photos to share with the Audrey LaRue cyber–fan club. The next thing he did was dash off a long thank-you to his friend in Hollywood.

A few days afterward, Rich Later, Audrey's business manager, received that thank-you, forwarded to him by the friend of the friend of Marty Weiss. Rich was dressed in a vampire outfit, checking the location of the Brothers of the Night meeting, when he got the e-mail. It made him furious. Livid. As livid as he'd been when Audrey, through Lucas, had agreed to go to this fat fuck's birthday party. It appalled him that angelic Audrey had sold out. She'd sold out, sold *herself* to that fat fuck, just like a whore.

Hell, maybe she *was* a whore. Maybe he had been fooled by a dirty, cheap whore. Rich was so furious that he decided to write Audrey another anonymous letter and tell her exactly how he felt about her whoring ways.

STILL WORKING THINGS OUT

(*Celebrity Insider Magazine*) Fresh off their getaway to a private island in Costa Rica where they reportedly flew to patch things up, Audrey LaRue, 28, and Lucas Bonner, 30, were spotted at a New York eatery deep in conversation. A source told *CIM* that Audrey is committed to Lucas, and has promised to cut back on the party scene. "She's been under a lot of pressure lately and just wants to have fun," the source said. "But Lucas is a homebody. He thinks the night scene in Los Angeles could be detrimental to her image and her career."

That didn't stop Audrey from stepping out with some gal pals. She was spotted at the popular Dime Bar in Los Angeles while Lucas was sharing a hip new sound in the music-loving capital, Austin, Texas.

In the Studio

(*Music Scene Magazine*) Audrey LaRue is back in the studio to put the finishing touches on her third album, *Frantic*, set to be released the end of this month. She is collaborating again with Lucas Bonner, who promises this album will "be a more soulful mix than the previous albums." Fans of the extremely popular LaRue will have a chance to hear her live when she embarks on an eighteen-city tour of the U.S. in July to coincide with the album's release.

Four

The third letter Audrey received from the guy who wanted her dead was fairly graphic in the details of how he would kill her if she didn't stop whoring.

It was the last straw for Lucas, who had found it in the mound of mail Rich, the business manager, had brought in.

"We have to get security," he said. "No arguments, Audrey. This is serious—this whack job could show up in one of your tour cities."

The knot in Audrey's stomach tightened. She'd gotten a lot of mail since she'd hit the major leagues, and some of it had been pretty weird. But nothing was quite as disturbing as the letters she'd gotten from this particular fan.

"I know just who you should get," Mitzi, her publicist, said as she painted her nails. They were in the artist's lounge of the recording studio, waiting for a booth to free up, along with a host of label reps and various hangers-on Audrey didn't even question any longer.

"Who?" Lucas asked, glancing up from the contract he was studying.

Mitzi held up her gloriously red nail tips and blew on them a moment before answering. "Thrillseekers Anonymous. Remember the guys who put the Costa Rica thing together? They could do it. They do that sort of thing all the time."

The knot in Audrey's belly was joined by a little fluttering. She hadn't thought of Jack Price in a while, but every time she did, she couldn't help but think of those blue eyes and those shoulders, and Jesus, that *kiss.*

"Perfect. I'll put in a call," Lucas said.

"Luke, not so fast," Audrey said quickly. "I have no idea what the expense is, or how this would work with the promoter's security while we're on tour or even if—"

"Leave it to me, sweetie. Remember our motto: You focus on the music, I focus on the business," he said with a thin smile, and flipped open his cell.

"But I—"

"Just please do as I ask," he said brusquely.

Everything in the room suddenly stilled—even Mitzi's nail polish brush froze mid-dip in the bottle. No one breathed, no one moved, but all eyes slid to Audrey. It embarrassed her. She knew Lucas had her best interests at heart—he always had—but she hated the way he spoke to her like she was a child.

She lifted her chin. "I would really like to know more," she said firmly.

With a snort of surprise, Lucas smiled at her. "Don't be a drama queen, baby. Let's just get through today's session, and then I'll take you to dinner and we can talk about whatever it is that's bugging you."

What was *bugging* her was that it was *her* name on the concert tour and the albums and the billboard charts. But years of watching her parents argue loudly in public had made Audrey the exact opposite. She couldn't muster the courage to talk to Lucas about his tone in front of all these people, especially people who were certain to leak it to some media outlet. So she bit her tongue, nodded curtly, and turned away. Mitzi's nail polish brush slid the rest of the way into the bottle, and Audrey could almost hear the collective breath being released.

She wished for all the world that she could be alone with Lucas and tell him exactly what she thought, but there was *never* a damn moment she was alone with him. She was constantly surrounded—she couldn't even go to the bathroom without everyone knowing it.

So Audrey did what she always did when this happened—she walked out of the artist's lounge and down the long hallway to the ladies' room, the only place she could get a moment of peace.

That night, while Audrey was writing music, Lucas let himself into their hotel suite carrying a leather bag. Audrey glanced at him and decided she must be tired, because for a moment, she thought the bag was moving.

It *was* moving—Lucas had brought her a small, furry, black-and-white-haired dog. "It's a toy Havanese," he said. "I named him Bruno." It was a gift, he explained, for the mix-up about the security this afternoon.

"But . . . but I don't want a dog, Lucas," Audrey said, staring at the little thing. "I'm about to go on tour."

"That's why I got you this carrying case," he said, holding up the bag.

"Thanks . . . but I don't want a dog."

Lucas looked at the dog, then at Audrey. "Wow. You sure know how to cut a guy off at the knees. I am just trying to make it up to you. I'll go see if they will take him back."

He looked so hurt by her refusal that, against her better judgment, Audrey stopped him. "No, don't. He's cute," she said, and smiled when Lucas grinned and handed her the dog.

On the morning of the day Lucas Bonner would meet with TA about security—something they told him they did *not* do, but had agreed, thanks to Mitzi, to at least hear the guy out—Jack saw a picture of Bonner with Audrey on the front page of the *Star,* running into the very popular Twist nightclub in L.A. The caption read,

Is Marriage in Audrey's Future?
What the Stars Say!

Jack looked at the line ahead of him—four deep and a woman in front of him with a cart piled high. He glanced surreptitiously behind him—the woman was trying to wrestle her toddler out of the shopping cart.

He sheepishly reached for the magazine and opened it up quickly, folding back the cover so no one would think he was actually reading the *Star*.

> *Star* asked astrologers if this is the year Audrey LaRue might find true happiness and marry her long-term boyfriend, aspiring artist Lucas Bonner. "Venus is in her seventh house, which makes this year ripe for love and marriage and meaningful partnerships," the astrologer told *Star*. "It will be interesting to see if this is the year Audrey and Lucas tie the knot. I think her seventh house is perfectly set up for it." Only Audrey knows, but one source tells *Star* that Audrey and Lucas were recently spotted in the diamond district in New York.

Jack quickly closed the rag and put it back on the rack, and only then noticed the woman behind him was reading over his shoulder. "I really like her music," she offered when Jack looked at her curiously.

"Yep," Jack said, and quickly turned around, feeling like an idiot.

Later that afternoon, when Lucas Bonner was in the TA offices, Jack discovered the man set his teeth on edge, and he couldn't figure out why. Granted, he wasn't crazy about Bonner's manner—it seemed false to Jack somehow. And it annoyed him that when talking about Audrey's security needs, he kept saying *we*.

He wondered how a woman as beautiful and vibrant as Audrey LaRue could have ended up with this guy. They didn't seem to match. Bonner was too intense for her.

What he wanted was a security detail for Audrey LaRue during her nationwide tour this summer, and Mitzi had led him to believe that TA staged security details just like they staged extreme adventures.

"We've had a couple of scary encounters with fans, a few threatening letters, and then there was the break-in at our condo. The police are investigating that, but we'd still like to take an extra precaution," Bonner said. "Those letters are giving us the creeps."

"Wait . . . did you *both* get letters?" Michael asked, confused by Bonner's liberal use of the word *we*.

"Well, no . . . Audrey did."

"Aha," Michael said, and frowned a little disdainfully. "So . . . what do you need from us?" he asked.

"I'm not sure," Bonner said, leaning back in his chair. "All I know is that we can't walk out our door without flashes going off and people screaming for autographs. Anyone could get to us."

Us? Did this guy really think anyone was dying to get to *him*?

"And besides, personal security is pretty standard fare nowadays. Britney has twenty-four/seven security. Lindsey and Mariah, too. It just makes good sense."

"Security is not really our scene," Cooper said.

"Right . . . but you *know* security," Bonner insisted. "You do all those adventures with people as famous as we are."

The TA guys all exchanged a look.

"Don't worry about the cost," Bonner added confidently. "We'd rather feel safe than worry about a few bucks here and there."

How nice for Audrey that this guy wasn't worrying about spending her money.

"We don't do security, but we'll talk about it," Eli reiterated, and stood up, indicating the meeting was over. "We'll give you a call."

Bonner stood, too, and shook each of their hands. "I look forward to working with you guys. Mitz says you're the best." He walked to the door.

Mitzi lingered and whispered to Cooper, "Just think about it. Promise me you'll *think* about it."

"Right," Cooper said, moving her to the door.

When they finally went out, and the door shut behind them, Michael turned around and shook his head. "What a waste of time."

"There are a dozen great security firms in town," Cooper chimed in. "Why us?"

"Because of you, Jessup," Eli said to Cooper. "You know Mitzi has a thing for you. This is her ticket into your pants."

"No way," Coop said instantly, shaking his head. "I have a girlfriend, and even if I didn't, I don't do publicists. You know what happened the time I dated Leslie."

"Don't tell it again," Eli said quickly. "I swear to God I can't hear it again without laughing my ass off. The last time you told it, I laughed so hard it damn near killed me."

"Too bad that's the gig," Michael said as he crossed to the little fridge they kept stocked with beer. "I was hoping for something really cool. Volcano diving, maybe."

"Yeah, too bad," Eli agreed, ignoring Cooper's glare. He squinted absently at a lamp. "I have to admit, I kind of like that new song Audrey's got out."

Jack paused in what he was doing and looked at the man he'd known all his life, since they were kids growing up in West Texas.

A man who, apparently, he really didn't know at all.

"You like 'Frantic'?" he asked incredulously. "You like a song that says, '*I'm frantic cuz I can't stop loving you, baby, oh oh oh oh*'?"

"Yeah, so?" Eli said defensively. "I *like* it! At least I'm not the one who's memorized the lyrics."

Jack shook his head and turned back to what he was doing. "I can't help but know them. There is a radio at the hangar and they play that damn song twenty times a day if they play it once. But hey, whatever floats your boat, there, pal," he said, holding a hand up to Eli. "Personally, I liked her better when she did alternative rock in dive joints around Austin."

"Austin?" Michael said, looking up from his rummage through the refrigerator for some beer.

"Five, six years ago, she was a staple in the live music scene there," Jack said. "I used to catch her gig when I was home. Really good stuff—not the pop shit she's singing now."

"Yeah, well, alternative rock doesn't make the billions of dollars pop makes. But as far as us getting into the security business, it's a no, right?"

"Right," Eli said instantly at the same time Cooper said, "Absolutely."

When Jack didn't chime in, the three turned and looked at him.

"What's on your mind, Price?" Eli asked.

What was on his mind was a teeny portion of those billions. This sort of gig could be a piece of cake, really. He knew a couple of guys who did it for a living. He could manage the thing for a substantial cut, and besides, he worked security in the service. He could really use a nice infusion of cash for his flight school.

There was one other thing. He could not stop thinking about that kiss on the beach in Costa Rica. "I'm just thinking out loud now," he warned them. "You know I've got this little project going on, and I could use some serious cash—along the lines of a million—to pump into it."

Michael whistled, but Cooper rolled his eyes. "That's not a little project, dude. That's a big damn deal. Flight schools aren't cheap."

No one knew that better than Jack. But it was what he wanted, and he was determined. "I'm just throwing the idea out there," he said. "If you guys could spare me for the summer, I could use the cash."

Cooper gaped at him. Eli smiled a little. And Michael, always the numbers guy, said, "How much do you think they are willing to cough up for security?"

"I don't know. But I am thinking enough that I could make up a substantial chunk of the mil I need."

"What the hell, Jack?" Cooper exclaimed with a frown. "You're not *seriously* considering—"

"You know how else I can get to a mil, Coop? I could really use the money. We do great with TA, don't get me wrong. But it's not enough to get me that flight school."

"You're crazy," Cooper said with a snort. "Do you have any idea how much *work* goes into providing security for someone like Audrey LaRue?"

He couldn't imagine Audrey would be any trouble at all. He'd handled her easily enough on that beach a few weeks ago. And besides, all it really needed was assembling the right people to do the job. "You know I did security in the service. And remember Ted Evans? He does this for a living. I would use his group if he's willing to do it."

"You're kidding," Michael said disbelievingly when it was clear Jack was really serious.

"Look, we're not signed for any films this summer, and you guys can handle the business for three months without me. Like I said, I could really use the cash, assuming Guitar Boy is authorized to spend his girlfriend's money like he says he is. If you're okay with covering for me, I am going to give Ted a call and then Bonner and see what I can work out."

Jack's three partners looked at one another, then at him. Eli shrugged. "I'm okay with it," Michael said.

Cooper groaned. "It's always something with you!" he said. "But what the hell? Whatever blows your skirt up."

Jack grinned. "Thanks, guys," he said. "You won't even know I'm gone."

Five

Eight Weeks Later

A big, sleek, and disturbingly conspicuous black limousine, flanked by two county sheriff patrol units, and followed recklessly by a Geo metro and two SUVs, hurtled onto the tarmac of the private Orange County airstrip where Jack was waiting.

He glanced at his watch—they were only eight hours late.

This was not what he'd call an auspicious beginning, but Jack was determined to start this job with a good attitude. He reminded himself that he stood to profit a sizable chunk of change for two months' work. Over the last couple of weeks, in meetings with the tour people, the label people, Lucas Bonner, and the men Jack had assembled to do the security, he'd had to push down the nagging thought more than once that perhaps this wasn't a good idea. The work wasn't bad, but navigating the tour sponsors was tiresome and Bonner seemed like a royal pain in the ass.

"Twenty-four/seven coverage," Bonner had barked at him like an army general.

"I got that," Jack said.

Now that the planning stages were over and they were about to implement, Jack thought if he kept a low profile and just did his job, it couldn't be that big of a deal.

The limousine came to an abrupt halt a few feet away from him, as did the two patrol units, from which four sheriff's deputies spilled out. They collectively hitched up their gun belts and sauntered to the back of the limousine, positioning themselves between the limo passengers and the eager cretins in the vehicles following them.

The front passenger door flung open with such force that Jack was surprised it didn't snap off the hinges. Mitzi emerged and hopped toward him in skin-tight white jeans, a tighter leopard sweater, and shoes with heels that were completely impractical for doing anything other than getting laid.

He had to admire a woman who could strut her stuff on stilts, and Mitzi Davis could strut with the best of them.

"Jack!" she shouted.

"Hey, Mitz," he said, and popped a piece of gum into his mouth, enjoying the bounce of her boobs as she came to a halt before him.

"*So* sorry we're late, baby," she said breathlessly.

"Eight hours late, Mitz. I hope that's not a sign of things to come."

She took off her shades and peered up at him. "*Eight* hours! Oh, doll, you got my message, right? Audrey did *The Tonight Show* last night. We couldn't possibly get to the airport any sooner, especially in this traffic. Did you see it?"

"The traffic?"

"*No*, silly!" she cried, swatting his arm. "*The Tonight Show*!"

"Ah, no," Jack said. "So you got everyone and everything together? We need to get going," he said as paparazzi jumped out of the Geo metro and the two SUVs and started firing off shots around the sheriff's deputies of the LaRue limousine.

"Oh look," Mitzi purred, "it's *impossible* to keep the media off Audrey's tail. She is probably the most popular pop star in the *world* right now. Do you have any idea who I had to sleep with to get *The Tonight Show* for her? But it was worth it—Jay *loved* her."

"Fabulous. Let's go," Jack said, and patted the railing of the steps leading up to the ten-seater Audrey's label had made available to fly her to the inaugural show in Omaha. They would take luxury tour buses from there.

Jack could scarcely contain his excitement.

"Let's get her moving," he said, nodding toward the limo.

"Keep your shorts on, sweetie," Mitzi said with a wink. "I'll get them."

Them. Jack assumed Lover Boy would ride along, but he had a feeling that *them* went well beyond the two primaries.

He was right—as Mitzi turned around and strode back to the limousine, the driver of the limo had opened up the doors of the vehicle and people were beginning to spill out while the paparazzi jostled each other for shots. Two women rolled out, then Bonner and couple of guys with cigarettes in hand, and then another guy who looked like a stoner they had picked up at the beach. And finally, Miss Audrey LaRue, the woman for whom Mitzi would sell her firstborn if it would convince the media that she was the World's Biggest Pop Star.

She might be that, but Jack was also reminded that she was just about the hottest woman walking on the planet today. He was both pleased and a little chagrinned that he had not embellished a thing about her body in his memory. Slender frame. Long legs. Silky hair and a mouth that could make a guy hard just looking at it.

She was wearing enormous shades, a beat-up cowboy hat, denims that looked ancient (for which she'd probably paid a fortune), a white cowboy shirt tied in a knot just below some very nice breasts that he fondly remembered squeezed up against his chest. And of course, she had on the obligatory cowboy boots.

She was also carrying a purse the size of Kansas. What *was* it with women and purses?

Audrey didn't seem to notice the frenetic activity around her as the paparazzi snapped photos and people grabbed bags and a couple of guitar cases. She was talking on her hands-free cell phone, the little mic curved around to her mouth. She seemed completely oblivious to the world as she began to move toward the plane, her free hand slicing through the air as she carried on a very animated conversation. She paused only once, glanced over her shoulder and shouted something at someone as cameras clicked, then turned and continued on her way, still talking.

She strode across the tarmac with legs that looked to be about ten feet long, her free arm swinging, her mouth moving with every step until she came to a halt directly in front of Jack and glanced up.

He smiled. "*Hey.*"

"Hello." She kept her eyes hidden behind the sunglasses. "Look, I have to go," she said.

"Go where?" he asked, momentarily confused.

She pointed a perfectly manicured finger to the little mic. "I'll call you later to see what's going on, okay?"

She wasn't talking to him, but Jack was pretty sure she was looking at him, although it was hard to tell behind those ridiculous shades.

"Okay, yeah. Later," she said. Her phone call apparently over, she reached into the enormous leather state-of-Kansas she had slung over her shoulder. "So. You're going to keep the freaks away from me, right?" she asked.

Sort of an odd way to start the conversation. "Yes."

"Great," she said, and produced, of all things, a tiny little black-and-white fur ball. "Will you see to it that he is walked before we take off? Also, I'd like some *chilled* bottled water."

Jack was stunned.

Audrey thrust the leather bag and dog at him. Not a dog, really, but a wind-up toy that growled and wore his fur in a stupid red bow above his eyes.

"Hello?" Audrey demanded.

"Excuse me?" Jack asked. "You want me to *what*?"

"Just make sure Bruno gets walked," she said again, putting the dog down this time.

"What *is* Bruno?"

"A Havanese. Here is the leash."

"Wait, wait," Jack said. "You don't have someone to do this?" he asked, horrified that she would expect him to *walk* something, much less something trying so hard to be a dog.

"I've got a *lot* of people to do it," she said meaningfully, and held out the leash again.

Jack glared at her. But he took the leash. And the little rat at his feet began to paw his leg.

"Oh, and don't forget the water," she said. "Thanks." And with that, she jogged up the steps and disappeared into the interior of the plane.

Jack didn't move. He was actually incapable of moving, he was so taken aback. Had she really just done that? Had she really just pushed her living toy off on him?

"*Diva*," he muttered irritably beneath his breath, and looked around for a place to let the thing do his business.

Since Jack was not authorized to fly the label's plane, as luck would have it, he had to ride in the seat facing Audrey's for the flight to Omaha.

If she noticed him, she gave no indication. When she wasn't making calls and talking into her earpiece, she kept her nose in some papers. She only looked up a couple of times, wearing a very thin and very forced smile. Jack couldn't tell if she was in a snit because she didn't get her water, or if it was because he'd shoved Bruno back at her and said, "*Here.*"

He couldn't understand her problem. Was she just rude, or did she have a problem with his providing security? If she did, she damn sure should have said something before now.

He couldn't help noticing that the other passengers didn't seem to notice her at all. Lucas Bonner had popped open a couple of bottles of Cristal champagne the moment they had cleared the runway, proclaiming this flight a celebration of his finishing an album—and the group had proceeded to party like it was 1999.

Not Audrey. She kept her head down.

For the first three hours of the flight, Jack gritted his teeth. He tried not to look at her legs, or the tantalizing view of her breasts that the deep vee of her shirt afforded him. He tried not to look at her mouth and think of that kiss, or hair that begged for a man's fingers. He *tried* not to . . . but Jack had nothing to do but watch her and wonder why the hell she wouldn't speak to him or at least *acknowledge* him. She *knew* him. And the longer the flight went on, the more obsessed Jack became with making her at least *look* at him.

He finally nudged her with his foot.

Audrey lifted her gaze without lifting her head. "What?"

"I thought I'd try and say hello again," he said. "I don't think you heard me clearly the first time."

"*Hi*," she said impatiently, and dropped her gaze to the papers again, as if she were being bothered by some punk kid.

All right, that was it. She had weaseled her way onto his beach and his lap, and he'd be damned if he was going to be treated like a bothersome gnat. So he shifted forward, arms on knees, his hands dangling between his legs. "You *do* remember, don't you? Private beach? Moonlight? Dancing?"

"Me on your iPod?" she muttered without lifting her head. "Of course I remember you. I said hello, didn't I?"

"Right before you ordered me to fetch you some water and walk that thing you call a dog. And *then* you got downright frosty."

That prompted her to look up. "*Frosty*? I'm not *frosty*, I'm *busy*. Most people understand that. And it's not a *thing*, it's a *dog*."

"That's not a dog. That's a child's toy. And you are definitely frosty."

Her mouth dropped open. Then she quickly closed it and frowned. "*Jesus*," she muttered. "Okay, Jack. Try and understand—I am about to go on my first nationwide tour, so I'm just a little preoccupied with my job. Maybe you should be focused on *your* job, which is providing security, you think? We're not going to be beach buddies. We won't even see each other that much. Let's just establish that as a ground rule, and that way, neither of us will expect anything. All right?"

"Wow," he said, leaning back. "That may be the warmest welcome I have ever received."

She shrugged. "I'm just saying. I've got a lot going on."

"So much that you can't even say hello?" he asked incredulously. "Most humans, regardless of how busy they are, say hello if only to acknowledge they've met before. And I thought, seeing as how I am going to keep some whack job from getting to you, that you could at least extend me that small courtesy."

Audrey sighed and placed her hands primly on top of the papers in her lap. "*Hello!* Okay? Are you satisfied?"

"No."

"What more do you want from me?"

"Manners," he said. "I want some manners."

She blinked with surprise. And then she glanced over her shoulder, to where Bonner was sitting on the arm of a chair, telling some outrageously long tale to the delight of the other passengers, and Jack suddenly clicked to it.

"Is *that* it?" he asked incredulously, glancing at Bonner. "Are you afraid I'll mention our little dance to your boyfriend?"

Audrey's eyes flew open wide, then just as suddenly fell into a narrow glare. "*No.* He wouldn't believe you anyway. And besides, there is no point in telling him, because it was just a stupid little thing. The sooner you get over it, the better off you will be."

Jack chuckled low and leaned back. "You think that kiss was *that* good?" he asked. "What makes you think there was anything to get over?"

Audrey colored and she frowned. "Whatever," she said, sounding suddenly uncertain. "Can we please agree that we'll both just do our jobs?"

"I'm definitely going to do my job," he said, smiling a little at the blush in her cheeks. "But lighten up, okay? I'm not here to give you a hard time. I just want some basic courtesy."

Audrey's blush deepened. She made a sound of disgruntlement before slouching down in her seat and lifting the papers so that she couldn't see him.

Jack didn't bother her again. But he sat smugly confident in one thing—she hadn't forgotten that damn kiss any more than he had.

When they at last arrived in Omaha, the passengers rolled off the plane—and were put in a waiting limo. Jack, Audrey, and Lover Boy took a separate limo and a different route to the hotel.

When they arrived, Audrey's assistant, the cute redhead Jack remembered from Costa Rica, had already handled everything. The hotel folks were waiting for Audrey and Boy Toy in the back, where they would be let in via the kitchen and escorted to their room to avoid the small throng of fans who'd gathered out front.

Once they were inside, Jack checked in with his guys—three of them were taking shifts in the lobby and on Audrey's floor—and then checked into his room.

He had changed his clothes and was headed for the gym to work off his frustration—and the sudden desire for sex—when someone knocked at his door. When he opened it, the redhead swept inside. "Hey," she said, obviously in a hurry as she ducked under his arm. "We haven't formally met. I'm Courtney, Audrey's assistant."

"Jack," he said, extending his hand.

She smiled seductively as she took his hand in both of hers and shook it. "You look like you're running out, so I'll be quick. Audrey left the earpiece that goes with her phone on the plane. There's no one who can go get it, so Audrey asked that you go back for it. I'll make a quick call to the plane to make sure someone is there to meet you."

Jack said nothing at first. It took his mind a few minutes to absorb the notion that anyone on this tour thought he was Audrey's personal gopher. Audrey especially. Courtney lifted a brow; Jack smiled and pulled his hand free of her grip. "I can't do that, Courtney," he said congenially.

"Oh, but you have to do it. No one else can be spared."

"Sorry. No can do," he said, and still smiling, he gestured to the door.

"Well . . . what am I supposed to tell Audrey?" Courtney asked uncertainly as he opened the door and held it open.

"Tell *Audrey* that I said to remember she hired me to keep her safe, not to pick up after her or walk her damn rat. So if she asks me to do something like that again, she can find other security."

Courtney blinked with surprise. "*Oh*," she said uncertainly. "Do . . . do you really want me to tell her that?"

He leaned down so that he was eye level with her. "Word. For. *Word*." He straightened up again.

"Oh-kay." Courtney looked at him like she thought he was nuts and slowly stepped across the threshold.

"See you," he said, and shut the door.

Jack never did make it to the gym. But he did find a bar that was serving tall beers. Buckets of them, fortunately, because he needed a good belt now that he was realizing he might have made the biggest mistake of his life.

Six

The next morning, Audrey could hardly open her eyes when Lucas shook her. He was dressed, ready to go to the Qwest Center to oversee the setup for the show.

"Hurry up," he said with exasperation, shoving her lightly as she burrowed deeper under the covers. "You need to rehearse the 'Take Me' number and get through a sound check before three."

"I'll be there," she muttered, her eyes sliding shut again. "Just . . . just take Bruno to Courtney and send a car back."

"Audrey—"

"Just send a car!" she moaned.

She was exhausted, and it was Lucas's fault. He'd kept her up until almost two in the morning, trying to persuade her to fly to New York at the end of the month to attend some Hollywood muckety-muck's birthday bash.

Audrey had never met the guy and didn't want to go, but Lucas was wearing her down. "Mike Senate is like *the* biggest director in

Hollywood," he'd said as he dug through his luggage, looking for his black leather pants.

"That's great. If I were in the movie business, I'm sure I would be interested," she'd said as she'd gone over the song list.

"You *could* be in the movie business."

Audrey had looked up from her songbook.

Lucas had pinned her with a look as he pushed a hand through his golden, highlighted hair. "I'm serious, Audrey. Jessica Simpson made the leap to screen. You could act circles around her."

Sometimes, she wondered what planet Lucas was from. "I could act *circles* around her? I don't even act! I've *never* acted, and what's more, I don't *want* to act. I want to make music, Lucas. Why can't I just do that?"

"Because sometimes you have to do things to get ahead," he'd said irritably.

"I *am* ahead. I'm in a place I never dreamed I would be. How much further ahead do I need to be?"

"Jesus," he'd said, tossing his leather pants on a chair. "I just wish that you would *listen* to me—"

"I listen to you all the time—"

"Well, you're damn sure not hearing me now, Audrey," he'd snapped. "Here's what's wrong with your little fantasy of having made it. Pop stars die a painful death after the age of thirty. You are twenty-eight. You need to think of the future and what you are going to do when this gig ends."

But it had been more than Audrey could think of last night. She was stressed from all the last-minute preparations for the show, and honestly, seeing Jack Price yesterday had stirred something in her she wanted to pulverize to a powder rather than acknowledge. And Lucas wanted her to fly off and meet some director?

On top of that, on the way out of town yesterday, she'd gotten a call from her sister Gail, who told her that her brother, Allen, had been missing for two days.

"*Missing*?" Audrey had cried as fear clutched at her heart. "What do you mean *missing*?"

"I don't mean he's been abducted or anything," Gail had said with a snort. "I think he went out on a bender. But his probation officer is pissed, Audie—she says she is going to have his probation revoked this time."

Audrey had to ask her to repeat the last part, as the party had already begun in the limo, but whatever Gail said was lost. When they pulled to a stop at the tarmac, she got out so she could hear her sister, oblivious to the sheriff's deputies, or the paparazzi behind her—they were just part of the normal landscape these days—and was hardly even conscious that she was walking, so intent was she on the conversation.

Her heart was beating wildly as she listened to Gail. Allen would never survive in prison—so why did he have to do this? Why did he sabotage every chance he was granted?

"I don't know what to do," Audrey said to Gail. "I'm just about to get on a plane. My *tour* starts tomorrow, Gail—my first nationwide tour!"

"Well, I know he's real nervous about paying a lawyer," Gail said calmly. "His regular lawyer wants two grand just to show up in court."

Audrey didn't know why she was surprised; the calls from her family were usually about money. Just last week, Dad had called asking for money to buy a race car. Audrey had closed her eyes briefly, and when she opened them, she noticed Jack Price standing at the steps leading up to the plane.

Actually, she couldn't help noticing him—he was fine-looking man. His dark hair was wavier than she recalled, but his blue eyes were still killer, and the man could fit a pair of Levi's better than any man she'd ever seen.

They fit so well, in fact, that as Gail had cheerfully launched into how much money they needed, Audrey did nothing but gape at Jack through a pair of very dark sunglasses. It was funny—she'd met so many people, so many Hollywood types who landed on every annual beautiful list. But to Audrey, a beautiful man was the kind who had some meat on him, who looked as if he could hold up the globe in one hand and had the calluses to prove it, the kind of man who didn't mind working for a living.

"Audie, did you *hear* me?" Gail screeched into the phone.

"What? Yes, of course I did!" Audrey said, startled back to reality as she continued her march to the plane. "But I can't come to Texas right now."

"You don't need to *come* here," Gail said wearily. "Just wire Mom some money."

Okay, seriously—Audrey didn't begrudge her family a dime—but could they not act like she was their personal ATM?

"Fine," Audrey said.

Jack was watching her. That was the other thing about this business of fame—people made no bones about openly staring at her. It always made her feel like she had spinach in her teeth.

"Look, I have to go," she said to Gail. "I'll call you later to see what's going on, okay?"

"Okay. But can you wire the money today?" Gail whined as a slow and sexy smile melted onto Jack's lips.

"Okay, yeah. Later," Audrey muttered, and clicked off. Looking at Jack, she felt absurdly nervous, and for no reason, other than being this close to him reminded her of being this close to him once before, on a moon-drenched beach.

And that inevitably reminded her of the way his body felt next to hers, which made her feel confused. Which is why, she supposed, she had come off like a diva. She hadn't *meant* to be a diva, but she had learned that the only way to get people to back off was to be mean. Lucas kept telling her she had to do it or people would walk all over her.

It was more of a self-protective reflex than anything else that made her shove Bruno at him.

Jack had looked at her like she had just asked for rack of lamb or something equally ridiculous, and Audrey had thought that if he was making a nice chunk of change off her, he shouldn't be so averse to letting Bruno pee. Needless to say, the flight had gone downhill from there. She'd been completely rattled when he sat across from her, staring at her the whole time with that smug look on his face. She couldn't think, couldn't wait to get to the hotel and away from him; she had even left her earpiece on the plane.

But then Lucas had started his crap about going to Mike Senate's birthday bash, like she needed to add anything else to her schedule right now, like she needed to be thinking of *acting* instead of embarking on a tour that had her on pins and needles as it was.

At two this morning when she'd tried to sleep, it was all running around in her head, and she tossed and turned while Lucas worked on some song.

"What's wrong, baby?" Lucas had asked.

"I can't sleep."

"Let me get you something," he said, putting aside his guitar.

"No, Lucas, I hate those pills."

He paused and looked at her. "Do you want to sleep, or not?"

She did want to sleep. If she didn't get some sleep, she would crash. So she had taken the pills Lucas gave her, chased them down with a drink, and that was the last conscious thing she remembered doing before sliding off into a deep, peaceful sleep.

It seemed Lucas hadn't been gone even fifteen minutes before he was jostling her again, his hand surprisingly firm on her hip. Audrey felt so heavy, she felt almost dead. She forced her eyes open beneath the covers she had pulled over her head—it took a moment for her to remember exactly where she was. "*Stop it,*" she croaked, the fog in her mouth as thick as the fog in her brain. Her face felt mashed on one side.

"Get *up*," he growled, his voice unusually low.

Audrey groped for the top of the covers and pushed them back, then rose up on her elbows. She had to push her tangled hair out of her face, and when her head stopped swimming, she turned to look up at Lucas—and screeched.

It wasn't Lucas towering over her; it was Jack Price, his arms crossed over his big chest, a frown on his face.

"What the hell are you doing here?" she cried, scrambling off the other side of the bed.

"A better question is what the hell are *you* doing here?" he countered. "You were supposed to be at the coliseum two hours ago."

Oh no—*oh God*. Audrey glanced at the clock just as it turned to 12:36. "*Shit!*"

"Have a late night?" Jack drawled.

"None of your business," she snapped and realized that she was wearing nothing more than a pair of thong bikini panties and a camisole. She grabbed a pillow to shield herself, but it was too late. His gaze was smoldering.

"I guess it becomes my business when you aren't where you're supposed to be. It's my job."

No thanks to Lucas. "How did you get in here, anyway?" she demanded as she backed her way to the bathroom.

"I'm security, remember? Of course I have a key to your room. Lucas gave me the okay to come in when you didn't answer the phone."

The *phone* was ringing and she hadn't heard it? Never mind that—when she got ahold of Lucas, she was going to let him have it. Who did he think he was, giving a strange man permission to enter their room? "Okay. Well. You've done your job, I'm up, so you can go now," she said, pointing to the door.

Jack laughed and slid his big frame into a chair. "I'm not going anywhere without you, starlight. I will personally deliver you to the arena."

"Just send a car!" she snapped at him, which she promptly punctuated by backing into the wall and hitting her funny bone. "*Ouch. Ouchouchouch.*"

He grinned. "I *am* the car, kid. So if you'll just hurry up and do whatever it is you do, we can both put this ugly morning behind us." And with that, he propped his feet on the end of her bed.

"Get your feet off my bed!" she said as she slid to her right and into the bathroom, slamming the door behind her. But then she realized she hadn't brought anything in with her—like toiletries or clothes. Or even panties.

Okay, this was absurd. She dressed in less than this on stage. Right . . . but she had makeup and leather and somehow it was different when *one* guy was looking at her like that as opposed to an auditoriumful. Nevertheless, she was frantic about being late. So Audrey dropped the pillow and threw the door open. Jack Price raised one dark brow as she marched, head up, to the mountain of suitcases in the corner of the room.

She rooted through her bags, silently cursing Courtney. Why hadn't Courtney sorted through this stuff? A personal assistant was the one thing Audrey had agreed with Lucas she needed. So where was her so-called personal assistant? Why did she always have the feeling that Courtney was off plotting something?

Oh, right. She went to get the earpiece Audrey had left on the plane since High and Mighty Security Guy over there couldn't be bothered.

She opened several bags before she found what she needed and stood up . . . only a little too fast. She had to put her hand against the wall to steady herself. When she could focus again a moment later, she noticed that Jack had come to his feet and was watching her closely.

"Are you okay?" he asked, moving toward her, his expression full of concern.

"I'm *fine.*"

His gaze fell to her mouth and she felt something stir inside her. "How often are you taking pills?" he asked softly.

The question stunned her so that she reared back. "*What*? What are you saying? Who in the hell do you think you are?"

He didn't answer, but let his gaze drift down her body before lifting it to her eyes again, and in those really stunning blue eyes, Audrey could see Jack was onto her.

"Just shut up," she said angrily, and brushed past him, headed for the bathroom. "It's not a big deal and it is *so* not your business," she spat over her shoulder as she stalked inside. She slammed the door, turned on the shower full blast and scalding hot. She slipped out of her clothes and climbed into the stall, and the moment the water hit her, Audrey melted.

She slid down the tiled wall to her haunches, her vision blurred by the tears that suddenly welled in her eyes. With her fists pressed against her mouth, she silently sobbed.

But when Audrey emerged a half hour later, she was completely composed, an art she had learned the last year in the course of her dizzying rise to fame and fortune. She was wearing a very short skirt and a T-shirt that had been doctored to look torn at the neck and arms by someone who thought three hundred dollars was what the look was worth.

Jack was standing at the window now—not that Audrey noticed or cared. She padded across the room to the trunk that held all her shoes and threw it open. She could feel Jack's eyes on her as she dug a pair of Ugg boots out if it. She stood and smoothed her skirt. No one had ever made her feel quite as naked as she was feeling at the moment.

Not even Lucas.

A sliver of guilt jabbed her. Audrey swallowed it down as she bent over and pulled one boot on, then the other. Jack was still watching her, but his expression had a predatory edge to it. It seemed almost as if he were restraining himself from capturing her and taking her back to his cave.

She walked across the room, picked up the little bag that held her cell phone and lipstick and mints—no money, she never needed money anymore—and said, "Let's go."

She didn't look back to see if Jack followed, just walked. She could feel him at her back as they stood waiting for the elevator, his gaze burning her body every place it touched. She could feel the warmth radiating from his body.

When the elevator arrived, Audrey stepped inside and slumped against the wall. Jack pushed the button for the second floor. As the elevator sped down, he clasped his hands behind his back and said, "You don't need pills to sleep."

"Oh dear God," she muttered angrily as the heat of shame crept into her neck. "I *said* it's none of your business."

He turned his head and looked at her; there was something new in his blue eyes. Dear God, was it *concern*? "I know," he said calmly. "But you're young and about to embark on the ride of your life. Why screw it up with pills?"

"Don't try and understand, Superman," she said. "You cannot imagine what my life is like. I have a lot on my mind."

"My guess? It's not your life that's convincing you to take those pills," he said casually. "Either you're not getting what you need, or someone is talking you into it."

That drew her up short—she cocked her head and eyed him curiously. "What do you mean, *getting what I need*?"

Jack gave her a very lopsided smile. "Exactly what you think I mean, cupcake."

She gasped; he smiled as the elevator door opened. "After you," he said, and put his big hand on the small of her back, guiding her out.

Audrey suppressed another bothersome shiver. Honestly, who did this guy think he was?

Seven

On the way to the arena, Audrey stared out the window at the passing scenery, one shapely leg crossed over the other, one booted foot swinging dangerously close to Jack's leg. There was no conversation—for which Jack was thankful, for the girl could really infuriate him. *Pills?* Who was she, Janis Joplin?—Jack studied the smooth skin of her thigh.

That was not helping him rid himself of the image of her in skimpy underwear.

Dammit. He could throttle her for not getting up this morning, because he had a feeling it was going to take him a good long while to stop thinking about those panties.

He wondered what she was thinking—she looked miserable. But when they turned into the parking lot of the arena, there was a small group of young girls hanging around the gated entrance. When they spied the limo, they screamed and jumped up and down, waving at it.

"Oh!" Audrey said, instantly lighting up like Times Square. "Stop here, stop here!" she cried to the driver, and as soon as he rolled to a stop, she popped out. Jack did, too, moving instantly to where she had walked up to the group of girls, who had broken into pandemonium at the sight of Audrey.

"What are you doing?" he demanded of Audrey.

"Hold your horses, Rambo," she said, and turned a brilliant smile to the girls. Their screams pierced his eardrums, but Audrey didn't seem to notice it—she was all smiles, dipping down to speak to the girls, taking their CDs and posters and autographing them. He watched in amazement as she spoke to each of the two dozen girls gathered there, answering their questions, complimenting their outfits, and looking every inch a star.

When she had signed everything she could reach, she told the girls she had to go and practice, said good-bye, then turned a warm smile to Jack. "I'm ready now."

He opened the door to the limo and she stepped in, giving one last, enthusiastic wave to the girls as Jack followed her in and shut the door.

The driver continued to the arena.

Jack couldn't help looking at her. She was still smiling. He'd been in Hollywood for too many years, had seen too many stars refuse autographs or to acknowledge their fans. He was astounded, really, by her eagerness. "That was really nice of you," he said, meaning it sincerely.

"Are you kidding?" She laughed warmly. "That is the one bright spot in my day. Girls like that are why I started the Songbird Foundation."

"The what?"

She laughed again, the sweet sound of it a stark contrast to the way she had spoken to him the last twenty-four hours. She seemed almost a different person somehow. More real. More alive.

"I guess you wouldn't know about my foundation, would you? I set it up when my second album went platinum. It's an organization that helps disadvantaged girls get into music. I would have killed for a little encouragement at that age, a little constructive, progressive instruction. Mostly I got the *put down the guitar and do the dishes* sort of thing. So now that I'm in a position to do it, I really want to give girls the chance to rock and roll that I had to fight to get."

Jack tried to picture Audrey at the age of ten or so, guitar in hand. He had an image of a scrappy little girl with dirty knees and tangled hair and a determined glint in her green eyes.

"I was lucky," she said as the limo drove up to a pair of glass doors at the arena. "I asked my old music teacher from high school to help me set up the foundation, and she's been fantastic. In the first year, we gave two hundred girls from across the country scholarships to study music." She smiled broadly, obviously proud of that accomplishment.

She had every right to be proud.

And when she smiled like that, it went all through Jack, warming him from the inside out. She looked young and fresh . . . and beautiful. "That's really cool," he said. "Too many people don't give back until their accountants tell them to."

"Well, you know, Security Dude, we are always looking for donations," she said with a sly wink.

He smiled. "Just tell me where to send a check."

Her eyes widened with surprise and pleasure. "Seriously?"

"Seriously. I'd be happy to donate."

"That's *fantastic*!" she exclaimed, smiling like a kid at Christmas. "I am so . . . surprised and pleased."

He couldn't help chuckling. "You think Security Dude doesn't have a heart?"

"As a matter of fact," she said with a laugh, "*no*." But she laughed again, and continued to smile as they made their way inside.

But as soon as they stepped inside, Junior Birdman was quickly on them, stepping in between her and Jack, his hand on Audrey's arm, and her smile faded rapidly. "What the hell, Audrey?" he said curtly.

"I overslept—"

"Don't make excuses. How many times do I have to tell you that professionalism is just as important as talent in this business? If you get a reputation for . . ." He paused and jerked his gaze to Jack. "Is there something you need?" he asked coolly.

Yeah. He needed to kick him in the teeth, but he held up his hands and stepped back.

Bonner turned back to Audrey, effectively dismissing Jack. "Let me show you the dressing room," he said low, and forced her to walk with him. Audrey went along, Jack thought, a little like a lap dog.

He watched the swing of her hips as she walked away. Damn, but he wished he didn't find her so attractive, particularly since he suspected she was a wreck. She had to be—one minute she was a pill-popping diva who let a jerk like Bonner lead her around by the nose, and the next she was the same sultry, sexy woman who used to sing soulful ballads in Austin clubs. She was exactly the sort of multiple-personality woman Jack normally avoided at all costs.

Yet there was something about Audrey LaRue that had slipped under his skin that night on the beach, and he was having a hard time getting her out.

Yeah, but he *would* get her out—he was fairly certain he just was having a normal male reaction to having seen one very fine ass this morning. Besides, he reminded himself, he was only in this deal for the money. He damn sure didn't need anything like useless lust complicating his life. Especially not right now—he needed to have a meeting with his guys and the Omaha police the promoter had brought in to work the concert crowd.

As he walked in the opposite direction of Audrey, the image of her nearly naked began to fade from his mind's eye, replaced by thoughts about security.

But it was obliterated altogether a few hours later when Audrey LaRue, *Diva*, marched toward him, the *click-click-clicking* of her heels on the concrete floor sounding a little like the rat-a-tat of a machine gun. He glanced up from his conversation with his subcontractor, Ted, and noticed that she'd changed clothes. She was wearing a costume—hotpants and a fierce-looking bra-thing. The flat plane of her belly was exposed and her blond curls were bound up into two mounds on top of her head.

She was also wearing a new expression, and this one was full of rancor as she sailed to a halt before them, glaring at Jack, oblivious to Ted. "*Hello?*" she said, folding her arms across her middle. "Did you forget who you are guarding?"

"No," Jack said calmly. "Did you forget how to converse politely?"

He heard a tiny snort of surprise from Ted, but it was nothing compared to the wide-eyed gasp of indignation he got from Audrey.

"I beg your *pardon*? Ohmigod, do you *know* who you are talking to?"

"Yes, Audrey. We have established who I am talking to more than once. Look, if you have a problem, or a question, you only have to ask nicely. You don't have to come at me in full attack mode."

"*Attack* mode?" she retorted angrily and shifted a fire-throwing gaze to Ted.

"Hey, I'm gonna check that . . . that thing we were talking about," Ted said, and quickly backed away.

Jack hardly noticed—he was staring at Audrey, one hand on his hip. "Do you want to try that again and ask your question *nicely*?"

"I don't have a question, *Rambo*, I have an *instruction*. You are supposed to be guarding me. For the last two hours, you have *not* guarded me, and therefore, everyone who works at Qwest Arena has been dropping in to say hi and ask me questions that I really don't have time to answer. So I would appreciate it if you would just do what you are being paid to do and keep them away from me!"

"Good God, I don't even know where to begin."

"How about an apology and a promise you will do your job?"

"No apology," he said, working to remain calm. "Let's get one thing straight, Audrey. Your keeper hired me to provide security to you and your tour—not to be your personal goon. You have a dozen people around you who can answer the door for you."

"What do you mean, my *keeper*?" she demanded, glossing right over his refusal to be her bouncer.

"Your boy—the one who tells you how to think and what to do."

"Are you talking about *Lucas*?" she squealed incredulously.

For a woman as creative as Audrey LaRue, she sure was dense when it came to that guy. "Anyone else feeding you pills?"

She gaped at him in disbelief. For a moment, she looked as if she would hit him. Then something washed over her, some emotion he couldn't really discern, but in the next moment, he saw the fire in those pretty green eyes.

He knew *that* emotion. *That* was full-bodied, potent female anger. One would think that Jack, having seen that look more times than he could possibly remember, might have learned a lesson or two. He hadn't, obviously, because he smiled in the face of it.

"You're *fired*!" she cried.

"Sorry, but you can't fire me. I signed a contract and you don't have the luxury of getting rid of me just because you don't like me."

"Oh, yeah?" she snapped, squaring off with him, her hands on a perfectly trim waist. "Do you honestly believe that I cannot *fire* you when I am the one who *hired* you?"

"No, you really can't," he said gleefully, feeling absurdly triumphant. "Why don't you check that out with the chief? He can read the contract to you. And in the meantime, I've got a lot to do, so if you could just tell me if there is anything else besides needing a butler to answer your door so we can both get on with our jobs, I'd appreciate it."

"Ohmigod!" she cried incredulously. "I'm sorry—I guess I thought that as some freak out there wants to kill me, my security guy might want to keep a close eye on who is waltzing into my dressing room every fifteen minutes! But hey, you don't think you need to do that," she said, waving her arms and head so heatedly that the Mickey Mouse ear balls on top of her head bounced. "You have so many more *important* things to do. Great, well, if I end up dead or—"

"You are not going to end up dead," he said impatiently. "If you had asked me nicely, I would have gladly told you that everyone in here today has been checked out. The doors are secure. One of my guys is standing in your hallway watching who comes and goes, and there are police crawling around outside. You can relax. *Trust* me."

That seemed to appease her somewhat.

"If you need something, or have a question about what we're doing, all you had to do is ask."

"*Thanks*," she said, her voice full of sarcasm. "I didn't know how to talk to my employees until you came along to show me."

He smiled with false sympathy. "I know."

"*Ohmigod*," she muttered below her breath and turned sharply on her stiletto heel to go.

"Hey!" Jack said before she could march away.

She paused, tossed her head back and groaned to the ceiling, then spared him a glance over her shoulder.

He took in her outstanding figure once more, then smiled and said, "Nice shorts."

"Shut. *Up*," she said, and marched on.

And for the second time that day, Jack watched a very fine-looking woman walk away from him.

"Oh hey," Courtney said when Audrey threw open the door of the dressing room and stalked inside. "Did you find him?" she asked as she quickly shoved a magazine beneath a bag at her feet.

Audrey walked over to Courtney's bag and glanced down. She saw the distinctive top of an issue of *Inside Celebrity* peaking out. "Yeah, I found him," she said irritably. She was furious with Jack, and furious with herself because she was actually *pleased* that he liked her shorts, which was just ridiculous because of *course* he liked her shorts; *all* guys liked her shorts. That was why she wore the shorts on stage, because her audience *liked* them.

Still, when he said he liked her shorts; she felt a funny tickle in her groin, the rat bastard. She couldn't even remember the last time Lucas said he liked anything she wore. Well, never mind that—she was not going to spend the next two months with some guy in her employ who told her to ask nicely and then lectured her about her manners, or sleeping pills, or anything else.

She leaned down, picked up the magazine Courtney had tried to hide. "I thought we weren't going to read those magazines anymore," she snapped at Courtney, and threw it across the room, toward the lone trash can. It fell a few feet short.

Courtney blushed and glanced at her feet. "I'm sorry, Audrey. I just can't stand it when I see something about you." She looked up and attempted a smile.

Honestly, Audrey had the feeling this perky young woman was just waiting to plunge a knife in her back. Lucas said she was overly paranoid. Maybe so, but at the very least, she was fairly certain that Courtney couldn't wait to read any bullshit written about Audrey.

But that was one battle she didn't need at the moment and she turned away from Courtney, pausing to pet Bruno, who was hopping around her feet, wanting her attention. "I need you to get Lucas," she said as she moved to her costumer, who was still waiting to adjust the outfit Audrey was wearing when she'd stormed out.

"Lucas is in a meeting."

Audrey sighed to the ceiling. "I don't care if he's in Siberia. I need to talk to him."

Courtney exchanged a look with Trystan, Audrey's lead dancer, who was watching everything from a fake leather couch. "Okay," she said. "I'll get him."

"*Thanks*," Audrey snarled, and watched her slink out before turning to glare at Lucy.

"All right, let me pin the shorts," Lucy said quickly.

"Please hurry," Audrey said. "Trystan and I still need to rehearse the 'Take Me' number . . . right, Trystan?"

"Sure, Audrey," Trystan said cheerfully.

Sure, Audrey. God, how she wished everyone could be like Trystan. *Sure, Audrey. We know that you are debuting your show to the biggest audience you have ever played to tonight, and it would be nice if we could be supportive of you instead of telling you to ask your questions nicely.*

A moment later, as Lucy worked, Courtney returned with Lucas on her heels. Courtney deliberately picked up the magazine Audrey had thrown across the room and put it in the trash, and exchanged a look with Lucas.

He frowned. "What is it?" he asked Audrey as Trystan shut the door behind him.

"It's the security guy," Audrey said. "I want him fired."

"*What?*" Lucas exclaimed, looking around at the others in the room. "Why? What happened?"

"*Nothing* happened. That is exactly the problem, Lucas. People have been dropping in all day, unannounced, asking me questions and interrupting me, and I thought he was supposed to be watching the door."

Lucas looked at Courtney, who looked at the floor. He sighed and looked at Audrey in a way that said she would not get what she wanted.

"I want that guy *fired*," she demanded again.

"Jesus, Audrey, we really don't have time for this right now, do we?"

"Lucas! Some guy has been threatening my life! It was your idea to get security; *you* were the one who said I needed protection! So why don't I have it?"

"You do have it. If you don't want people coming in, Courtney will answer the door. Or Trystan. Or *anyone*, I don't give a shit! But Jack has some slightly larger issues to tend to than your door!"

"I thought the issue was *me*, Lucas. You know, *my* tour, *my* life."

He sighed again, then flashed a very patronizing smile. He moved to put his arms around her, but Audrey shrugged him off. Lucas was persistent, though, and finally got his arms around her and kissed her temple. "You're right, baby, that is precisely the issue. But it takes a cast of thousands to protect you because you are such a huge star." He kissed her again, on the top of her head, just like she'd seen him kiss his niece.

"I had a talk with Courtney. She will answer the door. So no more talk of firing Jack. We can't just fire him anyway—there's a contract."

Oh hell. She hated that Jack was right and, with a groan, pressed her forehead to Lucas's shoulder.

"I think I know what is upsetting you. I think you are worried about the show. But don't worry, baby. The show is going to be spectacular. There is some press here from L.A. Did you know that?"

"No," she muttered.

"And guess what?" he said, dropping his arms from her. "I've got a little surprise for you tonight."

"What?" she asked as he walked to the door.

"I'm not telling you—it's a surprise." He winked. "Just chill out, okay? No more throwing things at Courtney."

"I *didn't* throw anything at Courtney," she said, glaring at her assistant.

"Baby, *please* calm down," Lucas said. "I'll check in on you later." He reached for the door handle and glanced at Courtney. "Courtney . . . you will answer the door so people aren't bothering Audrey, right?"

"Of course! Whatever she needs me to do," she said brightly.

"Good. Thanks," Lucas said, and with a smile, he opened the door.

"Lucas?" Audrey called after him.

He paused, glanced over his shoulder.

"What do you think of these shorts?"

He glanced at her shorts and shrugged. "They're fine. Why?"

"No reason," she said, and turned away from him, holding out her arms to indicate Lucy should continue her repair work.

They rehearsed the "Take Me" dance routine, a really difficult number, while Lucy held Bruno. Courtney could not be bothered, complaining she'd already had to walk the dog twice today. But someone had to hold him—Bruno could not see all the hopping about and not want to join in. It was precisely the reason Audrey did not want a dog.

They rehearsed until Trystan begged Audrey to stop so he would have something left for the show. So Audrey left and ran some vocal drills with her vocal coach, then had a light meal which she could scarcely eat. Two hours before show time, she went into makeup, where she was surrounded by people who transformed her into a pop star while she held Bruno.

When show time rolled around, she had forgotten about everything but her performance. As she walked down a dark and narrow corridor amid the electrical and sound equipment, Audrey realized she was nervous. This was a huge production, much bigger than anything she'd ever been involved with. There were three jumbotrons, eight costume changes, and a set that looked like something out of the movies. She thought she had gotten over the nerves that came with walking out onto a stage alone a long time ago, but they had come back with a vengeance tonight. It was just inconceivable to her that anyone would pay sixty-five dollars a seat to listen to her sing. It was even more inconceivable that twelve thousand people in Omaha alone would do that.

But they had, and as she waited below stage to make her entrance—rising up through smoke into blue light—she could hear the crowd whistling and stirring, anticipating her arrival. Fred, her stylist, was still futzing with her hair until she batted him away. She stood there alone now, listening to the last song Lucas would play, regretting that she had allowed him to sweet-talk her into opening for her—he really wasn't that good, was he?

"Hey."

Although there were a dozen technicians around her, the voice startled her. She turned to see Jack standing just beneath a big loop of cable. He was wearing a black shirt and faded Levi's, and his pool blue eyes were amazingly luminous in the dark light.

"Just wanted to tell you to break a leg," he said with a wink. "If you sing as good as you look, you will have them drooling all over the arena."

She smiled in spite of herself. "Thanks."

He smiled, too; a warm, easy smile.

"Show time," the stage manager whispered. "Your mic'd, so no talking." He held up a flashlight to lead Audrey to the platform. Audrey picked up her guitar then turned around—but Jack was gone. She stepped through the cables and onto the platform, assuming her position as the band began to play a pretty melody. The platform Audrey was standing on shuddered into motion, and she felt herself being lifted up. She raised her head, looked at the lights swimming above her, and took a deep breath.

She was terrified. She was always a little terrified until she opened her mouth and the first note came out, clear and precise. Tonight, the terror rattled her bones.

But when she was lifted to the stage, and walked out into the smoke and lights to the deafening roar of the crowd as the smoke slowly cleared and they recognized her, she felt a current run through her like she had never experienced before. It was exhilarating, absolutely intoxicating.

"*Hello, Omaha!*" she shouted, and the roar of the crowd rattled the dome as the band quickened the beat. Audrey opened her mouth—and the first note came out clear, strong, and pitch-perfect.

Eight

The night was magical in a way Audrey had never imagined it could be. There was nothing quite as euphoric as the applause of thousands for a song well sung. Up until tonight, she'd never heard that applause from a group larger than five thousand souls. The shouts of her name, the whistling, the constant applauding—all of it infused Audrey with the desire to give the performance of her life. She sang like she'd never sung, danced through every song with fresh legs, her steps quick and feather light, and she smiled so broadly that her cheeks hurt with it.

Her only regret was that there were a couple of places she thought needed more work, but for the most part, everyone had performed fabulously. The show seemed to be over before it had even begun. She could have sung all night, could have danced until her heels were worn into nubs. She performed two encores. And at the end of the second encore, she noticed the lights shifting as she sang, and glanced to her right to see Lucas—*Lucas!*—strolling onto the stage playing a steel guitar. He was wearing his favored black leather pants, a trench coat, and shades. She continued singing, but the light stayed with Lucas.

When the song came to an end, she had no choice but to extend her arm in his direction and shout, "*Lucas Bonner on steel guitar!*"

The crowd roared their approval; Lucas bowed and then strolled across the stage in his little circle of light, wrapped Audrey in a tight embrace, and kissed her on the mouth—much to the crowd's delight—then forced her to bow with him, as if *they* had just put on the show of her life, as if *they* had sung and danced their way through this night.

They bowed twice more before Lucas grabbed her hand and pulled her to the platform that would lower them below stage. The cheering and wild applause seemed to crescendo as they descended.

"Good show!" the stage manager shouted below, clapping Lucas on the back as he hurried off. They were alone—the stage crew was on the periphery, manning lights and smoke canisters. It was dark where they stood; Lucas grabbed Audrey and kissed her on the mouth like he hadn't kissed her in ages.

"That was fantastic," he said, kissing her again and pushing her back, deeper beneath the stage, into the tangle of cables and wires. "What a fucking rush!" he exclaimed breathlessly, as if he'd spent the last hour and a half up there, making his feet move through intricate steps in stiletto heels, as if he'd managed to sing without sounding winded while strutting across the stage and into the crowd and back.

He pushed her up against some planking, his hand groping for her breast.

"Lucas—"

"Come on, baby, that was a trip," he said again as his hand slipped to her bare leg beneath the hem of her short skirt. "You totally turned me on," he muttered as his hand rode up her thigh to the apex of her legs.

Audrey gasped a little; her head dipped back with her surprise at the bit of arousal and the pleasure of illicit sex under the stage . . . even if it was, as it turned out, fast and hard and not particularly romantic. Lucas came all over her leg, but still, it was sex, and there had been precious little of that in the last few months. Besides, Audrey was too revved up from the show, too excited by how well it had gone to dwell on the coarseness of it.

But she could not dismiss the thought in her mind that the person she was thinking of when Lucas lifted her up and pounded into her was Jack.

Above, at stage level, in an area curtained off for the crew and for Audrey to make quick costume changes, Jack had stood and watched the entire show. It was an electrifying performance—he was astounded by Audrey's talent and her ability to relate to an audience of twelve thousand as if they were all squeezed into an intimate club setting. Granted, he preferred the soulful ballads she used to sing, but he was nevertheless drawn into this show. Audrey danced like a pro, her hips gyrating, her blond hair swinging. Her voice was beautiful. *She* was beautiful.

Perhaps the most surprising thing to Jack was that Audrey seemed happier on stage than he had yet to see her.

It was clear to him that Audrey was born for the limelight—she was mesmerizing, and it was no surprise that the crowd went wild for her.

It had been a great show, with no more than a couple of minor chinks . . . until Bonner wormed his way on stage and let the crowd know that Audrey was his. Jack despised Bonner in that moment—for no other reason than he had taken the last moment of a successful tour debut away from Audrey, had taken her away from the crowd, and had inserted himself where he didn't belong.

Now, with the lights up, the crowd had started to dissipate, the crew was breaking down the stage, and the lovers still had not emerged from the caverns beneath the stage.

Jack pushed down a strange twinge of jealousy and walked away.

He spotted them a half hour later when they finally showed up to the after party. Audrey was resplendent, absolutely glowing with the exhilaration of having pulled off an almost flawless show. Or a quickie beneath the stage. Okay, Jack wasn't certain about that, but he knew women, and he knew that look.

She bounced from guest to guest, receiving their accolades, signing hats and CD covers. Individual cameras flashed; Lucas pressed a drink into her hand as she stood and posed for a dozen pictures or more with fans lucky enough to have gained a backstage pass. Her smile never wavered, the glow never dimmed.

When she finally made her way to the bar, she spotted Jack and smiled so warmly that he felt a peculiar little tug in his chest. "Hey! What did you think of my show, Superman?"

He smiled at her glittering green eyes. "I thought it was out of this world," he said sincerely. "I predict you will be an even bigger star—you've got a presence on stage that is fantastic."

"Wow! Thank you," she said, beaming with pleasure. "I'll have to buy you a drink for that." She chirped to the bartender, "A glass of red wine, please—and whatever my friend is having."

"I'm good," Jack said to the bartender, and to Audrey. "I'm working, remember?"

As the bartender stepped away, Audrey shifted her gaze to Jack again. "So you saw the whole show? I mean, all of it?"

"Every number, every dance."

"So let me ask you something—what did you think of the lighting during the 'Take Me' number?"

"A little too dark," he said.

"Too dark!" She laughed. "What are you talking about? It's a very sultry song—it's *supposed* to be dark. You're probably not the sultry kind."

"What kind do you think I am?"

She peered at him closely, then winked. "The no-holds-barred kind."

"Audrey!" someone called, interrupting them before Jack could tell her she had pegged him exactly right.

She turned to her right. "Hey, Randy!" she said, throwing her arms wide and around the guy dressed head to foot in Prada. Everyone else in the room was wearing jeans. "Did you see the show?" she asked excitedly.

"I saw it and it was great. Perfect! But what was that with Bonner?" Randy, whoever he was, asked. "I hope that doesn't become a habit. You're spending a lot of money to promote your release. Not his release."

"God, Randy, it was just one song," Audrey said. "Hey, do you want a drink?" she asked, turning toward the bar.

"Audrey, listen, between you and me . . ." Out of the corner of his eye he saw Jack and paused.

"Oh, this is Jack, my security guy," she said, putting her hand on Jack's arm. You can say anything to him." She smiled up at Jack. "Randy is my agent."

Agents, managers . . . it was impossible to keep up with the entourage.

"Good to meet you," Randy said, shaking Jack's hand, but he was looking at Audrey. "I am just saying don't let Bonner get ahead of you, okay? Remember that you're the money—not him."

"You worry too much, Randy!" Audrey said cheerfully. "Lucas knows that. He was just having a little fun on the kick-off show. And everyone said it was great!"

Randy didn't look convinced, and frankly, neither was Jack. But Audrey was sipping her wine, beaming with joy.

"Okay, Audrey," Randy said and glanced around the room. His gaze fell on Courtney, who was sitting on a tabletop with her skirt hiked up so high that Randy was afforded a very nice view of her thigh. "I'll call you next week. Rich and I are headed back to L.A. in the morning."

"Rich, too?" Audrey asked absently as she sipped on her drink.

"He'll be back. He's going to try and make a show next week, depending on his workload." Randy looked across the room again. "Will you excuse me? I'm going to go say hi to Courtney," he said, and with a kiss on Audrey's cheek, he looked at Jack. "Later."

"Bye, Randy! Thanks for coming!" Audrey said after him. She watched him go then turned her beaming grin to Jack. "You look good in black—it's definitely a good color for a bouncer."

"I am going to pretend that was a compliment," he drawled.

"It was." Her eyes were shining like a pair of headlights on a dark highway. "I'm feeling strangely magnanimous." She laughed at herself. "The thing is, Rambo, when you aren't so full of yourself, you're pretty cute."

A smile stretched across Jack's lips. "That's interesting. This afternoon you wanted to fire me. Tonight you think I'm cute. You might want to slow down on the wine," he added, and casually reached up and pulled free a strand of blond hair that had become caught between her glass and the edge of her mouth as she sipped.

Her eyes sparkling, she lowered the glass. "Oh, I still want to fire you," she cheerfully affirmed as her gaze flicked to the open vee of his shirt. "But you're still cute."

"Interesting. I still think you're a diva . . ." He leaned in, his gaze locked on hers. "But you're pretty cute yourself."

Audrey laughed, but she also blushed. She *blushed*. Jack had no doubt someone was telling her how damned sexy she was on a fairly constant basis, but she blushed like a young girl. And when she blushed, she looked so damned appealing that Jack had the urge to kiss her. A strong, extremely volatile urge, and if he wasn't mistaken, she was looking at him like she wouldn't mind it at all.

There was probably no end to the number of men and women alike who wanted to kiss her, and if there was one thing that was fairly clear to him in his short association with her *Frantic* tour, she didn't need that from him. Nevertheless, he wanted to take her in his arms in the worst way, to feel her body against his, to taste her lips . . .

Audrey tilted her head back and smiled in a way that suggested she knew what effect she had on him. Fortunately, Jack was stronger than his testosterone and winked. "Later, twinkle toes," he said, and walked away, aware that she was gaping at his back with surprise and, knowing her, righteous indignation. He chuckled to himself.

But that blushing smile of hers stayed in his mind's eye the rest of the night and long after.

Jack had learned long ago that when a woman started to slip under your skin, the best remedy for getting her out was work. He'd stayed up to oversee the loading of the tour buses, and the ten semis that hauled the stage and equipment, and in doing so, saw Courtney and Randy engaged in a very passionate good-bye in the parking lot just before dawn.

He got only a couple of hours of sleep before he was back again the next morning with Ted, inspecting the bags to go into the cargo hold of

Audrey's bus, when Courtney came looking for him, dressed in a racy halter dress she'd worn all night.

"Hey, handsome," she said, pressing up against his side.

"Good morning, Courtney. You're up early this morning," he said as he moved away from her.

"What makes you think I got up instead of got in?" she asked with a wink. "Hey, you disappeared last night!" she said, playfully punching him on the shoulder. "Where'd you go?"

"I had work to do. Is there something you need?"

"No . . . but there is something I want," she purred, then frowned a little. "But right now, Audrey wants you, too," she said as she slyly touched his hip. "She's at the hotel."

He sighed and shifted his weight away from her hand. "Please tell Audrey I'm busy at the moment but I will talk to her before we leave for Minneapolis."

"I think you need to come," Courtney said with a subtle wink.

"Courtney—"

"There was a delivery for her this morning," Courtney continued. "She got another letter. And a bad review," she added with a slight roll of her eyes. "You would think the world had ended."

"Another letter?" Jack asked, missing the remark about the review.

"Mmm-hmm," Courtney said as her gaze skirted over him. "With a box of chocolates."

"Tell her I'll be right up."

"*Right* up? Can't entice you to a detour?" Courtney asked with a seductive smile.

Jack put his hand firmly on her shoulder and turned her around. "No detours," he said, and gave her a nudge instead of a boot, which, for a moment, he seriously contemplated doing.

He felt a rumble of concern. "I'll check in with you later," he said to Ted, and started for the hotel.

Nine

In the hotel, Audrey had surrounded herself with Lucas and anyone else who could form a shield between her and any lunatics lurking in the halls at that very moment.

She was seated at a table, mindlessly autographing a stack of photos to be mailed out through her fan club, but her mind was on the chocolates and the note that the bellboy had delivered early this morning. As Lucas was digging through the box in search of truffles, Audrey had opened the note and read a horribly vile wish to see her dead. She stopped Lucas before he bit into a chocolate.

Now the police had come, taking away the box of chocolates to be tested, reading the note, asking her the same questions she'd been asked in New York when she received the last letter. *Did she know anyone who would want to harm her? Any problems with the family? The boyfriend? The lover?* She hated the questions—hated even worse that they seemed to believe there was a never-ending well of people who hated her. Worse, they didn't seem to think there was much they could do about it. "These things are almost impossible to trace," one officer said.

And to add insult to injury, one of the policemen had left a newspaper on her table. She'd made the mistake of opening it while they waited for someone to make some calls—she'd forgotten who or where—and had happened upon the review of her show.

Unfortunately, the reviewer was perhaps the one person in the arena who hadn't enjoyed the show last night. He said her music was derivative of Mariah and Kelly, that the lighting was intentionally dark to cover up the fact that she was a little too old to be embarking on a career in pop, and that the only song that had stood out was the ballad she sang and played on acoustical guitar, backed only by a violin.

That was an old song of hers, the only one Lucas and her label had allowed her to keep on the new album.

"I'm only twenty-eight!" she said when she read the paper and tossed it across the table. "They make it sound like I'm *forty*-eight."

"It's Omaha," Lucas said absently. "Who cares what Omaha thinks?"

Well . . . *she* did. And so did the cop standing next to Lucas, judging by the way he was looking at Lucas. The review wouldn't have stung quite so bad if Audrey didn't believe she'd done really well last night.

She groaned, paused in the autographing to push her hands through her hair. She just wanted to leave Omaha for Minneapolis, just get the hell out of here and move on, move forward. With a sigh, she began to autograph again as Lucas, wearing his distressed jeans and a faded blue T-shirt that said ROLLING STONES FORTY LICKS on it, ranted to one of the officers in the room.

Audrey glanced out the window—it looked like a blistering morning, and reminded her of a gig she'd had in Austin once, at The Backyard, an outdoor music venue. It had been blistering that day, too, but it was one of the best sets of her life. It was all acoustic, just her and a guitar—no pop—just the ballads she loved to write in alternative folk style and then transform into alternative rock when she got bored with them. Those were the songs she loved creating, the songs that made her want to get out of bed every morning.

Sometimes she felt like she wasn't supposed to be where she was now, like she was living someone else's life. If it hadn't been for Lucas's idea to turn her into a star, she might have stayed in the safety zone of her old music the rest of her life. Left to her own devices, she probably never would have jumped out to experience all that life had to offer.

Oh, but she would have missed so much—she would have missed the taste of fame and the chance to sing to twelve thousand people. Her new release was sitting at number 4 on the charts, right behind Kelly Clarkson and just ahead of Pink. Wasn't that what every musician dreamed of happening?

But then again, if she'd stayed in Austin, she probably wouldn't have some freak scaring the shit out of her.

A knock on the door interrupted her thoughts; Lucas, still talking, opened the door, and without speaking, without even a gesture, turned around and walked back into the room, his mind on his conversation with the officer.

From across the room, Audrey's eyes met Jack's. He was standing at the threshold, his arm up and braced against the door jamb, the other hand on his waist. What surprised her was how she instantly felt safer with him in the room.

One thick, dark strand of hair hung over his eye as he took her in. "Are you all right?" he asked.

Audrey nodded.

He straightened up and walked into the room, closing the door softly behind him, ignoring the cops. He glanced briefly at Lucas's back, and Audrey did not miss the slight, but unmistakable look of disdain that glanced his features. "You should have called me," he said, reaching her at the table.

"I sent Courtney."

"I would prefer you call me the moment something like this happens. So you want to tell me about it?"

Audrey shrugged and glanced out the window. "There's really nothing to tell. A box of chocolates was delivered with a note from someone who thinks I am teasing him by sending signals to him, coded in my songs. And that he thinks I am such a whore and I should die. You know, the usual. I'd show you the note, but the police took it."

"When did the chocolates arrive?"

"About nine this morning. A bellboy brought them up from the front desk. They are tracking that down now, but they won't find him. Look at all the flowers," she said, sweeping her arm around the living area. "They've been running stuff up here every hour since we arrived."

Jack nodded, but he didn't look at the flowers. He just kept looking into her eyes, making her feel strangely exposed. It was almost as if he could see inside her somehow and knew how miserable and vulnerable she felt at that moment, how close she thought she was to crumbling. His scrutiny made her nervous and she abruptly stood up, tossing down her pen.

"Are you sure you're okay?" he asked again.

"I'm *fine*," she said, and turned away from his probing eyes so abruptly that she collided with the table there. "I just want to know when we are leaving. There is a lot I need to do in Minneapolis—we need to rehearse 'Frantic' because I am screeching the last few notes, and someone needs to do something about the lighting—"

"No, no, no!" Lucas interrupted loudly from his perch on the edge of the couch. He held one finger up to the officer as he spoke to Audrey. "The show is *fine*. We are not going to change things because some pimply-faced punk reviewer in Omaha thinks your set is too dark. Get a grip," he said sternly. "It's one fucking review." And just as abruptly as he had snapped at her, he returned to his conversation.

Audrey was so taken aback she couldn't even speak for a moment. Not that it mattered—Lucas was absorbed in his all-important conversation with the police and was not the least bit concerned with her feelings, which were, at that moment, edging toward a total meltdown. She despised that about herself—over the last couple of weeks she couldn't seem to get away from the feeling. It reminded her of her mother, who could fly into a fury without the slightest bit of provocation. Audrey had always thought her mother was highly fragile and that *she*—singer, artist, balanced soul—was the even-tempered, thoughtful one.

But at the moment, she could feel the heat of shame, embarrassment, *something*, creep into her neck, spread up to her face, and it was all she could do to shift her gaze to Jack.

His eyes said it all, blue eyes filled with loathing and pity and . . . and that was it, about all she could take for one morning. "When do we leave?"

"An hour, maybe a little longer."

"Great," she said, and moved for the door.

"Hey!" Lucas shouted after her. "*Audrey!* Where in the hell are you going?"

She answered by throwing open the door and striding through, her arms swinging, her gait determined. She had to get out of there, to go someplace where she could be alone and melt down in private.

Audrey reached the elevators and punched the down button. Several times. Over and over again in rapid succession until she was convinced the door was not going to open for her, at which point she turned and ran to the stairwell. She had made it down one flight when she heard the stairwell door open and close above her, and assumed it was Lucas coming after her to smooth things over.

Only she didn't want to smooth things over. She just wanted to be alone, and she didn't think that was asking too terribly much. Just someplace Lucas wasn't hovering and no one was demanding anything from her.

She made it as far as the sidewalk before he caught up with her, grabbing her arm and wrapping thick fingers around it to stop her. But it wasn't Lucas as she expected—it was Jack.

"Wow. You're fast. I'm impressed."

"Why are you following me?" she snapped, jerking her arm free of his grasp.

For some reason, that made Jack laugh, but upon seeing her murderous look, he instantly put up an apologetic hand. "It's a strange question, you have to admit. There is some freak out there who wants to hurt you, so it seems fairly obvious to me why I am following you. And besides, you almost killed your poor little rat."

Audrey gasped—he was carrying Bruno in the crook of one arm, like a football. She'd forgotten about him. She took Bruno from Jack and glanced across the street, where a mall with an actual green and trees and beautiful plants and a trail and a little river stretched for several blocks. It looked so pretty, so peaceful—and she'd almost made it, had almost escaped to privacy. "Can't I just go for a walk?" she asked, her voice depressingly small.

"Sure. But I'm going with you."

Audrey shot him a dark look. "I meant *alone.*"

He shrugged. "Sorry, kid. You know the only way I can let you walk over there is to go with you. Especially after getting the chocolate and another letter."

She knew it, but knowing it didn't aggravate her any less. "Fine," she said irritably. "Then come on." And with that, she began striding down the street, to the crosswalk. Jack was instantly at her side, walking along like he was on some Sunday stroll while Audrey marched faster and faster to outdistance him.

She couldn't do it.

When they reached a light, she shot a look at him. He was as fresh as a daisy, even though it had to be ninety degrees and very humid. Audrey stifled a scream and pounded on the pedestrian button several times. When she finished, Jack arched a brow.

So did Audrey.

He calmly reached around her and pressed the button on the front of the light post.

It dawned on her that she'd been pounding the pedestrian walk button for the wrong direction. She ignored his smile of amusement, and as soon as the light turned—which took a while, given her impatient button-pushing—she practically sprinted across the street.

Jack easily kept pace with her, and even put a firm hand on her elbow to slow her when they reached the green.

"Okay, all right, I won't run away," she said, pulling her arm free and stooping to let Bruno run. "But could I just have a little privacy?"

He gestured for her to walk ahead of him.

She walked on, her skin melting where his hand had touched her, her mind racing around thoughts of his hand on other parts of her body. It was ridiculous—after what she'd been through this morning, she was thinking of *sex*? Yet it wasn't just sex. It was something more than that, something like what she had felt on the beach that night. *Comfort.*

After a few minutes, she grew weary of trying to clear her thoughts of Jack and stopped dead in her tracks. Jack was apparently following fairly close behind because he collided with her back, catching her shoulders in his hand and twirling them both around to face the water. With his hands on her shoulders, his body against hers, he said into her ear, "You might warn a person next time," and let go.

Audrey didn't move. She took great gulps of air to calm her nerves and her racing heart as Bruno bounced around her feet, wanting to keep going.

She closed her eyes, willed herself to stop thinking of Jack. She wasn't supposed to be attracted to him. She had a boyfriend. Sort of. Even if Lucas was a colossal jerk sometimes, she was still with him. And besides, even if there had been no Lucas—and there was definitely a Lucas—Jack was an employee. No one got involved with their employees unless they were in a sitcom. Wait . . . what was she thinking? *Involved* with Jack? She'd made the mental leap from attracted to *involved*?

Good God, she had much bigger things on her plate right now, like the tour, and her missing brother, and the *I'm going to kill you* note, of course, not to mention the awful review that she could not seem to get off her mind. There was no time for a lot of ridiculous *Jack* thinking. He was just a sexy guy, that was all, a sexy guy who somehow seemed to understand her better than anyone else on this tour, and it didn't help that he went down on his haunches on the water's edge and looked about as sexy as any man she had ever seen.

But then he ruined everything by asking, in that sultry, husky voice tinged with a slight drawl, "Why do you let him talk to you like that?"

"Oh, great," she said irritably. "Just great. Now you're going to critique my relationship. Let's see, what else can I add to this day? What about bird flu? I haven't had bird flu. Maybe I should just heap that right on top."

He laughed and put his hand on Bruno's head when the dog nuzzled him. "I'm not critiquing anything. I just wonder how this ever got twisted around to where the dude thinks he is the star instead of you."

"He doesn't think he is the star," she said curtly. "He knows I am, but he . . ." Her voice trailed off as she struggled to think of the words that would explain Lucas. "I don't even know why I am having this conversation," she said irritably. "You wouldn't understand it anyway."

Instead of being insulted, Jack smiled. "Try me."

"No."

"Suit yourself. But I'm here if you ever want to talk." He stood up, folded his arms over his chest, and smiled so warmly that Audrey felt that melting thing again. "So are you going to walk? There is a lagoon just down the way. Your furry little rat friend can run around a little and you can count the ducks."

"*Ducks?*" As if ducks would somehow make her feel better. It was insane—she suddenly had the strong urge to explain everything to Jack. "You don't know where I came from, Jack," she blurted, drawing his attention back to her. "Just two years ago I was packing Lucas's boxers for a gig in Luckenbach, of all places, and now I am playing to sold-out audiences. Do you realize there were twelve thousand people in that arena last night? Twelve thousand! I owe that all to Lucas—if it wasn't for him, I would not be here today. So just cut him a little slack, will you?"

"I am sure he's been a big help," Jack admitted. "But if you think for one minute that you were playing to twelve thousand people last night for any other reason than your talent, he's really done a number on you."

Audrey snorted. "And now you're an expert on how a pop star hits it big. Well, news flash—I wasn't voted to be a pop star on *American Idol.* It took a lot of work and a lot of people for me to get where I am today."

"I'm no expert, but I'm not deaf, and I know talent when I hear it. This tour is about *your* talent. You're on tour because of your *talent* and not because Bonner had a great idea once. Believe me, if you had stuck with the music you used to play, you would still be playing to an audience this size. It might have taken you a little longer to get here, but you would have made it."

"The music I *used* to play?" she said, turning to face him fully. "And how would you know about that?"

Something changed in his expression that gave Audrey a shiver. "I know," he said, his gaze sliding over her body like silk. "You aren't the only one from Texas here. It so happens I caught a couple of your shows in Austin a few years ago."

"You're kidding," Audrey said flatly.

He lifted his gaze. "Swear to God I did."

"*Really?*" she demanded, trying to read him.

He leaned forward, so that they were almost nose to nose. "*Really.*"

He'd *heard* her? He'd heard the music she loved? There was an obvious question, one she absolutely did not want to ask because she did not care what his opinion was, but somehow, her mouth got ahead of her brain and she said, "So . . . what did you think?"

"What did I think?" His gaze dipped to her lips. "I *loved* it. I loved *you.*"

She smiled with unabashed pleasure. "You did?"

"I thought you were the best sound in Austin."

The best sound in Austin. There was a time when that was all she aspired to. He'd known about her in Austin, and then. . . . "Wait, wait," she said, shaking her head. "Wait just a minute. If you had heard me in Austin, then what was that whole *never heard of you* thing in Costa Rica?"

With a chuckle, Jack carelessly brushed a curl of her hair from her cheek. "Well, now, sweetheart, if you hadn't come off like such a diva that night, I wouldn't have felt so compelled to turn that ego of yours down a notch."

"*Diva!*" Audrey insisted angrily. "I don't have an ego!"

"Oh no? You seem to have a pretty healthy one to me."

"How would you know?"

He cocked a dubious brow. "Well, for starters, you bite a lot of heads off around you. You're not very polite, as we have discussed."

Was that true? Did they *all* think she was a diva? But she wasn't, not even close! She was really very nice— Wait. What was she doing? "Oh my *God*," Audrey said, and with one arm, shoved him aside as she began marching down the path again. "I am not going to try and explain myself to you!" she shouted over her shoulder.

"Fine. But don't go far—we didn't budget for me to follow you around like your dog when you're having a tantrum."

"I'm not having a tantrum! I just want some time alone without you telling me what a diva I am, or without anyone threatening me or . . . or whatever!" she exclaimed, her hands wildly punctuating the air around her. "Is that asking too much? Is a little alone time asking too much?"

"Of course not," he said congenially. "This is your show. If you want some time alone, you need only ask for it. You don't have to stomp off like a PMS-ing fourteen-year-old when you don't instantly get your way. Just let me know when you want me to arrange it."

She seethed at his insolence. "All right. I am letting you know that I want you to *arrange* it, Rambo. I want you to arrange it *right now*."

He grinned in that sexy, lopsided way he had of smiling and Audrey suddenly needed to be away from him and those blue eyes. She turned and ran.

She knew how stupid and immature she must look, and okay, probably a little diva-ish. But at least she felt in control of whatever it was that was happening inside her.

When she had put sufficient distance between them and was nearing the walk down to the lagoon, she whipped her head around to see where Rambo was—right behind her, of course—and missed the jogger who was running up the incline from the lagoon altogether. Their shoulders collided, and it startled Audrey so badly that she shrieked.

"*Sorry*," the man said breathlessly as he ran by.

In that split moment of the collision, Audrey feared the worst—she feared the freak had found her and her heart stopped. She gasped, clamped a hand over her heart as the man ran by; at almost the same moment, Jack grabbed her, clamping an arm securely around her shoulders. "See? Yet another reason not to stomp off in anger—you don't watch where you are going," he said soothingly.

He was making light of it, but he knew what she'd thought—she could hear it in his deep voice, which wafted over her like a protective blanket, and Audrey lost it. Her frayed nerves and the tangled emotions Jack evoked in her—the small truths he uttered seemed to unravel her perceptions of reality. She had no idea how he did it, but she somehow turned into him and blindly managed to put her hands on his face.

She kissed him.

But Jack suddenly grabbed her arms and held her away from him. "*Don't*," he said, his blue eyes full of warning. "Don't do that. Because if you do it again, I am going to give it right back and a whole lot more. Do you understand me?"

She didn't speak, just panted as she gazed at his lips.

His eyes narrowed. "I mean it, Audrey. Don't start something you can't or won't finish."

She still didn't know how it happened—whether she grabbed him or he grabbed her—but she was kissing him, again, and it was no small kiss. She was devouring him, trying to eat him up, swallow him whole. It was a monumental moment, a jarring wake-up call to all her senses, and suddenly her entire body felt more alive than she'd felt in weeks, months, maybe even years. Desire raged through her like a wildfire, spreading quickly and with deadly consequences. Every protest, every reason her mind conjured up to stop her, Audrey tossed aside like so many bits of bread for the ducks.

Jack responded by twirling her around and pushing her up against the trunk of a tree. His lips began to press more urgently against hers; his hands swept down her arms, to her waist, and then up again, to either side of her breasts. She plunged her tongue wildly into his mouth, relishing his guttural moans of approval, and the feel of him pressed hard against her.

The fingers of one hand splayed against her breast while the other swept around to her back, down to her hip, pressing her against him, against the hard ridge of his arousal.

Audrey pushed her hands through his hair, caressed his ears and the breadth of his shoulders. She moved seductively against him. Her blood was pounding in her veins; her pulse was racing and making her breathless. She had never felt such massive, consuming desire, had never wanted so badly to throw a man to the ground and ride him.

It was, thank God, the sound of an approaching jogger, the sound of hard breathing that was not hers or Jack's, that brought her to her senses. It took all of her willpower to turn her mouth from his, to push against his chest and her unconscionable lapse of judgment.

But he still had his arm around her and a lustful look in his eye. He discreetly caressed the peak of her breast with the palm of his hand.

"*Stop*," she whispered, and closed her eyes. "We have to *stop*. I'm sorry. I . . . this is insanity."

"Is it?"

"Yes! I don't *want* . . . I mean, this isn't what you think."

He leaned in, trapping her with his arms and his eyes against that tree. "I think it's *exactly* what I think," he said huskily, and nipped at her lips.

"What?"

"I think you need to be with a man, Audrey. I think you need it worse than any woman I have ever met. You don't need pills, sweetheart, you need—"

"*No!*" she exclaimed, and shoved hard against him.

His arms fell away. His eyes roamed over her face, and he pushed a curl behind her ear, then reluctantly dropped his hands altogether. "I will tell you this once," he said, shoving his hands in his pocket. "Don't. Do. That. *Again.*"

"No, of course not," she said weakly, and turned away from him, pressing a hand to her forehead, where she felt a sudden and searing pain. "I don't know what came over me," she muttered, playing back in her mind how she had practically attacked him, almost thrown him to the ground and ripped off his clothes in a public park in Omaha. What was she thinking? "I just *lost* it," she said. She glanced at him from the corner of her eye.

Jack was watching her closely, his expression still hungry, his body still hard.

"Look," she said, stepping away from him and skittishly pushing a hand through her hair, "I apologize. That . . . that *definitely* will not happen again," she said, pointing to the space where they had just been standing. "I mean, I'm not *that* whacked out."

A wry smile tipped the corner of Jack's mouth.

"Okay, wait. I obviously don't mean that like it sounded," she said instantly. "But I will never do that again. I can't believe I just did that. I mean, you're really not—"

"Okay, okay, I get it," he said, and turned around, whistling for Bruno. The dog instantly came running from a stand of bushes. "We need to get back . . . unless you want more time to look at the ducks."

"Ducks?" She snorted and shook her head. "No. No, I really need to get back." She moved forward, anxious to get back, to put some distance between her and Jack. When she paused and looked over her shoulder, he was walking behind her, holding Bruno like a football again. "I . . .

that really was just a reaction to stress," she said, feeling a desperation to explain. Or perhaps to convince herself—she wasn't certain. "It didn't mean anything. I don't want you to think—"

"Audrey," he said, looking ahead on the path. "You don't need to say more. I get it. Let's go."

"Right," she said, and began to walk, head down, her heart spinning in her chest.

Critic Picks for the Week

(*Minneapolis Star Tribune*) Whether or not you buy into Audrey LaRue as the next great American pop star—particularly without benefit of *American Idol* to propel her into that superstardom—it's hard not to get caught up in the buzz over her first national tour. The American Diva puts on a show with everything the public wants: pyrotechnics, sensual dancing, and the chops that have the tone of greatness behind them. Don't miss this show—it's guaranteed to rock you. (7:30 p.m. Fri. $33–$58. Northrop Auditorium, University of Minnesota)

BLOGGING CRITICS

Your Source for All Music

CD Review: Audrey LaRue—*Frantic*

Frantic, Audrey LaRue's third pop album, made its debut in July and had the firepower to go platinum in the first two weeks. But it is a jumbled bag of emotions delivered in a confusing mix of rock and pop that leaves the listener wondering if LaRue knows what she's singing. "Take Me" is either LaRue's attempt to sing a pleading balled or to head bang her way through a successful tour. She alternately screeches her firepower and then breathlessly falls off in "Frantic" and "On the Wall." She does demonstrate a depth of talent in the more sultry offerings of "Sweet Dreams" and "Without You," whose lyrics are contemplative and show a side to LaRue's talent not likely to be seen on tour, where sexy pop and dance are showcased. When LaRue sings a ballad, one can believe she has loved deeply and lost even deeper. But this album of pop lacks the maturity of a seasoned songwriter and performer—there is nothing to distinguish her songs from other pop artists who populate the charts, with the exception of perhaps LaRue's age, which, at 28, is five to seven years older than most of her competition.

a diva in the making?

(*Us Weekly*) Does Audrey LaRue have what it takes to be a diva? Sources say the stress of her first nationwide tour is getting to her. "She threw a magazine at her assistant," a source reveals, "because she can't handle distractions." LaRue's publicist, Hollywood veteran Mitzi Davis, said the report is ridiculous. "Nothing happened," she avows. "The tour is going great."

Ten

That kiss at the lagoon was hot enough to rouse a dead man, but it was nonetheless a huge mistake, and Jack was going to make damn sure it did not happen again.

Frankly, he didn't know if he was insulted or amused by the whole thing. He'd never had a woman launch herself at him in quite that manner, then just as quickly fall all over herself to assure him she had just made a colossal mistake, and that it would not, come hell or high water, ever happen again.

It wouldn't because now *he* was in charge. But he was right about one thing: Audrey LaRue needed someone to make love to her. *Real* love to her—and he hoped she had good luck with that because it would not be him.

Fortunately, Audrey kept her distance during the first week of the tour. Jack and his guys rotated through the tour buses, but he managed never to end up on Audrey's. They made it through Minneapolis and Grand Rapids without incident—either the kissing kind or the ugly letter kind. He and Audrey avoided each other—when he saw her coming, he went in the opposite direction. She apparently was employing the same avoidance technique, for he rarely saw her, and when he did, she was usually with Casanova, who, Jack wryly noted, continued to show up in her encore and do his bit.

But that didn't matter to Jack—the only thing that mattered was that he remain as invisible as possible to Audrey. He didn't want to be near her, didn't want to smell her perfume or the sweet scent of her hair. At their tour stops, he managed it just fine. There was a lot of work to do; he didn't even see her until show time. When the lights went down and the smoke began to fill the stage, Jack would stand back, his eyes trained on the stage and band and crew, watching everything but her.

But he could not avoid her voice, and his head, his senses, were filled with it. And what a voice she had—explosive, powerful, but alluringly seductive. There were some songs she sang that gave him a chill, others whose beat and tone were so persuasive that he couldn't help but move a foot. Yet it was the ballads, the love songs and the haunting melodies of love lost and love survived that really moved him. He marveled at her ability to convey emotion and struggled to fathom how someone, born of flesh and bone and blood like him, could produce such a surreal sound as she did.

He knew she was destined for greatness.

But once the songs were over and the lights came up and the inevitable after party was in full swing, he would see her from the corner of his eye, talking and laughing and looking beautiful, and his thoughts would flash back to the beach. Or the lagoon. And he would feel something inside him tug a little harder.

It was making him crazy. He didn't need thoughts like that clouding his mind. He didn't need to be near her, didn't need to catch her eye across the room as he did every once in a while and feel something flow between them. He just needed to do his job and get back to his life and his flight school and the plane he had left half torn apart in a rented hangar in Orange County. He just needed to keep his head down, his mind focused on his work and the wiring specs he'd brought along, and everything would be fine.

That was his standard operating procedure, ever since Janet Richards, the girl for whom he had developed a massive crush when he was seventeen, dumped him. He tended to retreat into extreme sports or flying. Something as far removed from women as he could possibly get within the bounds of earth.

It was only a couple of months. But if a person was counting—and he wasn't, not really—it was seven weeks. A man could do anything for seven weeks if he put his mind to it.

That was his intractable belief until the day of the shoes.

It started when Bonner decided to stick his nose in Jack's business. When they were loading up for Cleveland, The Assclown tracked Jack down and insisted he ride in the tour bus.

"Why?" Jack asked.

"Because I caught your boy over there," Bonner said, nodding at Ted, "about to do Courtney before I stopped him. You're lucky I didn't call the cops."

Jack scoffed. "Why should he lose out on what she's offering to all the other guys? If you'd called the cops, she would have hit on them, too."

"Whatever," Bonner said dismissively. "The point is, you need to make some adjustments. *You* need to be on the bus—no one else."

Jack did not want to be on that bus—he would rather be strung up naked between two light poles than get on that bus. So he argued with Bonner that his guys were the real trained bodyguards, that he was really along to coordinate the security effort.

Lucas wouldn't hear of it.

"We hired *you*, man. *You* need to be there, and I think that the fee we are paying you buys us you on that bus. Audrey won't feel safe with any other guy."

Jack paused and squinted at Bonner. "Did she say that?"

"Look, dude, I know her better than anyone. Trust me. I know what I am saying."

The Assclown had no clue what he was saying, but Jack was stuck. Without a word, he turned and strode away from Bonner to grab his gear and give Ted the good news that he'd be riding Audrey's bus.

How in the *hell* had he ended up on this gig, anyway? What stupid brain spasm had he suffered that actually made him think he could endure this bullshit? Forget it—he was beginning to believe he would rather earn every penny for his flight school through his work with TA than this, even if it took him one hundred years to raise the dough he needed.

And it had only been a week. One *week*.

When he boarded the bus an hour later, Courtney was on hand to greet him, smiling broadly as she leaned over the stairs leading up to the interior, and in doing so, revealing her cleavage. "Hey, Handsome," she crooned so loudly that Jack wondered if she'd started her happy hour, "I hear we're going to be bedmates."

"Don't get your hopes up," he said as he entered, brushing past her when she refused to move to let him past.

But Courtney was cheerfully undeterred. "Let me show you where you'll sleep," she said, and led him through a small area that doubled as a kitchen and lounge, to a dark hallway that housed some coffin-like sleeping berths. Just the sort of accommodations every man dreamed of getting. Jack shoved his bag onto the top bunk, then turned around and walked back to the so-called lounge area, and sat down, cell phone in hand.

"What are you doing?" Courtney asked, taking a seat directly across from him and leaning forward again.

"Making a couple of calls," he said, and shifted his gaze to the ground to avoid Courtney's breasts.

For two hours, he avoided those breasts completely. He chatted with the representative from local security they'd hired for the Cleveland performance, which would present a different set of challenges as it was an outdoor venue. He checked in with the guys in L.A., too.

"Hey, how's it going?" Cooper asked cheerfully.

"Different," Jack said.

"The women? Or the job?" Cooper asked with a snort. But when Jack didn't answer immediately—he was uncertain *how* to answer it—Cooper laughed. "Don't tell me you've already gotten yourself into trouble."

Jack frowned at Cooper's laughter and quickly changed the subject. "Anything I need to know about?"

"Women, apparently."

Jack closed his eyes. "About work, Coop."

"Oh yeah. Remember Lindsey, the production assistant on *War of the Soccer Moms*?" he asked, referring to a film the Thrillseeker guys had worked on and a woman Jack had tried hard—and unsuccessfully—to date.

"Cooper," he said wearily.

"I thought you might," Cooper continued. "She got married over the weekend."

Jack blinked.

"That young director everyone is talking about—Sam somebody. Anyway, apparently they met on a set and it was love at first sight."

"Thanks for sharing," Jack said. "What about work?"

Cooper laughed again. "Don't let it get you down, pal. Someday, a woman will be able to see past all your obvious issues and phobias and—"

"*Cooper*," Jack said again, only more forcefully.

"All right, all right," Cooper said, and managed to get over his amusement, telling Jack about a new film that had cropped up on their radar screen—a remake of *The Jetsons*.

When Jack finally clicked off—and not before Cooper could get one more good-natured dig in—he was relieved to see that at least one of his strategies had worked. He'd been on the phone so long that Courtney had grown bored of him and had wandered to a different area—about two feet away—to look over Lucy's shoulder as she flipped through some fashion magazine.

In addition, Fred, Audrey's hairstylist and makeup artist, had rolled out of one of the coffins and had wandered into the lounge area, where he stood, yawning and scratching his bare belly. As Jack put his phone away, the two lovebirds decided to come out of isolation from the back bedroom.

Assclown came first. Jack was fascinated by his appearance—his hair was carefully messed up and sprayed into place. He was wearing a pair of jeans that rode low on his hips and made him look like a toothpick. The muscle-man tank did nothing to dispel that illusion. Jack had been in Hollywood a long time, had seen lots of guys who had paid a lot to be put together—but he'd never known anyone who looked like they'd paid so much to be put together.

Audrey followed behind, carrying a guitar. In stark contrast to the leech she called boyfriend, she looked perfectly natural and pretty damn good. She wasn't wearing any makeup, her hair was knotted at her crown, and little corkscrew curls floated around her face. She was dressed in a pair of cut-off shorts, which, intentionally or not, flaunted a pair of the shapeliest legs he'd ever had the good fortune to view. She also wore a T-shirt that had the words GRUENE HALL, GRUENE, TEXAS curved around a drawing of an old dance hall.

As Bonner took the lone empty seat—no surprise there—Audrey looked around and realized the only seat left in the lounge was the one next to Jack. Her eyelids fluttered with a little panic; she shifted her gaze to Courtney, who was in another of the captain's chairs, leaning over the arm to read the magazine with Lucy. Audrey opened her mouth to speak, but closed it again, and glanced at Jack from the corner of her eye.

He winked.

Audrey did not smile as she carefully took the seat next to him, taking great pains to sit on the very edge of the couch, her back ramrod straight and stiff, her guitar in her lap. Without speaking to him, she strummed a few chords. She seemed very self-conscious.

She paused in her strumming and adjusted a string, then struck another chord. Jack leaned back, slung one arm over the back of the couch behind her, and stretched his legs in front of him, crossing them at the ankles on a stool next to her.

Audrey paused and looked at his feet. Then she slowly turned her head and looked at him over her shoulder.

He lifted a questioning brow. "Don't let me stop you."

"Who said you were stopping me?" And as if to prove it, she turned away, folded over the guitar, and began again to strum a melody.

She'd played a couple of stanzas when Bonner suddenly looked up from a stack of mail and peered at her, listening for a moment. "No," he said, shaking his head. "No—that's too subtle."

"What?" Audrey asked, sounding confused.

"The chords are too subtle," Bonner said, swiveling around to face her. "You need it to *pop*," he said, making a gesture like he was flinging something. "You want something strong and vibrant to form the skeleton of the song, not soft." He sang a few da-da-*dums* to demonstrate.

From where he was sitting, Jack could see a bit of color bleed into Audrey's cheeks. Her hand curled around the neck of the guitar. "But

I like soft," she said. "It's what I do best. This is a song about a love gone cold. It's not pop."

"So?" Bonner said with the sensitivity of a bull. "That's not what you are making the bucks to write and perform. Think *pop*, Audrey."

"I do think *pop*, Lucas, but I like to write other stuff, too, and—"

"Why waste your time?" Bonner interjected as he turned back to the mail. "We've got enough on our plate without you trying to add any more to it."

He focused on the mail again, effectively dismissing Audrey. Her neck turned redder, and she glanced at the group at the table—who had stopped reading the magazine and were watching what happened between Audrey and Lucas.

It infuriated Jack. He spoke without thinking. "Why not let her do what she wants? She's the star—she obviously knows what she is doing."

He didn't know who looked more surprised by his question, Bonner or Audrey, but they both looked at him as if he had lost his mind. Apparently, he had. What did he know about it? The only thing he knew with any certainty was that Lucas Bonner made him want to punch a wall every time he was around him.

And Bonner was quick to give him a snide laugh. "You a music producer now, Tex?" he asked, then abruptly shot forward, his arms on his knees, his gaze intent on Jack. "What the hell do you know about Audrey's music?"

"Lucas—"

Bonner threw a hand up to cut Audrey off before she could stop him. "No, I'd really like to hear what this guy has to say about your career, Audrey. Maybe he's got some profound insight I need to hear."

"Jesus, Lucas," Audrey moaned.

Jack chuckled low in his chest, then slowly sat up, braced his arms against his knees just like Lucas, and leaned forward, so that their faces were just inches from each other. "I don't have any profound insights for you, Luke. Just a piece of friendly advice."

"Oh yeah?"

"Yeah. My advice is to get off her back. Audrey is the reason you're riding a big fancy tour bus. Not the other way around."

Lucas blinked, and somewhere, in the peanut gallery, someone sucked in their breath. But from the corner of his eye, Jack saw Audrey grin. *Grin.*

"You sonuvabitch," Bonner growled. "If you think I can't break that contract and kick you off this tour—"

"Go ahead," Jack said cheerfully. "You'd be doing me a favor."

"You motherf—"

"Lucas!" Audrey exclaimed frantically. "Ohmigod, just let it *go.*" She put her guitar aside. "It's okay. I don't want to write anything right now. I want to go shopping."

That statement made Lucas forget Jack for the moment. "*Shopping*?" he echoed incredulously. "We're on a bus, baby. How are you going to shop?"

"She means on-line," Courtney said.

"No, I mean in Cleveland," Audrey said emphatically. "I want some new red heels. The ones I've been wearing on stage are killing my feet."

Lucas snorted, fading back into his seat. "You can't go shopping."

"Why not? We've got time."

"No, *I* don't have time," Lucas said. "Do you have any idea what sort of work I've got to do when we get there?"

"I wasn't talking about you," Audrey said, trying very hard to be cheerful about it. "I was talking about me. Courtney can go with me if you're worried about it."

"Oh, right—Courtney is going to be a great help when you are recognized and mobbed. And besides, where are you going to shop? Some mall?"

"No, not a mall—I'm sure they have some shi-shi shopping in Cleveland. Courtney—"

"You are not going with Courtney," Lucas snapped and suddenly stood up. "You're not going."

"Oh yes, I am," she said firmly.

"God, Audrey, why do you make me crazy with this shit?" Lucas groused. "Do you really need to go shopping?"

"I don't need to, Lucas," Audrey said, gaining her feet. "But I *want* to. And the last time I checked, I wasn't shackled to this bus."

"Fine," he said with a loud sigh. "Go shopping. But take him with you," he added, pointing at Jack.

"What? No way," Jack said instantly. He had way too much to do, and besides that, he hated shopping. Despised it, abhorred it, loathed it.

"She can't go by herself!" Bonner snapped. "Someone has to be with her and you've got enough men here you can spare a couple of hours to keep an eye on her. That's what you agreed to, Price: *personal security*. I think that means you need to be where she is."

"I don't know if *that's* really necessary," Audrey argued, looking suddenly panicked. "Courtney can—"

"For the last time, Courtney *can't*."

"Hey!" Courtney said, pouting.

"No, Courtney," Bonner said, and strode angrily to the back of the bus in six steps.

Audrey watched him go, smoothing the palms of her hands on her bare legs.

"I don't know why he thinks I'm such a bad choice," Courtney pouted.

That seemed to snap Audrey out of it; she looked around like she was seeking an escape, and seeing none, she picked up her guitar and walked solemnly to the back of the bus, disappearing into the back bedroom.

Jack idly wondered how many times she had chased after that asshole. However many times it had been, it had been that number too many. He sighed, propped his feet up on the swivel chair Bonner had vacated, folded his arms across his chest, and closed his eyes.

He wasn't going shopping with anyone.

Seven weeks.

Eleven

Of course they had a huge argument inside the bedroom—or rather, Lucas had one. While he accused her of trying to sabotage her career, Andrey couldn't think. She could imagine a group of people on the other side of that flimsy door, ears pressed to the faux wood.

It seemed Lucas was furious about everything, but mainly the song she was writing. "You promised me you would focus on more pop songs for the time being."

"I never agreed to anything like that!" Audrey argued. "Why would I agree to stifle the only side of me that seems real anymore?"

"Oh for God's sake, Audrey!" he said churlishly, "You're *real.* But right now, we're on a different journey than the one you've been on all these years." When Audrey frowned, he took her face between his hands. "Baby, when we get to where we're going, you can write all the ballads and love songs and alternative tunes you want. But right now, I need you to focus. Do you know how huge you are? Do you know your new album is number *two* this week on the charts? Do you know that we have another sold-out performance tomorrow night? It's not your ballads that are selling, it's your pop."

"Yes, of course I know that, Lucas," Audrey said, pulling his hands from her face in frustration. "But I also know that I have to collaborate with another songwriter out of Austin, or you, on every single pop song I write because I just don't have that in my soul like—"

"Dammit, don't *ever* say that out loud!" he chastised her. "Do you want all those kids that come to see your show to believe that you don't have in *your* soul what you are putting into theirs?"

She was sick of listening to Lucas, sick of doing what he thought they ought to do. She understood his vision, understood the reasoning behind it—but sometimes she felt like he was making her climb a huge mountain. She could see the top of the mountain but could not seem to get there.

And all this talk about souls just made her feel like an even bigger gimmick. Unfortunately, there was no way out. Not at the moment, anyway, with only three cities of a twenty-city tour under her belt.

As Lucas lectured her, Audrey was even more determined to go shopping. She needed some space from the tour and, more importantly, from *him*.

As tense as it was between them—which, Audrey thought dolefully, was more the norm than the exception these days—it seemed forever before they reached the Ritz Carlton in Cleveland, where they would get a night in a real bed before they were on the road again.

There was a crowd of curious onlookers as they disembarked, but three men who Audrey recognized as being with the security team were waiting outside the bus for her and surrounded her as she stepped out, moving with her as she walked into the hotel. Someone in the crowd shouted *Audrey!* and she waved blindly as they hustled her inside, straight to the elevator, and up to her room.

An hour later, after she'd showered and put on a little makeup, and Lucas had gone off to make some calls, Audrey listened to Courtney and Lucy chat about their sex lives—Courtney doing most of the talking—as she tried to plot her escape.

"*My* fantasy," Lucy was saying, "is to be taken as a sex slave to a pirate or something. You know, the kind who ties you to a bed and then has his way with you."

She and Courtney giggled. "I love that idea," Courtney said. "But I'd have more than one."

"More than one what?"

Courtney shrugged. "Slave or pirate. I'm not picky." Lucy howled at that.

"What about you, Audrey?" Courtney asked, eyeing her closely. "Do you have any sexual fantasies?"

She instantly thought about Jack tying her to a bed and having his way with her. "I don't know," she said quickly. "Courtney, please call Jack and tell him I'm ready to go shopping."

"I thought you weren't supposed to go," Courtney said, exchanging a look with Lucy.

Audrey glared at her. "Just *call* him."

"Okay, fine," Courtney said. She picked up the phone and dialed, and Audrey heard the lilt in her voice when Jack answered. "Oh *hey*, Jack!" She told him that Audrey wanted to go shopping, then paused as Jack apparently said something. "But . . ." Courtney said, glancing at Audrey, her hand on her nape, "she *wants* to."

He wasn't backing out on her. She needed this. And if she allowed herself a moment to think, she might even admit she needed to see him. "Give me the phone," she said sternly, putting out her hand. Courtney started to turn away, but Audrey made a grab for the phone, taking it while Courtney shouted, "*Ouch!*"

She turned her back on Courtney and Lucy. "Ah . . . Jack?"

"Yeah?"

His voice was so soft and deep that it knocked her a little off balance. "I, ah . . . I want to go shopping." She closed her eyes. "I mean, I would *like* to go shopping."

"So I heard."

"So? Are you ready?"

"I'm sending one of my guys with you."

Audrey's heart skipped a beat. She tried to think of which guy and could only think of Tad. Ted. Tom, whatever. That wouldn't work. That so would not work. She wanted Jack with irrational vigor.

"But *you* need to go," she insisted as Courtney trotted around to stand in front of her, smirking. Audrey turned away again.

"It really doesn't matter which of us goes, Audrey," he said calmly. "Really, Bucky is better for you—he's been a personal bodyguard."

"A personal bodyguard," she repeated as she racked her brain what to say. She felt like a fish out of water—she couldn't remember the last time she'd asked someone to come with her and they had refused.

"I'll send him up to your room right now. So, if that's it, I'll see you later, okay?" he said, and clicked off before she could respond.

She froze, acutely aware that Courtney was watching her. "Okay!" she said brightly, and smiled. "Just give me a couple of seconds."

She clicked off and smiled at Courtney as she handed her the phone. "Take the night off. You, too, Lucy."

"You're kidding," Courtney said skeptically.

"No, I'm not." Audrey smiled and picked up her purse. Her heart was racing, much to her annoyance. What was it about Jack that made her so skittish? He was just her bodyguard. This wasn't a *date*, this wasn't anything but a trip to get some new red shoes. She was *paying* him to go with her. She was paying him so well, in fact, that she didn't have a chance of earning the slightest profit on this tour—her business manager had told her that when Lucas had hired Thrillseekers Anonymous. He'd been fairly perturbed about it, actually.

So if she wasn't going to make a profit because of Jack, the least he could do was accompany her to get some red shoes. It was like Lucas kept telling her: if she allowed it, everyone would walk all over her. She had to stand up for herself, demand what was hers.

She began to dig through her purse. "What room did you say he was in?" she asked Courtney.

"I didn't," Courtney answered coldly. "Isn't he coming here to get you?"

"No," Audrey said, still digging in her purse. "He's not quite ready. So I'll just go there. What room?"

Courtney's eyes narrowed even more. "Six-fifteen," she said. "It's just down the hall—we've got the whole floor."

"Great. Thanks," Audrey said, and picked up Bruno, stuffed him into her Balencia bag, and slung it over her shoulder. With a little wave of her hand, she walked out, aware that Courtney and Lucy were staring at her.

At the door of 615, Audrey nervously adjusted the bag on her shoulder and bit her bottom lip. "*Don't be stupid*," she muttered, smiled at Bruno when he poked his head out of the bag, and forced herself to knock on the door.

But when Jack opened the door a moment later, it was not clear to her who was more surprised—Jack, because she had shown up in spite of his brush-off, or her, because the man was wearing nothing but a towel wrapped around his waist, and he looked . . . *hot*.

So hot that she felt like an awkward sixteen-year-old and weak at the knees.

Jack, on the other hand, looked completely composed—and annoyed. "Audrey," he drawled in that wonderfully low voice, "do you speak English?"

That certainly snapped her out of any stupidly awkward feelings she was having. "Yes. Do you?"

"I think I was speaking English when I told you that I would send Bucky to take you shopping."

"I don't know Bucky," she said irritably. Somewhere behind her, she heard a door open. The last thing she wanted was for someone on the tour to see her hovering around Jack's room, and she suddenly moved forward, brushing past Jack—and making contact with bare, damp skin.

She dropped her bag on the end of his bed. Bruno hopped out and began to inspect the bedspread as Audrey faced Jack.

He was still standing at the open door, looking completely baffled. "What are you doing?" he demanded. "And please get that thing off my bed."

"I am waiting for you. I want to go shopping. Down, Bruno."

Bruno hopped to the floor.

"Audrey, I—"

"Do you think you could shut the door?" she asked, gesturing to the door. "I don't think everyone needs to hear you try and weasel your way out of your job."

He frowned, but let the door swing closed. He put his hands on a pair of trim hips. "I am not *weaseling* out of anything." He nudged Bruno away from his foot.

"Look," Audrey said, reverting to the person Lucas had taught her to be. "I want to go shopping. I am not asking you to carry my bags or try anything on, I just need someone to go with me, obviously, since some maniac wants me dead, and as I am paying you to protect me, it seems perfectly reasonable for you to accompany me. I *expect* you to accompany me. What's so hard to understand?"

"What's so hard to understand about Bucky? He's part of the team."

"Like I said, I don't know Bucky." She sat hard on the edge of Jack's bed. "Unfortunately, I only know you."

"But you would know Bucky if you allowed him to come along. He's a great guy."

"Don't care," she said stubbornly, and crossed her legs as she idly studied a nail. "Can you hurry it up? I need to make this quick."

He sighed. "Okay," he said. "I'll go. But I'm making a couple of rules."

She snorted.

"First," he said, ignoring her snort, "If you want me to do something for you, ask me nicely. I do not respond well to being ordered."

"I didn't—"

"And second," he said, walking over to the bed where she was sitting to tower above her, "No kissing. Do *not* kiss me."

Audrey's heart instantly started pounding at just the suggestion of a kiss. "Don't worry. I am *so* not going to kiss you," she muttered.

"Good," he said, and suddenly leaned over, caught her chin in his hand, and forced her to look up into his crystalline blue eyes. "Because if you kiss me again, I am going to lay you down wherever we are and fuck you like you need and want to be fucked."

Audrey's insides melted. She looked at his chest, his broad shoulders, the soft down that tapered to a line that disappeared into his towel. "What's the matter, big guy," she asked breathlessly. "Can't control your urges?"

With a chuckle, he gazed at her mouth, and she felt dampness between her legs. "Not when I'm provoked and kissing a good-looking woman, no," he said, and traced the pad of his thumb over her bottom lip. Audrey melted a little more. But he let go, straightened up, and walked into the bathroom.

She released her breath and covered her face with her hands a moment. "*Kiss* you?" she called after him. "Are you insane? I told you, that was just stress or something. I am *not* going to kiss you!"

Either he didn't hear her, or he didn't deign to respond—she heard nothing but the sound of stuff being moved around. She leaned forward, bending at the waist, hoping to see inside the bathroom, but couldn't.

She sat back up and picked absently at the spread as several confusing and uncharacteristic thoughts jumbled her mind. Bruno hopped up beside her and sat by her hand.

Just what was so bad about a stupid kiss, anyway? Okay, besides the obvious—she was the boss, he was the employee, she had a boyfriend, he had a . . . she didn't know what he had and didn't care. "No sir, you don't have to worry about me," she muttered, and leaned forward again, trying to see him in the reflection of the mirror.

He stepped out of the bathroom so suddenly that she jumped. He smiled a little at her obvious surprise as he walked to his bag on a chair and pulled out some boxer briefs.

With a wink, he reached for the towel at his waist.

Audrey quickly looked the other way as her pulse picked up another notch.

"There's one more thing," Jack said casually as he presumably dressed. "I don't like to shop. You might say I *hate* to shop. So whatever it is you want, we're going in, we're getting it, and we're out of there."

"I don't think you get to decide that."

"I have a lot to do, Audrey. I really don't have time to baby-sit."

"Baby-sit!" she exclaimed, whipping around, and just as quickly turning away again as he was standing in his boxer briefs like he'd just walked out of an underwear ad.

"Baby-sit," he said again.

She heard him digging through his bag. A moment later, he walked past her, wearing a pair of unbuttoned jeans and leaving a waft of cologne in his wake.

"I have a legitimate need for security," she said, starting to get a little miffed as he shrugged into a crisp, white shirt. "What makes you think I don't have a lot to do, too? It's not like I have a lot of time to shop, but I need some shoes, so I am going to go and get them. In and out."

Jack snorted.

"What?" she demanded.

He suddenly grinned. Her pulse jumped to a full staccato.

"I have yet to find a woman who is in and out," he said. "And I'd be willing to bet dinner that *you*, of all women, can't do it."

She put aside the image of him shopping with a variety of women to say, "That is a very sexist statement, Muscle Man. You must be hanging out with high-maintenance princesses. *Some* women have a lot more to do than spend your money."

"So is it a bet or not?"

"Absolutely!" she said confidently.

"Good. You shop for anything besides shoes, then dinner is on your considerable nickel, sweet cheeks," he said, and blithely tucked the tails of his shirt into his open pants. "If you go in and get your shoes and get out of there, it's on me. Deal?" he asked, punctuating his challenge by zipping up his pants.

"Deal," she said. It would be steak. She could definitely do with a little red meat.

"Come on, let's go," she said and stood, headed for the door.

"Not so fast."

Audrey paused and glanced over her shoulder.

"First, ask me nicely if I am ready."

"Oh for God's sake. Are you ready, Jack?"

"Almost. And you aren't going out like that."

She glanced down, confused. She was wearing a low-slung linen skirt, a spaghetti strap camisole, and some slinky kitten-heeled sandals. "What's wrong with what I have on?"

"Not . . . a damn thing," he said as his gaze raked over her. "But you need a hat and some shades. Didn't Genius teach you anything about moving around *incognito*?"

Audrey reached into her bag and pulled out a pair of Chanel shades and shoved them onto her face, knowing they covered most of it. "Will this do? I don't have a hat."

He sighed and gestured to her hair. "We're going to have to do something with that," he said. "Try and put it up," he added as he walked around to his bag. He rummaged inside and produced a New York Mets baseball hat, which he held up for her to see.

"The Mets?" she said, peering at it. "I thought a good ol' Texas boy went for the Rangers or the Astros."

"A good ol' Texas boy does, unless his brother plays for the Mets."

Audrey made a sound of surprised delight. "Your brother plays for the *Mets*? I *love* baseball! I can't believe it. Ohmigod, is it Parker Price?"

He stuffed the hat on her head. "It's Parker all right. What's that look? You thought the Price boys couldn't play a little ball?"

Audrey smiled wryly, took the hat off her head, and handed it to him. "I'm not surprised the Price boys can play ball. I'm just surprised one of them is playing for the Mets," she said as she put her hair up in a ponytail.

"Play your cards right, and I might take you to see a game sometime."

He said it as if they had known each other for ages instead of only days. Audrey stilled only slightly, but it was enough for Jack to notice. "I'll get you tickets," he amended himself, and thrust the cap at her again.

She took it, threaded her hair through the hole in the back, and fit the cap on her head, tucking up curls of blond beneath it. When she'd finished, she turned around for Jack's inspection.

He let his gaze drift over her, long and slow, and nodded. "You'll do."

Audrey laughed. "Okay. Let's go."

"Uh-uh," he said.

"What now?"

He frowned playfully. "Aren't you forgetting something?" he asked, and looked meaningfully at Bruno, sitting at her feet, peering up at her.

"Oh my goodness. Bruno!" She scooped him up and put him in her bag. "*Now* if you are ready, I will show you how a *real* woman shops."

A pained look came over Jack's handsome face. He sighed, pressed his lips together, and nodded.

Audrey couldn't help laughing.

Twelve

In the third shoe store and the sixth chair he'd occupied since this "in-and-out" shopping had begun, Jack shifted the packages on his lap: two pairs of shoes, three blouses—at least he thought they were blouses—and the enormous bag in which Bruno was patiently awaiting his next outing.

Jack had decided in the first shop that if women ever ruled the world, they would do well to torture male terrorists into talking in just this way. There was absolutely nothing more painful than watching a woman pick through racks of clothes or shoes, particularly if they held up each article of clothing that caught their eye, and asked, "What do you think? Too pink?"

Was there such a thing as too pink? Wasn't pink just pink?

Jack was staring at the shoes on the wall (Why did shoes have names? Did shoemakers really believe women walked into establishments such as this and ask for the *Maria* or the *Bethany*?) when Audrey cleared her throat in a loud and obtrusive manner.

He turned his head to the right—and almost dropped his packages.

She was standing before him, her legs planted apart, her linen skirt gathered even higher above her knee. On one leg, she wore a dark red leather, over-the-knee, stiletto boot. On the other foot, she wore the spikiest, reddest, badass stiletto sandal he'd ever seen on a woman.

She bent slightly at the waist and looked at the shoes, then straightened and looked at Jack, her expression very serious. "Which one?"

Was she *kidding*? Both shoes made him want to drink heavily—he couldn't take his eyes from her legs.

"So?" she asked in a low voice. "Which do you think?"

Which did he think what? They were both killer. He wanted to put her on her back right there, in the middle of this fancy little shoe store, and have her wrap those shoes around his back.

She shifted her weight to one hip and waited for him to speak. When he didn't, she turned the foot encased in the stiletto sandal, and with a sexy smile, she asked, "Which do you think would do best on stage?" She slid that leg a little closer to him. "The sandals?" She turned again, sliding the leg in the boot toward him. "Or the boots?"

Jack swallowed down a lump of intense lust and lifted his gaze to hers. "I don't know which would do best," he said sincerely, "but personally, I think I prefer the boots."

She smiled seductively. "Aha . . . a *boot* man."

"Did either of those work for you?" a woman suddenly trilled, her voice slicing across the moment. Jack suppressed a groan as the saleswoman appeared between him and Audrey. "Oh my," she said, nodding approvingly. "Those are lovely."

"Which do you think?" Audrey asked.

"It depends on what event you're shopping for," the saleswoman said, boggling Jack's mind even further that she could break this sale down to a single event.

Audrey leaned around her and smiled pertly at Jack. "I think I'll take them both," she said, and turned, waltzing like she was on a runway across the store to where she'd left her shoes.

The saleslady chuckled. "She has the legs for either style." She glanced at Jack. "I can tell that you are a veteran of shopping with your wife."

Jack started. “She’s not—”

“Don’t worry, hon,” the woman said, putting her hand on Jack’s shoulder. “It won’t be much longer. I think your wife has found what she was looking for,” she said with a wink.

Of course the saleswoman was speaking of the shoes, but nevertheless, as she bustled off to divest Audrey of her money, Jack’s stomach did a weird little flip.

Audrey lost the bet, though she argued that she shouldn’t have been held to the terms of the bet because she’d stumbled onto such a great sale, and no one in their right mind would have passed up 50 to 75 percent off designer shoes. But Jack held up her packages as proof that she had shopped, and therefore, lost.

Audrey gave in. She called Lucas’s cell and, thankfully, got his voice mail. “I’m going to dinner,” she said. “A steak place, the Brasa Grill or something.” She glanced at Jack. “With, ah . . . with Jack. I owe him,” she added hastily, as if she needed to explain. “Ah . . . see you later.”

She was relieved Lucas wasn’t around. The last thing she wanted was for him to show up at dinner. Frankly, she was looking forward to dinner with someone other than Lucas for a change. Every time she and Lucas went to a restaurant, he spent the whole meal watching to see who noticed Audrey, or pushed his latest plan to make them fabulously rich.

It would be nice to have dinner with someone who wasn’t worried about who she was or what important press person was in the area or her career. Fortunately, so far, no one in Cleveland seemed to know or care who she was.

Audrey was in such a good mood that she removed her ball cap. “I’m not going into a restaurant looking like I just ran the bases,” she said to Jack, and then reached into one of her many bags. She withdrew a sheer blouse to dress up the linen skirt and pulled that over her head. Then she dug through another bag, withdrew a shoebox, opened it up, and took out a pair of gold beaded sandals.

When she had finished, she turned to Jack and smiled. “How do you like me now?”

His gaze turned sultry. "I like you," he said low. "And you look fantastic."

If there was one thing Audrey had learned in her life, it was that there were two ways a man could tell a woman she looked nice. One was to say, "You look nice," with a quick smile and a pat on the hand or the shoulder. The other was to say, "You look fantastic," with a gaze full of the promise of fabulous sex. That was exactly the way Jack was looking at her, and a shiver shot down her spine and landed squarely in her groin.

She knew she should look away, shouldn't encourage that look any more than she already had, but she didn't. She couldn't. She couldn't even speak, and just held his gaze, believing with everything she had that he was feeling the desire flow between them as acutely as she was.

It wasn't until the cab had pulled up in front of the Brasa Grill that she could finally draw a breath. A helpful salesclerk had directed them to the restaurant, and it was, as promised, a happening place. At the entrance was a patio lounge; the tables were already full at seven o'clock.

"Oh God," she said when she saw the crowd. She felt defeated, trumped in her illicit outing before it had begun.

"What's wrong?" Jack asked, peering over her shoulder.

"There are too many people." As if in agreement, Bruno whimpered.

Jack looked at the crowd, then at her. "I have an idea," he said. "Are you up for it?"

"Anything."

He asked the cabbie, "Is there a park nearby?"

"Yep. Just a mile or so from here."

"What about a Wal-Mart?" Jack asked.

"A *Wal-Mart*?" Audrey echoed laughingly.

He took her hand, wrapped his fingers securely around hers. "Trust me," he said.

She did trust him. Remarkably, she *did*.

Jack directed the cabbie to a Wal-Mart, where they picked up a blanket and some wineglasses. Then they stopped at a liquor store, where Jack went in alone and emerged with two bottles of very nice wine. The last stop was a barbeque joint. He bought chicken and the accoutrements for everyone, including the cabbie and Bruno. After that, they headed for a park. Any park. And Jack paid the cabbie to wait.

For the first time in a long time, Audrey felt like a normal, regular person, the sort of person she used to be when she would drive to gigs in her Honda with an amp in the trunk and the trunk roped shut around it. She was sitting under the stars with Jack, drinking excellent wine and eating moist, tender chicken, with Bruno chewing happily on a rawhide bone ("You *do* like him," Audrey had accused Jack when he picked it up at Wal-Mart. "Do not," he'd said with a smile. "He's just a rat."). It didn't get any better than this.

The tension she'd created by kissing Jack at the lagoon was gone. They were comfortable together, like a pair of old friends enjoying a lazy summer evening. She looked at Jack stretched long on the blanket, propped up on one arm, and watching some people at the far end of the park.

"So tell me something about yourself, Rambo."

He gave her a wary smile. "What do you want to know, starlight?" he asked as he polished off the last of the chicken.

She wanted to know everything—how old he was, where he went to school, if he'd ever been in love. She wanted to know which of her songs he'd heard first, if he ever danced, if he had a family that drove him nuts, like her. "Start with the obvious," she suggested.

"Like?"

"Like . . . any great love in your life?"

"You don't beat around the bush, do you?" he asked with a winsome smile. "Honestly?"

"Honestly."

He sighed. "Yeah . . . I've had the same great love most of my adult life."

A wave of disappointment swept through Audrey, which she immediately dismissed as asinine. Good for him! He'd found that one great love, the thing that eluded most people. "What's her name?" she asked breezily, stabbing a little too hard at a piece of chicken.

"She doesn't have a name."

Audrey glanced up. "What do you mean, she doesn't have a name?"

He grinned. "The great love is flying." At Audrey's look of confusion, he casually moved her sleeve away from the chicken it was about to touch and said, "You know. Planes. Helicopters. Dirigibles."

"You can fly?" she asked, happily surprised and curious.

"Yes."

"*Dirigibles?*"

He laughed. "Okay, I was kidding about the dirigibles. But just about anything else with wings," he said.

"Ooh, tell me," she begged him.

Jack had flown everything—big planes, small planes, propeller planes and jets. He told her about his years in the service where he'd learned how to fly. And then he mentioned his desire to teach others his love of flying.

Impressed, she smiled broadly. "You have a *flight* school?"

"Not yet," he said with a proud grin. "But I'm working on it. It's why I took this job, to be honest." He told her about the hangar he'd rented in Orange County, the plane he was rebuilding (*rebuilding*, she noted, as if that were an everyday task, like changing a flat tire), and how he hoped to be up and operational in two years' time. She watched him as he spoke of his dream, could see the excitement in his blue eyes, the pride he took in his work. She understood it, too—she felt that same pride with her songwriting, knew the sort of thrill of having achieved something special when one song out of one hundred turned out to be really good.

What she envied about Jack was his ability to pursue his dream on his own terms—to pursue what *he* wanted as opposed to what the world wanted from him.

"But . . . I thought you were part of a stunt group," she said, when he'd finished telling about the work he'd put in on his flight school.

"Thrillseekers Anonymous," he said, and laughed a little as he poured more wine for them. "Yeah, that's another little venture I'm into."

"Stunts?"

"Stunts, yes . . . but we're really all about the sports." He told her more about TA, how he'd grown up with his partners Eli McCain and Cooper Jessup in West Texas. He laughed as he talked about how, as boys, they'd developed a love for sports—football, baseball, basketball, rodeo—whatever sport they could play. He told her that when regular sports got to be too easy, they began to create their own.

"How do you create your own sports?" she asked with a laugh.

"Well, you start by diving into old mines that have been filled with water. Or creating dirt-bike trails through the canyons. Or you make a game out of breaking horses without a bit. And when you get tired of that, you build things that look a little like cars and a little like trouble and race them across fallow wheat fields."

Audrey could imagine three boys racing across empty fields. "How exactly did you parlay that into a business?"

"Oh, I didn't," he said, shaking his head as he pushed his plate away. "Eli and Cooper did that. By the time we finished college, we were into the extreme side of sports in general. We'd done it all—white-water rafting, rock-climbing, canyon-jumping, kayaking, surfing, skiing—name the sport, and we'd tried it. Except flying." He grinned and leaned back. "I wanted to fly, but the only way I could afford to learn how was to join the Air Force. Coop and Eli weren't as interested in flying as they were in jumping off buildings and blowing things up, so they headed out to Hollywood to hire on as stuntmen. They got their start working on some of the biggest action films in Hollywood, and before too long, they were choreographing some big-picture action sequences."

"What about you?"

"Me? I was in the service. That's where I met Michael Raney, our fourth partner. He and I met on a couple of classified missions, discovered we both had a love for extreme sports, and started hanging out when we could." He chuckled low and shook his head. "Raney and I did some crazy shit. But when I came to the end of my tour, Cooper and Eli had come up with the idea to start up Thrillseekers Anonymous. It sounded good. So I came out to Hollywood to work with them."

"In the sports club," Audrey said, nodding.

Jack grinned and playfully tweaked her arm. "Woman, have you heard a word I said?

"Of course!"

"Then what is our motto?"

"Aha!" she said. "You didn't say. I am sure I would have remembered it."

He leaned forward, his face just inches from hers, and said low, "TA is a members-only club. Our motto is *Name your fantasy, and we'll make it happen.*"

She laughed at him, but a fantasy popped into her head, one delicious fantasy inspired by Jack Price, and she smiled.

He raised a brow at her smile.

Emboldened by the wine, Audrey asked, "Any real women in your life? Mother? Sister? Girlfriend? Wife?"

"Definitely have a mother and two older sisters. But at the moment . . . no girlfriend and no wife."

She couldn't help grinning with delight at that news. "I'm disappointed, Security Guy. A guy who makes fantasies happen and there is no one in your life?"

"Not at the moment."

"Has there ever been?"

"Depends on what you mean by 'ever.' I fell in love with Janet Ritchie when I was seventeen—you know, that kind of all-consuming love you think you could die for. But I can't say I have had that since she dumped me." He chuckled. "I've had a couple of serious relationships, and girlfriends . . ." He looked at Audrey. "But not a love I'd die for."

She swallowed hard. "What about Courtney?"

"What about her?"

"She's obviously interested. And she's cute."

"Oh my God, are you serious?" he asked, falling to his back with feigned shock.

"Don't you think she's cute?"

Jack snorted and came back up on his elbow. "Guy rule number one: In the company of a beautiful woman, never say aloud if you find another woman as beautiful, or, God forbid, more beautiful than your current companion . . . as if that is even possible."

A smile spread across her face. "You think I'm beautiful?"

"Darlin', I think *all* women are beautiful. But you? Dangerously so."

Her belly flipped in a most delicious way. "For what it's worth," she said, leaning toward him, "I think you're pretty cute yourself."

His smile faded. He wrapped his fingers around her wrist and pulled her hard to him, heedless of the picnic between them. He rolled over, bringing her on top of him. "I warned you about provoking me, sweet cheeks."

"I didn't kiss you," she responded pertly.

"Then I'll have to kiss you," he muttered, and pressed his mouth against her cheek, then her eyes, and slid to her lips.

Audrey tasted the wine he'd drunk and the chicken he'd eaten and teasingly bit his lip. She relished the feel of his arms around her, his hands caressing her back. But then he rolled again, so that Audrey was on her back and he on his side, his hand on her belly, moving to her breast as his mouth covered hers. His tongue swept inside hers, feeling her teeth and the flesh of her mouth. His hand drifted up, to the column of her neck, then down again, to her breast, cupping it, feeling the weight of it.

She moaned softly as he squeezed her nipple between his fingers, and pressed against him, feeling his erection hard against her hip bone.

"Do you have any idea what I want to do to you right now?" he growled, and kissed her again.

She knew what she wanted him to do to her, and lifted her hand to his neck, entwining her fingers in his hair, then letting her hand drift down his body, to the taut muscles of his arm, the hard wall of his chest. The more her hand moved, the wilder Jack's kiss became. She could feel herself becoming wet, could feel her defenses and common sense eroding.

His hand moved from her breast, gliding down her belly, to the top of her skirt, and then to her bare knee. He caressed her knee before slipping his hand beneath the hem of her skirt, between her legs.

He stroked her inner thigh, making her skin tingle where he touched her and her body fire deep in her groin. "You make me crazy, Audrey," he said. "I don't know what it is about you, but you make me crazy."

She smiled with great satisfaction and lifted her hand to touch his face. He lowered his head to her again, kissing her gently now, letting his hand slip higher under her skirt. It occurred somewhere on the fringe of her brain that they were in a park, in a public place. Anyone could walk up on them now, and while she supposed a part of her thrilled to the idea of being caught, a larger part of her knew it could be disastrous. But she could not bring herself to stop him any more than she could stop herself. As his fingers brushed against her crotch, she moaned, urging him on.

He began to stroke her over the fabric of her panties as he kissed her, making her wetter. She could feel his cock thickening against her. She was not conscious of anything but him and his touch, both alarmed and titillated by the response he evoked within her. When his fingers slipped inside her panties, into the slick folds of her skin, she gasped into his mouth.

It had been a lifetime since she had wanted a man's touch as badly as she wanted his. She wanted it with a ferocity that was unknown to her—her blood pounded in her veins, her heart beat like a drum against her chest. He stroked her, his finger swirling around her, then sliding down and sliding deep inside her. Then another finger. Then three.

Audrey was lost. She rode his hand as he began the seductive rhythm of lovemaking. It was not supposed to be like this, she was not supposed to want the seduction, but she pressed against his hand nonetheless, as a furious, anxious heat began to build in her.

When his thumb touched the core of her while his fingers performed their dance, she gasped again, turning her head away, lifting against him.

"Easy," he whispered as he continued to stroke her, inside and out. Audrey felt herself falling away all too quickly, shuddering against his hand as a massive wave of release moved through her. The life bled out of her; she could feel her body melting onto the blanket and closed her eyes.

Jack slowed his hand until she lay motionless, completely spent. Only then did he remove his hand and straighten her skirt.

Slowly, Audrey opened her eyes. He was gazing at her, an unfathomable look in his blue eyes. He kissed her tenderly, stroking her cheek with the back of his knuckles, smoothing her hair with his hand.

"What are we doing?" Audrey whispered.

He shook his head and kissed her once more. "I haven't the slightest idea."

They lay on that blanket, not talking, just being, until Bruno began to paw at Audrey's hair, reminding them that it was time to go.

There were photographers waiting when they arrived back at the Ritz.

"Great," Jack muttered. Audrey was startled by the number of them—she had forgotten about their constant presence in the few hours she had spent with Jack, and she didn't like the jarring return to reality.

She and Jack said good night, careful not to touch one another, the only hint of their feelings in their eyes. When Audrey entered her suite, Lucas was waiting for her. "What happened?" he asked instantly. "I thought you were at the Brasa. I came looking for you, but you weren't there."

"Oh," she said, fumbling with Bruno to avoid his direct gaze. "We ended up at some diner. The Brasa was so crowded and it looked like there would be a wait."

"A *diner*?" Lucas said disbelievingly, peering at her. "What diner?"

Audrey blinked. Then laughed. "Hell if I know. Do they have names? It was just some diner. Hey, look what I got!" she exclaimed, pulling out her boots.

She showed him everything, chattering about the sale she'd found and how good Bruno had been. When she was certain he wasn't going to ask more, she excused herself to clean up and get ready for bed. In the privacy of the bathroom, as she changed clothes, the bottle of sleeping pills rolled out of her bag.

Audrey picked up the bottle and looked at the little blue pills. Jack was right about that, she thought, smiling softly to herself. She didn't need pills. She needed a man to make love to her.

She poured the contents of the bottle into the toilet and flushed it.

Rich happened to arrive at the Ritz at the same time as Audrey LaRue, having just flown in from L.A. From down the drive where his cab had let him out—"Looks like some celebrity," the cabbie said—Rich saw Audrey run inside, the security guy on her heels, carrying her bags.

"*Whore*," he whispered as he watched her from the sidewalk with a handful of other curious onlookers.

In his room, Rich took out his folder of press clippings he kept about Audrey, and shook his head as he leafed through them. "Such a damn *whore*," he said again, and got up, scratching his bare ass as he walked to his computer to pull up the letter on which he'd been working.

THE OFFICIAL FANBLOG OF AUDREY LARUE

Got txt that AL was at Brasa Grill, and me and KK91 went 2 see her and get her hancock, but she didn't show! bummer! that's cool we went to BK and met some guys and KK91 wants to hook up with this one guy and she wouldn't meet him if we hadn't gone to Brasa to see AL, so thanks AL!! you rock!!

120 comments

hot pics!

Audrey's Curvy New Look!

(*Us Weekly*) It's all curves for Audrey LaRue! On tour with her new album, *Frantic*, sources report that Audrey makes at least eight costume changes and struts some of the best curves on the music circuit today. "She's not afraid to show them," says designer Kate Raymond, who created Audrey's costumes for the tour. "She's healthy and it shows." Audrey is partial to Prada, according to a source close to her.

Thirteen

Rich delivered the paper to Audrey across the hall later that morning. "Thought you'd like to see this," he said cheerfully, and dropped it on the table next to a room-service tray that held two covered dishes and a coffeepot.

"Thanks, Rich," she said with a smile she could not seem to wipe from her face. "When did you get in?"

He blinked, then sighed irritably. "Ah . . . last night? Didn't you get my message?"

"What message?"

Now Rich's brows dipped into a definite frown. "The message that I was coming in last night," he said, a little too angrily to suit Audrey. "I called *three* times," he said, lifting three fingers. "The first time from my office yesterday morning. I got Courtney and left a message," he said, bending one finger over. "The second time on my way to the airport. Funny, I got Courtney again and left another message. And then the *third* time I called," he said, folding over fingers two and three, "was from the airport when my flight was delayed. *That* time, I got voice mail. Didn't you get *any* of those messages?"

"Ah, well . . . I was kind of busy, Rich," Audrey said. What was with this guy? She rarely spoke to him on the phone—she had people for that sort of thing.

"*Busy*," he spat, his frown etching deeper into his face as Lucas emerged from the bathroom, dressed in a robe. "I'll just bet you were."

"Hey!" Lucas exclaimed. "Careful! Audrey doesn't owe you an explanation!"

Rich checked himself. "I didn't say she did," he said haughtily. "It's just very frustrating to ask that a message be relayed and find out that no one has bothered to relay it."

"Okay, well . . . was there something you needed to talk to me about?" Audrey asked.

"I *assumed* you would want to know how the expenses for this tour were going—and here's a preview: you're spending too much money."

"Okay, that's the last thing I want to hear about this morning," Audrey said with a sigh of resignation. "So tell Lucas," she said, turning back to her breakfast.

"Uh-uh, don't tell me. At least not right now," Lucas said, waving a hand at Rich.

"Well," Rich said, shoving his hands into his pockets. "I'm not exactly certain what my utility is here if no one wants to talk about the money aspects of this tour."

"*Dude*," Lucas said with a bit of a laugh, "calm down. I'll catch up with you later."

Rich looked from Lucas to Audrey and the frown returned. "Fine," he snapped. "Later. In the meantime, do you think you could instruct Courtney to relay a message now and again?"

"*Yes*," Lucas said, and looked meaningfully at the door.

Rich glared at Audrey and stalked out of the room.

"Jesus," Audrey said. "What's his problem?"

"Who knows," Lucas said with a shrug as he helped himself to a triangle of toast.

"Remind me why we hired him again?"

Lucas shoved the triangle into his mouth. "Highly recommended," he said, and picked up the paper. "Did we get any press?" he asked, looking at the page Rich had left on top. "Excellent," he said, nodding.

Audrey got up and looked over his shoulder—there she was, climbing out of a cab.

"Good," he said. "The more press the better."

"Why?" she asked, feeling vaguely angry. She didn't like every aspect of her life being on constant display and could not understand why Lucas thought it was so great that it was.

"*Why?*" he echoed, as if it was a ridiculous question. "Because we need it. And because we told them where you would be. Of course you were supposed to be at the Brasa and weren't," he said with a pointed look. "Fortunately, they followed the trail here."

Audrey's breath caught in her throat. "You *told* them where I'd be? Told *who?*"

"It was a local Internet thing. You know—they keep track of what's going on around town. So we logged on and reported that Audrey LaRue was at Brasa Grill."

"Why did you do that?" she cried. "Why would you intentionally send photographers after me? You know I hate that!"

"Don't be naïve, baby."

"I'm not naïve, Lucas," she exclaimed angrily, slapping her palm on the table. "It's not like I don't have to live my life under a microscope as it is! Why would you do that to me?"

"Baby," he said soothingly as he tried to gather her in his arms. "Come on, you know the score."

"There is no score, you asshole," she said, wrenching free of him.

"A little preconcert press never hurt anyone. In fact, it helps."

"It doesn't help me have any semblance of a life. Did you think about that?"

"Hey," he said, holding up his hands. "I do what I do for us. One day you will look back on this and appreciate how hard I have worked for us."

Audrey rolled her eyes.

"Ooh-kay," he said, frowning. "Looks like we're going to have another day of violent mood swings, so if you don't mind, I am going somewhere else."

"You make it sound as if I am being childish for insisting on my privacy," she said, seething with anger.

"Why do you have to get so bent out of shape?" he shot back. "Why do you need so much privacy all of a sudden?"

Audrey immediately clammed up, but she was furious with herself now for saying anything. Furious with herself for having these warm feelings for Jack; strong, undeniably warm feelings. She shouldn't be feeling anything for him at all. She had a boyfriend. Granted, something had shifted between her and Lucas a long time ago, but nevertheless, she'd been with him for eight years and she was *still* with him. To have allowed herself to develop such intense feelings for another man made her question her character.

It was wrong.

She was no better than her father, whom she despised for having screwed around on Mom for as many years as he did.

But God help her, she couldn't seem to *stop* feeling this way.

"I've got to get ready for work," she said to Lucas, and walked into the bathroom. She turned on the shower, then sat on the toilet, her head between her hands. Okay, this could never work—no matter how much she liked Jack's attention, it just couldn't work. It was better to nip it in the bud than to let it go any further—it had already slid into treacherous territory.

That was easier said than done, of course—she'd thought of little else but Jack in the last couple of days. So to take her mind off him, when Audrey got out of the shower, she called Trystan and told him she wanted to review some dance steps.

"*Again?*" he asked reluctantly.

"Again. Come over."

When Trystan arrived, she tried to clear her mind by striking up a conversation. How was the tour, what did the dancers think of it? What did they think of the dance routines? How did they like the accommodations?

She was trying so hard to clear her mind that she scarcely noticed the number of people who came in and out of her room—Courtney, Rich again, dropping off reports for Lucas, a hotel maid, a bellhop bringing flowers, and a maid who removed the breakfast trays. She had walked by the paper Rich had brought in twice before she saw the envelope beneath it with the distinctive lettering: Audrey LaRue.

She recognized the font and caught her breath; she instantly began to shake as fear bled into her veins.

Trystan looked up when Audrey gasped and walked over to stand beside her. "What is it?" he asked, looking around the table like he was looking for a spider. Several moments passed before he noticed the letter.

"Oh," he said, grimacing. "Is it one of *those* letters?"

Audrey nodded and put her hand on his arm. "Pick it up."

"What? No!" Trystan protested.

"Pick it up," she said again, pushing him.

With a groan, Trystan shoved his dreadlocks over his shoulder and very daintily picked up the letter between two fingers.

"Open it!" she urged him.

He very reluctantly did so, wincing when he pulled out the paper. "No anthrax," he said, shaking the paper open. His brown eyes skimmed over the note, his frown deepening as he read, and then his eyes went wide. "*Eewe!* Now that is just *vile*," he said, and clasped a hand over his heart as he looked up at Audrey. "This guy needs to be locked up."

"*Shit!*" Audrey exclaimed, surprised and ashamed by the tears that sprang to her eyes. She whirled around, grabbed her cell phone from the end of her bed. She quickly dialed a number, but it wasn't until she'd told him that a letter had come that she realized she'd called Jack instead of Lucas.

"I'll be right there," he said.

She took a breath, then called Lucas. "I got a letter," she said breathlessly when he answered.

"Goddammit," he said, sounding irritated. "When?"

"I don't know. It was just . . . *here*," she said, gesturing wildly to the table.

Jack and Lucas arrived at the same time. Jack took the letter from Trystan; Lucas came to Audrey's side and wrapped his arms around her.

"Don't pay any attention, baby," he said. "That sick fuck can't get near you."

She wished she could believe him, but he'd obviously gotten close enough to leave another letter threatening to kill her, and she turned her face into Lucas's shoulder.

"When did it come?" Jack asked, fishing his cell phone from his pocket.

"I don't know," Audrey said, lifting her head from Lucas's shoulder. "I saw it lying on the newspaper that Rich brought me earlier."

"Rich? The business manager?" Jack asked, frowning a little.

"*Yes*, the business manager," Lucas said with a roll of his eyes.

"I thought he headed back to L.A. a couple of days ago," Jack said before turning around to talk into his phone.

"I honestly didn't think he was due back until this weekend," Audrey said to Lucas.

"He came back early," Lucas said. He put his hand against Audrey's cheek. "Now listen, you can't let this sick fuck get to you, because that is what he wants. He wants you to be so rattled that you won't do the show."

"Christ, the show!" she exclaimed. Lucas was right—she couldn't allow this maniac to push her off the stage and into hiding. "But what about security? It's an amphitheater. Anyone can get backstage—"

"He can't touch you, Audrey." This was from Jack, his voice clear and strong and determined, falling over her like a protective blanket. She pushed away from Lucas and looked at Jack, wanting to feel his arms around her, his breath in her hair.

"He can't come near you, I promise you that."

There was such hard determination in the way he said it that he made Audrey believe him. He smiled, his expression full of confidence. "I promise," he said again as Lucas's phone rang.

Lucas flipped open his cell and moved away from her.

Jack seized the opportunity to come near her, his smile radiating warmth and security as he walked across the room. "Are you okay?"

"Yeah," she said, nodding.

"Right now, we need to get you to sound check." He put a hand on her arm and squeezed it. "No worries, all right, starlight? We've got this completely under control. The only thing you need to worry about is putting on a kick-ass show." He turned his smile to Trystan, who seemed as mesmerized by him as Audrey. "Can you help her get her stuff together?"

"Sure," Trystan said, and began moving about the room, picking up a couple of bags.

"Better give him a hand," Jack suggested, and Audrey nodded, scooping Bruno up in her arms, her eyes following Jack around the room. When Trystan had her things together, she looked at Jack once more. He gave her a reassuring smile as she and Trystan went out the door. They were met in the hall by two of Jack's guys, who flanked her as she stepped across the threshold, sandwiching her between them.

"How you doing today, Ms. LaRue?" one of them asked.

Audrey glanced over her shoulder. Jack was watching her, his eyes full of reassurance. "I've had better days," she said, and turned around again, managing a weak smile for the bodyguards.

The local police conferred with Jack and the hotel staff, but they seemed to be getting nowhere. "Maybe it's a disgruntled employee," one of the detectives mused. Jack sighed—they'd been through this in Omaha. His own questioning of Rich Later left him wondering, but he couldn't put his finger on why, exactly.

"Can't help you," Rich said cheerfully when Jack asked about the letter. "I just dropped the paper off and went to the gym. Someone else must have brought it in."

"Yeah," Jack said, eyeing him curiously. Was he nuts, or was the guy wearing eyeliner?

"Weird, huh?" Rich remarked, and at Jack's look, he laughed. "You're barking up the wrong tree, pal. Why would I want to hurt Audrey? She's my meal ticket."

It was true, and Jack had nothing, really, but a funny feeling. At the same time, he hadn't ruled out Lucas. That guy was intent on exploiting Audrey, and Jack wasn't sure how far he would take it.

As usual, the letter was handed over to law enforcement, who made lots of noises about looking into it, but Jack knew full well that the minute the tour left town, the letter would drop to the bottom of their priority list.

Fortunately, in spite of the letter—and the inability of law enforcement to catch the bastard—Audrey's show went off without a hitch.

Frankly, Jack was amazed by Audrey's ability to adapt to anything in the course of a performance. He'd heard grumblings from the band and the dancers about the song "The Roar of an Angel" not coming off right. It seemed to him that it had sounded rougher each night, but in Cleveland, Audrey substituted one of her old ballads for the song. She walked out onto the stage wearing a long silky dress, carrying a guitar. And with just that guitar to accompany her, she sang a lusty, soulful song about secret love. It was, at least to Jack's way of thinking, magical.

He knew the letters frightened Audrey, but when she was working, she seemed okay, focused and determined to put on a good show. And over the next few days, she seemed to work around the clock. On the way to Pittsburgh, she rode in the bus with the musicians and changed out "The Roar of an Angel" with the old ballad, but put the ballad to a different beat. In Pittsburgh, she and the dancers revamped the routine to fit the new song, practicing up until show time.

She was completely engrossed in the change to her set, and the latest letter seemed to be a distant memory. The only thing that visibly upset her was the phone calls she had been getting from her family. This, Jack surmised from the number of times she said, "*Mom!*" into the phone.

Jack heard and witnessed it all—he was loath to leave her, given that two letters had found their way to her—but he was just as loath to hang around. The truth was that after that fabulous night in the park, he and Audrey rarely had a moment to speak. It was impossible—they were surrounded by assistants and hairdressers and dancers and managers and talent agents and musicians and a whole host of people with official titles whose names he could never remember.

He began to think that maybe it was better this way. He was realizing that it was damn near impossible to be near her and not want to touch her. He had no idea when he had crossed over from being mildly attracted to aching for her, but it had happened, and he wanted to kick his own ass for it. He couldn't help admiring the shape of her face, the curve of her hips, the gentle slope of her shoulders. He'd come to detect her scent among so many, the faint smell of magnolias, just like those that grew in his grandmother's garden and marked the memory of his youth.

He wanted her, just like the world wanted her. He wanted her so much that he was beginning to have very erotic dreams of her, of Audrey on his lap, gloriously naked and riding him with enthusiasm. Worse, he was having daydreams of her, imagining them in various settings—walking in Central Park in New York, or running on the beach in Malibu, or even at dinner with his friends.

Such daydreams were uncharacteristic, and in this case, really out of the question. He wanted her, but he worked to convince himself that the want was the product of being in close proximity to a beautiful woman. This was not something that could ever work out between the two of them. There was the problem of Bonner, and her fame, and so many other things that it made Jack crazy to think about it.

So he kept his emotional distance.

But on the way to Atlantic City, where she was scheduled to do two shows, Audrey made a call to someone who made her smile, and when she hung up, she asked Courtney to arrange a car for her when they reached the hotel.

"A car?" Lucas asked from his perch in the living area's captain chair, where he was strumming on a guitar. "Why do you need a car?"

"One of my scholarship kids lives near the shore. I want to surprise her."

Lucas shook his head. "We haven't got time for that, baby."

"I have time for it. I am free tomorrow morning. I don't have to be at the theater until three."

"We've got airtime on two radio stations in the morning," Lucas said. "You don't have time to go running off to pat little kids on the head."

Audrey's hands stilled. She slowly turned and gave Lucas a look so cool that even Jack flinched a little. "I'm going to pretend you didn't say that," she said softly. "And just so we're straight, *you* have two radio stations in the morning, Lucas—not me."

"No, *we* have two radio stations in the morning. They both expect you to be there."

"Only because you told them I would be there. But the spots are about your music. Not mine."

All of the bus inhabitants, smelling a good fight, looked from Audrey to Lucas and back again. Courtney was the most interested, and Jack had the feeling she fed off these arguments. Personally, he wished for once Audrey would plant a stiletto up the guy's ass, but in the end, Audrey did what she always did—she pressed her lips together and remained quiet.

He hated Bonner.

Hated him so much that he got the name of the kid from Courtney, and called and arranged the whole thing, including a car to drive Audrey the next morning.

If Bonner wouldn't take her, he damn sure would.

Fourteen

At five-thirty the next morning, Audrey's cell rang so obnoxiously loud that she almost killed herself trying to get to it so that it wouldn't wake Lucas.

"Hello?" she hissed into the phone. "*Gail*?" It had to be Gail. Only her family would call at such an ungodly hour, probably needing money or something.

"Hey, sweet cheeks."

The sound of Jack's voice made her pulse surge, and she quickly fought off the covers. "*Jack?*" she whispered as she retreated to the bathroom. "Has something happened? Did I get another letter?"

"No, Audrey, no," he said. "Everything is cool. When is the car picking you up to take you to the radio station?"

"Six-thirty. Why?"

"Wanna play hooky?" he asked softly.

A dangerous, inappropriate image swam through her head. "What did you have in mind?"

"Be downstairs in half an hour and I'll show you."

She wanted to, ah God, she wanted to. But how could she? "I don't know," she said, her voice full of the disappointment she was feeling.

"Do you want to see your scholarship girl?" Jack asked. "Because if you do, I have arranged everything."

Audrey gasped with surprise and delight. "You did *what*?" she squealed. "Are you kidding?" She instantly sobered. "Shit! I can't go. We've got radio this morning—"

"No, Bonner has radio. Let him do his own airtime without you for a change."

The suggestion was strongly appealing. She didn't like the way Lucas booked these sorts of things and then told her after the fact. And she would give anything to see her scholarship girl.

She couldn't believe Jack had done this for her, and smiled. "I'll be down in twenty minutes."

She had no idea how she did it—brushing her teeth and hair, dabbing on a little makeup and dressing at the same moment, then dashing off a note to Lucas to tell him he was on his own and to please feed Bruno. That would infuriate him. Nevertheless, in twenty minutes, she was striding through the slot machines to the front door.

He was there, leaning up against a blue car, one leg crossed over the other at the ankle, his arms folded across his chest. His shirt sleeves were rolled up, and his dark hair looked as if he'd run his fingers through it. He grinned when he saw her and straightened up.

"Okay," she said breathlessly, feeling strangely giddy. "I just have to hit the gift shop."

He didn't ask, but with his hand on the small of her back, he directed her to a row of shops inside the Taj Mahal. Audrey flew into the first one, picked out a stuffed bear, a T-shirt, and a pair of flip-flops. "This isn't exactly what I wanted to take, but it will do," she said as she signed the slip the woman behind the counter handed her.

With her sack of cheesy gifts, Audrey allowed Jack to lead her out to the car. She noticed as they strode up to it that it was the sort of car she would have driven pre–smash hit days.

Jack opened the front passenger door. Audrey peered at it. "This is the car?" she asked, hearing the disbelief in her voice.

"Yep. I thought we'd go with something small and unremarkable."

He'd just hit another home run, then. "But . . . who is driving?" she asked, eyeing the car suspiciously.

"I am. How long has it been since you were in a Ford Taurus?"

She laughed. "At least one hundred years," she said, and climbed into the plain car, tossing her bag onto the backseat.

It almost felt like they were Bonnie and Clyde, making a grand getaway. "She knows we're coming?" Audrey asked, trying to make her unruly curls look presentable in the visor mirror.

"Yep. Katie Parmer's mother is waiting for her daughter's idol to show up."

"How did you know it was Katie?" Audrey asked.

"I sweet-talked Courtney into making a couple of phone calls," he said with a wink.

"Oh my God. You *did*? Did you have to sleep with her?"

He laughed. "No . . . but she didn't let me off cheap. She called your foundation and they figured out who it was and called Katie's mom. I understand this is supposed to be a surprise for Katie and twenty of her closest friends."

"I can't believe you did this," Audrey said, her smile broadening, her heart and skin warming with delight.

He shrugged. "I thought it would mean a lot to the girl, and you, well . . . you looked like you really wanted to meet her."

"You have no idea how much I do! Jack . . . this is so . . . *nice*."

He laughed. "Don't look so surprised. I can be a nice guy when I want to be."

"But this is above and beyond nice. And I intend to enjoy every last moment of it because Lucas is going to kill me when I get back. I left him a note and told him he was on his own with the radio."

Jack kept his gaze on the road before them, but she saw the muscle in his jaw flinch. "That can't be too big a deal, right?" he asked evenly. "He's promoting his new CD, isn't he?"

"Yes," she said, and sighed. "You don't know Lucas. He can get really insecure about his talent and he just feels better if I'm there, you know? It's a support thing."

Jack looked at her, his blue eyes full of something she couldn't quite read. "I think he'll live."

"I don't know," she said, dreading the scene when she came back.

"Who knows? Maybe he'll finally figure out that he has to learn to stand on his own two feet," he said. "You don't owe him a career—you've got your own to build."

"But you don't know what all he has done for me," she said, feeling a little defensive of him. "It's okay," she said quickly before Jack could argue. "I really want to meet the scholarship girls. And if I don't take this opportunity, when will I have another one?"

Jack said nothing.

Audrey's cell phone rang. She fished it out of her bag and winced. Lucas. She put the phone back in her bag, unanswered. But she felt another nail in a coffin she hadn't even realized she was building—or really, even thought of building—until perhaps that very moment.

The phone continued to ring. Audrey smiled a little at Jack. "Thanks," she said, meaning it. "This means so much to me."

His jaw relaxed a little, and he smiled. "Don't thank me. It's a good thing you're doing."

Audrey grinned. Jack did, too.

He couldn't help himself. When the girl smiled, she could melt the polar ice cap.

The drive to Katie Parmer's house was short—too short, really—but well worth the trip. He'd never seen a child's face light up like Katie's did when she saw Audrey walking up the sidewalk to her door. The girl's face turned up to the sun like a daisy, her smile as brilliant as a handful of stars. Her wide blue eyes never left Audrey, and when Audrey sat cross-legged on the floor and asked Katie to sing for her, Katie filled her lungs and sang like she was auditioning for *American Idol*—which, if she kept this up, she would be one day.

Several young girls gathered around as Audrey showed them some basic chords on Katie's guitar. When Katie's mother—also glowing with delight, Jack noted—invited them to enjoy a cake she'd made, she seemed overwhelmed when Audrey hopped up and insisted on helping her. She got the paper plates and plastic forks, arranged the paper napkins in a fan on the kitchen table, and helped serve Kool-Aid punch to the kids.

With ten other girls and several admiring parents looking on, Audrey ate cake and asked the girls questions about themselves. Did they like music? Did they mind their parents? Did they have boyfriends?

Then it was their turn to ask Audrey questions.

Did she have to take music lessons? Did she get in trouble with her mom for dancing? What was her favorite song? And then came the inevitable question from Katie. "Is he your boyfriend?" she asked, pointing to Jack as a chorus of giggles filled the room.

Audrey smiled at Jack. "No," she said. "He's . . ." She seemed to have trouble explaining him. "He's my—"

"Bodyguard," Jack said.

Audrey laughed. "Well *I* was going to say friend," she said, "but okay, bodyguard." And with another laugh, she leaned down, still looking at Jack, and whispered something into Katie's ear. Katie was instantly giggling and turned to tell the girl sitting next to her.

"Great," Jack drawled to the woman standing next to him. "Even at the age of eight, females have the ability to make me squirm."

They stayed for three hours; Jack had to force Audrey to come away. He was loath to do it, but they were running out of time. She hugged all the girls good-bye, thanked their parents again, and finally, with Jack's hand on her arm, walked outside—and right into the arms of Lucas and the media coverage.

"Lucas!" she exclaimed as two television reporters put mics in her face.

"Your generosity needs to be seen by the world, baby," he said, and kissed her on the mouth.

"Miss LaRue! Can we speak to you about your foundation?"

"Ah . . . sure," she said, glancing nervously back at the blue-trimmed bungalow from which they had just emerged.

"It's okay," Lucas said, and gripped her hand tightly. "I cleared it with Katie's dad." And with that, he turned around, so that he and Audrey were facing the cameras together.

It wasn't long before the house had emptied and all the girls were swirling around, trying to be in the camera shot with Audrey. As Jack watched Lucas bundle Audrey into the town car he'd arrived in a few minutes earlier, leaving Jack to the Taurus, he figured that Lucas, in a snit, had figured out a way to get some of that much-needed Audrey LaRue fairy dust today after all.

He had to hand it to Bonner—he'd even managed to sneak in a reference to his own CD, which would debut next week. To the world at large, it looked as if Audrey LaRue and Lucas Bonner had set up the Songbird Foundation to help girls get into music.

How magnanimous of the pair. What a lovely couple they made.

He drove back to Atlantic City alone, fuming.

Jack didn't get a chance to talk to Audrey again that day, but he did speak to Lucas. Or rather, Lucas spoke to him.

"You pull a stunt like that again, and I'll kill you," Lucas said heatedly in the corridors around the stage.

Jack grinned and looked Lucas up and down. "If you think you can, big shot, bring it on."

Of course, Lucas backed off, but not without telling Jack what he thought of him, which went in one ear and out the other.

It wasn't until the rush before the show—they were late getting started because of a lighting malfunction—that Jack saw Audrey across a large, crowded reception room. She was dressed in black leggings, heels, and a studded leather bra, and had her hair piled high on her head. She caught his eye and smiled, and mouthed the words *Thank you.*

Funny how those two little words and that smile calmed the fury in him.

For the time being.

AUDREY PAYS A SURPRISE VISIT

(*Celebrity Insider Magazine*) Audrey LaRue is determined that young girls with talent and who are interested in learning music will have access to music education and lessons. She has set up the Songbird Foundation, which awards scholarships to girls with promise and desire but without the resources necessary to improve their talents. On Friday, boyfriend Lucas Bonner (*Speeding to Hell*, *August*) surprised Audrey with a visit to one of her scholarship students, Katie Parmer. They enjoyed a morning of music, games, and cake. As a result of her surprise visit, and the reports that followed, the foundation reports applications for funding are up thirty percent. Insiders say Audrey can sing, but she is a loser when it comes to playing LocoRoco with a group of 8–10-year-old girls. Rock on, Audrey!

Audrey Late for Tour Date!

(*Famous Lifestyles*) Insiders are rumbling about what's going on with Audrey LaRue's *Frantic* tour after Audrey showed up late to a performance in Atlantic City recently. Handlers say Audrey is exhausted from the grueling tour schedules, but a personal friend tells *Famous Lifestyles* that Audrey was late returning from a party in a nearby town. "Audrey can't handle the pressure of touring," the friend says. "She tends to drink when she is stressed, and lately, she's been stressed a lot." The source reports that Lucas Bonner, an aspiring rock artist and Audrey's longtime boyfriend, is concerned about her and is monitoring the situation closely. (Reps for LaRue and Bonner deny the story.)

Fifteen

The Audrey LaRue entourage was in high spirits when they moved on to Baltimore and Washington, D.C., after two very successful shows in Atlantic City. With the changes to the set list, everyone was happy, the show was really streamlined, and Lucas's CD had opened to a decent start.

Everyone was happy except Audrey, who had received a lot of "*We're on it*" responses from law enforcement about the letters. But even more stressing was getting news about trouble at home.

Granted, there was *always* trouble at home, but Audrey was usually spared the daily drama because of her job and notoriety. Her family called when they needed money, and even then, they usually put Gail up to it. Allen, her brother, the freckle-faced tagalong who had grown into a man with a horrendous substance abuse problem, called every once in a while to assure her he was doing great.

Audrey had no doubt in those instances on the phone he *was* great—but it never lasted. Gail would call a few days later and tell her that Allen had screwed up again.

The grip of his addiction was impossible to break—even monthlong stints Audrey had put him through in some of the best treatment facilities in the United States couldn't seem to break him of the desire to abuse his body and spirit. She worried that Allen just didn't have the strength of character to stop.

He promised her he did. He promised her each time that he was done with drugs, that he was going to stay clean. And just like he always did, Allen relapsed at the worst possible moment. He'd gone missing right when she'd started out on the tour, but he'd surfaced a few days later—again, like he always did—a little beat up but relatively unscathed. His probation officer, Farrah Jakes, told Allen and the family in no uncertain terms that if he pulled a stunt like that again, she would throw him in jail for violating the terms of his probation.

So once again, Allen had tried to walk the straight and narrow and had almost succeeded.

Until recently.

Until just about the time they hit Atlantic City, which was when Gail and Mom started calling, telling Audrey she needed to do something, that Allen was out of control.

"What can I do?" Audrey demanded of her sister. "I'm in *Atlantic City*. I am on a nationwide tour. I have a huge responsibility to a lot of people, so I am not sure what I can do to help him now."

"Great," Gail said curtly. "Thanks a lot. Leave all the family shit to me."

"I'm not leaving it to you, Gail, but I don't know what I can do. Do you think I should cancel my tour and come home because Allen has relapsed again?"

"No, but I think you could do *something*. Can't you get him into that rehab place again? What is it, Hazeltown?"

"Hazelden," Audrey said. "He's been there twice now. Do you really think a third time will magically do it?"'

"Just call them and talk to them," Gail urged her. "And then maybe you can come down one weekend and talk to Allen."

It was a never-ending battle. Audrey's family seemed to think she should drop everything—in spite of the countless number of livelihoods that depended on her—and rush home every time Allen was teetering on the brink of ruin, even though Allen had been teetering on the brink of ruin for two decades. If she had run home every time there was a close call, she would never have achieved what she had.

At least that's what Lucas kept telling her. "Forget him, baby. He's a loser."

"That's my baby brother you are talking about," Audrey said. "He's *not* a loser. He's really a good guy—he just can't seem to get his shit together."

"That's because he doesn't want to," Lucas said. "He feeds off the drama."

His dismissal of Allen angered her. "That's just stupid, Lucas. Of course he wants to do better. But he lacks the skill or whatever it is that makes normal people say no to drugs."

Lucas had given her a very condescending smile and patted her on the shoulder like she lacked the skills to understand a loser when she saw one. "Don't let that bullshit get in your head, baby. We've done half of this tour and things are going great. Just shut that noise out until we land in L.A., and then you can send them more money and clear everything up. All right?"

It was a callous thing to say . . . but it was also true. They wanted her money. They wanted her to send Allen away so they didn't have to deal with him. She couldn't blame them—she wasn't in Redhill, Texas, her hometown, like they were. She didn't have to face the dysfunction every day.

Yet Audrey couldn't turn it off like that. She remembered the chubby-faced kid who followed her everywhere, the one who thought she'd hung the moon. He was her little brother, the one she'd practically raised in those years after Mom and Dad had split up and they were bouncing from house to house.

There was good inside Allen. She just wanted to find the right person to help him rediscover himself. Her family didn't seem interested in that anymore.

She tried to get Allen on the phone, but he avoided her—he knew what she was going to say. So Audrey continued on with the tour, trying to do what Lucas suggested and keep the noise from her head.

After the Baltimore show closed, the band took Audrey and Lucas to a club, where they jammed with local musicians. That was recorded in the papers Monday morning as they headed for Washington.

In Washington, Courtney found another letter addressed to Audrey. *You are such a slut, Audrey*, the madman wrote. *How much longer should I let you live?*

This time, the letter was delivered by a bellhop in a bouquet of flowers. The police were working on tracing the delivery and who might have had access to it, but as with the chocolates, the flowers were ordered online, and the delivery van left unattended in several locations before arriving at the hotel.

"These things are really hard to trace," the cop said, just like the cops before him had told her.

"Weird," said Rich, who gathered with the rest of the crew when the letter was discovered. "You'd think he'd be easy to catch. It's almost like he's stalking you. I wonder why he wants to harm you? I wonder what he thinks you did to him?"

"Rich," Jack said with quiet warning. "Maybe now is not the time to voice your thoughts."

Rich shrugged. "Maybe." He shifted his gaze to Audrey again. "It just seems very odd to me."

"Okay, pal," Jack said. "Why don't we give her some space?"

Jack didn't have to do that—Rich hadn't said anything Audrey hadn't already thought of.

Only Jack could assure her, in that quiet way of his, that she was safe. There was something about the way he said it, something about the look in his eye and the set of his jaw, that made Audrey believe him. So she went on with the show in Washington on Tuesday night in confidence and did two encores.

The crowd always enlivened her, made her blood pump, made her feel invincible. So much so that when she was leaving the MCI Center that night, a large crowd had gathered at the exit to wait for her. Still riding a euphoric high from the show, she strode to the barriers the city had erected and reached for the notebook one young woman held out to her for an autograph.

"What's your name?" she asked.

"Krista."

"Are you into music?"

She didn't hear Krista's answer, didn't hear anything but Krista's angry "*Hey!*" at the very same moment someone grabbed Audrey's arm with two hands and tried to yank her into the crowd.

The sick feeling of being grabbed filled Audrey with hysteria. But Jack was there instantly, coming between her and the man who tried to grab her. The only thing Audrey saw was her attacker's cold black eyes before Jack dragged her away. Everyone was pushing and shoving—the crowd was yelling and barriers were going down. Jack moved her away from it all, his massive arms lifting her up and around and away from the crowd.

"Calm down," he said. "Take a breath."

"*Jack!* Oh, thank God! Was it him?" she asked frantically. "Is that the letter guy?"

"I don't know," he said. "But the police have him."

Audrey twisted in his arms, peering over his shoulder as two policemen manhandled the guy away from the crowd.

"It's him," she said frantically. "I know it was him! He was going to *kill* me."

"He wasn't going to do anything like that, sweet cheeks. We were right there—he never would have had a chance." He tightened his embrace around her, two steel bands that felt unbreakable, and still, she trembled. "Now listen to me, Audrey. He doesn't have you. He isn't going to get anywhere near you. Right now, he is headed for a little R&R behind bars. Relax."

"I'm okay," she muttered into his shoulder.

"No you're not—you're shaking like you shake your booty during 'Frantic.' And while I am personally a huge fan of that particular number, you have no reason to shake like that now because I have you and no one is going to get near you. So stop before you make me do something stupid."

She smiled into the hard wall of muscle that was his shoulder and lifted her gaze. "Like what?"

He smiled a little crookedly. "Use your imagination, girl."

"Audrey! Jesus, what the hell?"

She felt a huge wave of disappointment as Lucas suddenly appeared from nowhere. Jack's grip of her loosened, and with a murderous look, Lucas put his hand on Jack and shoved him.

"Hey, watch it," Jack said coolly.

"Will you just step back and let me speak to my girlfriend?" Lucas snapped, and instantly turned toward Audrey. "What the hell happened?"

"I don't know . . . I was signing autographs and somebody grabbed me—"

"Where the hell was your security?" he asked, flashing a menacing look at Jack.

"Right there, Lucas, they were *right there*. I—it was *my* fault. I went running over there to sign autographs and the guy grabbed me so fast."

"From now on, I don't want you to let her out of your sight for a moment!" he railed at Jack.

"Listen, Bonner—"

"He won't!" Audrey said, her voice pleading. She looked at Jack, held his gaze. "He won't leave my side, he promised."

Lucas grumbled something about how he'd better not, and with an arm around her shoulders, he marched her to the tour bus.

In their hotel room, he tried to comfort her in his way, but his attention turned to groping, and Audrey pushed him away. "Come on, Lucas. I just had the scare of my life!"

"Turn a negative into a positive," he said, his eyes on her breasts. "A little reconnection never hurt anyone who just had a scare."

"Funny that this is the time you choose to reconnect. We've had sex once in three months, maybe longer, and that was a big grope under the stage."

"And that is my fault? It's not like you're ever in the mood! You're always tired or bitchy—"

"*Bitchy?* What the hell is that supposed to mean?"

"Come on, Aud. You know how you can get after a long rehearsal or a show."

"No, Lucas, how do I *get*?" she demanded.

"You can be a bit of a diva, okay? *Not tonight, Lucas, I am so tired*, or, *turn out the light, I have a headache*," he said, mocking her voice. "Sound familiar?"

"Hey!" she exclaimed angrily. "I said that *once.* Most of the time, you're jamming somewhere. It's not like you're in here with me."

"Maybe that is because you have an attitude."

"Maybe the attitude is, I'm *tired*. It's grueling being on tour."

"Like I don't know that? I'm on tour with you, remember?"

"You're backstage somewhere, Lucas, but you aren't the one performing!"

His eyes narrowed. "I would be if you would lighten up a little. I don't care what your talent manager or the label says, Audrey. It wouldn't hurt you to give me a couple of spots in your show."

"Oh Jesus, here we go again," she sighed, and fell into a chair. They'd had this argument more than once—yet they kept going around the same thing. It wasn't Lucas's show. It wasn't even his style of music. To give up "one or two" spots on the concert list would be giving up one or two songs people had paid to hear *her* perform.

"No, we're not going again," he said, and swiped up a denim jacket.

"So where are you going?" she cried, panicky at the thought of being alone after that scare.

"Out," he said, and let the door slam behind him.

Tears suddenly filled Audrey's eyes. She grabbed a pillow, buried her face in it. She had never wanted this. She had never wanted to be afraid of strangers or to fight with Lucas, but that seemed to be all they did nowadays. When they were driving a Honda around Texas, they'd been happy. The moment she'd hit it big, something had changed, and it felt to her like it had been a steady downhill slide between them since then. She didn't know how to talk to him anymore. She no longer knew how to get her thoughts and wants and feelings across to him.

There were so many little things that bugged her. Things that were beginning to add up to something big and weighty, and she didn't know if she could live with it or not.

But she didn't know if she could be alone anymore. And when had that happened? When had she become so dependent on everyone else for her happiness and well-being?

Maybe she really was a diva. Audrey closed her eyes, tried to keep from crying and tried to think what to do. But it was a miserable, traitorous fact that all she could seem to think of was Jack, of his arms around her, of his quiet, confident voice.

She took that image with her into the bathroom, where she ran a hot bath. And when she slipped beneath the surface of the hot, soapy water, the image of Jack changed. He was naked, his body long and lean, his chest broad, his erection enormous. In her fantasy, he slid his cock into her body instead of the fingers she slipped inside herself. It was his body that stroked her in that tub, his hand and mouth that drove her to an explosive end. And when she climaxed, it was his clear blue eyes she saw, his sexy smile and his flesh dampened with the exertion of making her come.

She slipped deeper into the water, until it was up around her chin, and closed her eyes. A single tear slid from the corner of her eye and dropped into the water.

Sixteen

"Now? Why? We're leaving in two hours!" Courtney demanded, as if Audrey was being unreasonable when she called the next morning and asked Courtney to come to her room as soon as possible.

Audrey didn't know how to tell Courtney that she was afraid to be alone without it being spread around the whole crew, so she said, "Do I need a reason?"

There was a moment of silence. Audrey squeezed her eyes shut.

"I'll be there as soon as I can," Courtney said curtly.

And she arrived with an attitude the size of Texas, striding in and flipping her red hair over her shoulder as she carelessly tossed her tote bag onto a chair. "Okay. I'm here."

"Just help me get my stuff together," Audrey asked, and turned away from her.

"What stuff? It's already together."

"There is more in the bathroom that needs to be packed."

Courtney said nothing, but marched into the bathroom, where Audrey could hear her throwing her things into a bag. Literally, *throw-*

ing things into the bag. And when she emerged again carrying Audrey's small vanity case, she let it drop next to Audrey's other bags.

Audrey was on the verge of telling Courtney to find another job when a knock at the door startled her. She tensed as Courtney stormed to the door and threw it open. The door blocked Audrey's view of who it was, but Courtney suddenly broke into a wreath of smiles and her body language changed dramatically. Her weight slid onto one hip; her hand went to the necklace that hung low to her cleavage. "Well hello there," she purred.

"Hello, Courtney. Is your boss around?"

Courtney's smile faded. "Where else?" she said tightly, and turned away.

Jack stepped inside the room; above Courtney's head, his gaze met Audrey's, and he smiled. "Bus leaves in an hour," he said. "I thought I would make sure everything is cool up here and see you out."

"Everything is cool," Courtney said.

Jack smiled again, but his gaze did not move from Audrey. She felt herself coloring slightly and turned back to her tote bag. "Thanks," she said. "I appreciate it."

"You ready to load up?" he asked, and from the corner of her eye, Audrey saw him pick up her bag.

"Yeah . . . whatever is left Courtney can tend to."

"Lucky me," Courtney muttered.

"Lucky you have a paycheck," Audrey retorted as she picked up Bruno.

If looks could kill, Audrey would be splayed on the floor right now, her guts spilling all over the carpet, courtesy of Courtney. Where was the animosity coming from? Since when had Courtney despised Audrey as much as she seemed to now? She really had to speak to Lucas about this. She saw no point in having a personal assistant who hated her.

But at the moment, Jack had two of Audrey's bags and was nodding toward the door. "You want to go?"

"You don't have to do that," Audrey said. "I can have someone sent up for them."

"I'm right here. And I would rather get you and your things on the bus sooner rather than later."

"Why?" she asked, her smile disappearing. "Did we get a letter? Did you see something?"

"Audrey," he said easily, and with a reassuring smile. "We didn't get a letter, and I didn't see anything," he said as Courtney disappeared into the adjoining living room. "Our guy from last night is still in jail."

"It's him, isn't it?" Audrey whispered, clutching Bruno tightly to her.

Jack smiled. "Don't worry about that, starlight. Come on. Let's get on the bus."

"It *is* him," she said, her eyes going wide, her mind flashing around how close she'd come to death. "You don't want to tell me, but it's him."

Something in his expression changed, something that seemed almost sad.

"What?" she demanded.

"Actually . . . I don't want to tell you that it's *not* him."

That cold shiver she felt was the fear creeping under her skin again.

So the tally for the last twenty-four hours went something like: boyfriend troubles, assistant troubles, and one crazy letter-writing slasher on the loose, who was *not*, as one might have thought, the guy doing the grabbing last night. That was just your random fan trouble.

Audrey didn't think things could get much worse, but the bus had hardly cleared the Washington suburbs en route to Raleigh, North Carolina, when Audrey's cell rang.

She glanced at the caller ID, saw her mother's number, and groaned. Mom rarely called her cell phone and hadn't since the last time Audrey had been home in Redhill and Mom had been offended that she'd received so many calls. "It's just rude," she'd said as she slapped an enormous bowl of potato salad on the table. "You got no respect for us, Audrey."

"That's not true! I do!" Audrey had protested. "But I'm trying to run a business from Redhill, and believe me, it's not easy. There's not even a *Kinko's* in this town."

"It's rude. And you won't find *me* calling that damn phone unless it's an emergency, because I got enough respect for you not to call while you're in the middle of something and expect you to talk to me."

And Mom was never one to go back on her word. Once she'd cut you down, she followed it up with action. So Audrey could be assured that if Mom was calling, it was an emergency.

It had to be Allen.

As usual when it came to her family, her instincts were right on. Mom dispensed with any of the usual greetings and said, "Well, thank God you answered. Allen's in the hospital."

"Oh *God*," Audrey exclaimed. "What happened?" she asked, dreading the answer. "Is he all right?"

"No, he's not all right," Mom said tersely. "He overdosed is what they're saying."

"Oh *Jesus*," Audrey moaned.

"It's a bad situation, but not so bad that you need to take the Lord's name in vain."

"Sorry, Mom," Audrey said. "How bad is he hurt?" she asked, aware that everyone on the bus was turning to look at her. She would have made a quick exit to the bedroom, but Trystan was standing in the hall, his bag at his feet, the contents spilled around as he searched for something. So she inched around in her seat, putting her back to them all as best she could. "Gail said he'd been clean the last couple of weeks," she whispered.

"We all thought he was doing good!" Mom said a little too sharply, then sighed again. "I don't know what he got himself into, I really don't. I thought he was doing good, but the next thing I know, they're calling me from the hospital. Anyway, I think you better come on home, Audrey."

Audrey's heart stopped beating. "What do you mean? What—he's going to *live*, isn't he?"

"How would I know? I'm not a doctor! They say one thing one day, then something else the next, and the bottom line is, he ain't woke up since they brought him in. So you better come on home, honey."

She caught her breath, closed her eyes. If something happened to Allen, she would die.

"So when are you coming?" Mom asked.

"I don't know," Audrey said. "It's really hard to get away—"

"Well, I know you're a big star now, and I know you probably don't want nothing to do with Redhill, but I'm talking about your *brother*. You can't just turn your back on your family."

She hadn't turned her back on her family! Why did her mother always have to do this? Why did she always have to blame Audrey for all her troubles? "That's not it at all, Mom. It's just that I'm in the middle of this tour, and a lot of people are tied up in it, and it's really hard to just *cancel.* I've committed to these shows, and if I have to reschedule, I can't just call them on the day I'm supposed to be there and tell them I am not showing up." God, what was she *saying*? She was really making excuses when her brother was lying unconscious in the hospital?

"Well. You do what you think is right," Mom said, her voice cold. "I just thought you needed to know that your little brother might not ever wake up. I got to go now. Gail's at the hospital and she needs to get home to the kids."

"Mom, I—"

"Like I said, Audrey, you do what you think is right," Mom said, and hung up.

Damn her. Couldn't she just once try and understand what Audrey's life was like instead of hating her for having escaped that hell hole? With a groan, Audrey dropped her head back against the headrest and sighed.

"What's going on?"

She opened her eyes; Lucas was squatting before her, concern in his eyes. He put his hand on her knee, massaging it. "Who was that?"

"Mom," she said, conscious that everyone was straining to hear her.

She didn't particularly want to air her family dysfunction in front of everyone—which included Courtney, and Mitzi, who had flown in for a couple of days, and Lucy, Trystan, and *Jack*, for Chrissakes—but then again, there was never a time that she was ever alone, so she said, "My brother is in the hospital."

"Oh *Jesus*!" Mitzi, her publicist, cried. "What happened? Does the press know about it yet?"

"I didn't ask," Audrey said, the thought never having crossed her mind. "Apparently he did something really stupid," she said to Lucas. Dammit, her eyes were welling again. She would really like to go one whole week without crying about something.

Lucas squeezed her knee. "Is there something we can do? Maybe get him into rehab somewhere?"

"No," she said, shaking her head. "It's worse than that. He's in a coma. I need to go home, Lucas."

An expression of disgust and anger washed over Lucas's face. He knew all about her dysfunctional family. Before they'd moved to L.A., she and Lucas could hardly last a day in Redhill before they headed back to Austin. Someone was always drunk or angry or otherwise making the holiday or family occasion miserable.

Now, Lucas was looking at her like he thought she was insane to leave this tour for them. "You aren't really thinking of going to Texas," he said, his voice full of disbelief.

"Of course I am. He's in the hospital and he hasn't woken up. He might *never*," she said as she struggled to keep the tears from falling.

"What about your responsibilities *here*?" Lucas demanded. "You are on a huge nationwide tour! You can't just cancel in the middle of it!"

"I just need a couple of days—"

"You don't *have* a couple of days!" he shouted. He suddenly stood up and started pacing the small living area of the tour bus while everyone watched him, their heads moving like they were at a tennis match. "This is too insane to be believed! You have a single climbing like an ape up the charts, you are playing to sold-out audiences in major markets, and lo and behold, your fucking little brother fucks up again, and suddenly, you are going to jeopardize everything to run and watch him wake up and go out and do drugs all over again!"

No one said a word, no one so much as breathed. Audrey wanted to kill Lucas. She wanted to grab him around the neck and squeeze those words from his throat. She could feel the heat of shame creeping into her face and avoided looking at everyone else. "Thanks for airing my family's troubles to everyone," she said evenly. "And for the record, I don't want to jeopardize anything. But I don't want to lose a member of my family, either."

"I'll take her," Jack said calmly.

"Oh great," Lucas said, throwing his hands up. "Studmuffin is going to take her. And how do you propose to do that?"

Jack's expression turned hard. He slowly came to his feet. "I will get a plane and fly her there. We can leave after the show tonight and meet up with you in Nashville. That gives her two days."

"That won't work," Lucas said, shaking his head.

"Why not?"

With an incredulous laugh, Lucas looked around at everyone, apparently looking for someone to join in. "Where are you going to get a plane, pal?"

"Don't worry about it. I can get a plane."

"Can you get one by tonight?" Audrey asked.

He shifted his gaze to her and his expression instantly softened. "No problem. If you want to go to Texas and see your brother, I will take you."

"Thank you, Jack." She stood up and looked at Lucas. "I am going to Texas."

"Wait, wait," Lucas said, grabbing her hand before she could escape. "Okay, look, if you have to go . . ." He was, obviously, understanding that things were not going his way, and Audrey could almost see the about-face in him. "I should really be there with you—"

"No!"

"But I need to go ahead and make sure everything is in order in Nashville. So I can meet you in Redhill."

"I'll call you," she said quickly, not wanting Lucas anywhere near her. "Just let me go and see about him and I will let you know if I need you to come to Redhill."

He didn't look as if he agreed with that plan, but everyone was watching him. Audrey pulled her hand free of his grasp.

"Okay," he said reluctantly, and exchanged a cold look with Jack that would have sent a shiver down most spines. Audrey stepped around Trystan's stuff in her haste, and Bruno leapt over it, trotting after her as she made her way to the bedroom to make some calls.

There wasn't anyone in Redhill who could help Allen, and she wasn't entirely certain she could, but she was the only one with a prayer of helping him. Unfortunately, her responsibility felt just as huge on this end. She hated letting down so many people on her tour; she hated toying with her success. Yet how could she not go to Allen? She felt both responsibilities like a rock around her neck, one that felt like it had the weight to sink her.

She punched through a series of numbers in her BlackBerry, looking for a doctor she knew in Redhill, when the door opened and Lucas entered. Audrey tried to keep from looking annoyed, but she really didn't want to see him right now.

"You know, I forgot something," he said.

"What?" she asked idly, her attention on her phone.

He walked over to where she sat, pushed her BlackBerry away so that she had to look at him. He put his hands on either side of her face. "I forgot our deal," he said softly. "You concentrate on writing and performing, and let me concentrate on the rest. I thought that was what I was doing, but I realized that you can't be very creative while you are worrying about Allen."

"You're right," she said evenly. "I can't."

He smiled and kissed her. "You go on, then. I will follow if I need to. Don't worry about the tour—I'll handle things here. And leave Bruno with me. I'll take care of him." He stood up, walking out of the room to let her make her phone calls.

She damn sure didn't need his permission, and she wished he'd quit granting it like she did.

Seventeen

Jack called Michael and told him he needed a jet.

"Any particular kind?" Michael asked, as if he were asked to produce jets out of thin air every day. But then again, no one ever knew with Michael—Jack believed he could produce Osama bin Laden if someone would just ask.

"The usual," Jack said, referring to the small Cessna jets TA used to ferry celebrities to their extreme adventures.

"Going on a little trip?" Michael asked.

"Yep."

"Did you say where to?"

"No. Redhill, Texas. Closest airport would be Dallas."

"Ah," Michael said. "That explains everything."

"I'll need to pick it up in Raleigh and return it in Nashville."

"Done," Michael said.

"Thanks," Jack responded.

"Just one question—and this is merely to feed the animals in the office—why the hell do you need a plane?"

"Just a quick trip," Jack said as nonchalantly as he could. "Audrey's brother is in the hospital. I'm going to run her out there between shows."

"*Audrey*," Michael drawled.

"Yeah, *Audrey*," Jack echoed, frowning.

"You're flying her and her main squeeze to her hometown?"

Jack shifted uncomfortably in his seat. "Just her," he admitted.

He heard something that sounded like a definite snicker on the other end before Michael said, "Okay, so just to make sure I've got this—you are flying *Audrey* to her hometown, where you will, presumably, meet Mom and Dad and hang a couple of days. Is that right?"

"Do you have a point, Raney?" Jack asked irritably.

"Just a question—have you two set a date?" He laughed at his lame joke.

Jack sighed. "If you are through with your juvenile needling, can you get me a plane?"

"Hell yes, I can get you a plane," Michael scoffed, and thankfully turned the conversation away from the ridiculous to the logistics of getting Jack a plane.

The plane was waiting for them at a private airstrip outside of Raleigh that night. At 1 a.m., Courtney and Ted—who Jack suspected had hooked up recently—drove them there. Ted helped him load a couple of bags onto the plane, then escorted Audrey across the tarmac.

Once she was inside, seated in one of the leather bucket seats at the table in the back of the plane, Ted made noises about getting Courtney back to the hotel.

Jack saw him out, saw Courtney skip around the town car to the front passenger side, and with a roll of his eyes, shut and locked the cabin door.

He glanced back at Audrey. "Everything okay?"

"Yeah," she said, looking around the cabin. "I'm going to try and get some sleep if that's all right."

"Sure," he said. "We ought to be out of here in about fifteen minutes. It's about a two-hour flight to Dallas."

"Okay."

"Buckle up," he reminded her as he stepped into the cockpit. But she'd already leaned back, her eyes closed. She looked, he thought, very tired.

He shut the door behind him and went to work. A half hour later, having reached a safe cruising altitude, and having cleared through the various towers in the area, Jack cranked the volume on his iPod. A touch on his shoulder almost sent him through the roof.

He jerked around as he ripped one earbud out of his ear. He frowned at Audrey's gleeful laughter.

"Oh my God!" she cried. "You almost ejected!"

"Most people knock," he said, turning his attention back to the instrument panel.

"I *did* knock, but you were hooked up to your iPod." She leaned over his shoulder to look out the windshield; a curl of blond hair fell off her shoulder and tickled his cheek. "Wow. It's so *black* out there."

Yes, it was very black, which was why he needed to keep an eye on the instrument panel and not the curve of her breasts. "I thought you were going to get some sleep," he said.

"I can't," she said. "Too many things on my mind. May I sit there?" she asked, pointing at the copilot seat.

"Help yourself," he said, and watched as she stretched one long, bare, and very sexy leg into the space, and followed it with another. "Seatbelt," he reminded her as she settled in.

Audrey dutifully strapped herself in, then began to peer at the instrument panel, leaning over to read the labels. "It is very cool that you know how to fly this," she said, reaching for a dial. Jack caught her wrist—she looked at him, then at her wrist.

"I'd rather you not touch anything," he said. But he couldn't seem to let go of her wrist, until Audrey lifted a golden brow. He reluctantly let go.

She smiled, her eyes glittering with amusement. Jack looked straight ahead, into the night.

"What did you think of the show tonight?" she asked.

"Fantastic. It always is."

"Really?" she asked, as if she was somehow surprised by his answer. She twisted in her seat as much as she could beneath the seatbelt to face him. "Let me ask you something. Do you think the 'Pieces of My Heart' should come before or after 'Frantic'? I've really been struggling with that—I don't know if I want a slow and easy lead-in to 'Frantic' or a slow and easy comedown from it. We've tried it both ways and I can't decide which is best."

Jack had never paid much attention to the order of the songs and shrugged. "I don't know. It seems okay the way it is."

"Hmm," she said, her eyes narrowing. "I don't know. Maybe I'll move it to the top of the set list. You know, start out slow and easy."

He said nothing, figuring she had plenty of people around to weigh in with opinions on that one.

"Which is your favorite song?" she asked.

" 'Complicated Measures,' " he said instantly and chuckled at Audrey's gasp of surprise.

"You're kidding. That one is slow and—"

"And one of your old songs," he interjected. "I wish you'd do more of the old stuff."

Audrey grinned. "I'm a little partial to the old stuff, too." She sang a few bars of "Complicated Measures," her voice clear and beautiful. Jack began to nod his head along in time to the music, and with a laugh, Audrey paused. "Come on. Sing it with me."

Jack snorted and shook his head. "I fly. You sing."

"Come on," she said again, nudging him. "You've heard it enough times." She began to sing again, and Jack sheepishly joined in, squawking along with her in a voice that reminded him of a pack of dogs howling at the moon. In a matter of moments, Audrey was doubled over with laughter. "You're *awful*!" she cried gleefully.

"Thank you," he said, grinning.

"You win—you fly, I sing," she said cheerfully, and beamed a smile at him that seeped into his pores. Audrey hummed a little more of the song then looked at him again. "Why do you like that song the best?"

He didn't know precisely. It was a love song, and he loved how sultry her voice sounded when she sang it. Almost as sultry as she sounded now, singing it softly beneath her breath.

"It just seems more like you," he said.

"Really? How so?"

He had no idea how, only that it was true. "I don't really know," he admitted. "But I think you have more of life and living in you than the pop songs can convey, and in the ballads, it really comes out."

"Living?"

He looked at her. "You know—good times and bad times. Heartache and happiness. You're a whole lot more than bubble gum."

She held his gaze, nodding thoughtfully, then looked out the window, at the splatter of lights in the black below that marked towns. "My life has not been bubble gum, that's for sure."

"Mind if I ask what's going on with your brother?"

She shot him a suspicious look.

"Never mind."

"Sorry," she said, relaxing. "It's just that when someone asks me a question, I have this instant fear that they are looking for something to give the tabloids." She sighed and shook her head. "Talk about paranoid."

"I think you have every right to be paranoid."

She smiled a little. "But I knew a long time ago that I could trust you. It's just habit."

That made him feel good.

"My brother," she sighed, and settled back in the chair and folded her arms across her midriff. "Where do I start? How about with this: He was one of the most talented guitarists in all of Texas. At least I firmly believe he had the potential to be. When we were kids, we used to hang out in the garage and play guitar to cover up the sound of my parents' fighting."

Jack looked at her—she smiled sheepishly. "Mom and Dad hated each other by the time Allen was born, and not a day went by we weren't reminded."

"Ouch."

"Yeah, ouch. Anyway, my sister Gail, she just took off with her boyfriends when they would start up. But Allen and I were too young, so we hung out in the garage. He's two years younger than me," she said. "And he used to worship me. I could have told that kid to jump off a bridge and he would have done it with a smile on his face. And he *loved* playing guitar—a whole lot more than I ever did," she said with a laugh. "Ironic, huh?"

"A little," Jack agreed. "Does he still play?"

"I don't think so," she said. "We were close until we hit high school, and you know how that goes. He had his friends, I had mine. We didn't hang out in the garage anymore. I kept playing and Allen . . . Allen was playing games at that point. I just never understood what happened to the dream."

"The dream?" Jack asked.

"Yeah," she said, nodding, looking at him again. "We had a pact—we'd get out of Redhill as soon as we could and form a band. We were determined to go to Austin and get some gigs. When I graduated, I was seventeen. I promised Allen I would go to Austin first and figure out where we were going to live and how we could get a band together. He wanted me to stay, you know, because of Mom and Dad . . ." Her voice trailed off and she turned her head so that he could not see her face. "My parents are a piece of work—none of us wanted to be stuck with them. And Allen was the baby, but I . . . I had to get out of there," she said, her voice going soft. "I couldn't take it."

She stopped there and absently ran a finger over the hem of her shorts. "I *had* to get out," she said again. "But I told Allen when he got out of high school he was going to follow me, and I'd have a place for him. Only he never came. He quit playing guitar altogether, and the next thing I knew, he was getting into trouble all the time. Needless to say, it went downhill from there."

With a sudden smile, she rubbed her hands on her arms. "We weren't exactly the model family," she said. "It's kind of cold in here, isn't it?"

"There's a jacket hanging behind my seat," he said, motioning with his head.

Audrey reached around him and grabbed his old Air Force jacket. She slipped into it backward, so the back of the jacket covered her front. The thing engulfed her. She wrapped her arms around her and crossed her legs.

"Did you ever see Allen after you left home?" Jack asked.

"Oh yeah," she said. "It was a couple of years before I could get up the money to go back to Redhill, but by then, I'd met Lucas, and he had a car and would drive me."

At the mention of Bonner's name, Jack clenched his jaw.

"But half the time, Allen wasn't around. He would take off with reprobates and get into all kinds of trouble. He's had a lot of odd jobs, but nothing permanent. He just keeps drifting."

"So what happened to Allen this time?" Jack asked.

Audrey shook her head, and the light in the cockpit caught the shimmering gold highlights in her hair. "I don't know. Mom was pretty vague, but it was definitely drugs." She bit her lower lip, lost in thought, and then suddenly straightened up and looked at him again. "What about you, Jack Price? What's your family like?"

The exact opposite—his parents were rock solid, his two older sisters as protective of him and his brother Parker as they were of their own kids. He and Parker had left Midland, where they'd grown up in the shadows of the auto body shop his father had owned, but the rest of them were still there, still getting together on weekends, still as close-knit as they'd ever been. "We're pretty tight as a family," he said, wishing Audrey could know what that was like. "Everyone gets along."

"Wow," she said with a laugh. "You don't know how lucky you are."

Oh, but he did—he'd known too many people in his life from screwed-up families that he very much appreciated his.

"I can't trust anyone in my family," Audrey continued, and twisted to face him again. "Do you know that my father sold himself to a celebrity talk show and told them a bunch of crap about me? Stuff he made up from nowhere," she said, flinging a hand out to indicate *nowhere*. "He got fifty thousand dollars for it! And then he had the nerve to ask me why I was upset!"

"That sucks," Jack agreed. "It is the price of fame, I guess. I've seen it with a lot of people I work with—the number of friends and family you can just be yourself around dwindles pretty fast."

"*Exactly*," Audrey said. "My dad never showed any signs of turning on me until a lot of money was dangled in front of him, and then suddenly, I'm his meal ticket. You ought to see the house I built for him—well, you will, because you can't miss it if you go to Redhill. But I told the builder, just build what he wants. Dad wanted this huge mansion in a town of three-bedroom, two-bath ranch houses. It's ridiculous." She looked off again, shaking her head. "I don't know who I can trust anymore."

He knew. And at least in one case, he suspected he knew better than Audrey. He debated telling her his suspicions about Lucas. "Are you sure you can trust everyone around you today?" he asked carefully.

To his great surprise, she laughed. "Hell no! Do you honestly think I don't know who would sell me out in a minute?"

Her answer surprised him—there was a glimmer of hope that maybe she did see through Lucas Bonner. "You do?" he asked.

"Of course!"

"But . . . but you seem so tight with him—and you let him tell you everything."

Audrey's brow sank into a deep frown. "Who tells me everything?"

Shit.

"Who are you talking about?" she demanded.

"Who are *you* talking about?"

"Courtney!"

"Ah," he said with a nod. "Good call."

"Are you talking about Lucas?" she asked, clearly miffed.

Jack groaned softly. Sometimes, when it came to women, he really had a knack for walking into a buzz saw. "I guess I am," he said wearily.

Her mouth dropped open. Then snapped shut. For a moment. "You really are something else," she said.

"You're not the first woman to have that opinion," he said with a snort of amusement. "But I don't respect a man who will use a woman to further his own ends."

"What is *that* supposed to mean?"

"Audrey," he said, looking at her, "don't you think it's just a little questionable that every time you end up in a tabloid or the paper or on the Internet that he is with you and, nine times out of ten, taking credit for something that is all you?"

"No, I don't think it's questionable. There are cameras stuck in my face everywhere I go, and Lucas and I are together a lot. Of course he shows up!"

"He shows up in the photos because he practically demands it," Jack said as all his common sense flew right out the window into the blackness around them. "He won't let you be your own person. He wants you to be *his* person. He wants to use your career as a stepping-stone to his own. Look at what he did at Katie's house. He didn't want you to go, but the moment he knew you had, he capitalized on it."

"That's ridiculous," Audrey said, but she looked uncertain. "He was promoting Songbird Foundation."

"Which just happened to coincide with the release of his CD."

"Dammit, Jack, you and I have . . . we've . . . well, we're *friends.* But that doesn't mean you suddenly know all about me and Lucas."

"I think you have a right to know that he is using you and that you can chart your own course without him."

"I *am* charting my own course."

"Oh really?" he asked. "So it was your idea to go pop and to do this nationwide tour?"

Audrey blinked.

"And your idea to hire security and choreographers and Courtney?"

"He is my manager, Jack. That is what managers do! They handle all the business stuff," she said, with a flutter of her fingers, "so that people like me can concentrate on the music. If I didn't concentrate on the music, there would be no business at all, would there?"

He'd obviously upset her, and he couldn't really say why he'd done it. What did it matter to him if she let Lucas Bonner walk all over her? "You're right," he said. "You're the music. You have a tremendous talent."

She folded her arms across her middle and looked out the window. After a moment, she asked softly, "Do you really think so?"

She looked suddenly and strangely vulnerable sitting there, a young woman uncertain of her talent. "Sweet cheeks," he said softly, "when you sing, I swear to God I see angels standing around you. I don't think there is another female artist on the charts today that has even half of your talent, and there is not another artist, male or female, whose music moves me the way your music moves me. That is the God's honest truth. Don't ever doubt your talent."

A grateful smile spread across her lips. "Thank you," she said, and put her hand on his forearm. "You have no idea what that means to me." Her smile broadened. "But you're wrong about Lucas."

"I'm not, either," he said.

"Yes, you *are*," she said cheerfully, and let go of his arm as she moved to get out of the chair. "I'm going to try and get some sleep now, okay?" With one last smile, she went out, leaving Jack to feel warm and sentimental and, God help him, incredibly horny.

Eighteen

They were in Dallas by three that morning, and thanks to Courtney's ability to pull a few strings, a Cadillac sports car was waiting for them. From there, without traffic, it was about an hour's drive to Redhill, which sat smack in the middle of absolutely nothing just southeast of Fort Worth.

Redhill, where Audrey had grown up with two parents who, having divorced ten years ago, still argued about everything. The town was nestled between a feed lot on one end and a tool and dye operation on the other end, and flanked by two opposing houses on hills that overlooked the towns. Audrey's father lived in one, her mother in the other.

Dad still owned the two-bay auto mechanic shop, but he rarely went in anymore. He preferred to hold court at the sprawling stucco and red-tiled mansion Audrey had built for him on the hill so that he could see over the town. He had insisted on being the general contractor for the job, and the result was a hodge-podge of design ideas that made the place look schizophrenic. There was a large lap pool in back that he had promptly turned into a pond, and a barn where he kept various cars in various stages of repair, and a stand of pecan trees that needed pruning. Dad wasn't much on upkeep—the house was surrounded by car and motorcycle parts, and the crowning glory, a guitar-playing frog that had once sat on top of his shop.

Across town, on the other hill, was Mom's house, an old Victorian that had stood on that hill since the town was founded. Always the martyr, Mom had insisted she did not want a new house when Audrey could afford to give her one. She swore she was fine in the family's three-bedroom, two-bath shotgun and she didn't need a big fancy house.

But then she saw Dad's.

Audrey bought the house Mom had coveted since they were kids. She tried to have it renovated, too, but Mom fought her every step of the way. Tile or wood floors, Mom? Neither—the old floors were fine. Pool or no pool, Mom? What a silly question. The result was a dated interior Mom insisted was too big and too hard to clean, and God forbid she should have anyone come clean it. When Allen was sober, he stayed there and kept up the lawn. When he was gone, two garden gnomes Mom had salvaged from the old house stood sentry in front of rosebushes that never bloomed.

As they drove toward Redhill, Audrey was sickened by the possibility of Jack meeting all of her family at once. Individually, they weren't so bad. Together, they were a redneck convention.

By the time they rolled into town, it was about four-thirty in the morning, and Redhill was absolutely dead. The two lights on the main street through town blinked yellow, and the only car they passed was a cop, who eyed them very suspiciously. A Cadillac in this town could only mean a couple of things: drugs or a funeral procession.

She directed Jack to the outskirts of town, where a hospital had been built in the eighties. Apparently, someone had believed there would be great growth in and around Redhill, because the hospital sat on a huge plot of land with plenty of room for expansion.

They parked in a vast and empty parking lot. Dread began to fill Audrey. There was never a pleasant homecoming, but this one really worried her. She'd tried several times yesterday to get hold of Mom. Before last night's show started, when everything was arranged, she had tried again to get Mom on the phone. There was no answer. And again after the show, but still there was no answer at the house. And of course Mom didn't have a cell phone.

"Why on earth would I want one of those?" she'd complained when Audrey tried to give her one.

"I don't know, Mom. So you can be in touch with the world?"

"Well, as you are the only one out in the *world*, Audrey, I don't think it's necessary. The rest of us here on Planet Earth seem to do just fine with the old-fashioned telephones."

God, if her mother could only see that, from the viewpoint of the rest of the world, Redhill was more like Mars.

Jack smiled reassuringly. "Chin up, sweet cheeks. Someone would have called if it was really bad."

How odd, Audrey thought, as they strode side by side toward the hospital entrance, that Jack could read her so well after such a short acquaintance.

When they walked through the hospital doors, they were assaulted by the smell of antiseptic. There wasn't a soul about but a chunky, fifty-ish woman behind the desk. She wore thick round glasses and a shampoo set that Audrey was fairly certain she'd received at Dot's Hair Shop.

As she approached the desk, the woman looked up and smiled warmly. "May I help you?"

Before Audrey could speak, another woman appeared from absolutely nowhere and shrieked, "*Oh my God. OH MY GOD!*" Jack instantly stepped in front of Audrey, as if he expected her to be attacked. But the woman—more of a girl, really—ran into the little half-moon area behind the reception desk and threw a stack of medical files on the counter. "You're *Audrey LaRue*!"

"For heaven's sake, Melissa!" the other woman exclaimed as she straightened her glasses, which somehow, Melissa had managed to knock askew in her eagerness to get in front of Audrey. Melissa ignored her—she was beaming at Audrey.

The other woman rolled to one side in her chair and heaved to her feet. "Can we help you, miss?" she asked again.

"Can I have your autograph?" Melissa squealed.

"Ah . . . yeah, sure," Audrey said, and looked around for a piece of paper. Melissa pushed a folder in front of her. "Are you sure you want to do that?" Audrey asked, pointing to Steve Helgenstien's medical file.

The older woman calmly removed the medical file and placed a notepad in front of Audrey. Audrey gave her a quick smile of gratitude and signed the notepad.

Melissa snatched it up and stared at it, wide-eyed. "Oh my GOD," she said again, and whirled around, picked up the phone, and punched the key pad.

"Now then. Can we help you?" the woman asked wearily.

"Yes," Audrey said, trying to ignore Melissa, who was now looking curiously at Jack. "I'm looking for my brother. I think he's a patient here."

"Where is Lucas Bonner?" Melissa asked.

"He's not here," Audrey answered quickly and looked at the other woman.

"A patient, you said?"

"Yes, ma'am. Allen LaRue."

"Allen LaRue. Let me just look in our records," she said and carefully took her rolling seat again, seemingly oblivious to Melissa's whispered phone conversation.

"*Hurry*," Melissa said frantically before clicking off. She immediately dialed another number.

"Oh, this thing is so slow," the woman said with a sheepish shake of her head at the computer. "Give me just a minute."

"Great," Jack muttered. Audrey glanced around. People dressed in colorful hospital scrubs had started to move into the lobby. In took only moments before they were arriving in twos and threes, all of them looking at her like she was an exotic animal in a zoo.

"Please hurry," Audrey said to the woman.

"Excuse me, is Audrey signing autographs?" some woman asked Jack.

"I, ah . . . we'll see," he said.

"And who might you be?" another woman asked him, smiling brightly.

"Jack," he said, and smiled right back.

Honestly, it never seemed to matter how often this happened, Audrey could never get used to it. The dozen pairs of eyes studying her sandals, her shorts, and the curls that had cost three hundred and fifty dollars to perfect made her feel terribly self-conscious. She could feel their scrutiny of the rings on her fingers, the dangling diamond earrings, and her Prada bag.

But what was even more remarkable was that while the horde was closing in around her—or rather, around Jack—the woman in front of her at the computer did not seem to notice them at all. Her face was screwed up in a frown of concentration as she peered at the computer screen.

"Allen LaRue, you said?" she asked again.

"Right." The reception area was quickly turning claustrophobic. "He came in yesterday." It suddenly occurred to her that they might have taken him to Dallas. If only she could have reached her mother on the phone! If they had taken him to Dallas, it could not be good. "Maybe he was transferred to Dallas?" she offered, dreading the answer.

"Hey, Audrey," someone behind her called out. "My brother went to high school with you. Greg Baker. Do you remember him?"

"Ah . . ." Audrey turned and smiled at what were now a dozen people. What did they all *do* here in the middle of the night? Patients could be having seizures while they stood up here gaping at her. "Sure," she said, looking down at the little munchkin of a woman. "He was in band, right?"

"No. Shop. He said you were in his history class."

"Oh," Audrey said, nodding thoughtfully. "Of course." She had no idea who Greg Baker was. "Oh yeah, I remember Greg. Tell him I said hi, will you?"

"Did you go to high school here?" the woman asked Jack.

He smiled that knee-bending smile of his and shook his head. "Midland."

"*Midland?*" another woman cried out. "I went to Midland! What year were you there?"

"Way too long ago to remember anymore," he said. "You would have been in grade school."

Several of the women tittered.

"Any luck?" Audrey asked the woman at the computer.

"No, hon, I can't seem to find him."

"That's because he was discharged today, Delores!" someone shouted from the back.

"Well, it doesn't say so here," Delores said, punching some more keys. "Are you sure?"

"Audrey, did you write that song 'Going Home' about Redhill?"

"Umm, I think that's a Kelly Clarkson song," Audrey said.

"Are you sure? I could have sworn you sang it."

"I'm . . . really sure," she said.

"If you're looking for your brother, they sent him home to your mom," the only male in the room, an orderly, said. "You need a ride over?"

"No, thanks," Jack interjected. "We've got it covered."

"Well, it doesn't say here that he was discharged," Delores said sternly. "All this technology they are making us use isn't worth a flip if it doesn't work right."

"Will you sign an autograph?" another woman asked.

"Where's Lucas?" someone shouted at her.

"Audrey, please don't leave until I get your autograph. My Allison would *kill* me if I saw you and didn't get your autograph," a nurse said, digging in her purse as another woman passed a prescription pad around.

"I can't even find a record that he was ever even here," Delores insisted.

"Delores, for God's sake, he went home!" Melissa snapped at her before turning another wide grin at Audrey. "I love your new album. You know, I've heard a lot about you around town, and I told my husband, I said, 'You know, that's just jealousy talking. I think she's probably real nice.' And look, you *are*!" she said, clasping her hands together gleefully. "You're just so nice and pretty and *I* think you're really talented."

"Thanks," Audrey said weakly and took the church bulletin someone thrust at her and signed the back of it.

"Is he your boyfriend?" Melissa asked, eyes narrowed.

"No," Jack said.

"You want to be mine?" a female doctor asked to the delight of the others.

A half hour later, they'd escaped, and Audrey pulled the Cadillac into the circular drive in front of her mom's house. She turned the car off and looked at Jack. "Sorry about the hospital. But I think it is only fair to warn you it was probably pretty tame compared to this leg of the journey," she said, pointing to her mom's house.

He smiled and touched her cheek. "It's okay. I knew you were popular before I flew you down here."

Audrey laughed.

He glanced at the house. "Now what?"

"Now? We go inside and wait for everyone to get up."

"Okay. Let's go," he said.

They approached the front door like they were approaching enemy lines. Audrey motioned for Jack to stop once they reached the porch, and then very carefully moved a small gnome from his guard post at the door and picked up the key upon which he'd sat. She replaced the gnome and let them into the house.

The front room, done up in lace curtains and blue carpet, smelled of Ben-gay, tomato sauce, and cigarettes. There was not a sound or light in the house, so Audrey put her bag down near the same blue plaid couch Mom had owned since the beginning of time—it reeked of cigarette smoke—and looked at Jack.

He glanced around the room, nodded to the blue La-Z-Boy recliner that was in front of the plasma TV. Audrey nodded; she sat down on the couch and watched as Jack moved to the recliner. Once he was settled, he looked at Audrey in the light of the gas lamp outside and winked.

"*Sorry*," she whispered. "It's the best I can do."

He grinned, folded his arms across his belly, and closed his eyes.

Audrey lay down on the couch, wrinkling her nose at the smell of smoke, and tried to sleep.

Nineteen

She must have slept, for she was rudely awakened by a shriek so loud and so piercing that she had to peel herself off the ceiling. It was her nephew, Logan, in his Bob the Builder pajama bottoms, screaming and pointing at her. "*Grandma! GRANDMA! Aunt Audrey is dead on the couch! And there is a MAN in here!*"

"I'm not dead, Logan!" Audrey said, trying to gather the kid in her arms. But Logan wriggled away and raced down the hall to the kitchen. "*Jesus,*" Audrey said, pressing a hand over her pounding heart, and looked at Jack.

Logan had awoken him, too. He was standing and looked as if he could have used a few more hours of sleep, but ran his hands through his hair just as Audrey's mother thundered into the living room.

"Hi, Mom," Audrey said. "Sorry—"

"What the hell, Audrey?" Mom exclaimed, clutching six-year-old Logan's hand and staring hard at Jack. "Can't you ring the doorbell like everyone else?"

"It was almost five in the morning when we got here. I didn't think you'd appreciate me waking you up at that hour."

"You could have called and let me know you were coming instead of giving me a heart attack," she said, eyeing Jack suspiciously as she clutched at the worn, thin cotton robe and put Logan in front of her. "I certainly would have liked to have known you were bringing a guest."

"I tried to call, I really did," Audrey said, fully aware that Mom wasn't really listening. "I tried a dozen times yesterday to tell you I was coming, but you never answered the phone."

"Well, how could I answer the phone?" Mom snapped, jerking her gaze to Audrey again. She put a hand to her short haircut, as if to smooth it. "I was at the hospital all day with your brother!"

"Right," Audrey said. "I'm sorry." She moved to put her arms around her mother, but could feel her stiffen and dropped her arms. "This is Jack Price. He's . . . he's—"

"I'm her bodyguard," Jack said, extending his hand. "A pleasure to meet you, Mrs. LaRue."

"A *bodyguard*!" Mom scoffed. "What do you need a bodyguard for?"

"It's a long story," Audrey said wearily. "We went by the hospital this morning when I got into town and they said Allen came home with you."

Mom softened a little and nodded. "He's upstairs sleeping it off like a drunk," she said with some disgust. "Maybe you can talk to him, Audie. I sure can't."

"I will," she said earnestly, and noticed that Jack was holding his bag. "There is a bathroom just up the hall there," she said, pointing toward the back end of the house. "Logan, will you show him the bathroom?"

"Okay," Logan said, his terror apparently forgotten.

When Jack and Logan had left the room, Audrey smiled at her mother. "Are you okay, Mom?"

"Why wouldn't I be?"

"This business with Allen surely has been hard on you."

Mom pursed her thin lips as if she had to think about it and shrugged. "You do what you got to do. I'll put some coffee on."

"Can I use a bathroom upstairs?" Audrey asked, picking up her bag.

"You can use whatever you want, Audrey. This is your house."

Oh dear God, how many times would they have this conversation? "No, Mom, it's yours. You know that."

But Mom had already headed back to the linoleum cave of a kitchen.

That was it, all Audrey was going to get at this stage of the game. No *how are you*, or *thanks for coming*. Nothing but a wave of resentment that would build until Audrey couldn't stand it another moment. And with only a couple of hours' sleep, Audrey was hardly in the mood for it. She headed for the bathroom upstairs.

Once inside, she locked herself in and looked around. White tile floors, pink tub and toilet, and for some strange reason, a yellow sink. She had tried very hard to get her mother to accept the help of a design team, but her mother wouldn't have it. "I always liked this house the way it was. I don't need to do all that California-type stuff to it. And I don't need any advice," she'd said, clearly insulted by the offer.

Lucas's theory was that Mom was jealous of Audrey's success. But Audrey wondered what sort of mother was jealous of her daughter's success? Audrey knew it was more than that—Mom had seemed to dislike her way back before she even knew she could sing. In fact, Mom was the primary reason Audrey had left Redhill at the age of seventeen. It wasn't her parents' constant fighting, or the dead-end town, or the desire to sing. It was her mother.

Oh yeah, she'd wanted to pursue a singing career more than she wanted to breathe, but the truth was that singing was the only escape from Mom and Redhill that she could think of. What irritated her was that she had made her escape, and yet she *still* sought Mom's approval. In eleven years, nothing had changed.

Except that she had become famous. Unbelievably famous. Honestly, who would have thought one song, "Breakdown," would get the airtime it did, then spread by word of mouth, and then, by some freaking miracle, ride up the charts and stay there for weeks? Who could have predicted that her first album would go platinum? It was luck. A little talent, okay, but a lot of luck and being in the right place at the right time.

Of course, Lucas thought it was clever planning on his part—after all, he did get the radio stations in Austin to play the tune. But the rest of it? Even he couldn't claim credit for her rocket-rise to the top of the charts.

Funny, but Mom's dislike of Audrey had grown in direct proportion to the rise in her fame. Now the chasm seemed so impossibly deep and wide, she couldn't imagine a way to cross it. She'd been in her mother's house a total of three hours, and already she felt like shit.

Audrey washed her face, brushed her teeth, and brushed her hair, which, she couldn't help notice, reverted to its usual frizz without the constant attention of high-paid stylists.

A pounding at the door shook her out of her thoughts. "What?" she shouted, unconsciously reverting to her sixteen-year-old self.

"Give someone else a chance!" Allen shouted from the other side of the door.

With a gasp, Audrey vaulted over her bag, yanked the door open, and threw her arms around her baby brother.

"Hey, Audrey," he said, and lifted her up, twirled her around, and set her down again, letting her go with a pat on the back as he stepped around her into the bathroom. "You didn't need to come all the way out here."

"Of course I did—you scared us all to death, Allen! What were you doing in the hospital?"

"Nothing," he said with a shrug as he leaned up to the mirror above the sink and examined his beard.

"You don't go to the hospital for *nothing*," she said with a punch to his shoulder. What happened? Mom said she didn't know if you'd make it, and—"

"God, she's such a drama queen," Allen said with a roll of his blue eyes. In junior high, Audrey's best friend, Mary Alice Turner, used to drool over Allen's beautiful blue eyes. "It wasn't that big of a deal."

"It *was* a big deal, Allen," Audrey insisted, folding her arms implacably. "So what happened?"

He tried to look away, but Audrey caught his face with her hand and forced him to look at her.

"Come on, Audie. I have to pee."

"*What happened?*"

"I just overdid it, that's all." He tried to smile. "I smoked a little weed, and then I took a couple of pills, and the combo didn't work out."

"I thought you were sober," she said, dropping her hand.

"I *am*," he said sternly. "I mean, I *was*. But Gary Torrence came into town—remember Gary?"

Like she could ever forget Gary. He'd been the first guy to feel her up, and without invitation, too—right under the bleachers her sophomore year. "Please tell me you aren't still hanging out with him."

"Come on, he's a friend," Allen said. "Not all of us can hang out with big stars, right? Anyway, I was just partying with him—it's not like I *hang out* with him. Don't look at me like that, Audie! I swear I'm sober. It was just the one time."

"Famous last words," Audrey scoffed, and pushed him out of the way so she could dab a little concealer under her eye. "If I had a dime for every time I heard you say that—"

"Whatever."

"If you don't stay clean, you'll go to prison. It's that simple, bucko. You *have* to stay clean."

Allen laughed. "What's the matter? Afraid the press will get hold of it if I do? Poor Audrey LaRue," he said, mimicking an old lady, "saddled with a deadbeat brother."

"That's not it and you know it. I couldn't care less what the media says," Audrey said, ignoring the tiny voice in her that said she did care what the media would say. "I just don't want to lose you."

Allen laughed, put his hands on her shoulders, and playfully pushed her to the door. "I'm not going anywhere. The prisons are full of violent offenders and there are plenty waiting in the wings, so they aren't going to take up space with my ass. And besides, I'm not using again. So can I pee now?" he asked as he pushed across the threshold. With a wink, he shut the bathroom door in her face.

"I'm not leaving until we talk, Allen!" Audrey shouted through the door, but as she might have guessed, she got no response. She stared at the door another moment, but finally gave up—he wasn't coming out until she was gone, just like they were ten and twelve all over again. With a sigh of frustration, she headed for the kitchen and a cup of coffee.

Jack had been in a lot of uncomfortable situations in his thirty-seven years—some of them including assault rifles, some of them while he was hanging off rock faces he hadn't intended to be hanging from at all, some of them on good dates gone very, very bad.

But this had to be the most uncomfortable he'd ever been in his *life*.

He wouldn't be surprised if Mrs. LaRue wasn't cooking up arsenic in that coffeepot. She was mean and bitter and it showed in every craggy line on her face. On top of that, staring at him like they'd never seen a grown man before were Logan and his brother Dustin—two years older and sleepy-eyed.

Jack was never so happy to see anyone in his life when Audrey walked into the kitchen. "I'm back," she said sheepishly. The hint of dark circles shadowed her eyes; she looked tired and worn. But she smiled brightly at her nephews. "Hey, you guys," she said, opening her arms and hugging them both tightly to her. "I bet I have something in my bag for you."

"What?" Logan asked.

"Go get it for me and I'll show you. It's upstairs."

"You don't need to bring them junk, Audrey," her mother said as the boys ran to find her bag. "It just gives 'em the wants," Mrs. LaRue said.

"Oh," Audrey said, and glanced nervously at Jack. "It's no big thing."

"Not to *you*," Mrs. LaRue said, as if that should mean something. She shuffled to the stove in her Dearfoam slippers and fit strips of bacon into a frying pan. She hardly spared Audrey a glance as she nodded to the coffeepot. "I made some coffee. I assume you still drink coffee, or do you drink some of them healthy drinks they have in California?"

"Coffee is great," Audrey said, and took a cup touting a local insurance firm from the hodgepodge of coffee mugs on a little tree near the pot. She glanced at Jack. "Coffee?"

"Please."

She poured another cup and joined him at the kitchen table while Mrs. LaRue dug inside the fridge. When she emerged with a loaf of bread, she asked, "So why is it you need your own personal bodyguard?"

"Oh, no reason, really," Audrey said, flicking her wrist dismissively. "Lucas thought it would be a good idea just because."

"Because what?"

"Because . . . there have been a couple of stupid freaky letters," Audrey said, clearly trying to downplay the threat.

"What kind of letters?" her mother pressed.

"Well . . . the threatening kind," Audrey said. She forced a laugh. "Seems like there is some whack job out there who doesn't like my singing."

Mrs. LaRue frowned over her shoulder at Audrey. "I don't like the sound of that."

"I am well protected, Mom. See?" she asked, pointing at Jack.

"Maybe if you didn't wear those trashy costumes on stage, you might not get mail like that," Mrs. LaRue said matter-of-factly as she turned the bacon.

Audrey's smile disappeared. "What?" she asked, as if she hadn't heard her mother correctly.

"I said, put some clothes on, and maybe you won't get such hateful letters."

Hurt swelled in Audrey's features; she shifted her gaze to the table cloth. "I think there's a little more to it than what I *wear*."

"Then try something less revealing," Mrs. LaRue said. "It won't hurt to try and it won't affect your music any. Who knows, maybe your old mother is right."

Jack did not get Mrs. LaRue's problem. He really couldn't fathom it. Three hundred miles west of here, in Midland, was a woman who would be busting with pride if her son had made a big star of himself and would be overjoyed if he popped in on her. She would welcome Audrey with open arms even if she were a stranger.

This woman was working extra hard to make sure her daughter never came back again.

"I think she looks fantastic on stage," he said, and felt his heart nudge him when he saw the gratitude in Audrey's eyes. He sipped his coffee, shifted a cool gaze to Mrs. LaRue. "She's beautiful."

"I'm sure you think so, Mr. Price," Mrs. LaRue said with a wry smile. "She's paying you to think so, isn't she?"

"No, ma'am. She's paying me to keep her safe."

If Mrs. LaRue had a retort, it was lost when the two boys had skidded into the kitchen again, carrying Audrey's bag. "Here's your purse," Logan said, dropping it on Audrey's lap.

"What took you so long?" she asked with a wink as she thrust her hand into her bag.

"We were looking at the cars."

"What cars?"

"The cars outside," Dustin said. "There are a *lot* of cars out there."

Audrey instantly looked at Jack.

"I'll check it out," he said, and as Audrey told the boys to close their eyes for their big surprise, he got up and walked into the front room. Through the windows, he spied one TV van and two cars. Radio and print by the look of it, judging by the equipment and the people milling about her mom's lawn.

Probably someone at the hospital had clued them in. In a matter of hours, the entertainment world and all of its followers would know that Audrey's brother had fallen off the wagon, and really, Audrey didn't need this sort of publicity right now. He pulled out his cell, put in a call to Mitzi to warn her and to see if she could begin the damage control.

"Damn media," Mitzi said. "Always looking for dirt. I've got it, lover. You just make sure Audrey gets to Nashville in one piece."

When Jack returned to the kitchen a few minutes later, Audrey gave him a questioning look over the heads of her nephews, who were now playing with two identical iPod Shuffles. He shook his head, and Audrey relaxed, resumed showing the boys how to work them. The Shuffles, as it turned out, were loaded with her songs. "Now you can listen to me anytime you want," she said.

"Yeah!" said Logan in a very loud voice, unaware of how loud he was with his earbuds and music playing.

"They can't play with those now," Mrs. LaRue said, one hand on the small of her back as she pushed bacon around in the pan. "They need to get a bath and get ready for Bible School."

"I don't want to go today," Logan shouted, until Dustin pulled his earbuds from his ears and said *Sssh.* "I want to stay with Aunt Audrey," Logan added.

"You're going to Bible School, and I don't want any argument from either of you. I got enough to do around here without having to watch you during the day. Right now I want you to go pick up your rooms."

"I could watch them, Mom," Audrey offered.

"*Yeeees*!" the boys cried in unison. "Please, Grandma?"

Mrs. LaRue looked at Audrey with surprise. "You're going to be here that long?"

Once again, Jack could see the pain of her mother's words slicing across Audrey's features.

"I thought I'd stick around and make sure everything is okay," she said uncertainly.

"I think they'd be better off in Bible School," Mrs. LaRue said with a snort of disdain, and turned back to her bacon. "Go pick up your rooms!"

With a lot of grumbling, the boys went, their Shuffles in hand.

"So where's Gail?" Audrey asked tightly, and to Jack, she said, "Gail is my sister."

"You can ask her yourself," Mom said. "She just drove up."

As if on cue, Gail suddenly sailed through the back door. Like Audrey, she was somewhat tall, but unlike Audrey, she was also a little chunky. She had honey blond hair and was attractive, but a little weathered. She was wearing a short denim skirt and a low halter top. Her large breasts had no visible means of support that Jack could see, and hung down her chest. She was carrying a pair of espadrilles, her hair was a mess, and her mascara was smudged under her eyes.

She took one look at Audrey and her mouth curved into a warm smile. "*Audrey*!" she cried, dropping her shoes and hurtling toward her sister. "I knew you were here when I saw the cars outside!" she exclaimed as she grabbed Audrey in a bear hug. After a moment of squeezing the life out of her, Gail stepped back and examined Audrey from top to bottom. "You look fabulous! What are you doing here?" she cried, and caught sight of Jack. "Oh *hell*," she said, grinning like a Cheshire cat. "Where did *he* come from?"

Before Audrey could answer, Gail gave her a stern look. "You didn't break up with Lucas, did you?"

"Oh for God's sake, Gail," Mom muttered.

"*No*," Audrey said, shaking her head. "No, Lucas and I are still together."

Jack's insides clenched.

"Did you color your hair?" Gail asked excitedly.

"Highlights."

"Girl, it looks *good*. Maybe I oughta do that color." She abruptly let go and moved to the coffeepot. "Pardon me while I get some coffee—I really need it. I'm getting too old to stay out this late!" She laughed as she helped herself to a cup. "*Dustin! Logan*!" she shouted, her voice bouncing off the yellowed kitchen walls as she poured. "I'm home!"

Logan was the first to arrive, launching himself at his mother's legs. Dustin sauntered in a moment later, looking very sulky as he leaned against the door jamb.

Gail lifted Logan's face and covered it with kisses. "Go put some clothes on," she said.

"Take a bath!" Mrs. LaRue demanded.

"Take a bath," Gail cheerfully corrected herself. She shifted her attention to Dustin. "Don't look at me in that tone," she said playfully. "C'mere, baby."

Dustin reluctantly came forward. Gail messed with his hair, then hugged him tightly. Dustin never took his hands from his pockets. "See, baby? I'm home before you go to Bible School, just like I said I'd be. Now you go get cleaned up and dressed and I'll take you."

As Dustin slunk out, Gail turned the full force of her attention to Jack. She slurped her coffee as she sidled across the room and plopped down next to him.

"You are *cute*," Gail said. "Who are you?"

"Audrey's bodyguard," Mrs. LaRue said snidely.

"No, he's really . . . he's my friend," Audrey said.

"Some friend," Gail snorted. "What's your name, Cutie?"

"Jack Price. And yours?"

"I'm Gail Reynolds, about to be LaRue again in a couple of weeks. Audrey's big sis," she said, and made a show of leaning over Jack to look at his ring finger. "Oh goody." She winked at him, then shifted her gaze to Audrey. "Looks like you gained a little weight," she remarked. "Did you see *Us Weekly*? They gave you the prize for being the curviest."

"They what?" Audrey exclaimed. "What does that mean, that I'm fat?"

Gail shrugged. "Maybe it just means you're curvy."

"*Fat*," Audrey muttered, frowning down at herself.

At that moment, a man appeared in the doorway, looking even more disheveled than Gail. "Maybe it's not fat. Maybe it's the baby bump we've been reading about," he drawled.

"Come on, you guys," Audrey said, clearly uncomfortable. "How many times have I told you that you can't believe any of that stuff? I'm not pregnant."

"Uh-huh," Gail said, her eyes twinkling. "You and Lucas have been together for what, nine years? It's about time."

"Not if they aren't married, it's not," Mom barked.

Gail rolled her eyes at Mom's back and then turned to Jack again. "So what brings you to the middle of hell?"

"Can I have his attention long enough to introduce Allen?" Audrey asked, pushing Gail back with her arm. "Jack, this is my brother, Allen."

"Hey," Allen said, extending his hand to shake Jack's.

"Okay, that's Allen. You didn't say what you were doing here," Gail said again.

"Audrey came for me," Allen said with a sigh as he shuffled to the coffeepot. "I *told* you not to call her, Mom."

"Why shouldn't I call her?" Mom asked irritably. "Why should I have to deal with your crap by myself?"

"Well, what am I? Chopped liver?" Gail cried, and then winked at Jack as if she was playing some sort of game.

"You ain't even got a job, Gail. How are you going to pay for his foolishness?" Mom asked, pointing a fork dripping with fat at Allen.

"Maybe he could come to California for a while," Audrey suggested hopefully and looked at Allen. "You could hang out at the house and get it together while I'm on tour."

Allen shook his head. "Can't. My probation officer won't let me. And besides, I got to get a job here. I think I can get on at the tool and dye."

"That's your answer to everything, isn't it, Audrey?" Mrs. LaRue said coldly. "You just tell everyone to leave here. Well, I got news for you—your family is here. You can't just leave and act like they don't exist."

"Oh Mom," Gail said wearily.

"I don't act like that," Audrey said, her eyes wide with hurt. It almost seemed as if she were getting smaller and smaller and her family bigger and bigger. "I came as soon as I could. I was in the middle of a tour, but I left that to come home and be with my family, when apparently, I didn't even need to."

"You didn't need to come?" Mrs. LaRue said angrily. "Then who do you think is going to pay for his trouble? I sure can't."

Jack almost gasped with outrage for Audrey.

"I . . . I can't believe that is why you asked me to come home," Audrey said, her voice gone soft.

"I *can't* pay for it," Mrs. LaRue said, getting defensive. "And Allen sure can't, and neither can his worthless father. Oh sure, he can live in that big fancy house you built for him, but he wouldn't give a dime to us if he had a pocketful. Anyway, I read in *Parade Magazine* that you made six million dollars last year, so I don't think you'll miss it."

"You can have whatever you need. But I thought—"

"I know exactly what you thought," Mrs. LaRue interrupted her as she forked bacon onto a paper towel. "You thought you were going to swoop in and save Allen when you haven't even seen him for almost a year." She frowned with disdain and shook her head. "I don't know when you got the idea in your head that being a big shot music star suddenly makes you God's gift."

"Mom, lay off," Allen said.

"You want me to lay off? Then how about you lay off drugs for a change?"

"This is so embarrassing!" Gail cried. "We have this fine-looking man in our midst and we're going to fight?"

Audrey suddenly stood up. "You're right, Gail. There is no point. So how much?" she asked.

Every last one of them avoided her direct look.

"Come on, how much?" she asked again.

Allen shrugged. "Amber, the nurse down there, told me the hospital alone would probably want four grand. Can you believe that? I was only there a day, and they're gonna want that kind of money. It's highway robbery. They're just sticking it to regular people."

"It wasn't like they did anything but pump your stomach," Gail said. "It's almost like stealing."

Audrey closed her eyes. "Four thousand, then?" she asked.

"Ten thousand," Mom said calmly.

Gail gasped, and Allen paled and glared at his mother. But Audrey didn't flinch. She just nodded and put down her coffee cup. "I'll have it wired in today. If you will excuse me now, I am going to go throw up," Audrey said, and walked out of the kitchen.

"Wait, Audie!" Gail cried, and jumped up to run after her sister.

That left Jack, Allen, and Mrs. LaRue and the most uncomfortable silence Jack had ever experienced. Allen eyed him curiously as Mrs. LaRue slapped a platter of bacon on the table. "Help yourself," she said, and stalked back to the stove.

Allen grabbed three pieces and shoved them into his mouth.

Jack would not have guessed, not in a million years, that this was the crap Audrey had to put up with from her own family. He had a newfound admiration for her. It took a very strong and determined person to pull herself out of this shit hole and make something of herself. These people were unbelievably miserable.

Jack was a betting man, and at that moment, he was betting he and Audrey would be heading back to the airport just as soon as he could get their stuff together. And if she wasn't of a mind to go just yet, he was contemplating picking her up bodily and carrying her away from these bloodsuckers.

Twenty

So anyway, I told Danny's lawyer he could stick it, and if Danny wants to see his boys again, he'll just drop that whole thing." Gail paused to exhale the smoke from her cigarette. "Can you believe his shit?"

"No," Audrey said, staring into the little stream that ran behind her mother's house. The previous owners had made a little oasis out of the lawn and the stream, but since she'd bought the house for Mom, no one had weeded down here. The Johnson grass was as high as the fishing platform where she and Gail were sitting.

"I don't think it ever crosses his mind that all this fighting isn't good for our kids," Gail said, as if she were completely innocent. From what Audrey knew of it, she started the fighting more often than not. She couldn't guess how many times Gail had called to complain she didn't like who Danny was dating and refused to let her sons around the skank, as she put it.

But this morning, Audrey was content to let Gail talk, because her mind was a million miles away. She couldn't manage to accept that she'd been called home under the pretense of life or death to hand over ten thousand dollars for Allen's emergency room visit that was not, by any measure, an actual emergency.

That was beside the point, really—she would have handed over one hundred thousand if that was what they needed from her. What she couldn't accept was that they didn't seem to need *her*. In *any* capacity. She was nothing but a checkbook to them. Somewhere along the way she had ceased to be a sister or a daughter.

Audrey swallowed down tears of helplessness as she watched the minnows swim about and Gail went on about Danny. She didn't want to admit it to herself, but wherever she went these days, she felt like she didn't belong. She'd never felt as alone as she had the last couple of months, which was ironic, seeing as how she was *never* alone. But she felt lonely at her core, almost as if somewhere along the way she'd lost Audrey.

She didn't know what was important to her any longer, didn't know what she wanted or what made her happy.

The only ray of warmth she'd felt in the last few weeks was Jack. Just like the warmth that spread through her the moment she saw him walking down to the creek. He stood below the platform, his hands on his hips, and smiled up at her. "Ever catch anything from up there?"

"Snakes," Gail said. "Come on up here, sugar, and we'll keep you safe."

Jack chuckled, the sound of it so soft and familiar that Audrey wanted to fling herself into his arms, bury her face in his shoulder, and let him cover up the world from her sight.

She did the next best thing—she swung her legs off the side of the platform and jumped down.

"Hey, where are you going?" Gail asked as Audrey stepped in front of Jack and looked up at Gail. She felt his hand on her arm, and allowed herself to sink back against him, allowed herself to feed off his strength. "Don't know," she said. "Maybe to see Dad."

"Oh God," Gail said with an exaggerated roll of her eyes. "Remember Hayley Grant?"

"Sure. Blond and pretty, and everything I wasn't."

"Well, Dad's dating her now."

Jack's hand tightened around her arm, but he didn't move, just stood behind her, propping her up as Audrey tried to process the information. "Hayley Grant is a year younger than *me*," she said incredulously.

"That's why I am warning you," Gail said cheerfully. "Tell Mom I'll drive the boys to Bible School, okay?" she said as she lit another cigarette. "And if you see Allen, tell him to quit stealing my smokes! Man, I'll be glad when he moves out!"

Audrey relayed Gail's information to Mom, who was busy cleaning the kitchen and could only grunt something under her breath in reply. She didn't see Allen, either. When she asked, Mom told her he'd walked to town.

So a half hour later, after walking through what constituted a media gauntlet in Redhill (a Fort Worth TV crew, the local biweekly paper, and radio), and answering a handful of benign questions (*My brother is fine. The tour is going well.*), Audrey and Jack were standing in front of the godawful, million-dollar house Dad had built. They were staring at half of a car that was, inexplicably, on the front lawn.

"Looks like it might have been a Roadster," Jack said, eyeing it thoughtfully.

"It is half of a car," Audrey protested.

"But it's the good half," Jack said. "And he's still got the motor."

"What good is a motor without the car?" Audrey asked.

"There's my girl!" Dad's voice boomed at them from the front door.

He strode out onto the lawn, Hayley Grant on his heels. Unlike Mom, who seemed to shrivel up as she got older, Dad looked healthy and fit and even younger than his fifty-five years. He was handsome and he knew it—he'd had more affairs than Audrey believed even he could count. He grabbed Audrey up in a bear hug and squeezed her tight, jerking her back and forth like a dog with a chew toy before setting her on her feet. "I heard you were in town."

"Gail?"

"Nope. Hayley's mom works at the hospital. Oh hey, you remember Hayley, don't you?" he asked, stepping back and grabbing Hayley's hand.

Audrey forced a smile. "Of course." She stuck out her hand. "Hi, Hayley. You look *great*."

"Thanks!" Hayley chirped as she grabbed Audrey's hand and pumped it several times.

With a beaming grin on his face, Dad turned to Jack. "And who is this?" he asked.

Audrey quickly introduced him as her friend.

"Oh yeah?" Dad said. "What happened to Luke the Kook?"

"He stayed with the tour."

"Not surprised," Dad said, hitching up his pants. "That boy never missed a moment in the limelight, did he?"

Jack snorted.

"Speaking of limelight, Dad," Audrey said sternly, "could you please stop talking to *Entertainment Tonight*? That story about me singing a Pasty Cline number in a bar when I was six is a lie, and you know it."

"Oh hell, they love that sort of feel-good stuff," he said congenially. "Now if I could remember what you were *really* doing at six, I'd tell them that. But I don't remember," he said, and laughed loudly, clapping Jack on the back. "How about a beer, there, big guy?"

"Ah, no thanks. I'm working."

"Working! Boy, this isn't work!" Dad laughed. "Come on in and at least drink some lemonade. Hayley was hoping you'd come by, Audrey, so she whipped up a can of it."

"Y'all come in!" Hayley echoed.

Apparently this little fling between Dad and Hayley had been going on long enough for Hayley to set up house. Audrey reluctantly followed Hayley inside, but not before shooting Jack a pleading look.

Hayley led them all into a sunken living room. The floors were Saltillo tile and the furniture right out of Discount Barn. Plastic greenery adorned the valances of every window, as well as the corners and the shelving around a massive plasma TV. Above the fireplace hung the head of a stag, and at the other end, Dad had put up mirrors behind a built-in bar. The room looked like someone had smashed a Wal-Mart and a pub together.

"I have asked Gene a hundred times if I have asked him once to get rid of that car on the lawn," Hayley said as she swished to the bar in her kitten heel sandals. "But he won't hear of it! He keeps telling me he's going to get the other half and fix it up."

"Why don't you put it in the barn?" Audrey asked.

"Can't," Dad said, accepting a beer from Hayley. "Barn's full."

"What about the shop?" Audrey asked.

"Oh," Dad said, flicking his wrist. "I sold that a couple of months ago."

He'd *sold* the shop? The same auto shop that had been in the LaRue family since 1931?

"Can I get you some lemonade, Jack?" Hayley asked, a little too sweetly.

"No thanks," Jack said. He stayed back, leaning up against one of the posts that marked the entrance to the sunken living room, just watching.

"You sold the shop?" Audrey asked incredulously as she sank onto a bar stool. *"Why?"*

"I don't need that shop. It's more of a headache than anything else. Besides, I'm getting into NASCAR."

"How are you going to live?" Audrey asked.

"Whaddaya mean?" Dad asked with a frown. "We do fairly well on our joint ventures, don't we?" he asked, gesturing between himself and Audrey.

Unlike Mom, Dad had no problem accepting her charity—he accepted it with gusto. Their "joint ventures," as he liked to call it, was really a stipend she paid him every month. She'd originally offered to do it a couple of years ago when the economy wasn't doing so well and he was having trouble making ends meet. Somehow, the stipend had stayed in place.

"So what brings you to Redhill, Audrey?" Hayley asked as she poured lemonade for her. "You sure don't get down this way very often, do you?"

"Because it's almost impossible to get to within any reasonable amount of time," Audrey said. "And I've just been really busy."

"Oh I bet you have," Hayley said, nodding eagerly. She leaned across the bar and smiled brightly at Audrey. "We're so proud of you in Redhill. So what's it really like, being a big star?"

"Don't bother her with that, Hayley," Dad said sternly. "She comes home to get away from all that, don't you, girl?"

"Well, actually, this time I came home to see about Allen."

"Allen?" Dad said, still smiling. "Oh, you mean that bit of trouble he had a couple of days ago?"

"A bit of trouble? I thought it was more a matter of life or death."

Dad laughed loudly at that. "That's Leanne for you," he said, referring to Audrey's mother. "She can make a mountain out of a molehill like no one I've ever seen. You should have called me, Pumpkin. I'd have saved you a trip."

"Come on, aren't you a little worried about him?"

"Who, Allen?" Dad shrugged. "Way I see it, there's not a lot any of us can do. The boy is twenty-six years old. If he wants to throw his life away like that, who of us is going to stop him?"

"You know, I always thought he had those tendencies growing up," Hayley opined. At Audrey's questioning look, she said, "You know . . . drugs and that sort of thing."

She spoke as if she had any knowledge of Allen at all. When they'd been in high school, Hayley had been a cheerleader and very popular. Allen had been overwhelmingly shy and had hung on the fringes of his class beneath a crop of long sandy brown hair and baggy clothes. Hayley had no idea who Allen was, and the fact that she was trying to pretend she did made Audrey want to reach across the bar and strangle her. But instead, she said, as politely as she could, "I don't think he developed those tendencies until later in life. But he needs our help now."

"He'll work it out," Dad said jovially. "So how are you, kid? Have you had a chance to think any more about that race car?"

"*Dad*," Audrey said wearily.

"I'm just asking you to help out, Audie," he said. "I'm lining up sponsors as we speak." He swiveled around on his bar stool to Jack. "Did Audrey tell you about my plans?" he asked eagerly, and when Jack politely shook his head, Dad launched into a tale of how he was going to be the next great thing in NASCAR.

It was all Greek to Audrey. As he talked, she got up and walked to the big picture windows. Just outside was the pool, and beyond that, a long stretch of field that had been burned a crispy brown by the early August sun. Next to the picture windows was a bookcase on which several framed pictures had been artfully arranged. As Audrey perused them, she noticed they were all of Dad and Hayley in various locations. There was a picture of Dad and Gail and Dustin and Logan, and one of Allen and Dad holding up a huge fish somewhere.

There wasn't a single picture of Audrey. Her CD was sitting on the shelf below the pictures, but there wasn't a picture. She felt like an outsider looking in. Maybe she was an outsider. She'd left so long ago, it was hard even to remember what it was once like being here.

An hour or so later, when Jack was looking a little glazed in the eyes, Hayley announced she hated to run out, but she had to get to her aerobics class. Audrey took the opportunity to bow out, too, saying she had to get back to Mom's.

Just as Hayley was leaving, Jack's cell rang, and he stepped aside to answer it.

Audrey and Dad watched Haley drive away. "She's great, isn't she?" Dad asked.

"Yes . . . but she's younger than me, Dad."

"So? Age is just a number, Audrey Jane."

She nodded. "I guess it is, because you and Mom are the same age, only she seems so much older."

"Well," he said, hitching up his pants with a grin, "I work at it."

Audrey smiled and hugged her father. "I have to go back, Dad. I need to see what I can do to help Allen."

"Help him what?" Dad asked.

"Help him *what*?" she exclaimed. "He is on a path to prison! I swear it seems like no one cares about that but me!"

"Now watch it, Pumpkin," Dad said. "Don't come home and act all high and mighty with me. You don't have any idea how much help I have given Allen. You have no idea what it's like watching your only son slip away like I have. But there is nothing you or I can do about it. Until Allen wants to make some changes, all the treatment centers in the world ain't going to help him. You just haven't gotten to the point of understanding that like the rest of us. It is what it is."

Audrey's shoulders sagged. "You really believe that?"

Dad put his arm around her shoulders and squeezed. "Hell, I don't believe it, I *know* it. You're feeling guilty because you live in another world, but I'm telling you, don't. There ain't nothing harder to change than a drug addict and tiger's stripes. You can throw all the money at him you got, and it won't change a bloomin' thing."

Perhaps . . . but Audrey wasn't sure she was willing to throw in the towel just yet. "It just seems like there ought to be something I can do," she insisted weakly.

"Have you asked your mother?" Dad asked.

Audrey groaned and shook her head. "She can hardly even look at me, Dad. I don't know why she despises me so."

"She doesn't despise you, Audrey. She loves you. You just got to learn to look at this from Leanne's shoes. She always wanted to get out of Redhill."

"I've tried to look at it from her viewpoint," Audrey said.

"Well, try a little harder. So what do you think about that car?" he asked cheerfully as Jack strode into their midst.

"I don't have that kind of money."

"Sure you do. Jack tells me you are playing to sold-out audiences and that your talent is out of this world."

Audrey shifted her gaze to Jack and smiled. "He said that?"

"He damn sure did," Dad said with a big smile. "So if you got all those sold-out audiences, then surely you have a little extra dough for your old man, right?"

"It doesn't work that way," Audrey said. "I'll be lucky if I break even on this tour."

"Ah, come on, now," Dad said, his smile fading. "You've got money. I *know* you've got money to help out your old dad."

"I hate to interrupt," Jack said, putting his hand out to Audrey. "But if we don't get going, we'll never make that flight, and you have to be in Nashville today."

They had no flight to make, they had their own plane, and she didn't have to be in Nashville until tomorrow. Jack was trying to help her out.

Audrey put her hand in his. "You're right. If we don't go now, we won't make it."

"I don't give a shit about your flight. What about my car?" Dad demanded, his temper flaring into the danger zone.

"I'll have my business manager call you, Dad!" Audrey said, and gave him a quick peck on the cheek before allowing Jack to pull her away to the Cadillac.

Dad was still talking as she got in, his face getting red as he went on about something to do with his car.

"Remind me to have Rich call him," Audrey said as they backed out of the drive.

"Remind me to cross Redhill off my list of vacation destinations," Jack said dryly, and hit the gas, barreling down the road back into Redhill. Just before they reached the edge of town, however, he turned left instead of right and headed for the town's cemetery. He drove inside, parked under a huge pecan tree, and cut the engine.

"What are you doing?"

"What are *you* doing?" he asked, turning to look at her. "You don't need to be here."

"No kidding," she muttered, and slumped in her seat. "I told you my family is a piece of work."

"Audrey," Jack said, "I don't mind telling you that I have never in my life been closer to a Jerry Springer show waiting to happen than I have been in the last eight hours. These people don't need you, they want to use you."

The moment the words were out of his mouth, she began to tear up. It was maddening to be on the brink of tears so damn often! She squeezed her eyes shut, but two tears slipped out nonetheless and she swiped helplessly at them. "Ohmigod, I am so embarrassed," she said.

"Don't be. You can't help it." He put his hand on her knee and squeezed it. "But I don't think you are doing yourself any favors here, sweet cheeks. You're only adding to your stress. Over the last few hours I have seen you start to shrivel up like a withering vine."

"Really?" she asked sorrowfully, knowing full well it was true. She could *feel* herself withering.

"Really," he said. "I've got an idea. The plane won't be serviced for another couple of hours. You don't need to be in Nashville until tomorrow. I know a place where you can go to really get away from it all for a few hours."

“Ha,” she said, swiping at more tears. “I’ll give you a million dollars if you can find a place like that.”

“As tempting as that is, I’ll settle for just seeing you happy,” he said, and started the Cadillac again. “Let’s go say good-bye to your mom and Allen and Gail and get the hell out of here.”

Audrey had to admit—the prospect of getting the hell out of here sounded divine.

Twenty-one

Mrs. LaRue did not try and persuade Audrey to stay. She stood in the kitchen, methodically wiping her hands on her apron and nodding as Audrey explained she had to get back to work. When Audrey had completed her apology—in which she seemed to be pretty hard on herself, considering how they had treated her—Mrs. LaRue shrugged.

"I'm sorry you have to rush back." And then she walked to the stove and put a pot on a burner, as if she was going to make something.

Audrey seemed to shrink a little. "Okay. I'll give you a call in a couple of days to see how things are going, okay?"

"If you got time," Mrs. LaRue said without turning away from the stove.

Audrey gave Jack a helpless look, and he gestured for her to follow him. Audrey hesitated; she looked at her mother once more and then suddenly walked to where her mother was opening a can of soup. Mrs. LaRue did not turn, but continued doggedly to open the can of soup. Audrey put her arms around her mother and pressed her cheek to her mother's shoulder, then let go. "Bye, Mom."

"Bye now," Mrs. LaRue said without turning.

Jack worried they wouldn't be able to find Allen, but Audrey knew exactly where to look. Off the main square, in a coffee house that she said had once been a pool hall, Allen was sitting outside with two other men, sipping coffee and smoking cigarettes.

Audrey got out of the Cadillac and walked up to Allen. He smiled. "Hey, Audie. Want some coffee? You guys know my big sis, Audrey LaRue, right?" he asked, and then laughed. "Yep, this is Audrey LaRue, the one LaRue who escaped Redhill." He took a long swig of his coffee as his friends shook Audrey's hand and gushed that they loved her music.

Audrey graciously thanked them, then turned to Allen. "Think we might have a word before I go?"

"What, are you going?" he asked. "I thought you came to save me from myself."

"Doesn't look like I can do that," she said. "Can I speak to you a minute?"

Allen glanced at his friends, then nodded. "Sure, Audie. Whatever you want." He slowly came to his feet.

Jack watched the pair as they walked to the corner of the building. They looked a lot alike, he thought. Allen shoved his hands in his pockets and looked everywhere but at Audrey. Audrey, on the other hand, looked so earnest and concerned that his heart went out to her. Her desire to help was visible . . . just as visible as Allen's desire to be left alone.

In his lifetime, Jack had known a lot of guys like Allen—hell-bent on self-destruction, trying to erase something with drugs or booze. Someone like Audrey, who was driven to succeed, could not fathom how someone could be so motivated to fail.

Jack didn't understand it, either.

After about fifteen minutes of Audrey talking and Allen shrugging, she hugged him and walked away. With hooded eyes, Allen watched her leave, and as she climbed into the Cadillac—waving at Allen's pals, who were calling out to her—Allen shifted his gaze to the sky a moment, then wearily pushed away from the wall and walked back to his friends.

Audrey turned as Jack pulled away from the curb and looked back at her brother until she couldn't see him any longer, then finally turned around and settled back with a sigh. "Get me out of here, would you?"

Jack did precisely that. About an hour and a half later, having made one stop at a roadside fruit and vegetable market, they entered the lake resort of Possum Kingdom, much to Audrey's delight. "We used to come here when we were kids!" she exclaimed happily.

"So did we," he said. This is where I learned cliff diving."

"You're kidding!" she exclaimed. "So what are we going to do, rent a cabin?"

"Nah," he said with a laugh. "You're Audrey LaRue—only the best for you, sweet cheeks," he said, and pulled over before a length of chain that roped off a dirt drive. In a box beneath a rock, he found the key, and let down the gate. When he got back in the Cadillac, Audrey gave him a curious look.

"Just hold on," he said, and drove onto the dirt drive. They bounced down the drive, winding around native mesquite and oaks, and finally came to a halt before an old double-wide trailer house. It had been cared for—the shutters looked to have a new coat of blue paint, and geraniums lined the decking around the front door. The lake was just below the house, a short walk down a cliff where steps had been carved from the limestone, to a boat dock.

Audrey gave him a skeptical look.

"It's not the Ritz, I know," he said quickly. "But the Price family has spent some happy summers here."

Audrey's face instantly lit up and she squealed. "Oh how wonderful!" she exclaimed with delight and got out of the car, hurrying up the steps to the door.

The place smelled a little; no one had been up for a couple of months. As Jack walked around and opened the windows, Audrey investigated the place. It was comfortably decorated for a lake house—a pair of La-Z-Boys and couch, a big flat-screen TV. The kitchen was surprisingly large. Jack, Parker, and his dad had spent one summer refashioning a sliding glass door on the back side, which opened onto a sizable deck.

Over the years, the two weeping willows Jack's sisters had planted had grown up and now provided shade against the sinking afternoon sun.

"This is fabulous, Jack!" Audrey said.

He had worried that she would be disappointed—it was hardly the sort of accommodations she was accustomed to—but she seemed genuinely thrilled to be here.

"Can we swim? The lake looks so inviting. When we were kids, before Gene and Leanne began to hate each other," she said with a laugh, "we would go to the Cliffs."

"Know it well," he said. "My folks bought this lot when we were little. We always liked it because it's away from the tourist spots and is a little more private."

"Let's swim—oh, but I don't have anything to swim in!"

"Let me see what I can do," he said, and walked into the back, where the bedrooms were. He riffled through a dresser and produced one of his sisters' old swimsuits, which was well worn, but serviceable. Audrey laughed when he handed it to her—it was green with big white polka dots. "How stylish," she said with a grin.

But when she appeared a few minutes later, wearing the suit and one of his old shirts as a cover-up, Jack was fairly certain that suit had never looked so good.

"It's a little small," she said.

He let his gaze slowly sweep the length of her. "I guess that depends on your perspective."

Audrey laughed and gave him a sexy smile as she brushed past him and opened the sliding glass doors. "Are you coming?" she asked him over her shoulder.

"Are you kidding?" he said. "I'll meet you at the lake."

When he met her there a few minutes later, he was wearing some old shorts and flip-flops and was carrying a small cooler in one hand, an inner tube in the other. Audrey was already in the water, paddling around. He stood on the boat dock, watching her a moment, his thoughts in places they shouldn't have been—on her body. Inside her body, moving long and slow inside her body. What could he say? The woman was sexy to begin with, but awe-inspiring as she floated on her back.

"What's that?" she called up to him.

With a grin, he fit the cooler into the small tube, then got on his knees. "Come and get it," he said, and handed it to her.

In the water, Audrey opened the top of the cooler and laughed as she withdrew a beer. "Perfect!"

"Not yet," he said, and walked back to the little shack they kept on the boat dock. He turned the combination lock until it clicked open, then reached inside for two tractor-trailer inner tubes. He rolled them back across the dock.

"Oh, gimme!" Audrey cried, waving a hand. Jack rolled one off the dock and watched her swim to catch it. The other, he swung out with one arm at the same moment he jumped, landing perfectly within it. Audrey grabbed his foot with one hand and the cooler in the other and tossed him a beer.

Jack tethered Audrey and the cooler to his tube, and they spent the afternoon bobbing in the wake of passing motorboats as the rest of the world floated away from them. They drank beer, waved at passing skiers, and lied to each other about the heights from which they had jumped at the Cliffs when they were kids.

Audrey told Jack how she and Allen had commandeered a small outboard motorboat one year and had puttered across the lake, only to run out of gas. It was night before anyone found them, and she laughed when she told how much trouble they had been in. "Dad whipped Allen," she said. "But Mom saved me and told him she was going to punish me with kitchen duty the rest of the trip. I think I did it once," she said, laughing. "Allen never forgave me."

Jack told Audrey about the year he and two of his partners, Eli and Cooper, graduated from high school and had come up here, built a catapult on the dock, and used it to shoot cantaloupes from Jack's father's garden at passing boats until the lake patrol had come and taken their catapult away.

They laughed together like two people from the same neck of the woods who spoke each other's language. Their chatter was comfortable, their friendship easy. And it didn't hurt that Audrey was so damn goodlooking. Every time Jack looked at her, he felt something stir inside him, something that wanted desperately to be inside her. But he felt something else just as strong—a genuine, full-fledged attachment.

Who would have thought he could feel that for the woman who, just a few short weeks ago, he thought was the world's biggest diva?

When the sun began to creep behind the house in preparation for its descent, Jack rowed them to the steps leading up to the dock. He went first, taking the cooler up with him. On his second trip, he managed the tubes. And on his third trip, he laughingly hung a slightly inebriated Audrey over his shoulder and climbed up.

She laughed when he put her down on the deck, and wrapped her hands around his biceps. "Dude," she said, squinting up at him, "you're so *strong*." She caressed his arm for a moment. Jack was about to caress her back, but then she said, "I am starving."

"Great," he said, and put his arm around her shoulders. "Chef Jack showed up to cook for us."

Inside, Jack showered first, donning another pair of shorts and an old camp shirt that belonged to Parker. "Your turn," he said when he came out of the bathroom. "Turn the knob toward cold to get hot."

She blinked up at him.

"Plumbing job gone bad," he said. "Just do the opposite of what it says."

While Audrey showered, Jack checked on the steaks he had taken out of the deep freeze and left on the deck to thaw. In the storage room, he found a couple of bottles of cheap wine. With the fresh green beans and squash he'd picked up at the roadside market, there was enough to make a decent meal.

By the time Audrey emerged from the shower, he had snapped the beans and cut up the squash. He glanced up as she walked into the living room, wearing a pale blue slip of a sundress that shone against her skin. Her blond hair, still wet, curled around her face. She wasn't wearing any makeup, but she didn't need to—her eyes were large and sparkling. He couldn't remember a time he'd ever seen her look so totally relaxed . . . or sexier.

She paused at the table that held the flat-screen TV and the various framed pictures there. "Oh wow," she said, picking one up. "Is that you?"

Jack squinted at it—it was a picture of him at the age of twelve or thirteen, a skinny thing in short bathing trunks and with his hair sticking up in several directions. Standing next to him was his sister Paige, who, at that age, had been in her strike-a-pose phase, and Parker, still a little runt. "Yep. That's my brother Parker and my sister Paige. My other sister, Janet, must have been behind the camera."

"It looks like you have a nice family," she said, picking up a picture of his folks.

"I do," he said. "They're great people."

"Must be nice," she muttered as she put the picture down and wandered into the kitchen. "Can I help? It's been ages since I did anything in a kitchen."

"Sure. You can open the wine."

Audrey picked up the bottle and laughed, then unscrewed the top.

"Yeah, that's the Price family all right—only the best from the discount aisle for us."

Still grinning, Audrey poured the wine. She held it up to her nose, then to Jack's as he put the vegetables into a skillet to be sautéed. "It's good!"

He didn't know about that, but he was more than willing to drink it.

Audrey poured him a glass, then sidled around the bar and sat opposite him, sipping her wine as she watched him cook. "I have to thank you for today, Jack," she said with a soft smile. "I can't remember the last time I was so relaxed."

"Me either," he said, and grinned when she flicked the screw-off wine top at him. "I was thinking of you when I was showering." When Jack lifted a very curious brow, she giggled. "I *mean*, I was thinking that you . . . you were really cool today. My family isn't easy to deal with."

His gaze absently dipped to her breasts. "It was no big deal, sweet cheeks. Everyone's got a few whackos in their family."

"Really? Do you?"

He lifted his gaze to her glittering green eyes and realized he couldn't lie to her. "No," he said with a sigh. "We're disgustingly normal."

"I noticed," she said, nodding. "Pictures of the entire family, everyone smiling. You look really close, all of you."

"We are," he said.

"I would kill for that. I can't tell you how many times in the last two or three years, since I started getting so famous, that I just wished I had someone to talk to. Someone who really knew me and could advise me what to *do*, someone whose opinion I could trust implicity. That's what is hard about this job—I don't know what to do half the time. Do I endorse a line of jeans or not? Should I make a big deal over the cover art they came up with for my next release because I hate it? Do I go pop, or stay alternative?"

Jack knew what she meant. When Parker had moved into the major leagues of baseball, he'd called Jack many times for advice on how to handle various aspects of his fame, and his brother's fame was nothing compared to Audrey's.

"I feel like I am swimming blind sometimes," she said. "Even Lucas . . . sometimes I don't know if he has any better idea than I do." She laughed and shook her head. "Do you know that once we handed over fifteen hundred dollars to a guy who promised us he'd record an album with me? No contract, nothing but this guy's word. Of course he skipped town with our money. God, we were stupid."

He preferred not to think of the prick Lucas, and said blithely, "At least you won't make that mistake again." He picked up the platter of steaks. "I'm going to throw these on the pit," he said, and walked out onto the deck.

Audrey followed him and stood beside him as he placed the steaks on the grill.

"You're lucky," she said thoughtfully, her gaze on the steaks. "You're lucky just knowing you can trust your family. You're lucky you don't have to worry about them making up something about you to make a quick buck, or to tell the media your darkest secrets."

She looked away, out over the lake. "That's the hardest part about this fame business, knowing who you can trust."

"You can trust me, sweet cheeks."

She turned around, a smile on her face, her eyes sparkling. "Oh yeah, I *know*," she said playfully. "You made that perfectly clear from the get-go—not interested in the drama."

"That's right," he said as he flipped a steak. "Put down the stiletto and move away."

Audrey tossed her head back and laughed, giving Jack a glimpse of the young woman she might have been had she not been thrust so hard and fast into the spotlight. She looked happy and free, full of life and youthful beauty. Her eyes were glittering, the laugh lines around them telling of her personality.

Jesus, he wanted to kiss her, to make love to her. He forced his attention back to the steaks and said, "Still hungry?"

"*Famished.*"

They dined on the deck as the sun sank on the horizon. They polished off one bottle of wine and laughed as Jack unscrewed the top of the second. When they had finished the meal and put the dishes in the sink, they stood out on the deck, illuminated with a strand of Christmas lights.

"I could live out here, you know?" Audrey said wistfully.

"Nah," Jack said. "It's too remote. You'd be lonely."

"What's new? I'm always lonely."

Jack looked at her. "How can you be lonely?" he asked. "You're surrounded by people twenty-four/seven."

"I know. It doesn't make sense. But honestly? I never felt lonelier in my life."

He wanted to take her in his arms and promise her she'd never be lonely. He wanted to kiss that look from her face. But Audrey's cell phone rang. They both looked at the glass doors. "Don't answer it," he said.

She hesitated, but then shook her head. "It might be Allen."

Twenty-two

It wasn't Allen; it was Lucas. "Where are you?" he demanded. "I've been trying to get you all day."

"You have?" she said, and glanced over her shoulder as Jack walked into the house. "I guess I didn't hear it."

"Your mother says you left today, said you had to get back."

Audrey's head began to swim from the wine and the sun and the niggling guilt at having such a lovely time today. "Oh yeah. Yes, I told her that," she said, and put a hand to her temple. "But I just said that to get out of there because she was driving me nuts."

"Then where are you?" Lucas asked, his voice full of suspicion.

"At Dad's," she said, and turned away from Jack's gaze.

Lucas didn't speak for a moment. "You're at Gene's?" he said, his voice less accusatory.

"Yep. With him and his new girlfriend. She's younger than I am."

"Oh hell," Lucas said. "So where is Muscle Man?"

"Ahh . . ." Audrey squeezed her eyes shut. "Ah . . . not sure. He's around somewhere. I don't know."

That seemed to satisfy Lucas. "I needed to talk to you," he said, moving on without asking about Allen or Gail, or her, for that matter. "I have agreed to add a few tour dates—"

"What?" she exclaimed, opening her eyes.

"Audrey, listen. Your single has been number one for a month now. Your album just went platinum. We are sold out in every venue, and your business and talent manager and I think that it's worth the expense of adding a couple of extra nights to the schedule."

"But I have to be in the studio in two months and I have written exactly two songs, Lucas. I need time to write."

"We'll find the time. But right now, I think this is what we need to do."

"I don't!"

"Audrey," he said sternly, "let's please not argue about this right now, all right? Do you think it's easy holding down the fort while you're off dealing with Allen's shit? I just wish you would let me manage our career like we agreed without giving me grief every time I make a decision."

"So I'm not allowed to at least have a *say* in it?"

"Oh God," Lucas groaned. "Go have a cocktail or fifty with your family and I'll talk to you when you get back." And he hung up.

He *hung up* on her. Audrey's jaw dropped. She stood frozen for a moment, staring at the faded carpet.

"Is something wrong?" Jack asked.

Everything was wrong. Her *life* was wrong. "I just . . ." She just what? She just wanted something, something she couldn't name. She turned around and looked at Jack, tossing the phone onto a chair. He was leaning up against the bar, propped on one arm. His gaze followed the phone then shifted back to her.

"You just what, starlight?"

Audrey bit her lip. "Lucas added some tour dates," she said quietly. "He didn't ask me, he just did it."

"Cancel if you don't want to do them," Jack said.

"I can't."

"Why not?"

Because she had handed so much of her life over to Lucas, that she didn't know how to cancel tour dates, didn't know how it worked or what it would mean or even who to call. She felt helpless. "Because . . . because I really don't know anything anymore, other than I *want* . . ." Goddammit, tears were filling her eyes again.

"Audrey," he said, his voice full of concern. He was moving away from the bar, toward her.

"*I want you.*"

The words spilled out of her from a place she didn't even know she could tap. She reached for Jack, but he was there before her, taking her in his arms, holding her tightly to him. "I don't *want* to want you, but I do! And it's getting worse, Jack. I can't think of anything but you, I can't seem to feel anyone but you." As the words came out of her mouth, a fleeting panic swiped through her as she realized what she was doing, and she instinctively put one hand against his chest, pushing lightly. "Oh God help me, I am so going to hell—"

"No," he said, covering her hand on his chest and holding it there. "*Don't.* I want you, too . . . in the worst way," he said, and lowered his head to kiss her, his mouth moving hungrily on hers, his tongue tangling with hers.

She could feel her body heat through her dress, could feel her blood rushing to the surface. He touched her hair with his hand, caressing it, then moving to her face, angling her head up to his. She felt herself passing the point of no return, surrendering her heart to him.

Jack groaned deep in his throat and moved his hands down her body, over her shoulders, to the sides of her breasts, cupping them, squeezing them, then down her ribs, to her waist and her hips, lifting her and pressing her against his erection.

His mouth moved to her jaw, and he trailed a path with his tongue to the hollow of her throat, then down to kiss the crevice between her breasts. He slid farther down her body. She could feel his mouth, wet and warm through the fabric of her dress, burning her skin beneath. He slipped his arms around her waist, lifting her off her feet as he kissed her, twirling her around so that the backs of her legs were up against the couch.

He put his hand on her thigh and lifted his head. His eyes, as blue as a hot summer sky, were glowing. "I want to make love to you," he said as his hand slipped beneath the hem of her dress, sliding up her bare thigh to the thin strap of underwear that rode over her hip bone. "I want to fill you up and take away the loneliness."

No one had ever said anything as sexy to her. "Oh, *Jack*," she murmured, and took his head in her hands, nipping at his lips.

He caught her mouth with his and slipped his thumbs beneath the straps of her dress and slowly pushed them from her shoulders.

The dress slid from her body, drifting down to a pool at her feet. Beneath it, she was wearing nothing but a thong. Jack drew a steadying breath as his fingers skated over the breasts, tweaking her hardened nipples before sliding down to her waist. He turned her around, taking in the entire view of her.

"*Damn*, you're beautiful."

When he turned her around again, Audrey put her hands on his shirt and quickly ran down the row of buttons. Jack shrugged out of the shirt, and tossed it aside as Audrey ran her hands over his thick shoulders and pecs, and down his belly to his hips. She glanced up at him as she slipped her hand into the waistband of his shorts and unbuttoned them.

Jack gave her a demonic, hot-blooded smile. His erection was straining against the fabric of his shorts, but he grabbed her hand, pulled it away from their bodies while he slipped his other hand into the waist of her panties. "Uh-uh," he said with a wink. "You first."

He moved his hand to the swell between her legs, palming her. When Audrey drew a shaky breath, Jack chuckled wickedly and slipped his fingers into her slit.

She gripped his arm. "Are you particularly fond of these panties?" he asked. She shook her head. With a wolfish grin, he suddenly snapped the elastic and tossed them away. Now she stood before him completely bare, except for her recent Brazilian wax job. Jack's eyes greedily took her in before he pushed her down on the couch. When Audrey reached for him, he pushed her again, so that she was slouched against the back.

"Just sit back," he said, and moved between her legs. His tongue darted into her belly button before he painted a line down to the top of her sex. Audrey's breath was coming quicker; her hands gripped her thighs as he slowly pushed her legs apart and used his thumbs to spread her open. He dipped his head, teasing her with the tip of his tongue and his breath.

"*Ah God,*" she whispered.

He smiled at her. "I'm going to make you come like you've never come before," he promised, and dipped his head again, this time plunging his tongue deep into the folds of her flesh.

Audrey gasped as he nipped and sucked the kernel of her desire, two fingers moving deep inside her. She bucked against him, making mewling sounds of pleasure as Jack licked her to oblivion. And when she came, she cried out, arching her back, pressing into him.

He waited until she had come down from her high before sitting back on his heels. Spent, Audrey touched her fingers to his shoulder. He caught her hand and kissed it. "Jack. That was . . . that was *unreal.*"

He laughed as he stood up and pushed his shorts down. His engorged penis sprung free, and he took it in hand, stroking it almost thoughtfully as he looked down at her, sprawled on the couch. "You know what, sweet cheeks?"

She shook her head.

He grinned. "I think I can make you come *again.*"

She smiled and pushed herself up. "I don't know," she said as she reached for his sinewy thigh and pulled him close, so that she was eye level with his cock. "I think it's your turn."

He groaned as she removed his hand and closed her mouth around the tip of him. He caressed her head, moving slowly into her mouth and out again as she teased him with her lips and her tongue.

For Jack, her mouth forced him to exercise a Goliath-like restraint. He wanted to take her then and there, plunge into her, and fuck her with the strength of ten men. She teased his body to a precipice and he wanted to leap, to fall headlong into that sea of pleasure. He wanted it . . . but he wasn't quite through giving her pleasure.

He eased her back, put his hand under her chin. "Stand up," he said, holding out his hand to her. Audrey stood, slipping her arms around him. Her skin was baby soft and hot against his skin. He loved the way she smelled—a mix of sweet perfume and the arousing smell of a woman well satisfied.

He kissed her, then turned her around and pressed his erection against her.

"Do we have birth control?" he asked.

"Pill," Audrey panted.

"Good," he said, and reached for her breasts, kneading and tweaking them as she moved against his erection. "Remember what I said?" he asked softly.

She leaned her head against his shoulders as he kneaded her breasts. "Ummm."

"I'm going to make you come again," he uttered, working to keep from coming himself, and buried his face in her neck. He moved one arm to her waist, and with the other, he gently bent her over the couch. He moved a thigh between her legs and spread them apart, and with one hand on her breast, the other sliding down to her clitoris, he slowly pushed into her from behind.

He sank into heaven. Audrey groaned, lifting her hips to him as he stroked her, sliding into her warm depths, then slowly moving out again. Then sliding into heaven all over again.

He continued to lengthen inside her while he stroked her with his hand, swirling around the tip of her pleasure. Audrey moved against him, drawing him closer and closer to the edge of a monstrous release. Her body squeezed around him, pulling him in, and just as Audrey let out a sob of pleasure and her body convulsed around his flesh, he came with full force, shuddering to an end.

They were both panting; Jack slipped his arm around her waist and maneuvered them onto the couch without dislodging to lay on their side. As he stroked her arm, he marveled that he'd never made love quite like that, had never felt such an explosion of joy and tenderness all at once.

Maybe she felt the same way, for when his body slid from hers, she twisted about on the couch and slipped her arms around his waist before burying her face in his neck.

Sometime in the night, Jack awoke, stiff from sleeping on the couch. He picked a mumbling Audrey up in his arms and carried her back to one of the bedrooms. And when he lay her on the bed, she reached for him again, her mouth closing around his nipple, her hands sliding down to his cock.

They made slow, easy love. What they had to say to one another they said with their bodies and their hands. And when they'd both found fulfillment again, and Audrey had drifted into sleep with her lips curved into a dimpled smile, Jack had a crazy thought.

Maybe this could work. Maybe, just maybe, she would come to love him, too.

Twenty-three

Seeing Audrey asleep in his bed the next morning had a profound effect on Jack. He recognized all the tender feelings of being in love.

He woke Audrey with his hands and his mouth, and when they had given in to desire again, he kicked her out of bed with the playful admonishment to hurry—they had a long drive and a long flight ahead of them. Only then did Audrey notice the time, and with a squeal, she began shoving their loose things into their bags.

On the drive to the airport, they held hands. Audrey told him about a song she had written about growing up in Redhill and sang it to him. He told her it was beautiful, told her that he sincerely hoped one day she would do some of her old music because it was so stirring. Audrey was ridiculously pleased by the compliment and decided then and there to finish writing the song.

During the flight back to Nashville, she sat in the cockpit with him and made him tell her about his work in Hollywood. Neither of them addressed what had happened between them or what it meant, or where it might take them. Jack was content, like her, apparently, to bask in the lightness of new love, laughing and smiling and enjoying the moment that he knew would evaporate as soon as they landed.

Audrey was having the same incredible feelings for Jack, but in the back of her mind was a little worm of a thought that grew bigger and more insistent the nearer they came to Nashville: she had done the one thing she despised in others, the one thing she had believed she would never tolerate in a mate.

And while she felt a tremendous amount of guilt and disappointment in herself at some level, she also felt something that surprised her: *relief*. Relief! She had at last admitted to herself as well as Jack what was in her heart. She was relieved she'd acknowledged—perhaps not in the most productive way—that her relationship with Lucas was over.

It had been coming for a long time, but she had not been able to face it. Lucas was the first man who had been good to her. He'd taken an interest in her talent and her career, had helped guide it to where it was today. She wished she had ended it differently, she wished she'd done so many things differently, but she was relieved it was finally at an end.

The hard part would be telling Lucas, of course, but she had to do it as soon as she could.

They touched down around two, already late for rehearsal. On the tarmac, parked near the hangar, was a limo that Audrey was certain had been sent for her.

As Jack powered the plane down, he smiled at her, but his eyes reflected the growing trepidation she felt inside her.

"I'm just going to get my things," Audrey said, gesturing to the back of the plane.

He nodded, then ran his hand along her thigh and squeezed her knee. "I'll be right there."

Audrey crawled out of the cockpit and walked to the back of the plane, where they had carelessly thrown their things in their haste to be on their way. As she tried to sort out their things—an impossible task, given how her mind was racing—Jack surprised her by stepping up behind her, slipping his hands around her waist, and drawing her into his chest as he kissed her neck.

"I wish we didn't have to get off this plane," he murmured as his hands slid up to cup her breasts. "I wish I could fly you to the moon."

"What would we do on the moon?"

"These seats fold down into beds."

Audrey smiled and turned in his embrace, slipping her arms around his neck. "The moon is going to have to wait, unfortunately. I have a show to do. A dozen of them, actually."

"Ten," he corrected her. "Just ten." And he cupped her jaw, kissing her.

She returned his ardor tenfold until Jack at last lifted his head. He pushed her hair back from her face. "Audrey . . ." He smiled and gripped her hand. "I need to say this. I am crazy about you, sweet cheeks. I . . . I adore you. What happened between us was real."

She blushed. "*I'll* say," she said low, and kissed his chin. "I adore you, too, Jack." And oh, she did, she truly adored him, everything about him, and the way he touched her and looked at her and spoke to her like she mattered to him.

He smoothed his hand over her hair, his eyes moving over her face. "I think I'm falling in love with you," he said quietly.

"Really? I've already fallen."

He smiled, almost gratefully, she thought. "Then I guess the burning question is, where do we go from here?"

"To the moon and beyond?"

He smiled at her optimism. "I'm afraid we've got some complications with lift-off."

"Yeah," she said, sighing. "I have to figure out how to end it," she made herself say, finding it surprisingly difficult to say aloud.

"Today?" he asked hopefully.

It was enough that she had to end it—to say when seemed impossible at the moment. Did she tell him the moment she saw him? Wait until after the show and then walk onto the bus to tell him with dozens of people outside the door of the tiny bedroom? And what would she say? "*Great show, Lucas, and by the way, I am leaving you for Jack.*"

It was too overwhelming to think of, and she shook her head. "I don't know."

His smiled faded. "Well . . . *soon*, I hope."

"As soon as I can. But Lucas and I have had a long relationship. I can't just walk in and announce it's over."

"Is there an easier way?" Jack asked.

"No . . ." Her hands fell away from him. "But I have rehearsal and a show to do, and I have been with Lucas a very long time and he's been good to me. It deserves more than a *see-you-later*."

Jack turned away from her. His expression had changed; he looked doubtful.

"But I *am* going to do it," she said, trying to reassure him.

He looked at her. "I hope so, because I want to be with you, Audrey," he said earnestly. "I can't be near you and not be with you."

"Jack . . . I want to be with you, too."

"Are you absolutely sure?" he asked, his voice gone quietly rough. "If there is the slightest doubt, please tell me now."

She touched her fingers to his hand and looked in his eyes. "I'm *sure*."

He gazed at her a long moment. Audrey could feel her entire being churn with fear and dread and an overwhelming sense of love for Jack. It was a lethal mix, turning to acid in her gut.

Jack's jaw was clenched shut, as if he struggled to keep from speaking. "All right," he said at last. "I understand. But I have to see you."

"I'll do my best—"

"No," he said, shaking his head. "I have to see you." He sighed, ran his hands through his hair, and turned a full circle. "Jesus, but I never meant for this to happen. I never believed myself to be the kind of guy to hook up with another man's girlfriend." He looked up, his gaze piercing her. "But neither can I deny that there is something about you, girl, something that slipped under my skin from the first time we met. I can't walk away from what we've shared and pretend it didn't happen. I can't hear you tell me you want to be with me, too, and then wait for some magical moment."

"I know, but this is really hard, Jack."

"Yeah. It is," he said, nodding, and put his hands on his hips. "I know I am pushing you, I know I am demanding something I probably have no right to demand. Honest to God, I don't mean to be a prick about it—I really do understand this is a big complicated mess, but . . ." He paused, glanced at the ground a moment, then lifted his gaze to her. His blue eyes were swimming with longing. She knew—she felt it, too. "But Audrey, I look at you, and I see everything I have ever wanted. I look at you and I realize that an empty place in me is filling up," he said, touching his fist to his chest. "I realize that you really can't just fly to the moon with me, but if you love me . . . I *have* to see you."

"Okay," she said, moved by his speech. "Okay." But uncertainty filled her.

Jack grabbed her up and wrapped his big arms around her, holding her tightly as he kissed her deeply, almost as if he was afraid it would be the last time. Audrey's body responded to the urgency in his kiss, curving into him, her breasts hardening against his chest. But her conscience had grown to a roar, and she slipped a hand between their bodies, pushing lightly against his chest as she moved her head away. "Jack . . ."

He nipped at her lip, kissed her cheek, and stepped back. He shoved his hand through his hair, then touched her jaw. "I love you," he said restlessly. "I understand how hard this is for you, but I don't know how patient I can be."

She sucked in her breath and held it.

"Audrey?"

"Okay," she said.

It was show time in more ways than one.

Courtney was waiting for them in the limo, seated in the back with her legs crossed, Bruno on the seat next to her. Jack suspected she'd taken a little turn around Nashville before heading for the airport. She was like so many starlets he'd known—grabbing on to any vestige of fame that she could, unable to reach it on her own.

She smiled at him in a way that clearly suggested she would lie down in the backseat for him if he said the word when he climbed in behind Audrey. He ignored her.

"So!" Courtney said brightly, depositing Bruno like a bothersome child on Audrey's lap. "Did you two kids have fun?"

Audrey very studiously avoided looking at him, Jack noticed, and said evenly, "It wasn't exactly a party break, Courtney."

"Oh, I know. I'm really sorry to hear about your brother, Audrey," Courtney said with all the sincerity of a snake. "Just be glad you weren't here yesterday," she said with a roll of her eyes.

"Why?" Audrey asked.

"Adding those tour dates was a *bitch*. And Lucas . . ." She waved her hand and rolled her eyes. "Let's just say he is not in a good mood. Rich says it's ridiculous to add the dates, and unless you add ten, it's just going to cost you money, not make you money, and that really pissed Lucas off. They got into it."

"Great," Audrey muttered, and pressed her cheek to Bruno's body.

Courtney smiled at Jack.

Jack shifted his gaze to Audrey. He tried not to think of her in bed or the way she moved beneath him, her eyes closed as she gave in to ecstasy. He did not want to think of the way she slept, facedown, her limbs sprawled across him and the bed, her hair covering her face.

He wanted her. He needed her. He had felt more alive last night than he had in years, and he did not want to lose that feeling.

As Courtney asked about rehearsal this afternoon, Jack looked out the window and recalled the way Audrey had finally opened her eyes this morning, a catlike smile on her face as she enjoyed his attention to her.

How was it possible, Jack wondered, that in a matter of weeks, he had changed so much? He hadn't thought of his flight school, hadn't thought about TA. He hadn't thought about anything but Audrey, about keeping his hands off her, keeping her at arm's length just so this *could* not happen.

But with Audrey glancing at him now, her eyes full of the same sort of emotions he was feeling, he was certain that this was the woman he was supposed to be with, improbable though it seemed. He felt that as strongly as he'd felt the passion last night, as strongly as he felt the enormity of the wreckage they'd created.

He felt responsible, felt as if he must pull her up from that wreckage. That was all this story needed, the opening chapter—when he pulled her out of that wreckage.

Yet when they arrived at the coliseum, a feeling of foreboding grew in him, and the blissful feelings he'd been experiencing in the last twenty-four hours all but disappeared when he caught sight of Bonner standing out front with Rich, waiting for Audrey.

"There he is," Courtney said with a sigh. "Your manager."

Audrey, Jack noticed, avoided his gaze altogether now.

The driver hadn't even come to a full stop before Lucas opened the door and poked his head inside. "Hey, baby," he said as he reached for Audrey's hand. She quickly pushed Bruno into his hand, but when she stepped out, he put his arms around her and kissed her.

The heat of angry frustration crept into Jack's neck, and he shifted his gaze—unfortunately, landing inadvertently on Courtney, who was watching him closely.

She knew.

He grabbed Audrey's bag and stepped out of the car.

"How are you, okay?" Lucas was asking Audrey as Rich stood there, shuffling his feet uncomfortably and looking a little agitated, which Jack attributed to the dispute over added tour dates. "Everything okay at home?" Lucas asked.

"Yeah," she said, looking everywhere but at Lucas as Bruno scampered around their feet.

"I worried something more might have happened—I called your dad this morning and he said you were at your mom's."

"Did he?" Audrey asked, and smiled nervously at Rich. "You know Dad—he thinks he knows how to handle things." She shifted her gaze to Jack for only a split second, but it was enough that Jack saw her helplessness.

"Well, you're back now, that's all that matters," Lucas said, and kissed her again. "I missed you, baby. God, I missed you."

"Oh," she said.

"Rich and I need to go over a few things with you before you get to rehearsal," he said, letting her go save the arm he kept tightly around her shoulders. He glanced at Jack. "Get her bags, will you?" he said, and pulled Audrey along as they started walking to the coliseum, Rich walking alongside, his hands stuffed in his pockets.

Jack watched them go, consciously stretching his hand to keep from making a fist. He didn't even notice Courtney watching him until she stepped up beside him and folded her arms.

"She *is* cute," she said matter-of-factly. "I can see why you're hot for her. But she can be a real diva."

Jack slid his gaze to Courtney.

She smiled up at him and winked. "And besides that, she is obviously unavailable. But I'm not." She put her hand on his ass.

Jack grabbed her wrist and jerked her hand away from him. "You need to go to work," he said.

"Fine. It's your turn to pick up Bruno's shit," she huffed, and walked on.

Jack slung Audrey's bag over one shoulder, his bag over the other, whistled for Bruno to follow him. "Looks like it's you and me again, little guy," he said, and began walking, with Bruno hurrying to keep up.

After the meeting with Audrey and Lucas, where Rich explained the cost of the extra tour dates the idiot Bonner had added, Rich retreated to his hotel room, furious with Audrey. He closed the drapes, changed into his suit and cloak, then extinguished all lights but one at the desk. He swirled his cloak around him, dipped his pen in the special red ink he'd bought in D.C., and wrote a letter to Audrey, admonishing her for being such a whore. He'd had it with her—first Lucas, now that dumb jock from Texas. She was a slut and she needed to pay for it, which was precisely what he told her in his letter.

Crisis for Audrey LaRue!

(*People Magazine*) Platinum pop-star Audrey LaRue was dispatched to Dallas last week after her brother gave her family a scare. Allen LaRue, who has battled drug addiction for the last ten years, had an apparent relapse and was rushed to the hospital in Redhill, south of Ft. Worth. "A number of pills were pumped from Allen LaRue," said Dr. Randall of the Tri-city Regional Hospital. "It may have been a suicide attempt."

Audrey LaRue left her national *Frantic* tour to be with her brother. "She got there as fast as she could," a source close to the family said. "Audrey is very family oriented." As of press time, Audrey had rejoined the tour in Nashville.

Addiction runs in pop star's family

Audrey LaRue's brother rushed to hospital in desperate plea for sister's attention!

(*Famous Lifestyles Magazine*) Allen LaRue, the younger brother of mega-diva Audrey LaRue, was rushed to the hospital after a suicide attempt last week. "He was just trying to get her attention," an unnamed source said. "Audrey has turned her back on her family since she hit it big, but they obviously really need her. It was like once Audrey left Redhill, she didn't look back. Most people in these parts think that's wrong. Family comes first. Audrey is going to find that out the hard way." Allen LaRue, recently released from jail, has had his share of problems, including felony charges and continuing drug abuse. LaRue's reps could not be reached for comment.

Twenty-four

It was impossible for Audrey to speak to Lucas before the show that night—she went straight from the business meeting she had with Lucas and Rich about the added tour dates, the perfume line someone wanted her to start, and details about the studio dates Lucas had managed to secure, to rehearsal. Which—if anyone was keeping score, and Audrey was fairly certain that every member of the band was doing just that—was pushed back two hours because of her late arrival.

The looks she got were not exactly smiles. She didn't know what to say or do, really—she could hardly tell them she'd been in bed with Jack this morning and got a late start—so she just picked up her guitar and said, "Let's go."

After rehearsal, she wolfed a tuna sub Courtney brought her on the way to hair and makeup. "Have a good time last night?" Courtney asked with a bit of a salacious sneer. "Any of those fantasies come true?"

Her expression made Audrey's heart skip a beat—the girl *knew* something. It flustered her; she bent down to scoop up Bruno so Courtney wouldn't see just how much. "What happened to the stuff I asked you to do for the Songbird Foundation?" Audrey asked.

"Working on it," Courtney said, her knowing smile widening a little further.

"Work on it harder or I will find someone who will," Audrey responded just before sailing into the makeup room.

She scarcely had a moment to breathe; there was so much to prepare. But self-loathing thoughts kept creeping into her brain, thoughts that left her longing for Jack. Yesterday, everything had seemed so right. Today, everything seemed a mess.

At show time, she stood backstage, her stomach in knots, listening to Lucas finish up his opening set. The only comfort in that darkened passage was Jack, who caught her eye more than once and gave her a reassuring smile. As Lucas finished up his set, Jack walked behind Audrey, let his fingers trail over her hips, his hand rest on the small of her back.

Audrey shivered with the promise of his touch. She wanted to turn and throw her arms around him and feel the comfort of his body next to hers. But she didn't move, didn't turn. She felt him leave, disappearing into the dark, leaving her standing alone.

A moment later, Lucas rushed off the stage. He was grinning broadly and caught her up with one arm, kissing her fully on the mouth. "What a fucking *rush*!" he exclaimed, and kissed her again. "Feel the power?" he asked breathlessly. "I am passing it to you, baby. Go tear it up."

"Okay," she said, and squirmed out of his embrace. It seemed to her, in that dark passageway, that Lucas's smile faded a bit.

"I know you will," he said, his voice cooler. "I'm going to grab a beer, but I'll be right here when you go on."

She nodded, watched him walk away, watched him pause to throw his arm around the shoulder of his bass player and say something as they went. And she continued to watch him because she couldn't make herself turn around, couldn't make herself look into Jack's eyes. She knew he was somewhere just behind her. She could *feel* him.

She'd never *felt* Lucas like that in the entire time they had been together.

"Ready, Miss LaRue?" one of the stagehands whispered.

Ready? At this point, there was no refuge from her mess but the stage. "Yeah, Jerry, I'm ready," she said, and followed his flashlight trail down to the lift that would bring her up to the stage in a cloud of smoke.

A half hour later, when the set had been readied for her, Audrey put the guitar strap around her neck, closed her eyes, and hoped for peace from her raging thoughts for at least the space of her show.

But the stage betrayed her. If anything, her thoughts ramped up during the course of her show. It didn't help matters that her first song had to do with cheating boyfriends. It angered her—she didn't need to be reminded and stroked her guitar with a vengeance and kicked the mic stand over. When it came time to abandon her guitar for dance, she leapt into the routine like a lion, kicking higher and landing harder than she ever had before.

The crowd roared.

The next two songs were angry, hard-hitting tunes, and that suited her. But then she reached the acoustical version of her old ballad about a love gone bad.

You say you love me,
but I can't see any heart shining through your eyes.

The memory was heart-wrenching. Lucas really had loved her when no one else would.

My lips move,
but the words aren't mine, they taste like lies.

She closed her eyes, tried to think of Jack, wondering if he was standing just beyond the lights like he did every night, if he was feeling the force of the words. Did Lucas?

By the time the show had come to an end, she was exhausted, wrung dry of every possible emotion, her body feeling limp from the extraordinary exertion she'd put into the show.

"Girl, you were *hot* tonight!" Trystan shouted as he and the other dancers ran off the stage.

Audrey took her final bow, walked off into the dark on the opposite side, where she stood with two stagehands and one security guard. The applause was deafening. Bucky, one of the security guards, grinned at her. "You *rocked*!" he said. "I've never heard you sound so good."

"Thanks, dude," she said with a thin smile.

"No kidding," Bob, a roadie, added. "That was fantastic!"

Then why didn't she feel fantastic? The crowd was screaming—across the stage, Audrey could see Lucas frantically waving her on, and she knew she should go, knew she should walk out there and do an encore before it got too wild, but she couldn't seem to make herself. She didn't want to walk out there and share the stage with Lucas like she knew she would have to do. It seemed disingenuous somehow.

The crowd had begun to stomp, which was the point facility managers usually insisted she go back out. "Aren't you going?" Bucky asked, looking at her curiously.

She looked at Bucky, then at Lucas across the way, feeling almost paralyzed with indecision. It was the warmth at her back that saved her—she felt his hand ride her hip, his breath on her ear. "They love you, starlight. Go out there and give them what they want. That's the only thing you need to think about right now."

She moved then, walking back out on stage, accepting her guitar from one of the band members, hearing the screams of the crowd as the lights came up and a spotlight hit her. It was impossible to see in the crowd with the light shining in her face, but she could hear it and feel it, a living, moving thing, the rhythm of it matching the rhythm of her heart. The bass player started the encore tune, and Audrey struck her first chord on the guitar, and like a savage beast, the crowd quieted.

And as she sang her encore song, Lucas, who came on stage as he had every night since the first time he'd surprised her with it, smiled and winked at her as he played the guitar, and reached out his hand to her as he sang the harmony to "Frantic."

And for the first time, Audrey pretended not to see his hand and walked to the other end of the stage, singing out to the audience, using her guitar as a shield, wondering where Jack was as she sang, *I'm frantic when you're not with me, frantic when you're here*, wishing she could see him, knowing he was near.

The encore ended with Audrey and Lucas riding down into the bowels of the stage. And before they had disappeared from the audience view, Lucas grabbed her in a passionate embrace. As they sank lower, he did not let go, but began to grope for her in the dark, trying to push her under the stage scaffolding.

"Lucas," Audrey said, pushing him away. "*Stop* it." He groaned, ignoring her. Audrey panicked and slapped his hands away from her. "*Stop it!*"

He drew up, surprised. "What the hell is the matter with you? I'm just trying to love you, baby."

"I don't want you to *love* me under the stage like some whore," she said, pushing him again.

"*Whoa*," he said, throwing up his hands. "What the hell is wrong, Audrey? I thought you liked it when we got it on under the stage."

"No, *I* don't like it, *you* like it. It makes me feel—"

"It should make you feel hot, because you totally are," he said, reaching for her before she could complete her thought.

"*Cheap*," she said, knocking his hand away again. "It makes me feel *cheap*. Courtney does guys under the stage. Not me."

"Holy shit!" he said, glaring at her. "Pardon a guy for trying to make love to his girlfriend."

"You're not trying to make love to me, Lucas. You are trying to show off, and it's weird." She moved to pass him, but he caught her arm.

"What the hell is the matter with you?" he barked. "Are you on the rag? PMSing? Because you have been a bitch since you got back from Texas."

Audrey gasped. "Who the hell do you think you are?"

"Oh no," he said, shaking his head. "Don't pull that diva shit on me, Audrey. I *made* you."

"Lucas," she said, shaking his hand from her arm. "Just leave me alone, will you?" She shoved past him, walked through the scaffolding, and tripped over cables before she reached the lights where the crew was waiting. She didn't stop until she reached the after-show party room, which seemed to be part boiler room, part bar.

She walked in, smiling past the dozens already assembled, managing to respond to all those who told her that she and her show rocked as she made her way to the bar. She tried to help herself to a strong gin and tonic, but was intercepted by a well-meaning fan. When she at last got her hand on the drink, she downed it, feeling the burn of it all the way to her toes.

It did nothing to help the churning inside her. The room had filled with the usual group—the band and their groupies, the roadies and their groupies, the people who had won a chance to meet her and *their* groupies, a dozen or more people somehow associated with her that showed up after every show, and whom she'd never even met. As she helped herself to another gin and tonic, she tried to see over the heads of everyone crammed into that large square room, looking for Jack.

She couldn't see him anywhere.

More fans found her—she had no chance to look for him, no time to breathe.

It wasn't until a half hour later, when she had extracted herself from the clutches of one Sandy Winn, who proclaimed herself Audrey's most avid fan and then proceeded to prove that she was, indeed, a very rabid fan, by asking Audrey to autograph her shirts, hats, and canvas tote bags, that Audrey managed to slip away and help herself to an unprecedented third gin and tonic.

Drink in hand, she backed away from the crowd, stepping beneath a large vent and leaning up against the column, out from under the lights. She turned her face up, to the fan. Nashville was *hot*.

The touch of a hand startled her; Audrey almost dropped her drink. She took a quick look around before turning to Jack as his fingers wrapped around her wrist, pulling her into the dark behind the large column.

"Where have you been?" she moaned as he slipped his arms around her and pressed his lips to her throat.

"Right here," he murmured against her skin. He kissed her ardently, as if they had been separated days instead of hours.

Audrey's pulse surged with excitement. She broke the kiss and looked furtively to her right. "They might see us—"

"Did you get a chance to tell him?"

"No," she said, and shifted her gaze to the tuft of dark hair peeking out from the vee of his shirt. "I haven't had a moment to myself. But I will. Soon." Telling Lucas loomed like a beast in her mind, and Audrey suddenly threw her arms around Jack's neck and held him tight. "I miss you already."

"Me too, sweetheart." As his hand rode her nipple, he kissed her again. Her body reacted, her breasts began to swell. She was actually contemplating another illicit encounter when he suddenly stepped away and flashed a sexy smile that suggested he knew what his touch did to her. "More of that later," he said. "A whole lot more of that later. But right now, I think you better get back to your public." He untangled his fingers from hers as he moved back into the shadows, leaving Audrey full of a healthy dose of angst.

The angst intensified when she finally slid out from the shadows to see that Lucas, across the room, was staring at her.

Twenty-five

Lucas knew he was losing her—he knew Audrey as well as he knew himself, and he knew that something had happened in Redhill. Something had changed her.

Goddamn the LaRues. They were pure white trash and worse, stupid. God only knew what had happened, but he had a sneaking suspicion it had something to do with that fucking bodyguard he'd hired. He needed to have Audrey's lawyer take a look at the contract and advise him on how to get rid of that asshole.

But first, he needed to talk to Audrey. Right now, Jack Price was nothing more than a gnat on his ass—he had bigger problems if Audrey didn't get over this funk or crush or whatever the hell it was.

Jack was not about to get on the bus and try and sleep in some coffin-like berth while Audrey slept on the other side of the bedroom door with Bonner. So he made Ted do it.

"She ain't gonna like it, man. She likes to have *you* there."

"She'll get over it," Jack said as he tossed Ted his bag. "See you in the morning."

With a scowl, Ted climbed on the bus. Jack boarded the band's bus. The guys were still partying, however, and Jack wished for a plane. He could really use a flight right now, just him and the sky, alone with his thoughts.

He hadn't thought about anything related to his life at all in the last couple of weeks. How in the hell had he gotten himself into such a complicated mess? Why was it the first woman since Janet Ritchie that he had to go and fall in love with was Audrey LaRue?

He didn't know when his brain had deserted him, but he couldn't change it now if he wanted to. He was definitely into her—so much so that it scared him.

Exhausted and a little drunk, Audrey collapsed onto the bed in the bus, wrinkling her nose at the smell of the sheets. "Doesn't anyone ever wash these things?" she complained.

"I'll have that taken care of as soon as we get to Memphis, baby," Lucas said, and ran his hand down her back, caressing her. "You want me to rub your back?"

He knew her back always hurt after prancing around in stilettos for two hours. A long time ago, he used to rub her back every night. Audrey didn't mean to stiffen . . . but she did.

She closed her eyes when Lucas removed his hand. "Man, you're in a mood," he said gruffly.

"I'm just really tired, Lucas. And maybe a little drunk."

"Why don't you get a shower?" he said. "That always makes you feel better."

It did always make her feel better, and no one knew that as well as Lucas. A little stab of guilt made her sigh; she rolled off the bed and stumbled into the little cubicle of a shower, carelessly tossing her clothes onto the floor for Lucas to pick up.

When she'd finished showering, she wrapped a towel around her and stepped out into the bedroom.

Lucas was standing there, his expression inscrutable, holding a T-shirt out to her.

"Thanks," Audrey said, and quickly slipped it over her head.

He let his gaze move possessively over her body a moment and then said, "Here. You need underwear, too." And he held out a pair of boxer briefs.

It took Audrey a moment to understand that they weren't Lucas's and they definitely weren't hers. When the realization hit her, she jerked her gaze to her bag and saw that Lucas had dumped the contents on the bed. *He had gone through her bag.*

"*Thanks,*" she snapped, yanking the boxers from his hand and throwing them back into the bag. She dug through the pile for panties, her mind racing almost as fast as her heart.

"You slept with him, didn't you?" Lucas asked, his voice amazingly calm.

Audrey's hand stilled as she frantically thought of a way to answer that would soften the blow. When nothing came to mind, she sighed. The jig was up, as they say. "Lucas—"

"Just don't lie, Audrey, because you do it so badly."

She drew a steadying breath and turned to face him. "I slept with him," she said softly. "But it's not what you think."

"Oh yeah?" he asked, folding his arms across his chest. "What do I think?"

"I just . . . I don't know how to say this, but . . . but the thing is, along the way . . . I fell in love with him."

His gaze grew colder. "So . . . you've been fucking him all along, is that it?"

"*No!*" she said quickly.

"Since when?"

"Since last night."

Lucas didn't flinch. He was stunningly calm. "And you think you're in *love* with him? That's rich," he said with a sardonic chuckle. "Don't be stupid, Audrey. Don't confuse a little fling with love. This shit happens on tour all the time. Don't try and make it into something bigger than it is."

He spoke to her as if she were stupid, as if she didn't understand her own feelings. This was not a tour fling. There was something about Jack that touched her in a place she'd never been touched before. She hated how it had happened, but she wasn't going to let it go. She might never feel this way again in her life! And looking at Lucas now, she could see years of dissatisfaction stretching before her, and the constant wondering about what might have been.

"It's not a fling, Lucas. It's very real. I never intended for this to happen, I never went looking for it. It just . . . *happened*."

He laughed again. "Baby. *Audrey* . . . How can you be so naïve? It never just happens. Don't you get it? That asshole is using you."

"No he's not," she said, shaking her head and wishing desperately she hadn't had three drinks. "Jack isn't like everyone else. That's the thing—he doesn't need me for anything."

"Oh yeah, like I do?" he asked, smirking.

Audrey bit her lip and looked down.

"Oh, so *that's* the card he's playing. Okay, let's play it. Has he told you about his flight school?" Lucas asked. "What kind of scratch do you think he needs for that, huh? A whole lot more than he is ever going to make doing stunts."

Audrey rolled her eyes and shifted her gaze to her bag. She didn't want to debate and argue. She wished she could put her hands on a pair of panties—she felt terribly exposed before Lucas for the first time in years.

"Look," he said, touching her arm and making her look up. "I'm not going to pretend it doesn't piss me off royally that you slept with that fucking asshole. I won't lie—I am furious with you, Audrey. I thought I knew you, and I cannot believe you would do that to me after all we have been through together. This is not *you*. If we have problems, we talk. You don't go sneaking off behind my back to fuck around like your dad did."

That hurt, and he knew it. Tears welled in Audrey's eyes, but she angrily rubbed them out.

"You're so much better than that," he continued. "You're a good person—not a whore."

"God, Lucas, will you stop?"

"I am just calling it like I see it, baby. But here's the thing . . . I am willing to chalk it up to experience and work to get past it."

A lone tear slid down her cheek, and Lucas instantly reached for it, wiping it away with the pad of his thumb. "Just say you're sorry. That's a start."

She pushed his hand away from her face. "I *am* sorry," she said. "I never meant to hurt you, I swear I didn't. But I won't pretend it didn't happen or that it didn't mean anything. I love him."

Lucas's expression changed; for the first time since confronting her, he looked worried. "Audrey . . . baby, I don't want to see you make a huge mistake. I know things have been a little stale between us, but we are on *tour*, for God's sake. It's not the most romantic time of our lives, right?"

"You know as well as I do that this has been coming for a long time—"

"Oh yeah? News to me. Don't I even get the benefit of a discussion? Don't I deserve at least that? If something was bothering you, you should have come to me and said so. I would move every fucking planet from the galaxy to fix it if that is what it took, you *know* I would. It's not fair for you to throw away eight years of our lives just because things got a little rough for us and some guy rubbed his dick against you."

"Please don't say that. I know what you've done for me—"

"Oh, I haven't even *begun* to do for you," he said, his attitude changing again. "God, Audrey . . . you know how much I love you, don't you? You mean the world to me, and if I haven't said it enough lately, I'm sorry." He took her hand in his and kissed it earnestly. "I *love* you, Audrey. I have practically sacrificed my career to make yours. I mean, yeah, I am opening for you, I've got an album out . . . but it's just a hobby compared to the responsibility I feel toward you and your career."

"I *know* that." This was so hard. She just wanted to lie down now and close her eyes and think.

"I know you do, baby. I know you do. And if you think about it, I think you will understand that you're just reacting to the stress of the tour. That bodyguard isn't for you. You're a star, Audrey. He just wants to use you like everyone else."

"No he doesn't. You're wrong."

Lucas snorted disdainfully. "That prick was chomping at the bit to get on this gig. When his partners said no because it wasn't their scene, he came to me and practically begged me to let him do it. He told me he needed money—a *lot* of money—and I think he's figured out a way to get all the money he needs."

Her head was beginning to hurt; she sank listlessly onto the bed. Lucas sat next to her and began to rub her back. "I know that must be hard to hear, but I would never lie to you. That dickweed is no different than most of the people you meet on any given day. He wants a piece of the Audrey LaRue empire you're building, and since he doesn't have any musical or managerial ability, the best way for him to get what he wants is to get in your pants."

"You're wrong," she said again. "I know I can't convince you otherwise, but you're wrong."

"Okay," he said. "He's got you convinced. But what about me? I deserve more than a kick to the curb after all the years we've been together, don't I? You owe me a lot more than that. You owe me a chance to work on us."

Her headache was turning blinding. She needed to sleep—she hadn't slept much at all in the last few days and she was exhausted and confused. "No, I . . . I don't know. I really need to sleep."

He continued to stroke her back. "*Sleep*? You destroy my life and you want to *sleep*? At least promise me we'll have a chance to try and work this out. Give me a chance," he insisted. "I know the kind of woman you are, and this isn't it."

Truthfully, she didn't know what kind of woman she was any longer.

When she didn't respond, Lucas sighed. "Mother of God, I can't believe I am sitting here begging my girlfriend to give me a chance after she has slept with some fucking bodyguard."

"*Please* let me sleep," she begged him.

He pierced her with a hard look. "Then promise me."

She would have no peace until she did. "I promise," she said, hating herself for being so weak, hating Lucas for being right—because she *did* owe him more than just a declaration of her feelings for Jack. "I promise we can talk about it."

"I'll take it," he said gruffly.

She wrapped herself in a blanket and buried her head under a pillow, aching for Jack's warmth.

Lucas watched with a clenched jaw as Audrey slept. He wanted to strangle her, but he had to tread carefully—he was not about to let Audrey throw him out, not now, not after all he'd done to get them to where they were today. When he thought of all the work, of all he stood to lose, he saw red. Big swaths of scarlet red.

He really loved Audrey and he was stung to his mortal male core by her infidelity. He honestly didn't believe it was more than a fling. God knew he'd had his share of meaningless indiscretions along the way. People were constantly throwing themselves at Audrey, and he supposed he could see how it had happened—not that it made him any less furious. The key was nipping it in the bud, not letting it go any further than she'd already taken it.

He didn't try and get in bed with her. He couldn't stand to touch her, not right now. Not until he had managed to swallow down his hurt.

He slept on the couch in the front part of the bus.

When they pulled into Memphis the next morning, Lucas was the first off the bus. He marched into the hotel in a foul mood, and just happened to catch sight of Dickweed standing in the lobby, waiting for them. Every bone in Lucas's body snapped to attention, and he strode over to him, his hands clenched at his sides as he struggled to keep from hitting him. "You're fired, asshole," he said without preamble.

"Don't think so," Jack said calmly. "You can't terminate the contract without Audrey's signature, and I don't think she's going to do that."

"Oh, you don't, cowboy? Well, guess what? She already has."

He had to hand it to Dickweed—he didn't even flinch.

"Where is she?" Jack asked calmly.

Lucas scoffed at him. "Did you really think you could come between us? All I had to do was tell her that you were after her money and touch her in the right place—"

"*Whoa*," Jack said sharply. "Unless you feel like eating a fist for lunch, I'd stop right there."

Lucas laughed. "Okay, Price. I won't tell you how many times we made love last night. I'll leave that for Audrey to tell you. Asshole," he sneered, and walked on to the desk, his heart pounding, his palms sweating, and his desire to kill one Texan very, *very* strong.

He had them checked in and was back outside before Audrey managed to get off the bus. Truthfully, she looked like hell, and Lucas was glad to see it. He hoped she'd suffered all night. He had nothing but a big smile for her and caught her up in a hug before she could take a step. With his arm securely around her shoulder, he said, "Come on. Let's grab some coffee."

"No," she said petulantly. "I just want to go take a bath and try and do some writing."

"Come on, baby, can't you just spare a couple of minutes for your ex-boyfriend and a lousy cup of coffee?"

She looked up at him with big green eyes full of what he was certain was regret. "Okay," she said with resignation. "But just an hour or so, Lucas. I have to work."

"Just an hour," he said, and kissed her temple. Audrey pulled back, but he wouldn't let her go. If there was a god in his heaven, Jack Price was watching them now.

AROUND MEMPHIS

Daily Memphis Stylewatch: Audrey LaRue

Stylewatch scored a big fat whale this week when my editor and I spotted Audrey LaRue at an outdoor café, where the megastar was having coffee. She is in town for her *Frantic* tour, which, if press releases and press agents are to be believed, is playing to sold-out audiences across the U.S. Check it out—Ms. LaRue was stylin' in Memphis.

But never mind that—as my editor (who is an all-American male by anyone's measure) said, LaRue was *smoking hot* in her Juicy jeans. She wore some Weitzman sandals, a top that this blogger knew was vintage Chanel, and had the latest Coach bag designed to carry a BlackBerry and a dog. If anyone is interested, she had a cute little black-and-white dog and a no-fat latte. I know, I asked the guy at the counter. And okay, can I say Audrey couldn't have been more gracious? She allowed us to get this fabulous picture. And oh yeah, her dog's name is Bruno.

Tags: arts, performance, theater
Categories: News/Current events
Comments (240)

Picks & Pans

(*People Magazine*) Audrey LaRue, who splashed onto the national music scene with her hit single, *Breakdown*, shows she has the chops with her new album, *Frantic*. Her versatility is inspiring—she's rocking one moment, crooning tender love songs the next. The highlight of the LP is the title song, "Frantic," which makes the listener frantic to get the CD.

DOWNLOAD THIS: "Frantic"

Twenty-six

There was quite a lot of work to be done at the coliseum for security purposes. Jack, Ted, and company worked against the clock and the stage crew to make sure everything happened. It wasn't until late afternoon that Jack could even get backstage to check on Audrey.

He could hear the band in a room at the end of the corridor, the music sounding strange without the benefit of amplifiers. He could also hear Audrey's voice echoing down the hallway as he moved in that direction. She wasn't singing—but her voice was raised. He instantly thought of Bonner, and assumed they were arguing.

As he closed in on the room it became obvious, judging by the timbre of her voice, that Audrey was upset. "*We go over this day after day, and every night, it's the same thing—we completely screw up the bridge.*"

The bridge? Her remark was followed by muffled male voices, the strum of a guitar, and then Audrey again.

"I am so sick of excuses! I don't care how long we stay here, I don't care if we are an hour late getting on stage, I want that bridge to be perfect tonight!"

The last words were amplified when the door swung open and Courtney stepped out. The moment she saw Jack, she feigned staggering, a hand to her forehead. "It's hell in there," she said. "She's such a bitch today—what did you do to her?" she asked, and smiled wickedly.

"How long is rehearsal?" Jack asked.

"Until they get the bridge perfect, didn't you hear? Why so interested, Handsome? Gotta give Audrey a little something?" she asked, her gaze flicking to his crotch.

"Why so nosey, Hotpants? Jealous?"

Courtney laughed and casually drew a line with her finger down his chest. "I *am.* I wish you were as interested in all of us as you are in Audrey."

He caught her hand when she reached his belt and held it away from him. "Have you ever heard of sexual harassment? Besides, I thought you and Ted were looking at white picket fences."

"*Ted?*" She screwed up her face. "Did he say that? No way—I was just having fun."

Ted hadn't said anything, but Jack was fairly certain Ted didn't feel like they were just having fun. "That's really appealing, Courtney, sleeping with every guy on the job."

"Shut up," she said, frowning. "It's at least as appealing as sleeping with a woman who is practically engaged," she said, and walked on.

With a shake of his head, Jack stepped into the rehearsal room.

Audrey barely spared him a glance—she was bent over her guitar, working her way through the song. One of the guys in the band looked at Jack and rolled his eyes.

Jack stood to one side, listening to the rehearsal. He didn't have a trained ear by any means, but even he knew Audrey was way off today. Her guitar sounded out of tune and her voice strained. When she at last called off rehearsal—with a diva-like admonishment that they better have their shit together for the show tonight—he stood back and waited until the room had emptied.

Only then did she glance up at him as she put her guitar in the case. "One of the stagehands will be by to pick this shit up," she muttered. "So please just stay on that side of the room."

Jack lifted a brow. "Great to see you, too."

Audrey winced and sighed. "Sorry."

"What's up, sweet cheeks? You seem a little out of sorts today."

"Out of *sorts*?" She snorted. "You have no idea."

"You want to tell me about it?"

"Not really," she said low.

Okay, she wasn't in the mood to talk about her conversation with Lucas, clearly. But it wasn't like they could have a casual dinner later and discuss their next steps, so Jack pressed on. "I can guess that it didn't go so well with Lucas."

"Ya *think*?"

"Did he do anything? Did he threaten you in anyway?"

"*No*," she said, and frowned, as if that notion was out of the realm of possibility. "He reminded me of what we'd been to one another and how hard we had worked to get here, and how much he has done for me. And it was all true."

She glanced at the floor, avoiding his gaze, and Jack held his breath a moment, waiting for her to tell him she'd made a huge mistake, and that the mistake was him. He realized, with gut-sinking surprise, that if she did say that, he would be devastated.

But Audrey didn't tell him that. She looked up at him with green eyes filled with so much pain and confusion that he couldn't stay on the other side of the room. He was instantly moving, crossing the room in three long strides and taking her in his arms, folding her in a protective embrace.

"I don't know what to do," she said tearfully into his collar. "I just feel so *bad*. It doesn't seem fair somehow, and I feel so damn guilty!"

"I know," Jack said. "So do I."

"I don't know what to *do*," she said again.

He wanted to tell her what to do. He wanted to tell her that she was through with Bonner forever, and to just tell him so, to handle this like a man would handle it. But she wasn't a man, and there was a part of him—the part that had actually learned something in the course of the relationships he'd had with women in his life—that told him Audrey had to do this on her own. No matter how wrong their beginning, if they had any hope of a future, she had to do this.

"Okay," she said, pushing away from him. "Okay, I can't do this now, Jack. I've got to get ready for the show."

"Okay, sweet cheeks," he said softly, and ran his hand over the crown of her head. "I know it's tough . . . but we'll get through this."

"Yeah," she said unconvincingly.

"When will I see you?"

She shook her head; tears glistened in her eyes. "I don't know. I honestly don't know . . . as soon as I can get away, that's all I can say. I *need* to see you, Jack, I need to be with you. I just don't know how to do it without making a bigger mess of things than I already have."

"Okay," he said soothingly, and leaned down to kiss her, touching his lips to hers tenderly, cupping her face with his hand.

Audrey's fingers curled around his wrist, clinging to him as she sagged against him for a moment. God, he wanted to sweep her up and take her away from here. But Audrey righted herself, and with a shaky smile, she pulled his hand from her face. "I have to go." She stepped around him and walked out of the room.

Jack watched her with the uneasy feeling that it could be an eternity before he held her again.

Audrey went through hair and makeup preparation with the strange feeling she was standing outside of her body, watching herself. It didn't help that Lucas was hovering about, completely supportive of her, tolerant of her mood, and asking her what she wanted to do about the perfume samples that had arrived for her to check out without actually telling her what to do about them. A first.

And he beamed when the two-dozen long-stemmed peach-colored roses he'd sent arrived. There was a time, back in Texas, when he would bring her a single peach rose after every gig. It was about all he could afford based on what they would make in their cut of the door, but it had been their special little thing. Her belly churned when she saw them.

"Remember?" he asked her softly.

"Of course. I wish you hadn't sent them."

He looked taken aback, but quickly smiled. "How could I not?" He took the card out and handed it to her. Audrey opened it and read the message he'd written: *Don't give up on us.* She looked up at him; Lucas smiled again.

Audrey turned away.

This was the most attention Lucas had paid to her emotions in months, and Audrey wasn't sure she was up for it. It felt suffocating. She knew what he was doing—he was trying to put her on a pedestal, to let her know that he may have fallen down on the job of worshipping her, but that he was going to change.

It was weird—Audrey had wanted a change in their relationship for so long that having him suddenly attempt to change felt extremely cloying. She didn't want those things anymore. The time had come and gone, and she didn't want them.

And she did not like the feeling she was being pandered to, which she suspected was exactly what Lucas was doing.

She didn't find any refuge on stage, either. It seemed as if the concert was off by several beats all night. Audrey sounded sharp to her own ears, and even the audience, who were usually screaming for her, seemed more subdued than normal. The show went on forever, and by the time it finally ended—much to her great relief—she felt completely drained instead of the high she normally felt.

Which may have been the reason she changed the encore at the last minute. From the corner of her eye, she could see Lucas strapping on his guitar, preparing to walk out on stage and join her like he had since their first night. Not tonight. Audrey surprised herself and the band by playing an old ballad, "It's Just Me."

Lucas was not amused—she could feel his gaze burning through her as she sang.

Later, when they met up in the hospitality room, Audrey tried to avoid him, but it was useless. He would not be avoided.

"Good show," he said, sidling up to her at the bar.

"Are you kidding? It sucked."

"No, I'm not kidding," he said, and pressed his lips together, waiting for her to speak.

"I made some changes," she said, watching him. "What did you think?"

"What did I think?" Audrey knew Lucas well and could see the struggle in him to keep from lambasting her. "I thought it was great," he said at last.

"Great," she said, nodding. "Great." She left him with that and went in search of Courtney, wanting a ride back to the hotel.

It was almost four in the morning when Lucas entered their suite. Audrey knew it—she could hardly sleep with everything on her mind, and she was mentally kicking herself for not having thought of separate rooms. She heard Lucas moving around the living area, then stumbling into the bedroom, kicking her bag in the dark in the process. He finally managed to make his way into the bathroom and shut the door. A few moments later, he came out and slipped into bed beside her.

Audrey squeezed her eyes shut and tried not to move or otherwise let him know she was awake. But he moved close, spooning her, and pressing his erection against her back. A sound of disgust rose up from her throat and she jumped up, slapping his arm from her as she half stood, half fell out of bed.

"Baby, what's wrong?" Lucas asked, his arms wide, his eyes full of drink.

"What are you *doing*?" she snapped angrily.

"What do you mean, what am I doing? I want to make love to my girl."

"Ohmigod—do you remember *anything* that happened in the last twenty-four hours?"

"Do you think I can forget a single fucking moment?" he exclaimed. He fell back on the pillow, slung one arm over his eyes. "I just thought if we made love, you would remember what it was like between us."

"Jesus *Christ*! We haven't had sex in months!" Audrey said irritably. "And you decide *now* is a good time to pick it up again? It's like everything else today—you suddenly get the message, you suddenly start paying attention to me and you think it's going to change the way I feel."

"What am I supposed to do?" he shouted. "Maybe you want me to lie down on the floor so you can walk all over me in your high heels, huh? Would that make you feel victorious?"

"This is ridiculous," she said angrily. "You need to go sleep in another room."

Lucas moved his arm and looked at her. "I *what*? You gave me your word we'd at least get a chance to discuss this—"

"I'm not discussing anything at four in the morning, okay? This doesn't feel right, you being in here," she said, gesturing wildly about the suite they were sharing.

Lucas hauled himself up and fairly leapt to his feet. "I guess it didn't feel right, me being on stage with you, either," he said, as he marched around naked trying to find something to put on.

Audrey didn't say anything to that. There was nothing *to* say—he was dead on. She didn't feel right about it anymore.

Lucas found a pair of shorts and quickly put them on. He found a T-shirt, too, and as he pulled it over his head, he said, "I trusted you, Audrey. I trusted you with my *heart* and my *life*. I can't believe after all I've done for you, after all the sacrifices I have made to make *you* a star, that you are going to throw me out like some groupie."

"I'm not throwing you out. I am asking you to respect my wishes and leave!"

"I don't know what it means on your planet, but on *my* planet, when a woman asks a guy to sleep somewhere else, that's pretty much throwing him out."

She could feel a headache coming on again and put a hand to her temple. "Is it too much to ask that?"

He shot a look at her. "When are we going to talk?"

"We *talked*, Lucas. We talked yesterday and in the coffee shop this morning."

"You can't count that," he scoffed. "There were photographers and fans and everyone was gaping at us." He put his hands on hips. "We need a chance to really *talk*. You drop a bombshell like that on me, and it takes me a little time to get my wind back, you know? And even if I can't convince you to give me a chance, there's a lot to discuss if you're going to leave."

"Yeah, okay," she said, feeling that she was swimming in a sea of guilt again. "When we get to Little Rock, we've got some time there and we can talk then."

Lucas studied her for a moment. "Okay," he said softly. "But if you don't talk to me in Little Rock, I can't be responsible for what I will say or do."

She rolled her eyes and looked at the bed.

"One more thing," he said, watching her carefully. "Give me your word you won't see him, either."

She blinked. "*What*?"

"It's only fair! I at least deserve that much, don't I, Audie?" he asked, using her old family nickname. "I am begging you for a chance to at least be heard. But you're not going to hear anything I say if you are fucking him!"

Audrey's heart began to vibrate in her chest. "Get out of here," she said low.

"Promise me!" he cried frantically.

Twenty-four hours, she told herself. She just had to endure twenty-four hours and give him a chance to be heard. It was one day for all the days he had given her. And he seemed so desperate.

Audrey promised him.

MEMPHIS MUSIC SCENE

Audrey LaRue: Frantic
Lucas Bonner opening

Mid-South Coliseum, Memphis, TN

If there is one thing that can be said for Lucas Bonner, it's that he has a lot of co-writing credits on Audrey LaRue's latest offering, and everyone knows that he and Ms. LaRue are a hot item romantically speaking. He needs to cling to that, because as a performer, Bonner is a one-note pony. His opening set lacked the quality one would associate with LaRue, and the music was uninspired. Bonner might want to consider a full-time gig as her manager and hang up the guitar.

On a bright note, Audrey LaRue is beautiful, the rumors of her diva-like behavior notwithstanding. The girl has definitely got a set of lungs on her. The marketers must love *Frantic*, and I have to admit, it was great. But with the exception of some up-tempo pieces: "Frantic," "Breakdown," and "Take Me" among them, the other pop tunes sounded a bit generic. But LaRue turned it up in the second half of the show by singing some wonderful ballads. "Pieces of My Heart," "Complicated Measures," and "Loved Once More" were outstanding and included a soulful alternative mix. It was Diana Krall wearing leather—sexy and hot.

Twenty-seven

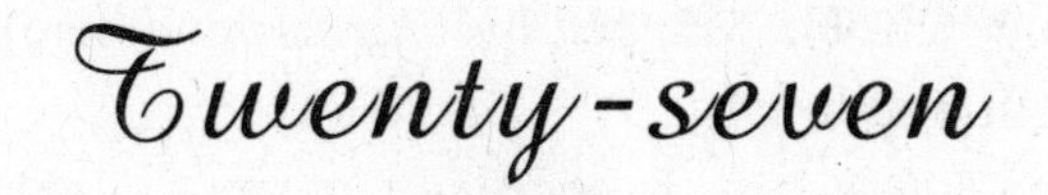

Jack was overseeing the loading of the buses the next morning when he saw Audrey get on the first bus. Alone. It was the first time he'd seen her alone since that moment in the rehearsal hall yesterday.

He took a quick look around, and moved in that direction.

"Morning, Joe," he said to one of his security guards as he opened the door to the bus.

"Hey, Jack," Joe responded with a wave, and seemed to think nothing of Jack getting on the bus.

Jack moved cautiously to the back, almost expecting Bonner or Courtney or some other constant presence to hop out of one of the sleeping berths and ask him what he was doing. Lucky him, there was *no* one on the bus. They were surprisingly and blessedly alone. The bedroom door was open, and with one last look behind him, he stepped across the threshold.

Audrey was standing at the end of the bed in that cramped little space, Bruno lounging on top of the bed. Her face lit with surprise and delight, but her smile quickly faded as myriad emotions scudded across her face. It seemed an eternity before either of them spoke or moved . . . but then Audrey whispered his name.

She lunged for Jack at the same moment he caught her by the waist, steadying them as she threw her arms around him and buried her face in his neck, kissing him. He wrapped his arms around her, pressed his face to her hair, breathing her in.

She cupped his face with her slender hands, nipping at his lips, kissing his face, his eyes. "God, I have missed you," she said between kisses.

"Are you alone?" he asked as he twirled her around and pushed her up against the fake paneling, his body responding wildly to her touch.

"I kicked him out last night," she said breathlessly as his hands roamed her body, and kissed him again, her tongue in his mouth, her body pressed against his. Jack slipped his hand beneath her blouse and caressed bare skin, moving up, to the perfect mound of her breast.

"I've been going crazy, wanting to touch you," he growled. "I see you on that stage and all I can think about is being inside you again."

Audrey moaned and kissed him again. Jack's hand moved lithely over every curve, palming her breasts, and then down, to the apex of the legs, cupping her through her jeans.

She gasped against his mouth; he pushed against the fabric, and she twisted her head away from him. "No," she said roughly. "I *can't.*"

"No one is coming," he said low. "It's early yet—we've got time."

"But I promised . . ."

Jack stilled, his mouth in her hair. "What do you mean, you promised?"

"I promised him," she said weakly.

Jack blinked. He pressed his hands to the panelling, effectively pinning her against the wall as he stooped down to look her in the eye. "You promised him *what*?"

"That I wouldn't see you until he and I talked—"

"Oh God—"

"I *had* to," she said frantically, seeing Jack's look. "Come on, Jack, give me a break here—this is a lot harder than I thought!"

"It doesn't seem too hard if you are promising him you'll stay away from me," he said as he struggled to see the situation from her viewpoint.

"Don't get me wrong, Audrey—I hate that this is so hard for you. But it will be over before you know it, and you don't need to . . . to *promise* him anything."

She sighed heavily. "The guilt is suffocating. I just can't seem to *think* straight."

Jack felt his gut sink again and straightened up, dropping his hands. "What have you told him?"

"I don't know, to be honest," she said as she sank onto the edge of the bed.

Breathe, Jack told himself. *Breathe*. "You don't *know*?"

"I mean *yes*, I told him I was in love with you—" She sighed again. "Actually, he'd figured out we'd been together. And as you might expect, he didn't take it very well. I told him that I was in love with you, I never meant for it to happen, but it did, and . . . and he thinks he should have a chance to redeem himself."

"It's a little late for that, don't you think?" Jack asked quickly. "I thought you and I had crossed some sort of line here."

"Right. I know . . . but . . ."

"*But?*"

She looked up at him, her gaze pleading for understanding. "But . . . I've been with Lucas a long time, and he's done a lot for me—"

"Audrey, wake up! Don't let him hold that over your head," Jack said, squatting down next to her. "He *wants* you to feel guilty because he needs you too badly."

"I think he is saying it because he *believes* it. We've been together a long time, Jack. It's very hard—for *both* of us—to just throw that all away. I owe him some respect, I owe him an explanation, and I owe him the chance to discuss it. It's not like he did anything wrong. *I'm* the one who broke the commitment." She winced when she said it, as if it was painful to mention.

"Audrey—"

"And I think he's right. I can't ignore all that he has done for me."

"Wait, wait, wait," he said, feeling a little desperate as he took her hand in his. "What are you saying? You're going to give him the chance? You have to realize that Bonner has a lot to lose if you call it off, and he's going to fight like a dog to protect what he's got with you."

She groaned, pulled her hand from his, and buried her face in her hands.

Jack earnestly squeezed her knee. "Think about it, Audrey. He doesn't have a prayer of making it without you, because he doesn't have the talent. There'd be no record deal, no slot as an opener. Have you ever noticed that every time you end up in a tabloid, it's usually someplace with Bonner? Someplace *he* suggested you go? He is using you to put his name out there. He's like Kevin to Britney—if you go away, he slides into obscurity."

"That's not true," she said, dropping her hands from her face with a frown.

"Like hell it isn't. He knows if you go, so does the boat to fame."

"Don't you think it's possible that he really loves me and doesn't want our relationship to end because of that?" she asked irritably.

"Of course I do. I know he loves you—he'd be a fool *not* to love you. But he's got a lot to lose besides you."

"*Jack!*" she said, and stood up, walking around the edge of the bed in that small space. "What else is new? *Everyone* around me is on the boat to fame. It's not just Lucas—it's the band, it's Courtney, it's the roadies, it's even Mitzi. It's even *you* if you think about it."

"*Me*?" he asked, surprised, straightening to his full height. "I'm not looking for fame!"

"Not the same sort of fame, but you're using me to get what you want."

Jack blinked. "What the hell are you talking about?"

"Your flight school," she said. "You are on this tour to make money for your flight school. We both know you couldn't make the kind of money you need with TA. But you can make it with me."

She might as well have kicked him in the kneecaps. "You're kidding, right?"

"No, I'm not kidding! It's true, isn't it? Oh don't look like that—I don't *care* about that. I'm trying to make a point. I'm just doing it badly."

"*I* care about that. If you think I am here with you now in the middle of this mess for *money*, then I won't take a goddamn dime. And just so we both are clear," he said, moving closer to her, slipping his finger under her chin and forcing her to look up, "it's not as if I forced you into this mess."

"Oh for God's sake, don't go off the deep end. I am just trying to make you understand that everyone who comes near me is into me for some other reason besides just *me*," she said. "And Lucas . . . Lucas was there at a time when no one was into me for any other reason but me, and I feel like I owe him."

Jack's frown deepened; Audrey whirled away from him. "Help me out here, Jack. I don't want to be with Lucas anymore. I want to be with you. But I want to end it fairly with him and what we did wasn't fair."

There were so many things he wanted to say, so many thoughts in his head, none of them particularly productive and all of them rooted in love and disgust and emotions he couldn't even name, emotions so strong he felt like he was drowning in them. He shoved a hand through his hair, put his hands on his hips. "Life isn't always fair, Audrey. Maybe if I came with you to talk to him," he said, thinking out loud.

She sighed and looked heavenward for a moment. "I just need a little space to handle this. When we get to Little Rock, I will speak to Lucas and figure out how I am going to finish out the tour, and then . . . *then* you and I can see where we're going."

She looked up at him with desperate hope in her eyes. He didn't like what she was saying, and he damn sure didn't agree with her. But he had no choice. She was caught in the middle. "We're not *going*, starlight. We've already gone."

"I know," she said softly. "Please help me, Jack."

He swallowed down a lump of galling disappointment, hating himself for having put his heart on the line with her like he had. He should have trusted his instincts, should have left well enough alone.

"*Jack*," she said, her voice soft and pleading. She stepped forward, put her hands on his shoulders. "I love you. I *love* you. But I have to end something that took a long time to build. I am breaking up with a man I thought I was going to marry one day."

That suggestion made him shudder with revulsion, but he forced himself to consider it from her viewpoint again, and he finally, reluctantly, nodded. "Little Rock?" he asked her.

She nodded. "Cross my heart."

He cupped her jaw and leaned down to kiss her. He couldn't help that he kissed her like he'd never see her again—part of him felt that way.

And then he walked out of the cracker box room and off that bus without another word, afraid of what he might say if he opened his mouth.

Joe was still standing where he'd left him, his arms crossed as he watched a crowd gather around the doors of the hotel, hoping for a glimpse of Audrey. When he saw Jack, he grinned. "Told them she hadn't come out yet," he said.

"Good work. You might want to step inside and tell her not to come out now," he suggested. "I'll wait here."

Joe stepped onto the bus to do just that.

As Jack stood outside, waiting and watching the crowd, his thoughts rushing through his head, he noticed Rich standing off to one side, one foot braced against the wall, smoking a cigarette. He didn't know Rich smoked.

Come to think of it, of all the people on this tour, he knew the least about Rich, and wondered what other habits Rich had that might surprise him.

Twenty-eight

They arrived in Little Rock a whole lot sooner than Audrey thought would be possible, which distressed her to no end, for she still hadn't figured out how to extract herself from one overly attentive Lucas. The drive had been excruciating—he wouldn't leave her for a moment and was so solicitous of her that she wanted to scream.

They arrived at the Peabody Hotel about three that afternoon, and Lucas had already arranged to have a car waiting for them. He gave Bruno to a pouting Courtney, and opened the door for Audrey. From the corner of her eye, she could see Jack standing off to one side, watching them, along with a dozen or more people who had gathered, shouting out her name as Lucas helped her into the car.

"Why don't we just go inside?" Audrey asked.

Lucas started the car as he frowned at Audrey. "Are you kidding? There's no privacy in there. I told Courtney to get everyone booked in and get your room ready for you."

"I don't want to be gone long," Audrey said, feeling weird about this. "I've got some work to do—"

"You don't need to work. We've got two dozen people along for the ride to do all the work."

"I mean write songs—"

"Which reminds me," he said, looking very thoughtful as they pulled out of the big drive in front of the Peabody. "I talked to the label folks this afternoon. They're not exactly digging the new songs you sent them."

"What?" Audrey cried. "I love those songs!" It had been a battle with the record label from the moment she signed—they wanted more pop and she wanted more of her old songs.

"I know you do," he said, and gave her a reassuring smile. "And I told them, it's non-negotiable. But after some discussion, I think we can work a deal where we do a little more of what they are looking for and then you can add a couple of songs you like. I secured their agreement we would work this out so that everyone was happy."

"Thank God," Audrey said.

"So tell me," Lucas said casually, "do you think your lover could negotiate with the label on your behalf?"

She slowly turned and looked at him in disbelief, wondering if her label rep had really even called, or if Lucas had manufactured the crisis to make himself some sort of hero in her eyes.

He glanced at her. "Well?"

"I never once considered it," she said. "I thought I would do my own talking for a change."

"You'd be the only huge music star to do it, then," he scoffed. "You've got a business manager, a talent manager, and a personal manager. Don't you think you have them for a reason?"

"I know why I have them, Lucas," she said, although that was a partial lie. To avoid conflict, she had always just agreed when he argued they hire this person or that person. "But I am ready to take control of my own career."

Lucas suddenly turned into the parking lot of a large public park. "Is that why we are going through this right now?" he asked. "Because you are ready to take on more of the management of your career? If that's it, why didn't you just say so?"

"I *did*."

"No you didn't. You might have complained once or twice, but you never once approached me in all seriousness and asked for some management control."

"And neither did you ever approach *me* and ask for management control. You just took it."

"Like I said, if that is what's bothering you, let's fix it."

"It's not that easy."

"Come on, Audrey," he said with a sneer. "Don't throw everything we are away just because you got laid."

He was trying to humiliate her, and it was working. "*God*, Lucas," she said with disgust, and threw open the car door, got out, and began walking across the park. Lucas was quickly beside her, his hand on her arm. "Slow down."

"I don't want to slow down!"

"Audrey, come on. There are a lot of people in this park."

There were quite a lot of people in the park, a lot more than she would have thought, given that it was almost four on a very hot afternoon. She was instantly suspicious. "Did you plan this, Lucas?"

"Plan what?"

"*This*," she said, gesturing wildly at the park. "Are photographers going to leap out of the bushes and ambush us?"

"What are you talking about?" he demanded.

"You know what I am talking about," she said angrily, and walked on, seeking shade.

"Audrey," he said, stepping under the cypress tree where Audrey had sought refuge, "we are fighting about nothing, really. You know how much I love you, right?"

"That's one problem. I don't know if you really love me or my fame."

"Ohmigod. If you don't know it by now, I don't know how I can convince you. It's amazing to me that the last eight years of our life mean *nothing* to you! You never told me anything was wrong. I'm not a mind reader, so how could I know you were so unhappy?"

"How could you *not*?" she countered. "Every time I tried to speak to you about it, you would put me off, act like I was bothering you somehow. You love my career, Lucas. Not me."

"That's not true," he said, and it went downhill from there.

They argued for what seemed hours, Lucas reviewing everything he had ever done for her, Audrey growing more determined as he spoke. He *had* done quite a lot for her, it was true, but he almost made it sound as if she were incapable of having made it on her own. Or that without him, she would still be playing gin joints in Austin.

She tried to explain to him that she had begun to fall out of love with him at least two years ago and that, try as she might, she couldn't seem to get back the feelings she'd once had for him. She told him frankly that she was beginning to resent him more than she liked him.

Lucas seemed genuinely shocked by such admissions. And worse, he seemed genuinely wounded. "I never knew," he said, over and over again. "I never knew."

When it was obvious there was no resolution, and the heat was beginning to wear on her, Audrey asked that they return to the hotel. They walked in silence back to the rental car. Lucas started up the car, but instead of putting it into gear, he suddenly turned to Audrey. He looked tortured, his face twisted with pain. "I'll do whatever you want," he said, sounding almost desperate.

"No, don't—"

"You want a new manager?" he continued, undeterred. "*Done.* You want me to sleep in another room? *Done.* Just . . . just don't dump me, Audrey. I love you. I love you more than you can ever know, and *I can't lose you.*"

"Please don't do this," she pleaded with him.

"Don't beg you to stay with me?" he asked frantically, tears welling in his eyes. "Don't beg you to give me another chance? What am I supposed to do? I thought you were the woman I would spend the rest of my life with, and now I am suddenly out on my ass. Please don't do that to me. At least give me a chance to get on my feet—"

"I'm not going to kick you off the tour, if that is what you are worried about."

"I am talking about out of your *life*!" he cried. "Don't you understand?" he asked as tears began to slip from his eyes. "Without you, I am nothing! I know it's true! I know that without you, I would be playing second-rate clubs in Austin. But for the first time in my life, I have a chance! I have a chance to make something of myself, and if you drop me now, I will never make it. *Please*, Audrey. I will do whatever it takes. I will do anything you want," he said, and leaned over the console, sobbing.

"*Ohmigod*," she whispered, and put her hand to his head. "Oh, Lucas."

And just like that, her heart twisted around again. She didn't love him any longer and she would never be with him, but neither could she push him off the ledge. By the time the day breezes had begun to die down, and the bugs were coming out, Audrey felt no closer to resolution than before.

"Maybe," Lucas said, his eyes dry now, holding her hand, "maybe you can just finish out the tour without making a decision. You know, take some time for yourself to think things through. If that asshole really loves you, he'll wait for you. I know I will."

She felt exhausted. And hungry. Taking some time to think things through sounded like a wonderful idea at that moment.

"Maybe," he continued softly, "when the tour is over, we could take a little time, just us. You know, see if we can't find our way back."

"I don't think so."

He gave her hand an earnest squeeze. "I won't push you. But don't give up on me yet."

Audrey sighed and looked at her lap. She was weary to the bone. "Yeah," she whispered. All the feelings and wild emotions she'd experienced in the last week were beginning to congeal and harden, and they were sinking her. She wanted this over, wanted it to end, but she couldn't seem to shake the guilt or the idea that she really did owe Lucas something.

Lucas smiled tremulously. "Thank you."

By the time they returned to the hotel, she felt ill.

Jack was having a conversation with Ted in the hotel bar when he noticed Rich walk by, on his way out the lobby door. He was wearing a long black coat and black dingo boots. "I thought he'd gone back to L.A.," Ted said.

"Am I seeing things, or is he wearing eye makeup?" Jack asked.

Ted squinted after Rich, but shook his head. "Didn't see him, but I wouldn't be surprised," he said.

"Why's that?"

"He's just an odd duck. Bill—you know, our guy who hangs with the drivers? He went along to pick this guy up at the airport one afternoon. TSA had obviously been through his bag, because when Bill picked it up, the front came open. He said there was some weird shit inside."

Jack looked at Ted. "Like what?"

Ted laughed. "Like . . . *vampire* shit. Fangs and a cloak or something like that. He's into some kinky stuff."

It occurred to Jack that Rich was always going off somewhere alone. During the day, he was Mr. Business Manager, wearing a suit, smiling and joking with the guys . . . but how long had he been wearing makeup? And how long had he smoked? What else about Rich did they not know?

Fortunately, Audrey and Trystan were revamping a dance number, so when she and a dry-eyed Lucas returned to the hotel, she was able to escape Jack and go straight to rehearsal. Lucas looked like a forlorn little puppy as she hurried off, but she didn't care—she couldn't be around him at the moment, not with her emotions sitting like a brick inside her.

But neither did she want to run into Jack. She just wanted to be left alone for a little while so she could think.

That was the problem with her life. It seemed like she was always looking for a little alone time so she could just think. It was her holy grail, the one thing she was constantly seeking, and she wondered if she'd ever in her life been alone long enough to think on her own.

She'd gone from her parents' house to Austin, where she'd almost immediately taken up with a bass player. After that got stale, she hooked up with Lucas. She'd never really been alone for any significant amount of time in her life. She'd never had to solve her problems all by herself. There had always been someone there to help her.

It made her feel messed up, almost as bad as when Lucas made her take pills to help her sleep. She absently went through the dance routines, except that Trystan kept stopping the dance, asking if she needed a break or wanted to review a few steps. Apparently, she was off again today. When she finally called off rehearsal—the dancers were looking ragged, but she could have kept on all night, trying to get it right—Trystan invited her to join the group for a drink.

"Do you mean it?" she asked. They never asked her for a drink anymore, not since the tour started. Frankly, it had always seemed to her that they wanted to get away from her as soon as possible.

"Yeah, seriously," Trystan laughed, although Audrey could see a couple of the dancers behind him exchanging horrified looks.

"Okay," she said, smiling a little. "That would be really nice. But I can't stay long—I've got to work on a couple of songs."

The look of relief on the faces of the dancers was not lost on Audrey.

Man. How bad was she really?

They walked a couple of blocks to a pub. Trystan had his arm linked with Audrey's, and on her right was Bucky, tonight's assigned bodyguard. She ordered wine, and after half a glass, she began to wind down. The banter was fun, too, as the dancers reviewed the show in D.C., where one of them had almost danced right off the stage. Audrey laughed louder than anyone.

But as it was with her life these days, they hadn't been in the pub more than half an hour before people began to notice her, and a small crowd began to form near the bar. Bucky sat at a little two-top, alone, between Audrey and curious patrons, watching them watch Audrey.

She finally gave Trystan a rueful smile. "I guess I better go," she said.

"Don't let them chase you off. At least there aren't any paparazzi," Trystan said.

"Right . . . but I need to work, and this is only going to get worse."

"Want me to walk you back?"

"No, that's okay. Bucky will do it," she said, nodding in his direction. She thanked the group for letting her tag along, smiling at how surprised a couple of them seemed to be, and said good night. To Bucky, she said, "Ready to blow this joint?"

"Only if you are, Miss LaRue." He stood up, his large body between her and the crowd that was straining to get a good look at her. She didn't make it out without being asked to sign a couple of coasters and a hat, but they were nice people and very complimentary of her talent.

On the street, because it was dark, Bucky insisted they take a cab. Unfortunately, there were none to be had.

"They've got to have a cab around here," Bucky said, more to himself than to her, and pulled a cell phone out of his pocket. "I'll just give Jack a call—"

"No," Audrey said quickly. "There has to be a cab around here somewhere. Maybe on that street corner," she said, pointing to the intersection, where traffic seemed heavier than the street on which they were standing.

"Okay," Bucky said congenially. "Let's walk down there."

"If you don't mind," Audrey said, "will you walk down there? I've got these heels."

Bucky looked at her feet and winced, then looked at the thirty feet it would take him to get to the corner. "Okay," he said. "But promise me you will stay put."

"I promise."

With another look at the intersection, Bucky jogged down the street.

It was just a moment of privacy, a single moment that Audrey was alone, and she relished it—until a man walking by knocked into her as he hurried across the street. He knocked into her with such force that she was shoved up against the brick wall of the corner of the pub. "*Slut*," he said beneath his breath as Audrey caught herself.

She jerked around—but the man had jogged across the street and into a dark doorway.

Was she just being paranoid, or was there something uncomfortably familiar about him? He had stark blond hair, and while she couldn't think of anyone she knew that was towheaded, she still had the feeling she knew him from somewhere.

"You all right?"

Startled, Audrey gasped when Bucky put his hand on her shoulder, jumping a foot in her skin.

"Hey, I'm sorry. I didn't mean to startle you," he said with a look of concern. "But you look a little spooked."

"It's nothing," she said, looking back across the street. "Some guy just bumped into me."

Bucky instantly turned in the direction she was looking.

"He's gone," Audrey said. "Let's just get out of here, okay?"

"You bet. I've got a cab," he said, and with his hand on her elbow, he moved her quickly down the street to the waiting cab.

At the hotel, Audrey moved through the lobby without looking left or right, Bucky close on her heels. He saw her up to her suite, walked in first, as all the security guys did now. Someone had left Bruno inside, and he came bounding forward, happy to see her. When Bucky was convinced no one was lurking in a closet, he leaned down to pet Bruno. "All clear. Good night, Miss LaRue."

"Good night, Bucky," she said, and locked the door behind him. She turned around, leaned her back against the door, and looked around the sumptuous suite. It was just like all the other sumptuous suites she'd stayed in since the tour began—they tended to run together—but this one was vastly different in one respect. In this one, she was blissfully and completely alone. "It's just you and me, kid," she said to Bruno. He wagged the nub of his docked tail with delight.

For the first time in what seemed like years, Audrey had total privacy. There were no band members jamming with Lucas, no Courtney, no hair or makeup people or dancers or managers of any sort.

And she relished it. She took a long bubble bath and paraded around the suite completely naked. She ordered in—steak, potatoes, and bottle of wine—and there was no one there to comment. She took Bruno out to a little patch of grass. She ignored her cell phone, which seemed to ring every fifteen minutes. She watched TV, laughing with delight at some of the programs, rolling her eyes at others and trying to remember the last time she'd had the luxury of time to catch a movie or a mindless TV show. Good God, it was like she'd been living in a tent in some foreign desert.

She was wearing a plush house robe and flipping channels when someone knocked lightly on her door around two in the morning. Bruno instantly leapt from the bed, barking frantically at the door. She thought a knock at this hour was strange and hesitated—she couldn't bear to face Lucas and another discussion. But she really didn't want her cell phone going off all night, either, so she reluctantly got up and padded to the door, stood up on tiptoe, and looked out the peephole.

There was no one there.

She slid back down to her feet, her brow wrinkled in a frown, a little perplexed. Who would knock on the door? Some of the band coming in for the night, just having a little fun? Or maybe the housekeeping staff? It was very strange—she impulsively pressed her ear against the door, but couldn't hear anything.

There was a slight flutter in her stomach as she put her hand to the deadbolt and opened the door the little space the chain lock would allow.

Thankfully, no one was outside her door. She quickly shut the door and slid the chain out and opened the door again, only wider. She peeked out—first one way, and then the other. Nothing. She looked down for Bruno and saw him sniffing a small wrapped package, his docked tail wagging maniacally.

On the top of the package was her name, pasted across the top. She recognized the script at once. Her heart skipped a beat or two. "Bruno, come here!" she said, and bent down to get him.

That was when she heard it. She stilled, straining to hear.

The box was ticking.

Twenty-nine

Jack answered his cell on the second ring. "Yeah," he muttered into the phone, not entirely awake.

"Jack!"

His eyes flew open at the sound of Audrey's voice. He'd been waiting for her to call, waiting for her to say everything that he privately felt desperate to hear. But she was crying, her words unintelligible. "What is it?" he demanded. "What's wrong?"

"*Bomb!*" she shrieked.

He swung his legs over the side of the bed. "Where are you?" he demanded.

"In the bathroom."

"Stay there until I call you," he said, clicked off, and grabbed his jeans.

He found Joe at the end of the hallway of the floor the tour occupied, right where he was supposed to be, watching a video on his iPod. "See anything unusual?" Jack asked as he motioned for Joe to follow him.

"Nothing," Joe said. "Why?"

"Someone left a package outside Audrey's door."

"You're kidding," Joe said flatly. "No one's been by here except the band and a couple of dancers."

"Anyone else?" Jack asked as they strode down the hall.

"The business manager and a couple of room-service types."

"What about the stairway?" Jack asked.

"I can see it from here. No one has been in or out of it all night," he said as they strode down the hall.

They halted at Audrey's door. The package was small and tucked inside the recess. Anyone could have left it there.

"*Shit*," Joe uttered.

"Call the police," Jack said, and as Joe stepped away to do that, he squatted down to check it out. There were no markings on it other than her name. He could hear the ticking, too. It sounded like a kitchen timer.

As Joe called hotel security and the police, Jack called Audrey on her cell and had her open the door for him.

Her face was puffy and red, and she was clutching Bruno so tightly the dog looked like his eyes were about to pop out of their sockets. Jack stepped across the threshold, saw the wild look in her eye, and ran his hand down her arm. "You're safe," he said, and picked up her guitar. "But let's get you out of here."

"It's really a bomb?"

"I don't think so," he said. "But we don't want to take any chances. "You have some clothes you can put on?"

She nodded dumbly and, without thinking, dropped Bruno and ran to the bathroom.

She emerged a few minutes later, understandably distracted, dressed in a T-shirt and jeans. She grabbed up her purse at the same moment she slipped on some shoes. "Bruno! Where's Bruno?"

The dog scurried out from under the bed and allowed Audrey to scoop him up and put him in her purse.

"Okay," she said. Jack extended his hand, and Audrey slipped hers into it. With a firm grip of her hand, Jack led her out, taking great care to step over the package. She clung to him as they made their way down the hallway.

Fortunately, the hotel management, recognizing the threat of a public relations disaster, was quick to react. They put Audrey on another floor. Jack escorted her to the room and stayed around when the Little Rock Police arrived to question her.

No, she didn't know anyone who wanted to harm her. No, she didn't know who'd left it.

"Can you think of anyone who might have left a gift?" one of the detectives asked.

"No."

"Boyfriend? Everything okay there?"

Audrey colored slightly and avoided Jack's gaze. "No . . . but Lucas wouldn't do that."

"Lucas? Who's Lucas?"

"My . . . my boyfriend, I guess you could call him," Audrey said as she wrapped her arms around her body. "We've been having some problems."

"Oh yeah?" the detective asked casually. "What kind of problems?"

From where Jack was standing, it looked as if Audrey colored even more. "The usual kind," she said.

"Since when?"

"Since a while. But he wouldn't do this. He's been giving me gifts, not bombs."

Jack wasn't surprised.

"So what is the nature of your problems?" the detective asked.

"What difference does it make?" Audrey asked irritably. "It's not him."

"Miss LaRue, you never know what can set a person off."

She groaned and covered her face with her hands a moment. "Falling out of love," she mumbled.

"You or him?" the detective asked.

"*Me.*"

"Is there someone else?"

"That is a very personal question," she said, glaring at the detective.

"Just covering all the bases," he said congenially. "I'm going to take that as a yes."

"*No*," Audrey said quickly, and lifted her head, looking right at the detective. "There is no one else."

Jack swallowed down the nudge his heart gave him in response to her answer. Of course she wouldn't own up to their affair. Not now. But deep inside, he wished she had.

"Let's see if we can't round up Lucas," the detective suggested, and looked at Jack. "Can you find him for us?"

Audrey didn't look at him, but drew her bottom lip between her teeth as she concentrated on her hands in her lap. "Yeah," Jack drawled, his gaze steady on Audrey. "I can find him." He turned and walked out of the room.

He could tell these local cops that it wasn't Lucas who wanted her dead. But he had a funny suspicion about Rich, and thought he might have a little chat with him by himself.

The box was not a bomb, but another letter wrapped around a little travel clock telling Audrey that next time, it would be for real. The clock, Jack and the detective thought, looked new.

"Any place you can buy these around here?" Jack asked idly.

"Not too far. A quick cab ride from here," the detective said, and looked at Jack. "Want to ride with?"

"Yep," Jack said.

On the way to the pharmacy, Jack put in a call to Michael.

"Yo," Michael said when he answered the phone. "It's Bob the Bodyguard. What's up?"

"Can you run a quick check on someone for me?"

"Sure," Michael said. "Friend or foe?"

"Don't know." He gave Michael the details and told him a little about what was going on.

"Damn," Michael said low. "And here I thought you were just having a grand old time. You and Hotpants are still dancing to the beat, right?"

"I'd appreciate it if you could get back to me as soon as you can," Jack said, and hung up.

The detective raised a curious brow. "What you got?"

Jack shrugged a little. "Not much, really. A hunch."

"Hunches are good," the detective said. "Talk to me."

Jack talked, laying out why he thought Rich needed an extra look.

The pharmacy did have a surveillance tape, which they handed over to the police. And Michael called back with some interesting news of his own. "Richard Later had a little run-in with the law about fifteen years ago," he said. "He was stalking an old girlfriend. She said he wrote her some nasty letters, although it appears the actual letters are missing from the file."

"That's interesting."

"What's interesting is that he caught up to her one night, talked her into coming over to his place, then got all weird on her. He was wearing a vampire outfit and tried to bite her."

"No shit?" Jack asked.

"No shit."

"Huh," Jack said, thinking. "Wonder why that didn't show up on the background checks we ran on everyone at the beginning of the tour?"

"Because his girlfriend refused to press charges. She didn't like it, but didn't think he needed to go to jail for it. He moved from Chicago to L.A. after that."

"I think we have our guy," Jack said. "It will take a little more to make a case, I suspect, but he's our man."

"Stick close to your girl," Michael said. "I'd hate for her to get bit." He laughed at his own joke.

They talked a little longer about work, but when Michael started nosing around about Audrey, Jack cut the conversation short. "Gotta go, pal," he said. "We've got a show tonight."

"Spoilsport," Michael groused as Jack hung up.

Jack called Audrey just as she'd managed to convince everyone that they could leave her alone. Lucas was especially resistant, but when Audrey threw a fit, he made his way to her door. "You're being foolish," he said, pointing a finger at her. "This is not me directing your life, this is just telling you what is."

"Go tell someone else what *is*," she said irritably. "It wasn't a bomb, they have a good lead, and I don't need to be watched like a toddler, okay? So please go."

Lucas went. She hadn't even locked the door behind him when her cell rang.

"I need to talk to you," Jack said without preamble when Audrey answered.

"*Now?*" She was drained and felt completely off-kilter.

He paused, and she wanted to kick herself for sounding so reluctant to see him. "I had hoped now. You've got a couple of hours before you need to be at the amphitheater."

"I know, but . . . okay," she said, giving in.

"I'm coming over."

Audrey threw the phone on the bed. It had been a very trying day—what she did not need right now was someone else telling her what to do. She just wanted to get to the amphitheater and do her show and then get the hell out of Little Rock.

Moments later, she heard his knock on her door, and Bruno began his hysterical barking.

Audrey marched to the door and looked through the peephole; Jack was standing on the other side, one arm propped against the jamb, looking very impatient. She threw the door open and glared at him.

"Uh-uh," he said, waving a finger at her. "Not that look."

"*What* look?"

"The aggravated look," he said as he walked in and shook the door from her grip, letting it slam closed. "The *diva* look."

"I don't have a *diva* look," she said. "I'm just exhausted."

"Oh yes you do," he said, and put his hand on her waist. "Not a good idea when I'm in this kind of mood."

"What kind of mood?" she asked, confused.

"*This* mood," he said, and yanked her into his chest and kissed her with the same sort of longing Audrey had felt for him the last few days. She wished for all the world she could just sink into him and forget about everything else, pretend that life beyond that door didn't exist.

Unfortunately, it did exist. He lifted his head, tweaked her nose. "What's the matter?"

"What's the *matter*? I've been a little busy being interrogated," she said, catching a breath as he tweaked her nipple through the fabric of her shirt. "And stalked. And oh yeah, someone left a bomb at my door. And I haven't slept."

"It wasn't a bomb."

"If it looks like a duck and quacks like a duck . . ."

"Okay," he said, "you've had a rough day. But I've got an idea to make it a whole lot better."

"Does it involve Ben and Jerry's Ice Cream?" she asked.

He laughed. "It could. Are you alone?"

"No. *You're* here." *Thank God.*

He smiled again. "Smart ass," he said, and lowered his head to hers again at the same moment he swept her into his arms and carried her across the room. He tossed her onto the king-sized bed and leapt on after her, breaking his fall with his arms on either side of her. When Bruno jumped up to join them, Jack pushed him off again. "Not now, Bruno. You have her all the time."

In spite of her promises, in spite of the many confused feelings she'd been having lately, Audrey could not resist his touch. She hadn't even realized how badly she wanted him until the moment he touched her.

He wrapped one leg over both of hers, then slid his hand up her ribcage and down again. "I tried to call you."

"Like I said . . . I was a little preoccupied."

He moved his hand to the waist of her jeans and flicked open the button. "Girl, you don't even know what preoccupied means," he said, and unzipped her pants. He slipped his hand inside, sliding his fingers between her legs. Audrey sighed with pleasure as he began to massage her. Jack covered her shirt and breast with his mouth, teasing her with his teeth.

Everything flew out of her head—her promise to Lucas, the bomb scare, her show. Somehow, Jack could push the entire world out of her room so that it was just the two of them. She felt incapable of anything when he touched her and she let herself go, falling headlong into the moment. She moved so that he could pull her pants from her body and push her legs apart and press his mouth to her panties.

It was incredibly sexy—she was soon sliding down the slope to fulfillment. He suddenly rolled onto his back, pulling her with him so she was on top. "Take my jeans off."

Audrey smiled pertly and undid the button of his jeans, then unzipped the fabric that strained over his erection and, with his help, pushed them down his hips. Audrey straddled him, rubbing against his erection.

"Take off your shirt," he said low, and greedily eyed her body when she did.

"And the bra."

Still rubbing against him, she reached behind her and unfastened the bra. Jack grabbed it and pulled it off her before surging up and taking her in his arms to kiss her. One hand slipped between their bodies and began to stroke her. "Can you guess how many times I have thought about this in the last forty-eight hours?" he asked softly.

"As many times as I've thought of you?" she responded as she pushed her hands through his hair. He groaned and took her breast into his mouth. She sighed with pleasure, let her head drop back, reveling in his touch.

He grabbed her by her hips and lifted her up, closing his eyes as she slid down his body, burying him deep inside her, moaning as she began to move on him.

Jack leaned back and took her breasts in his hands, his eyes closed as he enjoyed the way she moved on him. She braced her hands against his chest to move faster, feeling the pressure building within her body.

Jack suddenly surged up again; Audrey squealed with surprise when he rolled them over so that she was on her back. He grinned, buried his face in her belly for a moment, then flipped her over, onto her stomach. He slipped his hand under her abdomen and lifted her up, so that she was on all fours, and leaned over her, his mouth on her shoulder, one hand on her breast, the other sliding down between her legs.

"I've been going crazy thinking of you," he said. "I can't sleep, I can't eat . . . I count the minutes until I can be with you again, just like this," he said as he moved between her legs. He kissed the back of her neck, massaged her with his hand. Audrey was breathing raggedly now, wanting him inside her, pushing against him and grinding her body against his hand.

Jack drew a line with the tip of his tongue down her spine as he spread her thighs with his. He guided himself into her, slipping in slowly, groaning with the exertion of holding himself back to be gentle.

"No," Audrey moaned, pushing back against him. "Don't be easy, I don't want easy. I want you to *fuck* me."

A growl of approval escaped Jack and he pushed hard inside her, causing Audrey to cry out with pleasure. She dropped her head and began to match his rhythm, pushing back against him with as much force as he slid into her. Her back arched; she indulged the lustful desire that was roaring through her veins, feeling her body pitch toward an explosive release.

The stroking of his body was as frantic as the stroking of his hand. She moved wildly against him, moved with animalistic abandon, her body burning in every place they touched. He put his hand at her nape and urged her to bend down, then bent over her, his mouth in her hair and on her neck, his fingers moving magically against her flesh. "You make me hot as hell," he said hoarsely. "God, how I've wanted you like this."

Audrey panted, building to a release, all but sobbing with pleasure and bucking wildly as her body erupted. She cried out with the strength of it, and was followed a moment later by Jack as he thrust into her once more.

With his forehead on her shoulder, he snaked his hand around her waist, anchoring her to him as they both fought to catch their breath, and rolled them onto their sides. His breath was in her hair and on her skin as he pulled her to him.

Audrey closed her eyes and dreamily relived it all, her life held at bay.

But then Jack stirred and kissed her shoulder and pushed her hair back. "I love you, you know," he said, his voice low and hoarse with emotion. "I've never loved a woman like I love you."

Audrey opened her eyes; reality came flooding back in, carrying with it her feelings, scattered into a million unrecognizable pieces, and taking the fog from her brain. "I . . . I love you, too."

His hand stilled from stroking her belly. "A little more conviction would be nice."

"I, ah . . . I guess I was thinking about the show," Audrey said, and moved away from him. His hand slid away from her body as she moved; her skin felt cold where he no longer touched her.

"Wow. That's romantic," Jack said, sounding wounded.

"Sorry. I didn't mean that like it sounded," Audrey said as she slipped off the bed and picked up her pants and pulled them on. Honestly, she didn't know how she meant it.

Jack propped himself up on his elbow, watching her. "What's going on?" he asked quietly.

"Nothing," she said, but she realized that she couldn't seem to look at him.

"*Nothing?* We just made love. And here I am assuming that after yesterday, we're in a better place. Aren't we?"

"Sure," she said. She stole a glimpse of him, saw the look of utter disbelief on his face. "Not exactly," she admitted. "It didn't go as I'd hoped."

"Wait . . . *what*?" he asked, scrambling off the bed and grabbing his jeans.

"I can't do it, Jack," she said, throwing her arms wide. "I have tried every which way, and I can't seem to break his hold over me."

"How can you say that?" he exclaimed. "It's not like he has you in chains."

"Not physically," she said. "But emotionally. I have all this guilt and he . . . he's begged me to consider the impact of this on him."

"The impact on *him*?" Jack echoed angrily. He thrust one leg into his boxers and jeans. "No one likes to lose, I get that—but he's holding you hostage."

"Jack, please try and understand." She was so weary of begging everyone to understand her. "I don't hate Lucas like you do. I feel a certain responsibility toward him, and he is *begging* me—"

"Of course he is," Jack snapped. "He'll try everything he's got to keep you, but not for the reasons you think."

"I know the reasons," she said irritably. "I am not a naïve child. You're right; he needs me for his career right now. But I know him better than you, and I know that he just *needs* me to make this transition."

"Oh for God's sake," Jack said as he thrust his second leg into the jeans. "Not a week ago, the asshole couldn't give you the time of day, and if he did, it was to tell you how to run your life. And now suddenly he cares about you?"

"Jack—"

"No, Audrey, no *Jack* this time. You and I have something really amazing, and you know it. I didn't want it to happen like this any more than you did, but now that it has, I can't live off the grid, waiting for the one moment in your day you have to spare for me."

"That's not fair! I'm on tour!"

"And since you and I made that amazing connection, you have spent more time holding Bonner's hand than seeing me."

Audrey whirled away from him, feeling her insides begin to knot again. "This is not easy, Jack! Do you understand that? I didn't set out to hurt Lucas, and I don't find it so easy to just tell him to get lost after all these years! I can't even remember a time I was even on my own. And there is my business to consider . . ."

"I'm not suggesting I take his place in your business—is that what you think? Is he trying to convince you that I want to *manage* you?"

"No!" she said as she struggled into her bra. "But that's something I have to consider! I am too busy to manage my career and I need someone to do it."

"*Bonner?*"

"No, no, no! I'm just confused about a lot of things right now."

"Oh God—"

She suddenly whirled around and grabbed his face between her hands. "Jack, listen to me. Someone would like to see me blown to bits, Lucas can't handle the change in our relationship, I am on a tour with three dates just added, I have to be in the studio by October, and I *love* you, Jack, I *do*, but I need to figure some things out."

There. She'd said it. She'd said what had been rumbling around inside her the last twenty-four hours, making her ill with anxiety. The pain in Jack's eyes was difficult to bear, but she had to say what was true.

"Okay," he said, curling his fingers around her wrist, "I get it." He pulled one hand from his face. "I understand," he said softly as he pulled the other from his face.

She'd said what she needed to say, but now she panicked. She didn't want to *lose* Jack. "No, you don't *get it*; I can tell you don't *get* it. I hit so high so fast, that I got lost in the spotlight. I have endorsements I don't even know about, I have product lines for products I don't use,

I've signed with a major label but they don't like my songs. I am surrounded by people I can't trust, and I don't know who I am anymore!"

His jaw clenched, but his eyes moved over her face as if he really was trying to understand it.

"I'm not saying that I don't want to be with you, but only that I need a little time to think through some things."

"What is a little time?"

Audrey blinked. She had no idea. A day? A month? A lifetime? "I . . . I don't know," she stammered.

He looked stunned. He nodded dumbly as he buttoned his shirt.

"Say something!" Audrey begged him.

"I can't say I understand," he said slowly, tucking the shirt into his jeans. "But if you want time to think, I'm not going to stop you. And I won't lay a guilt trip on you." He looked up again, his blue eyes swimming with hurt. "Take all the time you need." He moved for the door, pausing to slip his feet into the sandals he'd worn.

"*Jack*," Audrey said as he reached the door.

He turned partially and smiled thinly. "Don't worry about it," he said, and walked out the door.

She'd wanted alone? She just got it.

Thirty

Jack moved through the rest of the day feeling almost as if his spirit had been left in that hotel room.

He went through the motions of security, but left the heavy lifting to Ted.

What really sucked was that Jack was so taken aback by how deeply Audrey's decision had wounded him. It was as if he and Audrey had spent years together instead of a few weeks—the hurt felt just as deep.

But he loved her, and that, too, went remarkably deep. Part of him felt as if he would die without her. Another part of him felt like a colossal schmuck for having fallen in love with her to begin with.

He should have trusted his initial instincts; he should have stayed the hell away from her.

They had only two weeks left on the tour, and as far as Jack was concerned, that was two weeks too long. He had to distance himself from her. He couldn't be around her and not be with her. He had to find the space where he could be himself, and not some damn dog moping around the door, wanting to be let in.

Just before show time, Jack assembled his security team and made some changes: Ted would be Audrey's go-to guy. Jack would focus on other aspects, such as the loading and unloading of equipment. The rest of their team—five in all—would rotate through the various points of their security just as they'd been doing all along.

"You sure about this?" Ted asked, squinting curiously at Jack. "She's not going to like it."

"I have my reasons," he said.

"Okay, boss," Ted said with a shrug. "Whatever you say."

Yeah, whatever he said. Jack left them to it, and took his new place for the show, as far from the stage as he could get. Tonight, when Audrey looked to the stage wings for him, she wouldn't see him, she'd see Ted.

The show proved to be excruciatingly painful, even at a distance. Jack could not hear Audrey's voice and not feel the desire bubbling up. He could not listen to the lyrics she'd written and not be moved. And perhaps it was his imagination, but he was fairly certain she had turned up the performance a notch. She seemed to sparkle more than usual, her dancing crisper, her music outstanding.

Talk about kicking a man when he was down.

When the show was over, he didn't go to the party room like he normally did. He left that to Ted and went instead to the buses and trucks, which would leave for Dallas at 4 a.m., just as soon as the set was broken. Along with the stage manager, Jack watched carefully as every bit of equipment was broken down and loaded.

One of the stagehands appeared with Bruno. With a sigh, Jack took the furry football and freed the stagehand from dog duty. With Bruno on a leash that stretched miles, Jack walked around the back of the buses, where he paused so Bruno could take care of business.

Something caught his eye. There was a man standing on the loading dock, in the shadows. Jack walked around and in between two buses, so that he could move closer to the loading dock without being detected. When he got closer, and could see the dock again, he started a little.

The man hovering about was Rich, wearing a long dark coat, one hand holding a lit cigarette, the other hand deep in a pocket of the coat. Over his shoulder was a small black gym bag. He stood back, as if he meant to be in the shadows, watching the loading.

He was waiting, Jack thought. *Waiting for Audrey.*

Jack stepped back, deeper into the shadows himself, but where he could still see Rich. He watched him as the roadies loaded, and when they went back inside the amphitheater, Rich moved. With a furtive look around, he walked to the first bus, Audrey's bus, and boarded.

Jack quickly followed, tethering Bruno to the bus's sideview mirror. He stood outside, waiting in the shadows. A few moments later, Rich reappeared and stepped off the bus and Bruno, bless him, went berserk. He had no idea that tiny dog could turn so ferocious.

It startled Rich; Jack stepped in front of him. "What's up?" Jack asked casually.

Rich gasped and quickly dropped his head so that Jack wouldn't see the makeup he was wearing. It was too late—Jack had seen the garish stuff around his eyes and mouth and the inexplicable dusting of white powder on his face.

"I was just putting some stuff on the bus," Rich said. "What's up?"

"You know the rules—no bags go on the bus until we're here to see it. It's a security measure."

Rich shrugged and looked down the lane between the buses. "I forgot."

"So what did you put on the bus?" Jack asked.

Rich looked at him from the corner of his eye. "A bag," he said. "That's all. It's hardly a security breach."

"You're probably right. But let's just have a look to make sure," he said, and grabbed Rich by the arm. "Why don't you show me what's so special about this bag that you had to load it yourself?"

"What the hell are you doing?" Rich cried, trying to yank his arm free as Bruno went for his ankles. "Get your fucking hands off me!"

Jack pushed him up the stairs of the bus. Bruno's frantic barking increased.

"The police questioned me and let me go—you have no *right*," Rich shouted, struggling against him. But he was a smaller man, and his strength was no match for Jack's. "Take your hands off me or I will kill you!"

"Before or after you kill Audrey?" Jack asked, and shoved Rich inside. "Where is it?"

"You're insane," Rich said, rubbing his arm where Jack had held him.

"I'll ask nicely once, and then I will crack your head open. Where the hell is it?"

With a roar, Rich lunged for him, but Jack had choreographed more fights than Rich had ever seen, and easily caught him, turned him around, and threw him down on the couch. He twisted one arm behind Rich's back and pressed his knee into the elbow. Rich howled with pain just as Ted bounded on the bus, alarmed by Bruno's frantic barking.

"What the hell?" Ted said, and moved to help Jack.

Jack found the bag Rich had hidden in a floorboard compartment beneath the carpet. He dropped it in front of Rich and unzipped it and proceeded to withdraw a gun, a weird pair of fangs, a blond wig, and a small bag containing the makeup Rich was wearing. There was also a laptop computer, an envelope addressed to Audrey in the same script as had been taped to the fake bomb, and a vial of something red and thick.

Jack looked at Rich and held up the vial. "What are you, a vampire?"

"I will have you arrested for this," Rich snarled.

"Twisted, man," Bucky said, shaking his head at the contents of Rich's bag.

"You people have no idea how much trouble you're in," Rich said angrily.

"Well, you can tell the cops all about it when they get here, which should be any minute now," Jack said, and pushed Rich down on the couch to wait it out.

Two hours later, Rich, who was as meticulous with organizing his threatening letters as he was with Audrey's finances, was on his way to the Little Rock jail. Jack left Ted in charge of making sure everyone got on a bus for Dallas, scooped up Bruno, and went in search of Audrey.

He was exhausted, having slept very little in the last twenty-four hours, and needless to say, his emotions had been through a roller coaster. He was drained of life, running on pure adrenaline. But he knew what he had to do.

Audrey knew something was up when she saw Jack striding down the corridor, holding a panting Bruno like a football. She was still reeling from the news that her business manager was the one behind the threats, that Rich, who had been taking her very generous pay for his services, was plotting to kill her at the same time.

It was almost more than she could absorb. "*Vampire?*" she'd echoed with disbelief when Detective Ruiz told her about Rich. "What do you mean, *vampire?*"

"I mean the dude is kinky," the detective said with a shrug. "But I think he's probably harmless. He's the sort to like the drama and the world of make-believe, but he doesn't have the guts to carry out any fantasy. In other words, he's not quite in touch with reality."

"How is this possible?" she asked Lucas. "I had no idea he was so obsessed with me. Didn't we check this guy out?" she asked Lucas.

"Of course we did," Lucas said, taking her hand and squeezing it. "But we didn't ask him if he had a vampire fetish."

"Not to worry, Miss LaRue. The guy won't be bothering you again."

Audrey hardly heard another word the man said about arraignment and bail and so forth. She was in shock. But Lucas listened, nodding and speaking for her.

She couldn't stop thinking that she didn't really know Rich. She had entrusted some very important matters to a man she really didn't even know. Honestly, she could count on one hand the number of conversations they'd had. It was absurd—how could she not have *known* him?

Worse yet, now she had a business that no longer had a manager and she didn't know her business any better than she apparently knew Rich.

When Lucas had left her in the dressing room to go and gather his gear, that's all she could think about. How could you be with someone day in and day out and not know them? How could you come so far without really knowing yourself?

When she saw Jack at her door, her stomach flipped. She knew instinctively what was behind his stoic expression . . . perhaps because she felt the same thing so keenly in herself.

"Can we talk?" he asked quietly.

She couldn't speak. But she nodded. Jack stepped inside, quietly closed the door behind him, and put Bruno down.

Audrey folded her arms defensively across her middle. "It was Rich," she said, her voice cracking. "*Rich!* I can't believe it—what did I ever do to him?"

"You didn't do anything. He's a sick puppy, that's all."

"Detective Ruiz told me that you were the one who figured it out and that you caught him."

Jack shrugged and glanced down. "You can relax for the remainder of the tour. You're safe now."

"Because you'll be there."

He didn't speak, did not rush to assure her he'd be there, that he'd always be there. He glanced up and held her gaze, and Audrey felt a larger piece inside of her crumble.

"What's going on?" she forced herself to ask.

"I'm leaving the tour," he said softly.

Now everything in her crumbled like a sand house. Her knees buckled and she sank onto a chair, gaping at him. "*Why?*"

"The real threat is gone now. You don't need me anymore."

"Of *course* I need you. I have two weeks left on the tour and I can't do it without security."

He smiled wryly. "Not exactly the reason I hoped you'd want me here, but then again, not much is as I'd hoped."

"Jack . . . you know what I mean. Of course I don't want you to go. I love you."

"But you need time. An indefinite amount of time."

She couldn't refute it.

"And I need space. I can't walk around here watching you and hearing you and not be with you. I've just never been very good at waiting in the wings."

"Can't you try and wait this out? I would wait it out for you. I would try and understand where you were coming from and wait it out," she insisted, while a voice inside her argued she would not wait.

"It's not the same thing—it seems like I'm waiting to find out who you'll ultimately choose. You'd be waiting for me to finish a job."

Her heart twisted, and Audrey sucked in a sharp breath. She hadn't realized it would hurt as much as this. She suddenly stood and went to him, placing her hand against his chest. She looked up into his eyes and her heart twisted harder. "Why can't this be easy?" she whispered.

He covered her hand with his and pressed it against his heart. "I wish I knew," he said, and leaned down to kiss her cheek. "I love you, sweet cheeks," he said low. "I love you more than I can say."

"I love you, too," she said. "But I don't know how to get to you."

He put his arm around her and rubbed her back soothingly for a moment. But then he let go and reached into his chest pocket and withdrew a card. "If you ever figure it out, you can find me here," he said, and gave her the card. "Be good, sweet cheeks."

"Jack—"

He stopped her with two fingers to her chin. He touched his lips to hers, then let his hand drift away. He opened the door at his back and stepped out, letting it close behind him.

On the other side of the door, Audrey's legs buckled at last, and she sank to her knees, bracing her hands on the carpet as grief racked her body.

AUDREY AND LUCAS: SPLITSVILLE!

(*Celebrity Insider Magazine*) Reps won't comment, but Audrey LaRue and Lucas Bonner are on the skids, according to a source. "There was a definite and visible strain between them at a Dallas hotel," the source says. Personnel associated with LaRue's *Frantic* tour say the split has been in the making for some time.

CELEBRITY BUSINESS MANAGER ARRESTED FOR TERRORISTIC THREATS

(*Arkansas Times, Little Rock*) The business manager for Audrey LaRue, singing sensation and pop star, was arrested Friday for making terroristic threats to Ms. LaRue. According to police, Richard Later, 42, has a history of stalking and menacing behavior against former girlfriends. LaRue could not be reached for comment.

Thirty-one

Jack had been back in L.A. for two weeks before he allowed the other TA guys to talk him into a night on the town.

"Think about it, man," Cooper drawled into the phone. "Women. Beer. And the best company a guy could ask for."

Jack debated it. In truth, he was tired of holing up at the hangar. When the weather wasn't clear, he worked on his plane. But when it was, he went flying, soaring high above the earth all by himself, into his little piece of the universe. It was the only place he was at peace. It was also the only place he could escape news about Audrey.

Shortly after he'd arrived back in L.A., the news broke about her former business manager, and her face, her beautiful smiling face, was plastered on every paper and TV tabloid in town.

"The usual place?" he asked Cooper.

"Yep," Coop said, and Jack could envision his buoyant smile. "The bar on Franklin Ave. We've been saving you a seat."

"See you there," Jack said, and hung up. And for the first time in a couple of weeks, he smiled.

Not only were the guys waiting for him, but so were their significant others. Marnie and Leah, Eli and Michael's partners, respectively, threw their arms around him at the same time. "Jack, you poor thing," Marnie said, pulling him to sit beside her.

"God, Marnie, don't say *that*," Leah cried.

"Why? What's wrong with me?" Jack asked.

Leah's eyes narrowed menacingly on Marnie. "*See?*"

"Nothing," Marnie said, ignoring Leah as she caressed Jack's shoulder. "We just really missed you, that's all."

Jack looked across the table at Michael and Eli, who were looking uncharacteristically sheepish. Cooper smiled a little, and his girlfriend, Jill, looked at Jack as if she'd never seen him before.

"What?" Jack demanded. "Why are you all looking at me like that?"

"So hey," Michael said, sitting up. "Did you catch that game your brother Parker played Monday night?" he asked, smoothly changing the subject.

"Yeah," Jack said, and grinned. "I taught him how to play ball, you know."

"Oh no, here we go," Cooper said with a playful groan. "Before the evening is out, he will have taught Eli how to rope a steer and me how to surf a wind."

"Don't deny it, Coop. You would be fish food right now if it wasn't for me," Jack said, and they were suddenly arguing about who had taught whom what, just like old times.

Jack thoroughly enjoyed the evening and even wondered aloud why he hadn't been out before now. He was beginning to believe he could put the summer behind him and move on with his life. After a few beers, he was talking about his flight school and how he'd figured out how to open it without the windfall of the tour.

No one questioned him about the tour; the guys nodded and added their two cents while the women chatted across them about sales and shoes, or something like that.

It was a comfortable, familiar evening, and Jack felt as good as he'd felt since he left Little Rock.

He felt good until he got home later and made himself a sandwich. He kicked back in front of the TV, was flipping channels, and landed on *Inside Edition*, a celebrity news show. He paused there—it was always good for a laugh, because he knew so many people who showed up on the half-hour broadcast.

But he was not prepared to see Audrey. Not a minute into the broadcast, they flashed a publicity picture of her up on the screen. The picture was followed by footage of her and Bonner walking out of a club on Sunset.

The anchor was saying something about her being in L.A. after the conclusion of a very successful national tour, and that there was some talk of her doing a tour in Europe.

Europe.

Jack clicked off the TV and put aside his uneaten sandwich, his appetite gone. He supposed a part of him still harbored a hope for Audrey. But that hope was effectively crushed by the footage of her with Bonner and the knowledge that she was on her way to Europe.

He turned off the lights and sat in the dark for God knew how long.

It had been so long since Audrey had actually driven herself anywhere that she could not remember when or where. At least Bruno liked it—he was stretched out as long as his body would go, trying to see out the window on their drive out to Orange County.

Fortunately for California drivers, Audrey found the airfield easily enough. It was Jack she couldn't seem to find. She drove through the hangars at least three times with no luck. She finally stopped and asked a couple if they knew where Jack Price had his plane.

"You're Audrey LaRue!" the man exclaimed as his gaze shifted to her boobs.

"I am," Audrey said, and picked up Bruno, obscuring the man's view of her body. "I am trying to find my friend. He has a hangar out here. Do you know him?"

"Ah, no," the man said, still grinning at Audrey. "But if you like, I can get in and we can drive around and look."

"Thanks, but I'll find it!" Audrey said cheerfully and punched the up button on her window and drove on. "Loser," she muttered.

She next saw an elderly man walking out to his car. This man seemed not to know or care who she was.

"Jack Price," he said thoughtfully, then squinted at the row of hangars. "Stunt man who builds planes in his spare time?"

Audrey's heart skipped a beat. "That's him!"

He pointed to his right. "The hangar with the blue door."

She peered down the lot to the hangar with the blue door. "Thank you!" But the man had already walked away.

Audrey drew a steadying breath and glanced at Bruno. "I hope you're ready, pal," she warned him. Bruno wiggled on the seat. Audrey took that as a sign he was ready and drove to the last hangar.

She parked behind the structure, away from the airstrip. She put Bruno on his gold-studded leash, got out of the car, and checked her appearance in the window's reflection. She'd worn her best skirt and heels for this, and a gauzy blouse that he always seemed to appreciate. Her heart was pounding as she walked to the door and knocked. She stepped back and waited, the throbbing of her pulse getting harder and harder. And she stood. And *stood*.

After a few moments, she cupped her hands around her face and peered inside the little window—the door opened into a tiny little office. There was a desk stacked high with paper and a motory-looking thing that acted as a paperweight. There was a file cabinet, a single chair, and several diagrams posted on the walls. And there was another door, which, she presumed, led into the hangar.

But there was no Jack. "*Dammit*," she muttered. "Damn!" It had taken her two days to get up the nerve to come out here. She turned around and leaned against the door. Bruno went up on his hind legs, his front legs pawing the air.

"Fine," she said, and let him off the leash. He instantly scrambled to the corner of the hangar to lift his leg. "Don't go far!" she shouted at him, and walked in the opposite direction. As she came around the front of the hangar, her heart sank with disappointment. It was closed. Jack was not here and God only knew where he might be. She should have called him, but she decided against it for the same reason she hadn't called him since arriving in L.A. First, she was afraid he'd hang up on her, and second, she really needed to see him. Just *see* him.

Oh hell, she should have called him! For all she knew, he was off on some TA adventure. Maybe even out of the country.

A plane landed on a strip a football field away from her, and Audrey stood watching it, debating what to do.

"Thanks for bringing Bruno."

The lusty timbre of his voice startled her, and Audrey whirled around, her hand on her heart. Jack was holding an ecstatically happy Bruno like a football again. He was wearing a black T-shirt that hugged his muscular arms and chest, and a pair of jeans that fit him so well, Audrey was grateful she didn't drool. He looked better than she remembered, better than she'd hoped.

"How are you?" he asked.

She nodded, not quite able to find her tongue.

His gaze ran over her, gliding over every curve, lingering in all the right places before lifting to her eyes again. "You look good."

"So do you."

Jack squatted down to release Bruno, then stood up, hands on hips, waiting for her to speak.

"How are you doing?" she asked.

He shrugged. "Working hard."

She nodded. She shouldn't have come; it was obvious he didn't want her here. "You don't seem very surprised to see me."

"Maybe that's because I'm a little stunned." He smiled a little, just a hint of that sexy, heart-melting smile that accompanied her to bed each night. "You want to come in?" he asked.

Thank you, God. "I'd love to."

He walked to the hangar and fished for a key from his pocket, unlocked it, and raised the door. Inside was a plane in a state of construction—or deconstruction, depending upon one's view. There were parts and pieces all over the floor.

"Wow," Audrey said.

"It's in better shape than it looks," Jack said. "I'm doing some rewiring right now, and some of it is hard to get to without taking the plane apart."

Audrey walked into the hangar behind him; Bruno scampered inside, too, sniffing each part.

Jack, however, did not seem in the mood to explain what he was doing, no matter how much Audrey would have liked to have known. He turned around and looked at her. "So . . . why'd you come all the way out here?"

The question jarred her. She had hoped for a coffee, a bit of chatting it up to break the ice. "To see you, obviously," she said. "I've really missed you."

"Huh," he said, and turned away, picking up a pair of gloves. "Didn't look like it on TV. Looked like you were still in lockstep with Bonner."

"Actually, no," she said, frowning at him. "It's over between me and Lucas."

Jack paused and glanced at her from the corner of his eye. "Over? Or do you mean you aren't sleeping with him, but still supporting his half-assed career?"

"*Over*. I gave him Courtney and my talent manager and told him to figure it out on his own. They're all gone. And I hired a new business manager—a woman—and a new talent manager, and I am talking with the label right now about the sort of music I want to produce."

"Personal manager?" he asked.

"Not yet. But I've talked to a couple of people."

"Wow," Jack said, nodding appreciatively. "You've been busy."

"Yep." She took a step closer to him. "I have been cleaning up my house."

He turned to face her fully then, his expression heartbreakingly hopeful. "I'm afraid to ask . . . but does all this housekeeping mean anything for us?"

She knew he would ask it; it was why she had come. "I don't know," she answered honestly.

His expression fell and he glanced uneasily at the floor, nudging Bruno a little with his boot. "Hell, sweet cheeks, you didn't really need to come all the way out here to tell me that," he said sheepishly. "I got the message the first time."

"I still love you, Jack," she said earnestly. "I know that sounds like a weird thing to say, but I do. I can't begin to tell you how I have . . .

have *pined* for you. God, I have missed you." In fact, she ached to touch him, but that didn't seem fair somehow.

"But I've also pined for myself in a way. Up until a few weeks ago, I didn't know what was real and what was manufactured. I finally figured out that for all of Lucas's talk of loyalty and how together we would soar higher and farther than apart, that he really kept me exactly where he needed me to be, to suit his own ends. I am flying higher out from under his shadow."

Jack sighed. "I can't blame you for wanting to fly solo."

She paused and pressed a palm to her forehead, wishing she had thought through more carefully what she would say. "You were right about him," she admitted. "It's funny how you can be with a person for so long and then suddenly realize they aren't really there for you. All the publicity and the deals—they were all about Lucas. I discovered that in some of the endorsement contracts I have signed, Lucas gets a large piece, whether I want him to or not. He had me convinced that, without him, I couldn't make it on my own. I *believed* that. I never would have believed otherwise until you told me I could do it."

"You *can* do it," Jack said.

"Yeah," she said, nodding, "I am starting to get that I can. I can handle my family—God save me, but Gail's new boyfriend wants to break into the music business," she said with a bit of a smile. "But I can handle that now. And my business, and my music . . . all by myself."

"So," Jack said. "You're flying high."

She nodded slowly. "I am going to Europe for a month. And then I don't know what I am going to do." She took a step closer to him. "And I know it's too much to ask, I know I am being grossly unfair, but . . . will you wait for me?"

He smiled sadly and touched her face with his fingers. "No, starlight," he said quietly. "That is unfair. And besides, those deals never work out for one of the people involved. If you want to be with me, I am standing here with open arms. I still love you, too. But if you need to go do your own thing, then you need to let me go, too."

She had known it would be his answer, but she had to hear it, had to see his face when he set her free. A single tear slid down her cheek, and

Jack impulsively reached for her hand. Audrey caught her fingers in his, wrapping them around his.

Her blood was churning; she was being swept away—with grief and relief—and yet she couldn't let go. Not yet. She moved closer, pressed her free palm to his jaw and stared into his eyes. She could see the same despair she felt, the realization that two paths had not converged.

"I will miss you," Jack said gruffly. "Just as much as I have missed you every moment of every day since I left the tour."

"Me, too."

He turned his face into her palm and kissed it, then let go of her hand. "I wish you the best, sweet cheeks."

"I know that, too." She wanted to stand there forever, to just look at him, impress the memory of him on her soul so that she would never forget.

There was nothing left to say. She swiped at the lone tear on her cheek and looked around for Bruno.

"Come on, Bruno," she said, patting her leg. He trotted over and waited patiently for her to hook him up.

Jack went down on one knee to pet the dog, his big hand covering the small body. "You keep an eye out for her, rat," Jack said, scratching behind the dog's ears.

Bruno danced excitedly. Jack smiled warmly at the dog and rose up to his full height again, stuffing his hands in his pockets. "Let me hear from you once in a while, okay?"

They both knew she probably wouldn't, but she nodded all the same. She was incapable of speaking, knowing that if she opened her mouth, nothing would come out but a gut-wrenching sob. So she pressed her lips tightly together and gave him a strange little wave before turning and walking away from him for the last time, leaving her broken heart behind, bloodied and useless.

new beau for audrey?

(Us Weekly) Audrey LaRue and George Clooney were recently spotted dining in Milan, Italy, at a popular eatery. A source close to Audrey tells *Us Weekly* that George bought an expensive little Cartier bauble for her, but that they are "just friends." But the two looked very chummy at a houseboat party on Lake Como the following weekend. "Absolutely false," says LaRue's rep. Clooney's reps could not be reached.

Thirty-two

Eli and Jack flew into New York a couple of months later to catch the Yankees' last series for the season with the Mets and to catch up with Parker.

They were lunching at a Soho bistro—or rather, Parker was lunching with his fiancée, Kelly O'Shay, whom he would marry in the off-season, over the phone while Jack and Eli watched him.

"China pattern?" Parker scoffed. "Kelly, darlin'—whatever you want is fine. You decide—huh? *No*, I am not advocating responsibility, I am trying to tell you in a polite way that we can eat off paper plates for all I care . . . No, I don't mean it literally, I just—"

He sighed and rolled his eyes heavenward. "Kelly, I have to go. Jack and Eli are starving. Okay, later." He hung up the phone and looked at Jack and Eli. "Shoot me. Seriously, one of you just shoot me. You would not believe how much crap goes into a wedding," he said, shaking his head. "She calls me five times a day to ask if I want pink flowers or blue candles or what I want the invitations to say."

Jack and Eli exchanged a look.

"What?" Parker demanded. "You think you're going to escape it? Whatever you may think, Eli, I can tell you right now Marnie has it all planned out. One day you will wake up and she'll hand you the tux and say, 'Be at the church in five.' "

Jack laughed, but Eli shook his head.

"She gave me a little more warning than that." He glanced at Parker with a smile. "Looks like we'll both be January brides, Park."

"Awesome!" Parker said, extending his hand.

Jack did, too, clapping Eli on the back. "The only thing that surprises me is that you held out as long as you did. Three years, now?"

"It wasn't me," Eli said. "I wanted to marry that ornery cuss the moment I came back from Australia. *She's* the foot-dragger. '*I've got goals I want to achieve, and they don't include baby-sitting you*,' " he mimicked with a fond smile. "But she came to her senses," he added with a wink. "Especially when I told her I was going to start seeing other women if she didn't. Nothing like the threat of another woman to snap them out of it."

"So . . . what about you, Jackie?" Parker asked. "Got your eye on anyone?"

"Me?" Jack laughed. "Yep. A Cessna. She's a beauty."

"Yeah, well, better not let Paige find out. She's making noises about hooking you up with a friend in Odessa whose husband died in the oil fields. Some freak accident."

"Oh man, not again," Jack said wearily. "Thanks for the warning." He didn't know what they were drinking in Texas, but lately, his sisters were hot on the trail to see him married and settled. They'd even come to L.A. a couple of weeks ago and grilled his friends about whom they could set him up with. "You would think they'd have enough to do with the kids and their jobs without worrying about me. I'm fine. I like the casual dating scene. No pressure."

"Bullshit," Eli said. "You're still not over her."

"Who?" Parker asked.

"Eli, dammit—"

"Audrey LaRue."

Parker gave a shout of laughter. "*The* Audrey LaRue?" he asked with a grin for his big brother. "Well, hell, of course. I should have known it when you took that job."

"Eli doesn't know what he's talking about," Jack said irritably, and looked around for the waitress. "Can you get a beer in New York, or what?"

"Like hell I don't," Eli said, clearly enjoying himself. "You've never been the same since you went on that tour. Good thing your friends are looking out for you, because guess what?"

"I don't want to guess what. I don't want to even *know* what. Parker, stand up and get the waitress's attention."

"She's playing in a Midtown club tonight."

Every fiber, every muscle in Jack's body froze. Even his breath. It seemed like minutes passed before he could breathe again and looked at a grinning Eli.

He winked at Jack. "She's playing in a Midtown club, not too far from the hotel. It's a charity event to benefit a foundation that helps girls get into music."

"The Songbird Foundation," Jack said absently. "It's tonight?"

"Whoa," Parker said, squinting at him, his laugh turned to awe. "I've never seen you look like this, Jackie. Are you all right?"

"He's all right," Eli said congenially. "He's just in love."

Jack had no intention of going. He didn't need to be rejected by the same woman an unprecedented three times. But when Parker sent a car around for them to head out to the game, Eli stopped him at the door. "Jack. Don't be a goddamn idiot," he said, then pushed him back inside the room and closed the door behind them. Jack stared at the closed door, knowing every moment he waited was one step closer to the club—the information for which Eli had left on the desk in their room, along with a ticket.

He didn't want to go; he didn't even want to see her. Hell, he'd just spent *weeks* purging her from every pore. But somehow he ended up sitting at a table in back, feeling antsy as the warm-up act stayed on stage too long. It was a trio of young women who had gotten their start, they said, because of funds from Audrey's Songbird Foundation.

Okay, Jack told himself. It was a noble cause. He'd just get a glimpse of Audrey, hear a couple of tunes, then book. She would never even know he'd come.

And he'd go back to the hotel and throttle Eli.

But when she came on stage, Jack lost all reason. He was mesmerized. Her hair had grown into long silky white waves that hung around her shoulders and framed her face. She wore a flowing, flimsy dress that skirted around her knees and showcased her perfect legs. She walked out holding the hand of a young girl who, like Audrey, carried a guitar.

They each took a seat on two stools. "Thanks for coming out tonight," Audrey said. "I can't tell you how much I appreciate your support. This is Anna," she said, smiling at the young girl. "She is so talented that she will knock me right off this stage." She strummed a few chords, then looked at Anna. "Are you ready?"

The girl nodded, and the two of them began to play. They sang three songs, three hauntingly beautiful duets. The crowd erupted with a roar of applause after each one. This wasn't a big arena like Audrey had been playing, but it sounded almost as big.

Then Anna left the stage and the lights focused on Audrey. "I am going to play a song I wrote about the stupid things we do," she said, garnering chuckles from the crowd. "I guess the first stupid thing I did was to get fired by my record label. No, no," she said, when a rumble went through the crowd. "It was a good thing. We had 'some artistic differences,' " she said, making invisible quotations with her fingers. "They wanted me to do pop, and I wanted to sing songs that I love. But amazingly, that wasn't the stupid thing."

The crowd laughed.

"Any of you ever let The One get away?" A couple of people whistled, and Audrey laughed. "Well, I did. He was the perfect man for me, and I did something really stupid. I walked away, and he didn't stop me. This song is called 'Don't Let Me Walk Away.' "

Jack hardly even breathed as she sang. His heart was pounding, his palms damp. Every word, every note she sang pierced his heart, took him back to that moment in the hangar.

You stand in the middle of the wreckage I've made of our lives,
and you watch me walk away.
Now you know what you never knew before,
and you send me on my way.

Baby, I've made mistakes,
but I know what I should have said.
This is my love, it's not perfect,
just don't let me walk away . . .

The melody was brilliant, the words piercing his heart deeply. He wasn't the only one who seemed to think so. Around him, conversation ebbed away, people leaned forward in their chairs. When she had finished the song, she stood up from her stool and bowed sheepishly to the thunderous applause. "Thank you," she said, smiling. "Thank you very much. We're going to take a break and bring out a chorus of young women you'll be hearing from in the future."

The crowd continued to applaud as she glided off the stage.

Jack stopped thinking; he was only feeling. He rose to his feet, his heart in his throat, and began striding through the tables toward the stage. When he reached the edge, a man as big as himself stepped in front of him. "Whoa, pal. Where are you going?"

"I need to speak to Audrey—I know her."

"Yeah, like everyone in this joint knows her. Back it up and don't cause any trouble."

"Look, *pal*," he said, "I am a friend and I want to say hello—"

"*Jack?*"

He saw Ted over the bouncer's shoulder and smiled with relief. If he could have reached him, he would have kissed him. "*Ted*," he said, extending his hand. "So you're still on board, huh?"

"Sure am!" Ted said with a bright smile. "Went to Europe with her. You want to say hello?" he asked, waving the other guy off. "It's cool, Andy. Jack had my job before me." Andy nodded and turned back to the crowd, and Ted gestured for him to follow. "Just let me tell her you're here," he said as they walked backstage.

Ted ducked into a dressing room and left Jack waiting in a dark corridor with a dozen young girls who were waiting to go on. They were giggling and wiggling around, adjusting their matching dresses, comparing them, and staring at him.

The door suddenly swung open, and light spilled into the corridor. Jack and the dozen girls turned toward the light.

Audrey was standing at the threshold, her hands on the frame, as if she was holding herself back. She looked beautiful. The fatigue that had dogged her on tour was gone. She looked healthy, with creamy skin, eyes as green as Christmas trees, and cascades of silky blond waves. "*Jack.*"

"Hello, Audrey."

She flew, flying solo past roadies, over cables, and through the sea of little girls, hitting him with such force that he stumbled backward. She peppered his face with kisses while the girls giggled.

"It's a dream," she said. "I must be dreaming. You found me! Oh God, I have missed you. Will you forgive me?"

"There is nothing to forgive, sweet cheeks," he said, catching her face to hold her still a moment. "But I won't let you walk away again."

A look of pure joy washed over her face. "Oh my God, I love you," she said breathlessly, and began to kiss him all over again while the girls squealed with surprise and giggles.

The feeling, in case it wasn't obvious to the girls, was entirely mutual. She would never let him walk away, either.

In the Hangar That Love Built

(*People*) "Love made this," Audrey LaRue likes to say. In a makeshift recording studio, built in the back half of a rented hangar, LaRue, who is arguably the hottest recording star at the moment, has released her fourth album, a soulful mix of folk and rock. *Billboard* magazine hails it as "truly unique sound." "I would never have made it had it not been for Jack," LaRue says, speaking of her fiancé, Jack Price. "He has inspired me . . ."

Epilogue

"This is so cool, Audrey!" Marnie said, holding up the magazine and the picture of Audrey's face that graced the cover. "It's a wonderful story, and the pictures are *great*. The hangar doesn't look near the dump it is in real life."

"Let me see," Leah said, and put down the knife she was using to cut limes to have a look. The TA boys and their significant others had rented a yacht to celebrate Audrey's spread in *People* and the fact that her fourth album had just gone platinum.

But they were much more enthralled with the article in *People*, because a photographer had taken pictures of them as a group. They had been at Audrey's Malibu beach house one night, sitting around a beach fire, laughing and telling stories and planning Eli and Marnie's wedding, which had just taken place a month ago. But the picture of them all, one of Audrey's favorites, was now in the magazine.

She loved it—they looked like a group right out of the movies. All of their faces shone with true happiness. Their collective future seemed to shine through, too, with Leah's pregnant belly swelling out of her pants with one month to go before baby Raney came into their lives, and Marnie announcing shortly thereafter that she, too, was pregnant.

As Marnie read aloud from the magazine, Audrey looked down at Daisy Raney, Leah and Michael's infant daughter, who was sleeping soundly in her baby hammock.

Audrey had the picture of all of them framed, and now it hung in her house right next to the picture of her and Jack, taken at Possum Kingdom.

His mother had taken that picture. They were standing on the deck, each of them holding an inner tube, having just come up from the lake. Her hair was wet and hanging down her back, Jack's messed up after he'd run his fingers through it. They were laughing at something Jack's sister had said. Of all the pictures of Audrey that had been snapped in the last few years, that one, taken with a disposable camera, was the one that she held dearest. That was the night Jack had proposed to her, the night they had made love under the stars.

"I have to show this to Eli," Marnie said, snatching the magazine back from Leah. "He wants Jack to build a hangar, but I think this one has some charm." She waddled up to the deck, her pregnancy nearing the last trimester. The guys were all up top, pretending to fish while they sat around and drank beer and one-upped each other.

"He really needs to build his own hangar," Leah said to Audrey. "What's he got—eight students now?"

"Ten," Audrey said proudly.

"Leah, come up here!" Jill called down. "You won't believe this sunset. You, too, Audrey!"

Leah grabbed the limes she had sliced for the drinks and checked on her baby. Daisy was out cold. She smiled down at her daughter then glanced at Audrey. "Are you coming?"

"I'll be right up," she said, and watched Leah make her way up the stairs.

She stood below deck, a lyric running through her head as she looked at Daisy. Her gaze shifted to her engagement ring, and she smiled. She had never believed she could be so happy, and had to pinch herself now and then to remind herself it was real. It seemed like everything had finally fallen into place—after being alone for several months, she had learned her business, had hired her own people, and knew precisely what she wanted to do.

She knew that she wanted Jack, too. Forever. Just when she feared she'd lost him forever, he came back into her life. That night in New York had been magical. They had reconnected in a way that defied human explanation. It was so right. It was so meant to be.

But it wasn't just that—her family had changed a little, too. Granted, Mom was still a cold fish, but she'd let Audrey redo her awful kitchen. And Gail had remarried, which Audrey thought was good for her sons. Dad had actually found another investor for his NASCAR venture, and surprisingly, he was doing really well with it. He'd married Hayley. Audrey was getting used to the idea.

Perhaps most surprising of all was Allen. Out of the blue, he'd learned he was a father. Who would have thought after all the stints in treatment and the threats by the court and the counseling that being a father was the one thing Allen needed. Since he'd met that little boy, he'd found his reason for living and he was a different man. He'd held on to his job at the tool and dye, and he'd been sober a whole year.

Lucas was something of a mystery—she hadn't heard from or seen him in over a year now. She heard about him every so often—someone told her he and Courtney had been an item for a short while. That didn't surprise Audrey in the least. She also knew he'd joined a band that was touring and opening with a couple of headliners.

Audrey sincerely hoped he was happy. If he could have only a fraction of the happiness she had found—

"What are you doing down here alone, starlight?"

She glanced up from Daisy and smiled at Jack. "I'm not alone," she said, and laughed.

He believed she was talking about Daisy, of course.

"Did you catch anything?" she asked as he slipped his arm around her shoulders and looked at the sleeping infant.

"No," he said softly. "I would have if Cooper hadn't gotten in the way. You would think a guy as talented as he is wouldn't be such a buffoon on a boat, but he's hopeless. Come on up, sweet cheeks. We all miss you, and we want you to play a few tunes for us."

"I would be happy to," she said. "And Jack? I *am* happy."

He grinned and kissed her. "Then that makes two of us."

Together, they went up on deck to join their friends and their future.